Tavia's Deception
Twelve Dancing Princesses Book Nine

Christine Young

ISBN: 978-1-62420-439-5

Credits
Cover Artist: Designs by Ms G
Editor: Christie L. Kraemer

Chapter One

London 1821

Tavia stood between her twin Tira and her cousin Larena waiting for a possible suitor. She swallowed her fear as well as her distaste for the marriage market. Only her older sister, Ella had what one could call a successful season. Ella met Drake Montgomerie at a ball just like this one and fell in love. Well, Eveleen met Logan and she too fell in love. Perhaps she should try a little bit harder but she wasn't sure she even wanted to fall in love or even get married.

No, on second thought, this was not what she wanted as she watched the males in the room devour them with their eyes. The man approaching made her skin crawl. She rubbed her arms in an attempt to ward off the chill encroaching. Praying the man was eyeing someone else, she looked down in hopes he would take the subtle cue.

Tavia and Tira Hepburn along with Larena Graham were the new charges of The Duchess, their auntie Charlotte, in London England. Aunt Charlotte took them dress shopping for their presentation gowns the week before, and now they appeared at one of the festivities of the season at St. Jame's Palace. The debutante ball this evening was at the invitation of the Duke of Somerset.

The man stopped at The Duchess and bowed, lifting her aunt's hand and placing a kiss on the back. The hairs on the back of Tavia's neck stood on end. She couldn't hear what they said but the next moment, the man, twirling his mustache, stood in front of her.

"Edwin, Edwin McMasters. May I have the honor of this dance?" he asked smoothly, his smile narrow and menacing.

With a quick look to The Duchess and the nod the older lady gave her, she understood she had no choice but to accept his invitation. When she stepped into his arms, nausea assailed her.

He was tall and thin, smelling of cigar smoke and alcohol. She counted the seconds as they moved around the dance floor. The palm of his hand was sweaty and hot. She thought she might gag. Tavia swallowed hard, wondering when she could end this politely.

"What are you doing?" Stunned she found herself maneuvered onto a dark balcony away from the men and debutants swirling around the room in their fashionable silk gowns. She was pushed up against a wall, his hands braced on either side of her.

"Making you mine." His mouth found hers and his tongue probed for entrance. She couldn't breathe. Trying to push him away she couldn't. She was shaking her head but he held it with hands on both sides of her face.

Inside she screamed no, but nothing helped. His tongue pushed her lips apart. She coughed, choking from the contact. Suddenly, Edwin sat on the ground, his legs sprawled on the floor, rubbing his jaw.

"Bloody hell!"

Her gaze ran the length of her savior from his well-muscled legs to his trim waist and farther to the width of his shoulders. He was the largest man she'd ever seen. He looked at her with his steel gray eyes as if he knew what she was thinking.

"The Lady Tavia Hepburn said no." The tall redheaded man offered his arm to her and escorted her back to her position by The Duchess before introducing himself. "James Macmurra at your service."

"I remember you." She blinked several times, her hand to her chest, trying to catch her breath. "Thank you for rescuing me." She flashed him a smile of gratitude as well as relief, perhaps even a tiny bit flirtatious.

"I'm glad to hear that. If I recall you were Jamie Lundin's partner at Drake Montgomerie's wedding." He turned to look at Tira. "And you were mine."

Recalling Ella's wedding to Drake, Tavia cleared her throat. "The wedding was a disaster."

"Let's not speak of that," James grinned at her. "May I have this dance?" He looked to The Duchess for approval.

"Of course, go on with you, enjoy." The Duchess waved them

away. "You're only young once. Enjoy."

Heat swept through her body. Anticipation at the thought of his strong arms around her left her breathless, perhaps a kiss. Broad shoulders and narrow hips, his feet planted firmly apart, she was mesmerized by his form and silver hue of his eyes. His gaze sizzled with some undefined message. She felt a sudden urge to test the feel of his red hair and beard.

She accepted his hand as he led her to the dance floor. His fingertips were calloused and her hand seemed to be engulfed by his. She stared at the floor, terrified of meeting his gaze, yet longing to do just that at the same time.

"Lady Tavia?" he asked, drawing her closer so he could position his hand on her back. They began to dance the quadrille, flying across the floor. The steps were rapid, skimming steps. He held her tighter, guiding her, managing to lead her around other couples.

The music changed to a Scottish reel with its own intricate steps. She didn't want to stop. These moments with her Scotsman were magical. He enchanted her. At the edge of the dance floor, he whirled her to a stop.

"James?" She was breathing hard and smiling at the huge man who could move with such ease and grace. "You amaze me."

"Would you like to cool off?" he nodded toward the balcony. "Just for a moment. I promise I'll be a gentleman."

Her hand rested on his chest where she felt the strong beating of his heart. She heard the rapid staccato of her own heart, pulsing. She wasn't sure she wanted him to be a gentleman. "I am rather hot." She waved a hand in front of her face wondering where she'd placed her fan.

Keeping her hand in his, he led her outside. The night air was chilly but against her heated flesh, it felt good. He paused at the edge, bringing her hand to his lips and placing a kiss on the back.

"Do you like to dance?" When he turned to her, his eyes sizzled beneath hooded lashes.

The touch of his warm lips sent a shiver of delight coursing through her. She moistened her lips. "With you I do."

"I like to dance to the pipes. They have a haunting quality about them, and I've always loved the sound." He slipped out of his jacket and placed it around her shoulders. The scent was of leather and a bit of rose

3

water then all James.

"Where in Scotland are you from?"

"Edinburgh I call my home now, but I grew up in the highlands. It's beautiful there. Whenever I feel lonely, I return. I've a hunting lodge I enjoy that lies by a loch. Are you cold?" He touched her forehead, gently pushing an errant strand of hair from her face and tucking it behind her ear.

"No." She could never be cold when he stood so close.

He folded his hand over hers where it rested next to his heart. He smiled at her. "Do you want to stay out here a little longer?"

She couldn't stop the slow bubble of laughter emanating from her. "Yes, but if we stay much longer, The Duchess will be here, pounding you on the back with her cane."

"I don't plan on doing anything that would cause that. If you look just beyond the drape there, you'll see your aunt. I don't believe she'll attack me unless I do something that would warrant that. I'm pretty sure holding your hand is fine even though I'd like so much more."

Her heart lurched beneath her ribs, hoping for perhaps a kiss. She and Tira had endless conversations about kissing. They both knew Ella had let Drake do things she shouldn't have done before the wedding, and The Duchess let them.

"You'd like more..." her voice trailed off as he ran a calloused fingertip across her lips. Her mind spun.

"I'm not a suitable catch for you, Lady Tavia. I'm a ship's captain, not a lord. Your family will never agree to a match between us. So, even though I would love to pursue this relationship, I won't."

"Oh," she murmured, disappointed by his statement.

"I'm leaving at the end of the week. Trust me you'll find someone suitable." He leaned against the balcony railing, holding her, gazing at her. His hands spanned her waist. She stood close to him, even closer than when they danced.

"Where are you going? I'd like to see the world, everywhere. If I could, I would love to go..." she couldn't think. The fingers of one of his hands left a heated path down her neck and across her collarbone. "Fayth went to Paris and Amorica lives in Maryland. Oh..." she gulped air.

"Should you do that?"

"No," he said before he dropped his hands. "I should be strung up by my thumbs, but I can't seem to help myself."

"Is The Duchess still watching? If she is, you haven't done anything that isn't acceptable."

Both hands were on her waist again. "I'm not about to test things. Are you hungry or thirsty?"

"We could go for a walk in the gardens," she suggested, wanting to find someplace where The Duchess might not follow, somewhere he might kiss her. She found that more than anything she wanted James to kiss her.

"That's not wise. I should put you back on the floor so a suitable man might ask you for a dance."

"I don't want to dance with anyone else. I didn't come to London to find someone who will marry me, a suitable man. I'm going to book passage on a ship. The only thing that matters to me is seeing the world."

He coughed and again, pushed a strand of hair behind her ear. This time his fingers lingered longer than the first time. "You would put your life in danger to see the world? You can't just find a ship and book passage." He sounded shocked. "The Duchess would never let you do that."

"Why would it be dangerous to book passage on a ship?" she demanded. "People do it all the time and survive to see another day."

"Because you would have no one to protect you. I can't let you do something so foolish. Your life and well-being are too precious."

At his words she stiffened. She could do and be whatever or whoever she wanted. "You have no reason to say that. Why on earth would you think my life would be in danger if I was on a ship."

Looking away for several seconds, he cleared his throat. "You are too innocent by far. I captain a ship and have done so for several years. My crew are no more saints than I am. The risk would be too great."

"Tavia, there you are." Tira appeared on the balcony with Larena. "Do you want to walk with us in the garden? You and James?" she asked. "Gavin and Jamie are coming too."

She turned to James, a dark expression gracing his face. She was sure he was about to shake his head no, but something seemed to change his mind. "Why not?"

"Why not indeed," she murmured, disturbed by his comment. He could at least act a bit more enthusiastic. Her presence with him suddenly seemed to be a burden. Still he stared at her, his eyes sizzling with some pent-up emotion Tavia didn't know how to define.

"We're bored with the dancing and Scarlett, Aunt Charlotte's companion, promised to chaperone. Our Auntie is sitting, resting.

"She looks tired," Tavia skipped ahead.

"The Duchess is going home soon but said she'd wait up for us. We're supposed to remember the talk we had this afternoon before the ball about how men think," Larena said. "She'll probably have her nightly brandy and a lemon bar."

James coughed then cleared his throat. She heard him murmur, "The way men think?"

The three couples headed outside where gaslights lit the gardens, the air redolent with the scent of roses. Tavia and James strolled behind the other two couples. Their carefree happy chatter filled the silence of the evening.

James offered his arm, and Tavia accepted his polite gesture. "My cousins and sisters used to visit an island near the McLellan castle," she began. "I miss those trips to the island. We had so much fun."

"Chaperoned, of course," James said as they strode past the other couples who had stopped to kiss.

She felt the distance between them growing even as she wanted so much more. "Absolutely not. None of our fathers knew about the island until Hunter, Allura's husband, appeared vying for her hand in marriage. None of our father's except perhaps the Laird McLellan even cared what we did."

James hand suddenly rested on hers. "You were impetuous as a child just like your thoughts now as a young lady of booking passage on a ship to see the world. You must take care," he warned.

"Well, it's not your life. I plan on living mine the way I choose." They stopped at a gazebo deep in the gardens.

"We should probably get back to the others." He leaned against the structure, turning her to face him.

"I don't want to go back." You need to kiss me, she wanted to tell him. Her hands rested on his chest as he settled her between his legs, his hands on the small of her back.

"People will talk." He closed his eyes, drawing air into his lungs. "I don't want your reputation ruined before the season has barely begun."

She laughed softly, "You see, I don't care about my reputation. If I'm doing something I've chosen to do with someone like you, then I'm happy."

"You should consider what people think in everything you do." He tightened his fingers and she enjoyed the subtle pressure.

"Do you? Do you contemplate what people think of you? Or do you just do what you want or what you believe is right?"

"Bloody hell, I'm a man." He brought one hand upward to rest on her shoulder, on her bare skin beneath his jacket.

At the sensation of his calloused fingers, she shivered. Yet she meant to tell him what she thought about males dictating to her. "Women should be treated as equals. At least that's what I think."

"Why?" he queried, his finger tracing a line along her jaw. "You are far more precious than I am."

She ignored his question, focusing on his lips instead of the conversation she didn't want to have with this man. "I've never been kissed before." Boldly, she touched his chin, felt the soft texture of his beard then drew her finger across his lips.

He stopped her, holding her hand in his. "And you want me to kiss you? Why me? Why not someone who has a title before his name? You could have so much more."

"Please," she said and not wanting him to say no to her she continued. "I want to know how I'll feel when a man kisses me. When you kiss me."

"I truly don't want to tell you no, lass, but it wouldn't be right." He kissed the tip of her finger instead. "I enjoy your company more than you should know, but I'm not the right man for you."

"Ah, kiss her," Gavin said from behind them. "If she wants you then you are the right man for her."

"Kiss her," Tira laughed. "She can't be the only one of us who isn't kissed tonight."

"Go on with all of you." He growled low in his throat. "This conversation is between the two of us. There is no room for eaves droppers."

"Really, you should kiss her. We'll give the two of you a wee bit of privacy, but when we finish the stroll through the garden and return, we want to hear that you kissed her," Larena said, all the while laughing.

The sound sent a primal shiver down her spine. She couldn't speak. She moistened her lips with her tongue, his gaze riveted on her mouth. "James..."

"You unman me you're so beautiful. But..." he watched her intensely, his large hand resting on the side of her face.

She was beginning to understand the power the subtleties of her body had over this man. Placing her hands on his shoulders, she leaned into him. "You can't, won't, kiss me. Perhaps I should kiss you then." She rose onto her toes, her breasts pushing against his chest.

"You play with fire, Tavia. Don't tease a man."

Was that what she was doing? Teasing him? She blinked several times, pressing into him and feeling things she'd never thought to feel. "Do you really believe I want some lord just because he has a title in front of his name? I'm not that shallow. I would take offense if you knew me better."

Her statement brought a chuckle from deep in his chest. "Do not take offense. I'm not marriage material. I spend most of my life at sea. Would you want that in a husband?"

"It's exactly what I want because I would like nothing more than to join him on his travels. Someone like you is perfect. You are perfect. We are perfect together," she stated emphatically.

"You don't know me well enough to make a statement like that. I might beat you when you disagree with me or don't do what I ask."

She was shaking her head, tendrils of hair falling from her swept up hair. "You would never do such a thing. A man's true character is always apparent to his male friends. Drake would have never asked you to be a groomsman at his wedding if you were an evil or mean man."

"Do you have an answer for everything?" His hands framed her face while he moistened his lips, his gaze blazing into hers with unrequited fire.

"Perhaps," she spoke softly, anticipating the kiss she was sure would come soon. She wanted to feel the warmth of his mouth on hers, taste the essence of who he was. He was so close she inhaled his breath.

"When I kiss you, I'll be your first," he murmured, his lips close to hers yet not touching.

"Yes, please." Her fingers wound into his hair. She felt the earth tremble beneath her feet, but it was his huge body shaking with desire she assumed.

"I shouldn't."

"Of course you should."

"Well, well, well, The Duchess would be interested in this. She might even have you keel hauled on one of your boats."

"Edwin. I'd know that high pitched whinny voice anywhere."

They broke apart. She was breathing hard. From the darkness, Edwin strode toward them. "You refused my kiss but you let a Scotsman kiss you. He doesn't have a title," he sneered. "And I do."

"Stand behind me," with one large hand James gently moved so he stood in front of her. His hands were fisted at his sides, and it seemed he rocked on the balls of his feet ready to fight, "What do you want?"

"Apparently the same thing you do," Edwin said approaching them. "Let me kiss her and I'll be gone."

"Never," James ground out through clenched teeth.

"You should let the little lady speak," he said with a sneer. "I bet she wants a real man, not a Scotsman or a commoner."

"I gave you my answer a few hours ago." Tavia poked her head from around James back. "No."

"Everything alright?" Gavin and Jamie approached with the girls.

"It will be as soon as this bloody fool leaves," James said. His hand touching Tavia's, she felt an inner strength permeate through her.

It seemed Edwin knew when the odds were stacked against him. "I'll have to try another time when you don't have this giant standing over you," he said looking over his shoulder as he walked away. "I will taste her."

"I don't like the way that man looks at you." James wrapped an arm around Tavia, pulling her against his hard frame.

"He's a lord. Do you think he's more deserving of a relationship with me than you?" Tavia challenged, beginning to understand the protective nature that defined James Macmurra.

"No. He might be a lord but he's a wastrel and cad," Gavin said. "I don't pretend to understand what is going on here, but you need to be wary of that man. He owes debts to a number of my friends, and he doesn't have the means to pay. I'm assuming he's looking for a rich heiress to finance his vices."

"Then he's trying to court the wrong girl. I'm not a rich heiress." She turned to James. "You're not looking for one..."

"That's right, I'm not looking for an heiress. I've made my fortune and have more money than I need or could spend in a lifetime of simple living."

"Enough of that," Tira pulled Tavia from James embrace and away from the men. Larena followed. "Well," she whispered. "Did he kiss you?"

~ * ~

"Dressed up again, I see. Where are you going tonight?" Seamus O'Malley, the first mate on James' ship, seemed to strip his thoughts bare as he scrutinized him.

James had been staring at the ledgers in front of him for what seemed like hours, a glass of whiskey on his desk. He glanced up, knowing he wasn't going to finish anytime soon. "Don't know, Drury Lane or Covent Garden. Not sure what the ladies decided on."

"Not your cup o' tea, if I say so myself. Don't see you going to the theatre for the fun of it or the opera. Who's the special lady who has you sweatin' buckets?" Seamus chuckled, rubbing his bristly chin. "Whoever she is, seems she's got you tied up in knots."

"I didn't know how to tell her I wasn't interested." James wasn't interested in the theatre, just a girl he had no right to court. Seems as if he was making a colossal mistake and wasting valuable time on something that was going nowhere.

"Looks like interest to me," Sean said. "You wouldn't have been starin' at those papers all afternoon. And it looks to me as if you've made no progress or is it just the little gal you're interested in and not the theater. Take her to your bed and get it over with then you can forget her and get on with your life."

"She's a lady, Seamus. Someone I have no business courting. I don't have a title or an estate to offer, and I certainly can't take her to my bed." He could certainly buy land or a home if he wanted to settle down and start a family. He had the means. James sat back, drumming his finger on the table as he let his mind wander to the possibilities.

"Don't be so noble. Love doesn't pay any attention to the things you just listed. If you're in love..." Seamus let the idea hang in the silence of the cabin.

"Love?" he murmured thoughtfully. "I barely know her. I believe you'd call it lust." But her beauty blindsided him the first time he saw her. When she talked to him, he was more entranced by the magic that was Tavia.

"We still sailing in a couple of days, or do you plan on another captain for this old vessel? You know you have men who'd love to command the ship and who are quite capable. Stayin' on land and courtin' the little gal might be the right thing to do. Otherwise, by the time we get back to port she could be wedded and bedded. You'd be the loser."

His thoughts settled on Edwin, his grimy hands touching her. He was one of those men who would stop at nothing to get what they wanted. If what happened last night was any indication, the odious man wanted Tavia.

"I can't do that." James rearranged the papers on his desk before stacking them in a pile to be read later.

"Won't?" Seamus questioned.

"It's best for her if I leave and don't look back." She wouldn't allow Edwin into her life so he didn't have that to worry about, just every other suitor in the ton.

"Did she say that? Did she tell you her life would be better without you? If you tell me yes, I'll call you for a liar."

"No."

"Well then, you best be doin' some serious thinkin' about your future and the lady you're about to leave behind. You're not gettin' any younger. Sometimes a man needs to settle down with a wife and children to make his life complete."

"And I see you did just that?" James leaned back, resting his hands on his stomach, grinning and feeling the humor.

"Had a wife once a long time ago." Seamus said. "And a little boy."

James sat up, concerned. "I didn't know. What happened?"

"She died and my boy with her. I was at sea and couldn't do nothin' about it. 'Nough said." He turned to leave then stopped. "James, we need a new cabin boy. I put the word out and told the harbor master just this morning."

"A new one? What happened to Mica?" This posed a new problem and one he'd have to deal with if they didn't find one.

"Decided he wasn't meant for life at sea. He was seasick most days, and the crew teased him unmercifully."

"Make sure we find one before we set sail in two days." James followed Seamus from the cabin. Down the gangplank he hailed a cab, giving directions to The Duchess' townhouse. He settled back, mulling over the conversation with Seamus.

He didn't like the idea of Tavia finding someone else, but he attempted to maintain his thoughts trying to convince himself. She would be better off with someone closer to her station in life, someone who would be there for her. Seamus' story confirmed his reservations. His first mate had been at sea and his family died. That wasn't a story he wanted to be told about his wife.

Yet no one else seemed to think the same way he did. He'd leave this to chance. If she was still a single lady when he returned, he'd court her. Satisfied with his decision he focused on the cargo and when it would be loaded. Seamus could oversee the loading so perhaps he and Tavia could go for a ride tomorrow in Hyde Park.

The carriage slowed to a halt. He strode to the porch and rang the bell, waiting nervously. This took more courage than battling a storm at sea. The butler opened the door and waited, a stoic expression on his face.

"James Macmurra, calling on Tavia Hepburn." He wiped sweaty hands on his pants.

The butler stepped aside then ushered him into the parlor. Apparently, he was the last to arrive. Jamie and Gavin sat in chairs sipping brandy, seemingly relaxed. The butler brought him a drink.

"Hope this is to your liking."

James leaned against the doorframe, holding his glass aloft, "Cheers." Either of you eager for an evening of opera at Covent Garden?"

Both men laughed. "Not here for the opera, just the ladies."

"So, you both have eyes for your lady. You plan on marriage when this is all over?" James pursued the topic that had been on his mind all afternoon as well as last evening.

"Can't say I've given it much thought. It's too soon." Jamie said. "She'd have to be willing to leave London. I've a life in Baltimore I won't leave."

"Me neither," Gavin said. "Larena intrigues me. She says outrageous things that take me by surprise and she makes me laugh. A man could do worse and," he paused in thought, "she's beautiful."

"You know how these things go," Jamie began.

"And how is that?" The Duchess stepped into the room then tapping her cane on the floor held each man's gaze for several seconds. As if to intimidate these men, as she walked she continued to tap her cane.

The staccato of the cane meeting the floor seemed to match his heartbeat. James ran a finger around his collar, waiting for the lecture to begin. "What would you like us to say, in for a penny in for a pound?"

"Mr. Macmurra, you do get to the point of things. I like that. Don't want to beat around the bush, I see. You've got places to go and time is of the essence. Well, I'm not going to live forever, and I want to see these girls find men who will treat them right. I've only had the opportunity to plan two weddings, and both went terribly awry. Not at all what I had planned, no, not at all."

"I would never hurt your niece," Gavin spoke up. "I mean it."

"That's not what I was speaking of," she looked to Gavin. "If you don't have marriage in mind, you should leave here at once and let someone who does have a chance to court her."

"I didn't mean it like that. I do have marriage in mind someday," his voice assumed a strange tone.

"What about you, Jamie Lundin? What are your intentions? Are any of them good?" she turned to Scarlett who brought in a plate of scones and refreshed the men's drinks.

Jamie cleared his throat. "Certainly not to hurt anyone. Tira enjoys my company, and I hers, but I'll return to the states in a few weeks. Perhaps by then we'll have a better idea what we mean to each other. Would you be happy with her leaving England?" He issued a challenge of his own.

"Whatever makes her happy will please me, and make the last of my duties successful where she is concerned. Then she directed her attention to James. "You know Tavia wants to travel. She wants to see what's on the other side of the sun. She believes with all her heart that she needs to follow sunsets and chase sunrises. A bit fanciful for my taste, but I believe she sees that opportunity in you. Don't disappoint her."

"Tavia has said as much to me. She brings to life something in me I thought long dead. I'm not sure myself what that means. My ship is leaving in two days. If you'd rather I left right now, I'll do your bidding. I won't be able to court her until I return."

"Ah," she waved her hand in the air, "you don't want to go to the opera. I understand." She leaned forward and cackling, "Tonight you will escort her to Covent Gardens, and tomorrow I expect you to ride with her in Hyde Park. She has her heart set on it and as you well know, I don't want to see any of my charges disappointed or unhappy."

James cleared his throat. "I don't have a title in front of my name or a home in London. An apartment in The Albany is what I call home when I have an extended stay here. My suitability is questionable."

"Fine, then you won't be taking her there or seducing her into your bed. That bit of information makes me feel much better. I'm going to tell it the way it is. If you're looking for something other than a chaperoned courtship, you are seeing the wrong ladies," The Duchess told them in her most formidable voice. "Both Scarlett and I are determined to make sure nothing untoward happens."

"You need not worry about me trying to seduce Tira. I would never bring her to my bed before we are wed...if we are wed," Jamie added hastily.

The Duchess held her glass to her lips for several seconds. James was sure she didn't swallow. When she set the glass on the end table, she closed her eyes for a moment before speaking, "I remember the late Duke. He promised much the same thing, as did my nieces' fathers. They were all rakes of the worst sort until they met their ladies."

"But the duke seduced you?" Gavin asked with a soft chuckle. "Who would have guessed?"

James began to enjoy this conversation and wondered where this would end up. "Of course you didn't let him." He believed the opposite, but for some reason he needed to see if The Duchess would be honest.

"On the contrary, I loved that man so much I would have done anything he asked and he knew it. Oh, he was arrogant or perhaps confident would better describe him, and his pride saw no end. He was a bit like the three of you only much more handsome. He had me in the palm of his hand the first time I looked into his gorgeous dark brown eyes."

James wanted to protest that he wasn't arrogant but perhaps he was. He possessed other sins, but he did have a few virtues.

Jamie seemed to stiffen. "I would never seduce Tira. She's an innocent."

"Balderdash. If given the opportunity there is not a doubt in mind you would use all the powers you possess to sway her into your arms and bed."

"I like to think of myself as a gentleman." He seemed determined to convince either The Duchess or perhaps himself.

"All three of you are gentleman, but you are men first. Would you expect anything else from a debutant besides innocence? They are beginners, and the girls know nothing about sex and how a man thinks. Except perhaps Larena, her sister does breed horses."

"How a man thinks?" all three asked at the same time, looking to the other as if they knew the answer.

"Yes."

"Enlightenment would be nice," James said, believing he had an idea about where she was about to go with her statement, and for some reason he couldn't fathom enjoying it. No wonder Tavia spoke her mind. The characteristic must be inbred.

"As you like. I mean to do just that." She paused in thought, watching the amber liquid as she swirled it in the crystal glass.

"You spoke to the girls about this yesterday. I remember how she told me I thought with a different part of my anatomy. Wasn't entirely sure what she meant."

"The Duke found this tiny cottage near a lake. It was beautiful and somehow we escaped our chaperone. He must have spent hours trying to figure out how to do it. That day it was raining so hard he didn't have to make up an excuse to take me to this spot he knew of."

"The cad," Gavin laughed out loud. "A man of my own heart..." His words died away.

"Perhaps I now have reservations about your intentions toward my niece," she directed the comment to Gavin before continuing her story. "We were both soaked to the bone by the time we were in the cottage. With a fire going, he set the mood for my seduction." She waved one hand in the air, "But I digress."

"To escape the chill of the night, he convinced you to take your riding habit off and spread it out to dry." James said, knowing it was something he would do with anyone of his female friends except Tavia. With Tavia he was determined to keep his hands to himself.

"Yes, well, his words made perfect sense. He did wrap a blanket around me when I had nothing but a few things on my person." She blushed, recalling the events. "It seems just like yesterday." A lone tear slipped from an eye to slide down her cheek. "I do miss William so."

"I'm sorry he passed so soon. His death must have been incredibly hard on you," James said. Suddenly on his feet then kneeling in front of the woman everyone called The Duchess because of how formidable she was. But at this tender moment she was Tavia's Auntie Charlotte. He held her trembling hands in his. "I hope I'm as blessed as you were when it comes to finding my true love."

She let him hold her hands for some time before she pulled away.

16

"I'm a maudlin fool. I'll be joining him soon enough. Which brings me to one of the finer points I intend to make today with you young men before you do something someone might regret."

Her emotional break down seemed to change the tone of this meeting, at least for him. He yearned for a relationship like the one Charlotte described, and he wondered if Tavia was truly the woman for him. In such a short time she touched something inside him he never knew existed.

"So," Jamie said, "what are these finer points you want to make?" He roughed his hands through his hair, seeming as touched by her story as she was.

"First," she began tapping the cane on the floor, "you three will make several promises to me right now, today, before I let you do anything more with my nieces."

"I'm sure I can promise anything you ask. It couldn't be too difficult," Gavin said with a cocky air to his words.

"You might be surprised. I'm guessing you've only slept with widows and perhaps a few women of ill repute. These women don't come with family and friends who will defend their honor or even care about what happens to them. You can come and go as you please with no repercussions to yourself, but women you bed can't say the same thing even if they are debutantes."

James reminded himself he had a lady in every port he visited. They were willing to have sex with him and just as The Duchess implied, he took them for granted. "What would you like me to promise?"

"There are several guarantees I need the three of you to make, but the first one is that while you are courting my nieces, you must promise me you will not have sex with any other woman." She waited, seemingly patient hands folded primly in her lap.

Gavin and Jamie were quick to answer, but James thought about the issues he had about courting Tavia and if he was truly wooing her, it would be months before he saw her again.

"What about you, young man?" She directed her question James' direction while she loudly tapped the cane on the floor as if intending to get his undivided attention.

17

Heat rose to his face, "Even if I wanted to, I'm not sure if I'm courting Tavia. My ship leaves..."

"I know, in two days. You cannot continue to use that fact as an excuse," she harshly interrupted. It seems you must make a decision right now and in front of me and your friends. Are you or aren't you going to see Tavia? If you have a lady in every port, you'll have to inform them you are no longer available. Can you do that?"

His heart thundered in his chest. He still had so many reservations, and the what ifs seemed to grow faster than he could possibly explain.

"Are you courting Tavia?" The Duchess persisted.

"Yes." He knew the answer would leave him with no regrets, not until he returned and if in the time he was gone, she found another man.

"Can you forgo your mistresses?"

"I have no mistresses." That part was true. He didn't keep anyone.

"Then my apologies, the ladies who wait for your arrival with baited breath," she spoke softly for the first time.

"If I have Tavia waiting for me here, I have no problem promising not to see other women. I will keep that vow." With his words, a weight was taken off his chest, and he began to look forward to this evening.

"To the second part, which will most likely be easier. Promise me you will not abscond with your lady to a cabin or to your ship in hopes of finding out if the two you are sexually compatible."

"Of course not," James was quick to say. "A single lady has no place on a sailing vessel carrying cargo. Your niece and I have already had that conversation."

"Good, my heart couldn't take another scenario such as the one Fayth and Jarret put me through. What about the both of you?" She directed her attention to Jamie and Gavin.

"I promise," they said in unison.

"Very well. Gavin, I've learned your family owns a hunting lodge. Are you positive?" She challenged the young man.

They all understood what she wanted to learn.

"I will not take her there for..." he stopped midsentence.

She smiled clearly pleased, "I would send my men to collect the two of you if you tried something like this. Drake took advantage of my wishes to see my charges happily wed. I was convinced Drake was the right man for Ella. The only one here who fits the category of suitor material is the only one unsure if he wants to court my niece." She directed her gaze toward James.

Her words shocked James. Most times confidence exuded from him. With Tavia he'd been unsure from the moment he saw her. He wanted her but knew she wouldn't desire a man who spent his time at sea, a man without a title, a man who had no place to call home save his ship.

Gavin and Jamie appeared as if they wanted to protest but wisely kept their mouths shut.

"What is the next promise?" James was beginning to sweat. The first two had been strange; the next one promised to surprise him as well.

"The hardest one of all is simple because it goes against everything that drives a man." She looked pleased with herself.

She managed to pry promises from all of them. Whether they kept them or not remained to be seen. Temptations waited around every corner.

"I wait in anticipation," James murmured, appreciating the elder lady more with each passing minute.

She cackled, pouring herself another brandy and sipping slowly, finally setting it on the table. He found himself holding his breath in eagerness.

She cleared her throat. "I was a bit parched. Let's get this over with. I've explained all this to my nieces. Men think with a different part of their anatomy than women. Be assured they don't know as yet exactly what I meant, but they are aware of the problem."

"And..." he didn't know if he was relieved or not. If she didn't explain anything about that anatomy, he thought it would inevitably be left up to him.

"I told my girls men think with their cock while they thought with their hearts."

~ * ~

Their evening gowns were hung and ready to put on, their makeup was strewn across the dressing tables, powders, eye paint, soot mixed with oil for the lashes.

"Don't use too much," Larena cautioned as she applied a shiny pearl powder on her face followed by a light rose-colored blush to her cheeks. "This is so much better than a white face."

"Do you think James will kiss you tonight?" Tira asked. "He really just has to and you have to let him. A kiss from the right man is heavenly."

"I have to do no such thing. Last night I wanted him to kiss me, but today everything has changed. If he does though, I won't object. I might even like it." Tavia smushed her lips together after applying a soft lip color.

"And why not? You know he's going to be away at sea for several months. You have to do it now so he'll remember you," Larena patted her hair into place and smiled at herself in the mirror.

"I'm leaving too," Tavia said softly, her hands shaking with fear of the unknown. "I've been taken on as a cabin boy on a ship, called the Firtha, sailing for Spain and Italy."

"You haven't!" Larena whirled on her cousin, her hands on her heart. "That can't be safe."

"I'm going to pretend I'm a boy so no one will be the wiser. Supposed to report for duty as the new cabin boy tomorrow afternoon so I'll be settled in when the ship leaves port. As soon as I'm ready, I'll have Tira take me to the docks." The closer she got to the time of departure, the more she reconsidered. So many fears assailed her.

"Do you even know what a cabin boy does?" Larena asked, clearly shocked at Tavia's statement. "They might have to do something totally inappropriate. They are boys, you know."

"I made inquiries." Tavia said, turning her back to her sister Tira for help with the corset. "They wait on the captain for one and carry messages from one end of the vessel to the other. I think I'm supposed to help trim the sails too."

"Well, I guess you could do part of that. Should find out how to trim sails sooner than later," Larena said sarcastically, eyeing her fingernails, "But why would you want to? You really should stay here in London where you won't be putting your life in danger."

"You know why. We're stopping somewhere in Spain and Italy. I can barely contain myself. I'm afraid I'll say something to James and he'll tell The Duchess and she'll lock me in tomorrow so I can't get away." Reciting all the places she was about to see left her breathless.

"I'm half tempted to tell her myself. This is really a fool's mission. When our auntie finds out we hid the information from her, she'll be furious. I don't have any idea what she'll do," Larena said.

"Tira and I went shopping this morning and I've breeches and shirts, bought strips of cloth to bind my breasts. No one will guess I'm a girl." She sported a huge smile, feeling a new surge of confidence.

"What about your hair," Larena said dryly. Even if you keep it tucked beneath a hat, you risk losing the hat in a brisk wind. How will you explain that? When all your hair tumbles down your back."

"Don't put a damper on this. I've got it all figured out. Tira and I discussed this escapade at length. I'm going to cut it off."

"No!"

"Yes, tomorrow after we get up, my first escapade will begin. I'm supposed to go riding with James, but I'm going to feign sickness. Once Tira has chopped it all off, we're going to the docks. I'll find the ship and board. Bought a duffel bag to keep my clothes in," she said proud of herself and the efforts she and her twin made for this adventure to succeed.

"Escapade is right."

"I'm going to the states after Jamie leaves," Tira said smugly, looking to her sister, seeming to ask for approval. "I'm going to stay at Ravyn's house in Baltimore, and I'm going to learn how to build ships."

"Really," Larena said, gazing at the twins as if they'd gone stark raving mad. "You're going to pretend you're a boy, too, and leave me all alone here? I don't like it that you're all deserting me."

"I'm sorry but we're pursuing our dreams." The twins ran to hug Lorena.

"You and Gavin will get along just fine. What are your dreams? You must have some or one even."

"I don't know," Larena said. "My passion is to ease the plight of the poor. I want to fight for all the injustices that have been done by the English government to the commoners."

"That's very noble. And you, too, would get more accomplished if you were a man," Tira said.

"Someone go peek and see if the men have arrived," Tavia said as she was putting the finishing touches on her hair.

"I'll go," Larena said and departed without a backward glance.

"Do you think she'll tell?" Tavia asked, afraid Larena would do just that. "I shouldn't have said anything. At least when you leave, you'll be with Aidan and Ravyn and Aric will visit from time to time. You'll have a home and you won't be on a ship and sleeping in the same place as the rest of the crew."

When she said the words, her adventure seemed more daunting and dangerous than when she planned it. She could not sleep with the crew. She'd have to find some place on deck where she could curl up and remain safe. This was a far cry from purchasing passage and having a room of her own. James' words came back to haunt her.

The door opened and Larena slipped inside, her back to the closed door. "They are here sitting in the parlor with refreshments and The Duchess is lecturing them."

"About what?"

"Promises. She's making them promise certain things. I didn't hear what exactly, but we can ask them tonight," Larena said breathlessly.

"I can only imagine. Do you think the promises are the same as the ones we made to The Duchess?" Tira asked while she finished with the fastenings on Tavia's dress.

"Probably not," Tavia said, trying to remember the three promises the girls made. "They couldn't possibly be the same."

"The Duchess wouldn't ask the same of the men. She could never make them promise not to go anywhere that was not chaperoned or unprotected."

"No, they'd laugh at her," Larena said.

"We promised to think with our heads not our hearts where the men are concerned," Tavia said, pausing a moment. "She most likely told them not to think with their cock."

"Close enough," Tira said. "What's a cock?"

"We'll have to find out. Whoever discover it first has to tell everyone else."

"Agreed."

"What do you think there third promise was?" Tavia asked. "It certainly wasn't ours. We promised to stay open minded and if they did something we didn't like, we had to tell them or her. Either one was fine."

Larena spoke up. "I heard her say something about sleeping with a different woman in every port. I don't know what the promise could be except not to do that."

"He really does sleep with a woman every place they stop?" Tavia's voice cracked. "Who does he have in London that he sees?"

Chapter Two

The girls entered the parlor, chatting with anticipation of the evening to come and eager to find out what The Duchess made their suitors promise. Tavia felt as if she floated on a magical cloud as they descended the stairway.

"We're ready," Larena said as she sat down next to Gavin. "I so want to see her sing."

James rose and helped Tavia to the chair where he'd been sitting. "A seat for you." He took a place behind her.

Jamie did the same for Tira. Scarlett entered with a tray filled with pre-theatre snacks. The platter held generous servings of apricot marmalade and cakes as well as lavender shortbread. The butler carried a pitcher of lemonade and glasses.

"I thought you all might like a snack before you leave. So I took matters into my own hands. Help yourself." The Duchess poured herself a glass of lemonade to replace the whiskey she'd been drinking previously. "I will expect a complete depiction of the evening on the morrow. So best you all pay attention to the play, not other things."

"Thank you," they all said.

"And we will certainly tell you all about our evening. Although I'm sure Scarlett will also tell you her version," Tavia said with a silent laugh, thinking about the differences in stories.

"This goes beyond anything I would have expected. Thank you for the food and drink," James said politely. "It's much appreciated."

The knuckles of his hands grazed Tavia's neck. She shivered slightly at the contact as he moved them in a gentle massage. She turned needing to see his eyes. When she did, the warmth emanating from them struck her, gave her pause even as her heart suddenly beat faster.

"Can I get you a plate?" James asked, letting his hand drift across her shoulder then linger at the base of her neck.

"Yes, please." She shivered at the sensations he created, wishing they were alone and not surrounded by so many people.

"I'll get you one," he bent low, speaking softly. His breath whispered across her flesh, reminding her of a sweet and very gentle spring breeze. She clenched her fingers in her gown.

A few minutes later he handed her the food and a drink. "Who is singing tonight?" James asked, handing the plate of food to Tavia.

"You mean you don't follow the opera?" Gavin asked, wielding a crooked grin. "I believe it's Angelica Catalani."

James shrugged his broad shoulders. "Don't know why I asked. The name doesn't mean anything to me, as I knew it wouldn't. And no, I've never been to Covent Garden nor did I ever think I would attend an opera."

Biting into an apricot cake spread with marmalade, his mouth full, Gavin enlightened him. "She's a famous Italian opera singer. Rumor has it after she sang for Napoleon, he was so enamored of her he refused to give her a passport to leave France. You will undoubtedly love her."

"I'm sure I will," James said with a slight chuckle.

"The food is quite good, Auntie," Tira said, smiling at Jamie. "Did Cook find some new recipes?"

"Yes, yes she did and she was dying to try them out. I'll leave you. I'm tired and intend to take a short nap. Scarlett will go to the theatre with you, so I've ordered two carriages. You have wonderful box seats. Now enjoy. Don't keep Scarlett up too late."

Tira turned to Jamie, "What did The Duchess ask you to promise? You can tell us. She made us promise things too."

"We heard about women in other ports," Tira slanted her statement toward James. "Do you really have someone waiting for you everywhere you go? The thought is hard to wrap my mind around."

"Are you sleeping with lots of different women? If you're going to court my cousin, you best stop those habits," Larena told him indignantly, her head tilted slightly.

A slow rise of color to James' face told Tavia what Larena overheard was most likely true. Suddenly struck with a wave of jealousy, she turned to him, "Tell me you don't."

James cleared his throat, pausing in thought for a few seconds. "Tavia, I'm not celibate; never pretended to be. If you want a man who is a virgin, then you don't want me. A man has certain needs..." It seemed he thought better of saying anything more.

"Then what else did you all promise? It's only right that we know so we can help you keep the vows you made to The Duchess," Larena asked, poking Jamie in the chest.

"We promised," James cut in, "that if we wanted to court you, we wouldn't have sex with any other women. I promised to forgo my women friends where we stop to load and unload our cargo. The others promised something similar."

"Then you're officially courting me?" Tavia asked, smiling and wondering what he expected from her now. "Am I to forgo all other suitors while you're at sea? That would be so boring."

"Tavia!" Larena said, with unexpected force. "That paints an unladylike picture. You must take it back."

"Seems fair to me," James said, roughing his hands through his hair. "But I would never hold you to that. You have a right to have fun while I'm gone. I'd never expect you to stay in the townhouse for all those months while your cousins go out with their suitors. But I would warn you to stay away from Edwin. I don't have a good feeling about that man."

"What did the rest of you promise?" Tira asked.

"The obvious," Jamie said, "Pretty much the same as James. We're not going to see any of our usual women friends for sex while we are courting."

"What else?" Larena asked, tapping a toe impatiently.

"Nope, it's your turn. What did you promise?" James asked, watching her with his intense brooding eyes.

"Not to go anywhere with you without a chaperone, which is obvious, but the promise comes because of her previous charges who had a penchant for doing just what they liked. They had this uncanny ability to lose their chaperones," Tavia said, knowing she was about to do the same thing.

"I also promised," he put her plate on the table and took her hands in his, "that I wouldn't abscond with you on my ship. So, if and when you are ever on my vessel, we will be wed, and The Duchess will have no say."

They revealed the other promises, laughing about The Duchess and her attempts to keep them safe from their suitors.

Entering Covent Garden, the halls were filled with people. Music played while they waited for the performance to begin and the sound of tuning instruments filled the hallways.

They found their seats a few minutes before the singing would start. James put an arm around her, and she leaned against him enjoying the feel of his muscular body next to her.

"She really does have a beautiful voice," she murmured, closing her eyes and imagining sailing on the ocean with James. She was going to be on a ship, but it wouldn't be with him. A small niggle of fear spiraled through her while she remembered all the reasons James quoted to her why she shouldn't sail by herself.

Her preparations had been meticulous. Her inquiry about the captain of the ship she would sail on were heaped with praise for the man. Nothing would happen to her. Tomorrow Tira would cut her hair. After that the two of them would go to the docks and she would walk up the gangplank and let the first mate know she was ready to perform her duties.

James would be angry with her when he found out what she'd done, but she'd be home by then and there would, of course, be nothing he could do about it. The Duchess would be furious with her when she read the note she'd already penned to her dear auntie. She didn't want to disappoint anyone, but she needed to follow her dreams.

"Tavia, Tavia, you need to wake up."

Her name whispered close to her ear caused her eyes to open. Disoriented, she looked around. "What?"

"You fell asleep and I didn't have the heart to wake you. Indeed, I enjoyed watching you sleep." He ran his knuckles across her cheek, all the while grinning.

She sat up, brushing hair from her eyes. Most of the pins must have come lose. "I..."

"You?"

"I was tired. My hair, what happened to it?"

"You were restless. Bad dreams? I think I can fix it." And in a few deft moves he repined her hair into an acceptable coif.

"How do you know how to do that? Never mind, I doubt if I want to know the answer."

"Would you like to get something to eat or drink a hot cup of coffee, a sandwich or perhaps some eel jelly? We can walk and find a vendor to buy something to eat."

"I'd like that." She yawned, knowing she needed to wake up because she still had a lot to do before tomorrow. She didn't want to miss the sailing and the harbormaster told her the ship would sail *with or without me*, a lowly cabin boy, and the captain was eager to leave port so he could return as soon as possible.

"The others are returning home. Scarlett offered to stay with us, but I assured her my vows were solid and you didn't need a chaperone. She was really tired, about to fall asleep on her feet."

Hand in hand they strode down the street, stopping at various stalls to purchase food and drink until the time was well past midnight.

"We should go home before The Duchess sends her men after us."

"I'll hail us a carriage."

Inside the vehicle she was suddenly met with a bit of yearning for him, "You're going to be gone how long?" she asked, suddenly realizing she was going to miss him and terrified as well as excited about what she intended. She was told the ship she was sailing on would be at sea for four months.

"Four months give or take a few weeks." His calloused finger trailed a path down her cheek, sending a flurry of sensations through her. "I wish it wasn't that long of a trip."

"Would you kiss me? Just once before you leave?" she whispered as she turned toward him, wishing she could see into his eyes.

"I'm not sure I dare."

"Why ever not. It's just one kiss." Unconsciously, she moistened her lips.

"I might not be able to stop. If I kiss you here," he touched her lips, "then I'd want to kiss you here, and here and maybe even here." He drew a line to her ear down her neck then across her collarbone before following a line just above her bodice, resting on her cleavage.

She inhaled sharply at the sensation as they drew ever closer to her breasts. "Just one."

"Women really shouldn't wear such tempting clothing," he murmured as his lips drew closer to hers.

"This is the fashion," she murmured. "What does it have to do with kissing me once? I assure you I don't mean to tempt you."

"Yet tempt me, you do." Instead of his lips touching hers, he traced a path across them with a finger. "So soft, is every part of you soft?" He moistened his lips.

"I don't know," she told him, having never thought about such a thing. Lord, but her throat was parched. She swept her tongue across her lips, touching his finger as she did so.

A soft rumble emanated from his chest as he pressed his finger on her lips. "You have no idea what you do to me. I don't think I can stop at one taste. I will have to try you again and again to see if you are just as sweet the second and third times."

"We are nearly there." She closed her eyes while she felt the warmth of his lips and tongue on her chin then either side of her mouth. His hands were placed on each side of her head, holding her still.

"True, but the carriage will wait until we are finished." He drew away from her, looking at her as if he'd never seen or kissed another girl. After the conversation today about promises, she understood that wasn't true. While she'd never been with another man in any way, he'd had many women in his bed.

"After tonight, I'll be able to tell my cousins I've been kissed."

"You would kiss and tell? I didn't think ladies did that," he murmured, his mouth finally descending to meet hers.

"Oh...no!" she cried as she was suddenly thrown into his arms, the carriage lurching sideways before grinding to a halt. She now lay sprawled on top of him, both hands on his chest. Trying to push away to sit upright, she found she couldn't move.

"Are you alright?" he asked, setting her to the opposite side of the carriage.

"I'm fine, maybe a little bruised. What happened?"

"It must have lost a wheel. I'm going to see if I can climb out that side then pull you out. Stay still. Any movement might topple this more. Do you understand?"

She nodded while she watched him push open the door and pull himself out. "Now you." He peered inside. "Can you maneuver yourself closer to the door?"

"I think so," her heart thundered in her chest. Her arms and legs ached. With all the strength she had, she pushed against one door, trying to reach the other and his hands.

After several tries and the rocking of the carriage with her movement, she was able reach him. He pulled her from the vehicle then ran his hands along her arms.

"Do you hurt anywhere?" he asked with concern.

"Everywhere," she laughed. "But I'll live. I've fallen from trees and off horses with more injuries than I have now."

"From now on you should stay out of trees and off horses." His voice held a slight hint of amusement.

She wasn't sure what to stay to this. "I haven't been in a tree top for several years now. I'm very sure of foot, but I'm not going to stay off horses. I enjoy a ride every now and then."

"Good then, if you just take out the gentler horses we will do just fine. Your hair has come undone again." He bent close to her, pushing the strands behind her ears. "Did you know it feels like silken fire?"

The driver of the carriage appeared from the other side. "If you help me right this thing, I can have the wheel back on in a few minutes and have both of you home."

"We'll walk. The townhouse is less than a block from here." James strode to the other side and in minutes had it righted.

"Heard you two talking," the driver said. "Are you both uninjured?"

"Except for a few bruises we'll be fine. Pick me up as soon as you've finished with the wheel."

A few minutes later, they stood at the door to the townhouse. "I certainly didn't expect this evening to end with a carriage accident."

"Neither did I," he said. "Do you still want that kiss?" Her back was to the door and he stood with his legs braced apart, his hands on her shoulders.

"Yes," she whispered softly, anticipation high. Before she left tomorrow, she wanted that kiss.

"Good," he said.

"My Lady Hepburn," the door opened and the butler stood just inside, illuminated by candlelight.

They jumped apart, Tavia turning away from him, "My goodness you frightened me," she said, her hand on her chest.

James stepped back, "My lady," he said, "I'll take my leave. Have a good evening. And I'll see you in four months."

Disappointed, Tavia watched him stride toward the carriage before she turned to go inside. The hour was late and all she wanted to do was go to bed, but it wasn't possible.

"Show my niece into the parlor."

Tavia had not expected The Duchess to be up and waiting for her. "Auntie? What are you doing?"

"Have a seat, child. You realize just how late it is." Her cane tapped on the floor several times.

"Not really. I know the others returned a while ago but nothing happened. He hasn't even kissed me." Tavia sat down, nervously smoothing her skirt and wondering what questions she would have to answer.

"So, you kept the man out in hopes he would kiss you?" The Duchess asked, a smile spreading across her face. "I'm glad to hear you are still very innocent and that your man is not trying to take advantage of that naivety." The Duchess kept her gaze focused on her.

She inhaled a long breath of courage. "I don't think he would. He didn't want to kiss me because he was leaving, but I know he would have if he'd had more time."

"What stopped you then?" The Duchess tilted her head and stared at her as if she tried to see inside her head.

Tavia gave a tiny shrug of her shoulders. "I don't know. A carriage accident and the butler opening the door."

"You're not hurt, are you?" The Duchess asked. "What happened to the carriage?"

"No, I'm fine. The carriage just lost a wheel." She folded her hands in her lap to keep them still. "After the theater we walked for a while and stopped at a few vendors for food and coffee. He's really a gentleman. Is that all Auntie, I need to get some sleep?"

"Sit with me for a few minutes," The Duchess said, her voice a bit stern. "Larena has told me you have something important you haven't spoken of yet. Would you care to do that now?"

"No," she was shaking her head and swallowing the curse she had for her cousin. "I have nothing to say. Larena is misinformed, that's all."

"Good, I was afraid you were planning on running to your ship's captain tomorrow and ruining yourself like Fayth did."

"I don't want to ruin myself. In time I want a husband and children, and I understand the repercussions if I was to do something so foolish," she told her aunt, knowing what she did plan might be considered just as foolish as what her cousin did.

"Go to bed then." She shooed her away with her hands. I'll see you when you wake up. You know you have a ride with Mr. Macmurra in the afternoon planned. So, make sure you get your beauty rest and you're ready on time. Wear the new riding habit I bought you."

"I will," Tavia walked to her aunt and gave her a quick hug and a kiss. "I love you, Auntie."

"And I you."

She raced up the steps to the room she shared with her twin. She closed the door then leaned against it, taking in deep breaths.

"Where have you been?" Tira asked, her brows drawn together in concern. "It seems I've been waiting half the night for you."

"With James," she said, whirling around the room, her skirts spinning around her.

"This whole time?"

"Where else would I have been?" Tavia asked indignantly. "We walked and ate."

"On his ship. I thought maybe you changed your mind about the cabin boy thing and like Fayth followed him to your ruined reputation."

"Tira," she said indignantly, "you know me better than that. I'm nothing like Fayth."

"I know, it's just we had plans and now we're a couple of hours late. I've tepid water here for your bath. It might well be the last one you get in the next four months," Tira said.

Tavia shuddered at the thought, realizing what her twin said might well be the truth. "Help me out of my clothes."

Time ticked by as the twins prepared for Tavia's departure. Tira raided the kitchen and filled Tavia's duffel bag with all kinds of treats. Some from last night's fare as well as an array of meats, cheeses and bread.

"Don't know what kind of food you'll get," Tira said.

"Leftovers most likely. From the information I learned about cabin boys, they're pretty much the lowest man on the ship."

"The food is packed as is your change of clothing. Now all we have to do is cut your hair."

"James said it was silken fire." Tavia ran her fingers through the length a moment of hesitation encapsulating her.

"It will grow back," Tira reminded her.

~ * ~

"Captain?"

"Yes, Seamus," James stared at the ledgers he still couldn't decipher because his mind was on Tavia.

"Ship's loaded and the new cabin boy arrived about an hour ago. If you want, we can set sail now."

"I believe I'll miss her." He thought of the feel of her hair winding through his fingers and her breath so close to him he could inhale her essence. It would not be hard to forego sex on this trip. Everyone would fall short when he compared them to Tavia. He'd never done that before, compared his lovers, but Tavia wasn't even a lover yet.

"Miss who?" Seamus asked, rubbing his whiskered chin thoughtfully. "Your debutante. Thought you didn't want anything to do with the marriage market and beginners."

"This one's different." She wanted to see the world, and bloody hell but he wanted to show it to her. He would have to win The Duchess' blessing, and he would have to marry her first. In four months' time if she was still single, he'd court her properly.

A few weeks ago, good God, a few days ago, he'd vowed never to marry. His life had been exactly how he wanted it. Now one, beautiful woman-child changed him. He was nearly a decade older than her. She wasn't a child, just innocent.

"You're smitten. She might not even be available when we return," Seamus pointed out.

"Set sail. The sooner we go the sooner we'll get back. Pray for smooth sailing. I don't want to waste any time on this trip. I'll join you as soon as I finish with these documents." He ran his hand through the papers, stacking them again then sorting through them, intent on finding the most important first.

"Don't rush. I got everything under control. The men tell me the boy climbs the masts like a monkey."

"Once we're out to sea, send the boy to me. I want to meet him. What's his name?"

"Tommy, no last name." Seamus chuckled. "Must be hiding from something or somebody."

"How old is he?" James asked, surprisingly curious about their new crewmember.

"Says he's fifteen but can't be a day over twelve. Nothing but smooth skin on his chin."

"Looks can be deceiving. Still..." his thoughts returned to Tavia and the kiss that never materialized.

"That all, Captain?"

"Go ahead, get this ship moving." His gut tightened, his instincts honed, as they always were when he sailed. Something was wrong. Yet Seamus gave no indication he sensed anything amiss.

He shook the thoughts to the back of his head, listening to the crew as they went about their duties. He heard the sails as they filled with wind and felt the subtle sway of the Firth as it moved from the docks to catch the current of the Thames heading toward the ocean.

Leaning back in his chair, he sipped the whiskey he'd poured earlier, once again his mind traveling backwards. He prayed Tavia could keep Edwin at bay. He spoke to The Duchess about the man and she agreed with him. Edwin would not be suitable for her niece, but that didn't mean it would stop the man, and now she had no one to protect her save The Duchess.

He sifted through the papers, finally finishing with them. He set them aside. He felt the change of the ship as it left the river and headed into the ocean, picking up speed.

The knock on the door didn't surprise him. "Come in."

"Tommy here."

The sight of the cabin boy shook him to the core, and he knew he had to school his features as well as his surprise. It was important that he think this out before he revealed what he knew.

"Tommy. Tommy no name. Why is that?" He watched her stop midstride when she entered before she had the look of a cornered animal. "Nice name." He drummed his fingers on the desk, trying to remember everything Seamus had told him about the new help and the subtle smirk in the man's eyes. The first mate had meant to see how he handled this and was most likely laughing right now. Seamus was probably at the door listening.

"Yes," she folded her hands in front of her.

"Heard you climbed the masts and handled the rigging quite well. Heard you were as nimble as a monkey." His glance riveted on her hands, which were bleeding. He clenched his fists, his anger simmering. He knew he had to discipline his emotions, but in this case it was damn hard.

"Yes, sir," she looked down. It didn't seem she wanted to meet his gaze.

"Your feet must be really interesting. You can't take your gaze off them. Look at me when I address you." He didn't know what to do. If he let her know that he knew who she was... Damn, but he didn't have an empty cabin, and the only place he could keep her was in his cabin, with him.

She wouldn't be protected sleeping with the crew nor would she remain safe sleeping with him for the duration of their trip. The crew would figure out he was a she before she could blink, and they would want certain favors he wouldn't allow with any cabin boy, let alone Tavia.

He was caught in the middle of an untenable position. The vows he'd made with The Duchess had just been undone but not by him. He would not return her to London pregnant with his child. He wouldn't. Or they would be married but not until they reached a port. Unless they made an unscheduled stop, that was months away.

"Yes sir," she said, looking up and biting her lip.

Her britches as well as her shirt were loose fitting, but he didn't doubt for a moment if she bent over the perfect roundness of her derrière would give her away.

"Are you enjoying yourself?" he asked for lack of a better question and trying for time to figure out his next move.

"Yes, sir."

"Do you know what your duties are?"

"Yes, sir."

"What are they?" he asked, wondering what exactly she would come up with.

"I'm supposed to wait on you and the other officers, and I'm supposed to take messages to various people and become familiar with the sails, lines and ropes and the use of all of these in all types of weather." It seemed she'd memorized her words.

"Good, very good, rest assured your only duty is to wait on me. You'll attend to all my needs and you won't leave the cabin unless I'm with you. Whatever happens I don't want you climbing the masts. Seamus," he yelled.

"Captain?"

"Hammock. In here. Now."

"Yes, sir," the man said with a chuckle that told James his first mate knew the cabin boy was a girl, but what he didn't know was that she was Tavia Hepburn, the debutant he'd been seeing, the one he intended to court.

James stared at her, hoping she'd apologize or tell him how sorry she was. "Nothing to say?"

She moistened her lips and his gut turned upside down. "What will your crew say?"

"They won't say anything. I'm the captain and they obey my orders as will you." What possible motive could she have for keeping up this ruse? She had to realize he saw through her disguise.

"Yes, sir."

It didn't matter whether or not she came forward, she was going back the minute they reached a port and he found a reputable captain. Then, perhaps she didn't know he recognized her. If that were the case, she'd never say anything.

"I don't want to be seen as someone who shirks their duties, Sir," she said, finally meeting his gaze. "I like climbing the masts. It's fun. Been doing it practically my entire life, well trees, that is."

Tempted to relax a bit and let her get a taste of the work she'd face if he allowed it, he struggled with his next words. "You cannot go up the masts. That is not a cabin boy's duties on my vessels," he lied.

"I misunderstood then? I apologize."

"You did."

"Captain? It's Seamus. Got the hammock." The first mate pushed the door open. "Where do you want it?"

James pointed to the side of the cabin just over the bed. If she fell out, at least she wouldn't land on the hard floor. *But in my arms.*

"You want me to put it over the bed?" Seamus seemed to question him.

"You heard me." Then he focused his attention on her. "Go to the galley and bring two plates of whatever they're serving. You can eat with me."

She darted from the cabin as if his room was the last place she wanted to be, not bothering to say, yes, sir or thank you, sir for rescuing me from your crew.

"When she's on deck, if you're anywhere near her, make sure nothing happens and bring me warm water and some salve. It won't take long for the crew to see the curves she tries to hide."

"Aren't you going above and beyond with the little gal? I'm sure you could find someplace safe for her to sleep other than your cabin," Seamus said as he made places for the hooks.

He debated telling Seamus the details. No one needed to know until he was ready. "Where would that be?"

Seamus rubbed his chin. "I'll try to think of somewhere. If you keep her in here, there will be talk. Some'll call you an abuser of innocents."

"And you and my other officers who know me will quash the gossip." His furry simmered deep inside. He'd looked forward to a quick journey then home to Tavia. Most of his crew had been with him for years, and he could trust them to be discreet, but there were a few who were new on this trip.

"Might not be as easy as you think. If they find out he's a she, they'll want a little of what they believe you're getting."

"Then we'll give them an extra night in port so they can see to their needs." James rose from behind his desk, pacing the room while Seamus set up the hammock.

"Think you got everything figured out, do you? Don't you doubt there will be surprises. What about the little debutant you got waiting for you at home? What will she think when she learns you had another woman sleeping in your cabin for the duration?"

"I'm sure she'll understand when I explain everything to her." She wouldn't though. If this lasted for the extent of the trip, she would think he kept a woman in his bed and she'd be furious even though it was her. She would think he broke his promise to The Duchess.

"If that's what you're thinking, you don't know much about women, Captain. Just sayin'."

"No more than you, Seamus O'Malley."

"There you go, hammock's up and functional. Now all she has to do is learn to sleep in the blasted thing. You goin' to give her lessons in that?" Seamus chuckled.

"Get your mind out of the gutter," James muttered.

The knock on the door didn't surprise him but, "Captain!" the panic in her voice did. "Can't get the door open."

When Seamus started for the door, James stopped him. "I'll get it."

Tavia stood in the doorway, loaded down with food and drink.

"Cook gave me everything in the galley. Didn't think I could carry it all."

"Best you build up those muscles, lad. Maybe the captain here will teach you a few things about boxing."

Her eyes grew wide. "Boxing?

Seamus took the tray from her and placed it on the small table in front of him.

"That's an excellent idea, Seamus. The boy should know something about fighting as well as protecting himself. It will give him good judgment too." James gave Tavia a solid blow to her back, sending her stumbling, instantly regretting his actions. If he intended to convince Tavia to go home by the next port, he would have to make her feel as uncomfortable as possible.

"Do I have a say in this?" She moved her shoulders up and down, trying to ease the pain from the blow.

"You'll love boxing. It's a manly sport and builds muscle." Seamus seemed to be enjoying this. "Got enough food here for several people. Mind if I join you?" he chuckled.

"Don't you have something to do? Like steering the ship."

"No, got one of the more experienced crew at the wheel. Don't need to take the helm for a couple of hours now." Seamus grinned.

"I'll make sure you get anything that's left when we're done. Need that soap and warm water." James reminded him.

"Aye, Captain." Seamus, seeming to realize it was time to stop baiting him, left returning in a few minutes with the requested items.

James nodded for him to leave. Her lessons and discomfort would begin now.

"If you need anything, send Tommy," Seamus said as he moved toward the door, grinning like a besotted fool.

When the door closed, "Come here," his voice gentled as he watched her hesitate.

"What are you going to do?" she didn't move.

"Don't be afraid. I'm not going to hurt you, just fix up your hands." He reached for her but she stepped back, distancing herself further.

"They're fine." She held them as if hiding the wounds from him would either make them go away or make him vanish. She probably wanted him to leave, but he wasn't going anywhere.

"Come here," he repeated in a firmer tone beginning to lose patience with her.

"Is that an order?" she moved another step back. "If not, I think I'll go and see if anyone has messages for you."

"It's an order," he growled. She wasn't understanding the situation and how she put herself at risk if she spent too much time with the crew.

Hesitating then slowly stepping forward, she stopped in front of him, hands still clasped tightly together behind her back. "What are you going to do?"

He watched the rapid pulse at the base of her neck. Bloody hell but he wanted to kiss her there. He wasn't a saint, far from it. "Fix these scratches and pull out any splinters embedded in your skin." He drew out a knife and heated it over the flames of a candle.

"No!" She stepped backward again, terror in her eyes.

"Tommy, enough of this game. When you need help you should learn to accept it." He rose, striding to her and guiding her by the arm, he settled her on a chair. "Give me your hands."

Reluctantly she set one hand palm side down on the table. Despite her reluctance to be close to him, he sat next to her. Gently turning her hand over, he examined the scratches and was relieved to find there were no slivers to cut out. He soaked a cloth in the water and rubbed soap over it before gently washing and rinsing the cuts then repeated his actions with her other hand.

He applied the salve then wrapped both hands with clean bandages. "Now they won't get infected."

"Infected?"

"Was that so bad?" He wanted to bring her hands to his lips and kiss them, show her just how delicate she was, but he didn't dare do anything so foolish. As far as he knew, she didn't know he recognized her and he meant to keep it that way until she revealed herself.

"No."

"Are you hungry? We've food and drink." He heaped a plate of food for her.

"I can't eat that much," she told him, clearly distraught. "What is the hammock for?"

"Sleep," he said with a grin. "What did you think it was for, hanging laundry perhaps?"

"Who is going to sleep there?" She broke off a chunk of bread and dipped it in the gravy before taking a bite.

"You."

The bread flew from her mouth. "Sorry."

He understood how wary she must be of him. After all he'd established ulterior motives of men to the best of his abilities when she told him she meant to sail the world.

"I told you that you would wait only on me." He smiled. "The last place I want you at night is with the crew." The look on her face told him he shouldn't have said that.

"Do you treat all the cabin boys like this?"

No, of course not, but this was a different situation. "Sometimes on the first night. You are so small. You wouldn't do well with the men. Not only would they tease you unmercifully, but they would go out of their way to pick fights. They are men, what else would you expect?"

"Oh," she chewed thoughtfully. "I guess it's alright then, but I'm not at all sure I can sleep in that thing let alone get in it. Isn't it an awfully long ways from the floor?"

"If it's too high, I'll lower it. Once you get in, you won't fall out. The sides kind of wrap themselves around you." Looking at it more closely it was pretty far off the floor. Seamus, the devil inside him, had put it there with a purpose. "Finish eating," he waved the fork he held in the air. "You need to eat everything on your plate."

The look she graced him with told him things he'd rather not think about. Just as always, she was going to do exactly what she wanted. Then she shrugged her slim delicate shoulders, "I'll eat what I want."

He watched her put food in her mouth, her manners impeccable, hardly ones of the likes of a cabin boy. She would never survive on her own in this capacity. His stomach rolled, thinking about what might have happened to her if she found herself on any ship but his.

"What's your story, Tommy with no last name? The tale must be

41

interesting. What brought you here?" He settled back on his chair, his arms crossed over his chest, his gaze riveted on her.

She gulped her wine, her eyes staring at him over the rim of her glass. "What's it to you?" She sounded defiant and obstinate.

"Just curious, your manners are impeccable. That fact tells me a story about that. Your lack of a last name does not." He shouldn't but he enjoyed her discomfort. The sooner she came to terms with the fact she was doing something so incredibly foolish and the sooner she realized these actions put her life in jeopardy, he could return her to London.

"What does that have to do with anything? You have good manners too," she was quick to say.

"I'm not a young man with no home, parents, or family of any sort. A young man who needs to take a job on a sailing ship as a cabin boy."

"So?" she challenged him, her chin jutting forward defiantly.

He leaned forward, "So," he began, "what I know and have seen of your tale, nothing matches. The facts don't go together."

"My story is my own and it's none of your business." Her lips pursed together even while her eyes narrowed, stubbornly remaining silent about herself. "If I don't wish to tell it, I won't."

He was more than curious about what she would tell him when she finally gave in, and she would if it took him all night. "Not when I employ you, feed you, keep you safe. I need to know if there is a family who will care about you and what happens on this journey. What if you die at sea? Who will I send the remains to?" They never took remains home, simply buried the person at sea, but he wasn't about to tell her that.

Her face paled. She suddenly found a great interest in the food on her dish where before, except for a few bites, she was merely pushing the food around on her plate.

"I have no family, no one who will care." Her gaze remained on her plate.

If anything, she was not a good liar. Where previously her face was nearly white it was now suffused in color. "I think you're lying."

""You've no reason to say something so absurd. Why would I lie? I've no motive. Lies are for people who have something to hide."

Aw, but she did have a motive and he understood what it was.

"Exactly. You're face turned the shade of a beet just now, which leads me to the assumption you're not telling me the truth or not all of it. Rest assured I will find out what you don't want me to know."

"Do you need to take a leak?" He asked, placidly waiting for her reaction, reminding himself as long as she wanted to pretend she was someone she wasn't, he was going to do everything in his power to change her mind.

Now her face was a ghostly shade of white. Silence pervaded the room while she stared at her plate. "I..." he watched her swallow.

He felt the cad, understanding her discomfort. "I'll leave and give you some privacy." Setting his napkin down, he strode from the room. "Never seen a boy so shy."

~ * ~

"Best you sit down, Auntie," Tira said. "You're not going to like what I have to tell you.

"What's this all about?" Charlotte asked, studying the white faces of the two girls. Something was afoot and it seemed to be bothering Larena more than Tira. "Where is Tavia?"

Larena and Tira exchanged glances. Then Tira spoke up. "She followed a dream."

The sick feeling she'd felt countless times before swept through her. "And what is that dream? Out with it. The sooner we get to the bottom of this the sooner I can correct her foolishness. If she needs rescuing, I'll call in some favors. Still have a few of those left."

Tira cleared her throat, "She talked to the harbormaster and he told her there was a ship that would be gone for about four months in need of a cabin boy. Tavia didn't want to be gone longer because it was the same amount of time as James. She signed on."

"Tavia did what?" Charlotte needed to school her thoughts and calm down. This could well be a nightmare worse than the one she experienced with Fayth. As a girl no one would let Tavia sign on to anything as a cabin boy.

"She wants to see the world, Aunt Charlotte." Tira said with a

43

small shrug. "I want to learn how to build boats. Auntie, I'm going to Baltimore after Jamie leaves. He doesn't know it yet, but he's going to teach me his trade. I'm sure Ravyn will let me stay at her house with Aidan."

"Of all the ridiculous stunts I've ever heard, Tavia's is the craziest of all of you. And you, Tira, you really think Mr. Lundin is going to let you into a man's world? That he'll hire you as an apprentice and teach you his trade? Really, how naïve can you be?" Anger as well as frustration seemed to simmer deep inside. What were these girls going to try next?

"I'm going to pretend to be a boy," Tira vigorously defended herself. "I've thought it all out."

To The Duchess she looked too smug and way too arrogant. "Not going to worry about that now. We have to find my niece and the two of you are going to help me."

"She's really at no risk, Auntie. We thought of everything to do so she won't be found out. She bound her breasts and I cut off all her hair so she'd look like a boy."

Charlotte groaned, closing her eyes. This was worse than she'd thought. "I know it's early but I need a drink. Bring me some of that brandy. I'm going to find out whose ship she's on and stop it."

Larena was quick to comply, and in a matter of a second The Duchess had a drink in hand.

"Tavia wrote a letter." Tira said, handing her an envelope then, seeming to think better of it, she began reading.

My dearest Auntie Charlotte,

I want you to know how much I love you and appreciate all that you want to do to help me find the perfect husband, one just like your duke. I do however need to follow my dreams to see the world. This might be my only chance and I have to take it.

I discovered a ship called the Firtha needed a cabin boy. After I made the inquiry, I signed myself on under the name of Tommy. Tavia cut my hair and I bound my breasts, so no one could see my curves. I've two pairs of britches and two shirts so I can clean them.

I'm a bit leery of sleeping in the same place as the rest of the crew, but I'm confident my disguise will keep my identity as a boy intact. James told me how men acted sometimes with women. Told me not to book passage, I wouldn't be safe.

Please don't be angry with me. I'll be back in four months and then I promise I'll behave myself and do everything you tell me. This was such a golden opportunity that I couldn't pass it up. Don't worry about me. I'll write to you from every port.

James will be back in four months also. So the timing is perfect.

I love you so much auntie.

Don't worry about me,

I love you,

Tavia.

At hearing the name of the ship, relief swept through her. She didn't approve of Tavia's choice, but now she didn't have to worry about her staying safe. James would protect her at all costs. If Tavia thought for a minute he wouldn't see through her disguise, she was truly ill informed.

"You look pleased suddenly. Why?" Larena asked.

Chapter Three

Tavia had never felt so embarrassed in her entire life. Why on earth would he want her to stay in his cabin unless he had some nefarious purpose? Then he asked her if she had to relieve herself. Well she did and of course he didn't show her where. Was there even a chamber pot in here?

Her pulse raced and her stomach rolled with strange sensations she couldn't define. He didn't know who she was, but he wanted her, a female, to sleep in his cabin. Of all the nerve, she would give him a piece of her mind when they returned and she could confront him on an equal basis.

Rummaging through his things and his cupboards, she found nothing. This was something she never thought about before. Then she found what appeared to be a privy of his own, and it had a door. *Of course, you ninny, it has a door.* Quickly, before he invaded her space, she finished her business.

She stared out the window, watching the moonlight shimmer on the waves. The ocean seemed restless. When she first saw James sitting at his desk, she was sure the adventure was over before it started. He didn't seem to recognize her though, and she thanked Tira for her wonderful help with the disguise.

Now that he left the room, the food on her plate looked a little more palatable. She sat down and began to eat, enjoying each morsel and sipping the wine. This was amazingly good, or perhaps she was just hungry. Her last meal was taken last night when she and James walked the street. She'd been too excited to eat before she left.

"You done?" He entered the room and she didn't even hear the door open and close. Somehow on his ship, he appeared intimidating where he was always the gentleman before. "Good, I see you're taking advantage of the food."

"I'm finished." She pushed the plate from her and wondered what humiliating thing he meant to do or say next.

"Pleasant night. Would you like to take a stroll on the deck? Most of the crew has retired for the evening." He smiled.

She sucked her lower lip between her teeth, staring at him. His motives might be innocent, but she didn't think there was anything harmless about him. "I..." she began.

"You don't have too. I'll just sit down then and write some notes about today." He began unbuttoning his shirt.

At the sight of him baring his chest, "Yes, I'd like that, a stroll on the deck." She needed to feel the wind on her face and smell the sea salt. "I've been inside all afternoon." She wanted to tell him it was his fault she was bored to tears.

"Good, then you can tell me all about your childhood."

She coughed on the sip of wine in her mouth, choking as it didn't go down right. He stood behind her, slapping her on the back as if that would stop the coughing fit. "You can stop now. That's really not helping anything."

"You're no longer coughing," he told her, grinning. "So, my gentle taps must have had the tiniest benefits."

His arrogance new no bounds, "Yes, of course."

"Are you ready? Do you have a jacket?"

"No, I..." She and Tira had not thought of something other than basic clothes to wear.

"I might have something in my trunk you can wear." Rummaging a few minutes, he pulled out a flannel shirt. "Here, this should ward off the chill of the night."

She slipped her arms through the sleeves and fastened the top few buttons. It fell to her knees. She rolled up the sleeves. "Thank you." She murmured, heading for the door and perhaps a few minutes of peace.

"You're welcome."

He didn't say anything about the size or make a comment about how tiny she was and for that she was grateful. "Is it always this beautiful?"

"To me." He was staring at her and she wasn't sure what to make of it. "The ocean calls to me and even in the foulest weather there is something magical to be seen."

She wanted to take his arm, feel the muscles beneath the fabric of his jacket. Last night left an impression in her head. He was gallant and understanding, so patient. Here he was...

He was the captain she supposed. He could behave anyway he thought right, and she was his cabin boy, his to command. They stood at the bow, the wind whipping through her hair.

"I've always wanted this," she murmured, watching the waves crash against the hull of the ship. "What port do we stop at first?" she asked, her gaze remaining on the ocean.

"Barcelona," he said, "but we might stop sooner if things go as I've planned."

"How is that?" she asked, suddenly realizing in the role of cabin boy she wouldn't be privy to any of his plans.

"Do you forget your station?" His voice was almost pleasant, yet deeply chilling and Tavia felt a wall of ice come sweeping down her spine to settle in her gut.

"No, sir," she said ever so quickly in hopes he wouldn't look into her eyes and discover who she truly was.

"Enough said. A simple question now, where did you grow up, what town or perhaps London?"

She was embroiled in lies so the more truths she could tell him the better and the less she'd have to remember. She would try to somehow parallel her own story. "In the east, near Scotland."

"So, you've decided to talk about yourself. Good, I'm glad about that. What about your parents?"

"Both dead," she lied, but in all actuality her father was dead too. When her mother died, he mourned so deeply he withdrew from life and his family. She couldn't tell James that because he was at Ella's wedding, and he might know those things about her family. Her father refused to attend Ella's wedding and walk her down the aisle.

"Siblings?" He continued with the questions his tone no longer cold or intimidating. It seemed he wanted to draw more information from her.

48

"Why would you care?" She knew though, he'd told her before. If she died, he wanted to know where to send the remains. "Never mind."

One eyebrow rose a fraction and his smile wrenched her heart. "I believe I've told you why. It's important the captain of a ship know things about his crew, intimate things."

"You need to know who to send my body to. Rest assured there is no one, none who would care about me. You can dump me into the ocean if it pleases you." His gaze lit upon her and it seemed she struggled to breathe as she felt the touch of silver fire.

"You don't need to be so sarcastic. Then you have no brothers or sisters, no aunts or uncles, no family whatsoever." He persisted, challenging her, trying to catch her off guard.

"What should I do if there is a storm." She changed the subject no longer wishing to tell her life story to this man. "Who will deal with the lines and the rigging?"

"A smooth change of topic," he said icily. "Same as during the day as well as the night. Unless you have my permission, you will stay in the cabin, and I've men who can do a cabin boy's job."

"Wouldn't there be something I could do?"

"I would not like it if I had to save you from the ocean. Storms are dangerous and the ocean doesn't give back what it absconds with." That icy tone returned as well as a brooding glare. James possessed a dark side, one she'd never seen.

"Ah, I see you're working things out with your cabin boy." Seamus stood beside them. "Thought I'd introduce you to one of our passengers. She is sailing alone so she said she'd welcome the company. This is Adelina. She is travelling to Barcelona to meet her husband. I've assured her this is a safe ship, and she need not fear a stroll on the deck."

Her husband thought it safe for her to book passage and sail. She wished she could confront James with the information.

"Adelina," James took her hand in his, "Please to meet you. James Macmurra at your service. If you need anything, don't hesitate to ask. This is Tommy, my cabin boy."

"James. Tommy." She curtsied, smiling prettily and tilting her head a bit to the side. "Tommy, you are awfully young to be a cabin boy."

"I'm fifteen," Tavia said defensively. A wave of jealousy swept through her, and she needed to remind herself Adelina was on her way to meet her husband. James was an honorable man and would never take advantage of her. Still, she was so beautiful. For a moment she regretted the male garb and her bound breasts.

"Ah, I see then, you've yet to sprout a few whiskers. Some boys don't mature as quickly as others. If you ever have the time and want to talk, let me know. Seamus is right, I'm a bit bored already, and we're only one day out."

"I will make sure she has some time each day. If I'm on deck and you would like to visit, feel free to come to my cabin." James said.

"Tommy stays in your cabin? Isn't that a bit unusual? He sleeps with the crew though," she challenged James.

"No, Tommy has a hammock in my cabin. I need to keep a close eye on him. It's his first trip and as you pointed out, he's a bit small. The crew, you know..." he let the statement hang. It seemed he expected her to finish it for him.

"I'm very good at climbing the masts and dealing with the rigging." She didn't like the fact they were talking about her as if she wasn't standing next to them without any concern for her feelings.

"Agile, are you? I'm sure I'd misplace a foot or a hand and fall to my death." She put a hand to her throat and sighed prettily.

"I climbed trees with my sisters." Trembling, she turned to James, "They are gone, my sisters are far from here. They are married with families of their own to take care of," She needed to learn to curb her tongue or she would let slip some clue that would unravel the truth. That was exactly what James had in mind.

"But now, thanks to this beautiful lady I know one more thing about you." He ruffled her hair. "Don't worry over your little mistake. I intend to learn everything there is to know about Tommy no name, including your last name before we are back in London."

He wouldn't learn anything she didn't want him to know about her until they were both in London and he was courting her.

"Well, there are no secrets where I'm concerned. I've been married for just two weeks. It was by proxy. I've never met my husband.

I truly hope I will at least like the man."

"I'll leave the two of you to chat. Don't go anywhere until I come back for you," James warned in that silken icy voice she was beginning to realize was an integral part of him.

When James was a distance from them, Adelina turned to her, "What do you think, you, a young lady, are doing parading as a cabin boy. It's the most foolish thing I've ever seen."

Taken aback, Tavia's heart raced and she gulped air. "I'm a boy," she tried to say the words forcefully.

"Anyone who looks at you can tell you are not a boy. While it seems you must have bound your breasts, you cannot hide the feminine curve of your hips. Does Mr. Macmurra know?"

Tavia was shaking her head wildly, suddenly questioning Adelina's words. "There is nothing for the captain to know. I'm a boy."

"Darling, you are truly precious, a breath of fresh air, I dare say. I won't tell on you. In many ways I admire you and I will be here for you, at least until Barcelona if you need anything. When was your last cycle?" she asked bluntly.

Tavia gulped air, "I never thought of that. Just recently, a week ago."

"When it comes, I'll give you everything you'll need. I can't imagine Mr. Macmurra sees you as a boy. Has he said anything or given any indication he knows you're a girl?"

"No, he doesn't. He truly believes me to be a boy." She paused, wondering if she dare tell this lady more. "We, James and I, courted for a short time was leaving on this adventure and I didn't want to be bored waiting for him so I decided to follow a dream."

"So, you are a dreamer. Once, a long time ago I was too. Now, I have no say in anything I do. Believe in yourself, Tommy. I'm not going to ask you your real name. I might inadvertently give you away.

"So, you are sleeping in a hammock tonight. Have you ever done that before? I hear they are quite comfortable. If the weather gets stormy, there is little fear of falling out of one."

"That's what James says too." The knowledge she had a friend if she needed one comforted her in so many ways.

"A piece of advice, woman to boy?" she asked.

"Woman to boy," she parroted.

"Don't call him James, only captain or sir."

"James could easily slip out, I'll try," she made a mental note to herself.

Adelina was leaning on the ship rail, "Don't ever do this either. That is how I realized you are a girl. This position shows off your hips, entices men to lust."

"You're a flirt and a bit of a tease, aren't you?"

"I was but I was sold to the highest bidder, and now I'm leaving my old life behind. It's a conversation for another time." She sighed into the night air. "I have no reason to want the life I've left behind."

"Do you regret anything?" Tavia asked.

"I'll know after I'm in Barcelona," she whispered softly, seeming immersed in her thoughts.

"I don't regret doing this, but I'll regret James' reaction if he ever finds out."

"How did you end up on his ship?" she asked. "You could have found yourself in a bit of real trouble if not for this accident. Or was it an accident?"

"An accident," she admitted, "a coincidence. I suppose I was blessed by an angel watching over me."

"Or a good fairy," Adelina laughed. "Now whatever brought you your luck, I'll pray it stays with you for as long as you need it."

"Thank you, I'll wish you luck too." Tavia started to lean on the railing then thought better of it.

"You are heeding my advice. I see." Adelina smiled.

"Do you really want to marry this man you've never met?" Tavia didn't think she would ever want to do something like that. Some men just made her skin crawl and suck all her energy from her body.

"Doesn't matter what I want. I've no choice," she said, seeming resigned to the situation in front of her. "In some ways it's better than my old life. Most ways," she amended. "You see, my little innocent, I was a whore and I had to service more than one man a night."

"You had no choice in that? You could have left, couldn't you?"

52

"If I wanted a roof over my head and food to eat, I had no choice. For me my life was a matter of survival. I was sold to an old man in desperate need of an heir. He wanted someone young enough and skilled enough to bring him to arousal so he would have a chance of siring a boy child. It's really nothing new to me."

"You don't have to honor this arrangement. I know James would help you escape."

"The man who bought me is very powerful, and he has the means to find anyone who goes against his wishes and make them regret it. No, I'll be fine."

"Captain says he'll be another half hour at least. He wants me to walk you back to the cabin," Seamus said, interrupting their conversation.

"I'm not ready to leave," Tavia said which garnered a look from Adelina.

"It was an order not a request."

"Will you walk Adelina back to her cabin after?" She recalled all James had told her and didn't want this sweet woman at risk.

"Yes," he said.

"Can I have one more minute with Tommy?" Adelina asked. "I'd appreciate the time."

Seamus nodded, scratching his chin before stepping back to give them some space.

Adelina brought her close and whispered. "If you're hoping to keep your secret, you really need to learn how to speak to your superiors. A mere cabin boy would never say what you just did. Remember, you take orders. You don't give or question them."

"I'll try but it really goes against the way I was brought up, which was do whatever I wanted when I wanted."

"Obviously," Adelina said, "but you have to promise me. This is serious if you want to remain the cabin boy Tommy."

"Promise and if you've got any other tidbits of advice or information, I'll take it. I do think I'm in a bit over my head in this situation."

They beckoned Seamus, "Thank you," she set a hand on his arm.

"Any time," he said, obviously a bit rattled by Adelina.

They were at her door and Seamus opened it for her. "Will I see you tomorrow?" Tavia asked.

"I certainly hope so."

Inside the cabin she rested, her back on the door, mulling over everything Adelina had told her. All the times she cursed her lot in life about the fact she was not born a boy and could not pursue her dreams. Adelina had to let men do what they wanted to her body. She had been lucky.

She stepped toward the bed and the hammock. So, she had to sleep in this. Running her fingers on the webbing, she wondered how the devil she was going to get into it.

She tried pulling herself into it, but the bed had a mind of its own and dumped her on James' bed. *I can't sleep in it if I can't get into it. I could spend all night trying and the results would be the same.*

This is ridiculous, absurd and irritating. She sat down at the table and poured a glass of wine from the decanter. She needed brandy, not wine. Poking her head out the door, she saw James standing at the helm. He didn't have to be there. He had men to do that for him.

She shut the door and rummaged through his cupboards finding a few bottles of whiskey then finally brandy. She poured herself a glass and settled cross-legged on the bed, staring at the hammock. Perhaps if it was lower, she would be able to pull herself into its welcoming arms.

One glass led to three. A few tears fell while she let the alcohol fill her with melancholy. This exciting adventure was becoming depressing and boring. Yet she was glad she met Adelina. If James intended to keep her confined in his room, at least she would have someone to talk to during the day.

She closed her eyes for a moment only.

An explosion sent her bolting to a sitting position.

"James!"

"Thought that might wake you. Why aren't you in bed?" he asked, striding through the room to the brandy bottle. "Hmm, a cabin boy with a penchant for the finer stuff. I don't remember giving you permission to get into my cupboards."

"Y-you didn't. I..." she swallowed hard, hearing that icy tone just beneath the pleasant voice.

"Don't do it again or," he paused as if in thought.

She almost blurted defiantly *or else what* but just in time remembered Adelina's words. *Don't give orders, don't question just obey.* "Sorry," she mumbled. "Not in bed because I can't get in the damn thing."

~ * ~

James let out a roar of laughter. "You probably can't get in because you're drunk. My cabin boy is drunk." He sat on the bed beside her and drank from her glass then pressed his leg against hers.

"I'm not drunk," she protested, moving to one side, trying to escape his big body and the warmth shooting from him into her.

"You look sloshed to me." He moved closer to her, letting his arm brush hers, pointedly trying to make her uneasy. At the edge of the bed, she had nowhere to go.

"I really should go to bed."

She tried to stand but fell back. He steadied her, his hands resting on her narrow waist before sliding up her ribcage. The feel of the bindings beneath his fingers sent him into a rage. This had gone on a day too long, yet he couldn't end this here. There was nowhere for her to go.

With no other recourse, staying with his original plan seemed necessary. He had to find a way to make her so uncomfortable she would beg to go home.

"You can't get in," he reminded her. "Unless you want my help. Have another brandy." He retrieved another glass and poured.

"Don't need your help."

"I'm not sharing my bed with a boy," he said, implying so much more. "Now if you were a pretty lass, I'd be happy to give you half of it."

Her emotions played across her face, but he wasn't sure what they were. Fear, anticipation, perhaps what he saw was longing then it was anger.

"Well, I'm not pretty or a lass," she told him indignantly. "You think I'd want to share a bed with the likes of you?"

"You are pretty," he disagreed with her, "but alas you are not a girl. It's a pity. We could have so much pleasure."

Her fists clenched. Ah, he found a way to make her angry. She knew about his promise not to sleep with any women on his travels, and now he all but propositioned a boy. Told her if she wasn't a cabin boy, he'd like to have her in his bed and in his arms.

"Is that all men think about, pleasure?"

He laughed again. "When you become one, you'll understand. I've a friend in Barcelona who would be happy to teach you how to make love to a woman. She is really very good at what she does."

"I don't want to be taught anything like that. I'm fine just the way I am."

Well, that much was true. "Of course you do. She'll teach you about a woman's most secret and private parts. How you can touch her so she will cry out your name. She might even take you into her mouth until you climax. You'll like the experience. I promise."

Tavia's face drained of color. Perhaps he went too far or perhaps not. Make her uncomfortable, was, after all his intention.

"No, sir."

"Perhaps I should find a lady a little closer to your age. You could start your own harem, a lady in every port."

"No, sir."

He liked it better when she said outrageous things. "A woman's breast are very soft and the tips so sensitive. She'll let you suck hers into your mouth. Ah the taste and texture is heavenly."

Next to him she squirmed, clearly bothered by his words that were meant to seduce. "The earlobe is sensitive too."

"I think you've said enough." Once again, she tried to rise from the bed.

This time he pulled her back, his fingers around her delicate and fragile wrist. He made gentle circles on the underside with his thumb, watching her as she closed her eyes. He had to stop himself or this game would be finished and she would be in his arms.

"Oh, I've not said nearly enough." His voice was a low growl. Bloody hell this was just the first night, how the devil was he going to last four months? He wasn't.

"Should you be doing that?"

"What?"

"Touching my wrists like that?"

"You can tell me to stop." He slowly ran a finger up her arm, watching as her eyes seemed to glaze over with pleasure. "This is something a man would do to a woman to seduce her," his voice so close to her ear he knew she felt his breath.

"Need I remind you I'm a boy?" she whispered softly, her body beginning to tremble.

"Just trying to further your lessons in becoming a man." In tormenting her, he'd seduced himself.

"Not in a hurry, sir."

"Hurry for what?"

"To become a man. Seems all men do is gamble, drink, curse and have sex. Doesn't seem like much fun to me."

"That's quite the list, Tommy. You like to drink a little too much. You're almost half way there."

"There?"

"So close to becoming a man. I can teach you to gamble but you have no money."

"I like myself just the way I am."

"But you could be so much more," he told her, rising from the bed. He slipped his shirt over his head then unfastened his britches. "It's a bit hot in here. Don't you think?"

Her eyes riveted on the bulge in his pants. He grinned, wishing he dare remove them but that might be too big of a shock for tonight. He had time and he meant to use it well.

"Yes, hot."

"You could remove your shirt." He baited her, watching for a reaction.

"Not that hot."

"Ah, well, suit yourself." He sat behind his desk and pulled out the ship's journal. "Got some work here. Do you mind?"

"No, sir, but can you help me into the hammock before you get too comfortable. I'm really very tired from doing nothing."

"You need to learn how to do it yourself. I'm not always going to be around to put you to bed." He'd love to put her to bed.

"If it was just a bit lower..." she looked at him then back to the hammock.

Seamus did this on purpose knowing she would have a devil of a time without his help. "Try it."

"Yes, sir."

She rose and standing on the tips of her toes, she clung to both sides and tried to pull herself up and into it. The Hammock flipped over, depositing her on the bed.

If she tried to get up in the middle of the night, she'd land on top of him, something else Seamus was responsible for.

"Try again," he encouraged, attempting to keep the laughter at bay. If this went on for much longer, he wouldn't be able to stop himself.

Time and again she fell until she lay sprawled on her back, breathing heavily. "It's just no use. I can't do it."

"You might have a valid point." In a matter of seconds, he was beside her, hand around her and gently lifted her into her new bed. Taking advantage of his position, he let his hands explore her hips and her derrière much longer than was appropriate. She didn't seem to notice.

"Now what? Do I get a pillow or a blanket? Something to keep me warm?" She asked, peeking over the edge.

"Cabin boys don't get those treats. But a willing woman would keep you so hot..."

It seemed she ignored his last statement.

"Really, I don't get a pillow or a blanket? That's hardly fair."

"Nothing's fair in life. You'll learn that soon enough. You could take your shirt off and wad it up to use for a pillow," he suggested smiling.

"Well, I won't be able to get a bit of sleep this way," she protested.

"You sure cause a man a lot of trouble." He tossed her a pillow and one of the blankets from his bed.

"You could have let me stay with the crew," she shot back.

"You drink the best French brandy and eat with impeccable table manners. Where most cabin boys would pick up the food with their fingers, you use a knife and fork. You have quite the tongue. Don't you understand yet that I give the orders?"

"Yes, sir," she seemed to grind out.

"That's better, much better. See you pay attention to the ship's rules of etiquette. You take orders from me but you don't give them. Understood?"

"Yes, sir."

She seemed to curl into a protective ball, her rear pressing against the lines of the hammock. If he thought to get any work done, he was a fool. Watching her sleep did nothing for his disposition.

He knew the moment when her breathing slowed, and she fell into what had to be an exhausting sleep. He made a mental note to speak with Adelina tomorrow and find out what they discussed.

As long as he could hear Tavia's breathing, he knew he wouldn't be able to sleep. Stepping outside, a mist filled the air and the wind had picked up. They were making good headway. He reached inside the cabin for his slicker before striding to the helm to speak with Seamus.

"The hammock's a little high." James watched the grin appear on his first mate's face.

"Thought you'd enjoy putting her to bed. How does she feel in your hands?" he asked through muffled laughter.

"If anyone else said that, I'd have them keelhauled. You're a lucky man right now. You have any idea what I'm going through?" Of course he did and that's what put the grin on Seamus' face.

"You can end the charade anytime. When you do, I'm sure you can seduce her into your bed. You know, I've been thinking. There's going to be hell to pay when she finds out the truth."

"Yeah, you're right. A few minutes ago, I almost seduced Tommy. Don't know what I was thinking. I just made myself miserable. She's not going to find out I know she's a girl. She's going to be so unhappy that she begs me to send her home."

"You want to bed her, 'fess up, and the last thing you want to happen is to send her back to London."

"In time I do, bed her that is." *But not until we are wed.* "If she returns, then when we finish this journey, I can court her the way she deserves. We can take the proper steps before we say our vows."

Seamus rubbed his chin. "What's that supposed to mean? Wed? You planning on tying the knot?"

"What you don't know about Tommy is that she is the girl I was courting while we were in London. I promised her aunt, The Duchess, I wouldn't sleep with any women while I'm away. The problem is she knows about the vow. If I tell her that I know she's a girl, she'll be furious with me. And if I tell her now that I've known from the first moment I saw her she's Tavia, well, I suppose you're right. There will be hell to pay."

"I'm not sure I followed that line of thinking. She's not another woman."

"To me, she is. At least that's what she thinks. And if I were to seduce her and make love to her, she would believe I broke my vow. She might not ever forgive me."

"Just tell the lass you know who she is. The sooner the better; the way I see this predicament you put yourself in. Mark my words if you don't tell her now, you'll regret your ridiculous decision."

"Sounds simple enough but that's not the way I planned this. I want to court her properly and marry her."

"You're going to have yourself wrapped up tight if you keep on this way." Seamus said.

James roughed his hands through his hair already feeling wrapped up tight. "I need to teach her a lesson too, which is why I'm proceeding this way. She thinks she can do anything a man does."

"And you want to teach her what?" Seamus continued to challenge him, and he didn't care much for the direction of his thoughts.

"That the world's not a safe place for a woman without a man's protection. She can't run off on her own any time the whim hits her."

"From what I've seen of Tommy, that's going to be a hard task. But I'm sure you're man enough to do that, if you survive the nights." Seamus laughed at his off key joke.

"Funny."

"Just tellin' it the way it is, Captain. Say, if you're going to stand out here why don't you take the helm and let me get a little shuteye. I'll spell you in a few hours."

"Go on, go to bed." James waved him off, ready to be alone with his thoughts and plans for Miss Tavia Hepburn.

The wind whistled, filling the huge sails with air. As storms went, this one was small and would speed their trip. At the moment they had a tailwind so there was no need to tack. Clouds covered the sky the darkness all-encompassing. Tavia, what was he to do with her?

She was asleep in his cabin. He needed to rest, sleep. He smiled at the picture she made dressed in boy's pants. What she didn't know was that even though they were baggy, they revealed more curves than the most elaborate costly gown money could buy.

They had yet to kiss, he mused thoughtfully. If he continued the path he had set for himself, it might be a very long time before he felt her lips against his.

Minutes ticked by and as the sun slowly began to rise, Seamus stood beside him. "You alright, Captain. Time for you to see to your lady. Have you figured out what to do?"

"Fine, just came to some decisions. You take the wheel, I'm going to see if I can sleep."

When he entered, she was no longer in the hammock. Instead she lay on his bed, curled up in a tight ball. He let out a long drawn out sigh, knowing he would have to wake her and help her back into bed. If he did that, well, he probably wouldn't sleep.

He set his hand on her back, "Tommy, Tommy you need to wake up and climb back into the hammock. "Tommy."

She rolled over, her eyes slowly opening, a small smile forming on her face. "Is it time to get up?"

His body tightened, thinking of all the things he wanted to teach her about lovemaking. She was so damn beautiful, and her sleepy eyed look sent his mind spinning. "No. What are you doing in my bed?" he asked even though he had a pretty good idea.

"I had to," she blinked several times, pursing her lips together and hesitating until she finally blurted out. "Too much brandy. I had to," she licked her lips, "relieve myself."

"And you couldn't get back into bed." If this happened every night, she'd fall into his arms. Then what was he to do?

"Yes sir, you're right, sir. No. sir, I couldn't get back in. Had a devil of a time trying to get out too."

"I'll help you up."

Once again she lay in the hammock just above his head. He watched it sway with the movement of the vessel. She didn't sleep though. She turned over then turned back, plumping her pillow only to do it all again.

He put his hands behind his head, closing his eyes, unable to watch her. His thoughts tumbled in different directions. He remembered the times he almost kissed her. Wish he would have. It would be nice to have those moments to remind him of her.

He could take a page from Drake Montgomerie's book or one from Jarret Kingsley's. He didn't know how Amorica, her oldest sister had found love, only that Damien Andrews had smuggled political and religious refugees from their homelands to keep them alive.

But he was different and he never wanted to force Tavia's hand. He might try to seduce her, but she would come to him a willing partner or not at all.

It could have been minutes but most likely it was an hour. "Breakfast," Seamus called out. "Everybody decent in there? Don't want to interrupt anything," he chuckled.

"Come in." Still clad in his breeches, he gazed upward just as she tumbled from the hammock to land on top of him. Her slight weight pressed against his body. When she pushed up, her hands on either side of his face, she stared at him. Her lips so close he could almost taste them. Bloody hell but he wondered if she knew just how beautiful she was.

When he saw her falling, he put his hands up to slow her fall. Even through the tight wrapping of her breast he felt their soft curves. Quickly he let his fingers slide to her waist. He shifted and with that slight movement, she was no longer on top of him.

"Got some food here if you feel like eating. You must have gotten some rest, Captain or something else. The sun's been up awhile. Want me to come back later?"

"It's not what it looks like," James muttered as she rolled to a sitting position, brushing her hair from her face.

"Looks pretty enjoyable to me. Or are you two just wrestlin'? More tips on how to be a man?"

James stood, fastening his britches and trying not to let his gaze wander to Tavia. "Set the tray on my desk. Get someone to bring hot water for a bath in about thirty minutes."

"Yes sir, one for the boy too?" He grinned shamelessly, seeming to enjoy every moment of James' discomfort.

When Seamus left, he turned to Tavia. "Can't you get out of it either?" He thought better of uttering the barb that was on his tongue. If he was going find a solution and end up unscathed, he would have to pay more attention to her feelings. This had to be difficult for her, but what had she expected?

"I could get out of it if I was six feet tall, but I'm not." She slanted him an angry look.

"Hungry?" At times changing the subject was the best idea. He was famished, and the fare sitting on the table smelled damn good.

"What did you and Adelina talk about yesterday?" Two sides of a story were always better than one. He'd talk with the young woman later today. She might be able to shed some insight.

"She was sold to the highest bidder." Tavia pulled off a chunk of bread. "I wouldn't reveal any of her secrets, but she didn't seem to be hiding anything."

"Sold, you say?" He poured her a cup of coffee before sitting down to eat.

"She was sold at an auction to an old man who wanted an heir." That was just like Fayth's father, but he wasn't an old man. All he wanted from his wife was a male heir, and all he got were girls. She shuddered, realizing she almost divulged that information to him.

"I'm not completely understanding. She seemed to be here of her free will. What you say just doesn't add up."

"She was happy about it, or maybe resigned. She was a whore and she thought sleeping with one man each night was much preferable than the life she previously had."

"Ah, my bath." Then, Adelina had never been a whore. Whatever she was pretending to be he meant to discover her story.

~ * ~

Adelina stood on the deck watching the breakers hit the side of the ship. She didn't know what would happen to her in Barcelona. Whatever life she was sailing toward, it would be fraught with danger, and she was alone this time. She tried to keep her spirits up, yet sometimes it was hard. Her task was a simple one.

She'd born children before. She didn't know what had happened to any of them, they'd been taken from her almost the instant she gave birth. One, a little boy she held in her arms for a few seconds. The others, she didn't know if they were boys or girls. She had four children, and she supposed given her circumstances, she was lucky not to have more. Adelina practiced her story.

"Weather's nicer today," Seamus stepped up beside her. "You talk to our cabin boy yesterday?"

For a few seconds she stared at him, trying to see if he knew the truth about Tommy. She supposed he did, just as she was sure the captain saw through the disguise too.

"I talked to him," she said, wishing for some insight into the first mate and where his loyalties were. "He's out of his element here. I'm glad the captain is helping him out some. The crew could be pretty hard on the boy."

"Enough about Tommy. You travelin' to meet a husband, I heard?"

"I am. I'm kind of like a mail order bride, only he bought me at an auction." She hoped that with each telling of her story, it would get easier. When she closed her eyes at night, her fears grew. Years ago, in London she knew her life was hell, but she understood how to deal with it. So much had changed though."

"You good with that?"

"Let's just say I accept it." At one time her life was not all that bad. Her family had enough money to live. They had food on the table and a roof over their heads. Then everything started to fall apart. Her father got sick then died after a lengthy illness. She looked for ways to make a living, whoring was just one of them. Meeting Drake Montgomerie and Logan Maxwell started her on a new path.

"Look over there," Seamus pointed to a pod of whales. "You can see them blow."

"Tommy would like to see that. I should get her." Adelina turned, but Seamus stopped her.

"Not a good idea right now," he said, his voice gruff. "Captain has him working on something."

"Something in the cabin? That can't be good." James seemed determined to do something, but what it was she couldn't guess.

"Best you don't interrupt them." Seamus glanced toward the cabin, his brow furrowed.

"I don't like what you're saying. The captain doesn't prefer young boys, does he? James wouldn't hurt the boy."

"No, didn't mean to give you that kind of impression. He just doesn't want to be interrupted."

"That boy's an innocent." She turned on Seamus. "Don't you think we should stop the captain?"

"You don't have to convince me about his innocence and stopping the captain might be detrimental to your health. No, not a good idea." Seamus leaned on the railing.

A few drops of rain started to fall, and the sun slid behind a wall of clouds. "Looks like our nice day is changing."

"Yup, there's a storm a brewin' for sure. Don't think the captain's going to survive the tempest he's creating." Seamus laughed so hard his eyes began to tear.

"Now you've got me curious. What do you know?" Adelina's head swam with scenarios that were all bad for Tommy. She felt an urgent need to rescue the cabin boy.

"In this case, curiosity will do you no good. If Tommy wants to confide in you, you might be able to help, but I recommend you don't get in their way."

Chapter Four

Tavia watched wide eyed as men filed into the cabin then the bathroom with steaming buckets of water. One after the other until no more men came. At least the room had a door and he would close it.

She wriggled in her clothes, wishing the water was for her. She could ask him if she could use the leftover water.

"May I go on deck? You obviously don't need me here." More urgent though was the need to escape.

"No," he told her, a wicked grin on his face. "On the contrary, one of the cabin boy's jobs is to scrub my back."

"I don't know how." Bloody hell but she wasn't about to scrub his back. If she did what he asked, she'd see him naked, touch him. Her heart thundered beneath her ribs. Closing her eyes, she tried to keep her imagination in check.

"It's not hard. Anyone can do it," he said as he slipped from his shirt before his pants followed suit.

Except for his small clothes, he was naked and standing in front of her. As he stared at her blood rushed to her face. "You don't have any clothes on, or at least not many."

"Tell me you've seen a man with no clothing on. How old are you?" His hands rested on the waistband of his last remaining garment.

If he took them off, she swore she'd run from the room. "Of course I've seen naked men," she lied. "A million of them, maybe more."

His laughter echoed in the small room. "Then you won't mind seeing me." He turned before he was stark naked, arrogantly and seemingly unconcerned striding into the bathroom.

Long muscled legs, a small tight rear and a waist that widened to broad shoulders. The sight of him mesmerized her. Her throat so parched she could barely swallow. She couldn't breathe either. No, she didn't mind seeing him, but she wouldn't admit it to him.

"I could go outside and send someone else in to wash your back. Adelina might not mind."

He laughed, gazing over his shoulder and for a moment she thought he might turn to look at her. "Want you, besides Adelina is a woman. She's not a cabin boy."

"No, sir. I won't do it."

"We talked about obeying orders, my orders," he said, one eyebrow slanted upward. "That's not a very good start. I'm sure if you try you can learn to do better."

She heard the water slosh as he sat down in the tub, the palm of her hands clammy, sweat dripping between her bound breasts.

"Ah... nothing like hot water to soothe aching muscles."

She wanted adventures, to see everything in the world, but she didn't bargain on seeing all of James or washing his back. At least not before they were wed. "I need a breath of fresh air, sir, Captain." She called to him, hoping he wouldn't hear. "I'm going outside for a minute or two, maybe three."

"If you leave this cabin, naked or not, I'll come get you and carry you back here," he threatened, his voice sending an icy chill inside her.

She couldn't have moved anyway. It seemed her feet were stuck on the spot where she stood. "You wouldn't dare," her voice wavered. She knew it was not prudent to challenge him so. She imagined his eyes drawing together and the shuttered look he sometimes slanted in her direction forming on his face.

"Try me," his voice sounded pleasant but the undercurrent of ice sent another chill down her spine his meaning implicit.

So why did the tone also send a wave of heat swirling inside? She bluffed but she was sure he didn't, sure he meant every word. Still, she hesitated. "I'll just sit down here and finish eating." She poured herself a cup of coffee and bit into a piece of cheese, chewing it slowly and waiting for another command, which she meant to ignore.

"You do little enough around here. Get your scrawny butt in here before I get out of this hot water."

"That's not by my choice." She thought better of defying him, but he was asking too much. If she was really a boy, would it be so outrageous to scrub his back? She had to admit this might be a cabin boy's job. When she first signed on, she intended to do everything, all the expected duties.

"Tommy, now." He sounded patient enough.

"Yes sir." She drank some of her coffee and let it slide down her throat, enjoying the bitter taste. It was tepid but it still tasted good.

Silence from the bathroom gave her a bit of confidence. She spread jam on the chunk of bread she tore off, relishing the sweetness. Then drank more coffee. She sorted through the food looking for another tasty morsel.

"Tommy!"

"Yes, sir," she said, enjoying herself for this one moment. He would have to find a way to make her come to him. As long as he was sitting in the tub, she wasn't worried.

One second she sat at the table, the next she was over his shoulder, his hand on her rear while he strode to the bathroom.

"Don't have any more patience for a lazy cabin boy."

"I was eating my breakfast. Didn't you want me to eat more food?" She was being obnoxious.

"You had plenty of opportunity before my bath, and you will have more opportunities afterwards. At this moment in time you have no choice. I won't have it any other way."

His hand on her rear sent a current of heat through her. She squirmed in his arms. "What are you doing to me?"

"Making sure you scrub my back," he said pleasantly.

His fingers squeezed and the gesture sent a tiny noise from her throat. "Put me down."

"I've told you, I give the orders and you obey. What do I have to do to teach you that simple lesson?" His fingers tightened again then moved slowly from one side to the other.

She struggled to free herself from his hold, but once more his hand held her still yet at the same time seemed to explore parts of her he had no business touching. "Please put me down." She sucked her bottom lip beneath her teeth, holding her breath, in hopes the simple gesture would stop the feelings coursing through her.

"If you promise not to defy me again," he said sweetly. "I would consider your wish."

"This is not appropriate." She tried to intimidate but fell short.

His laughter caught her off guard. "Appropriate? My dear little cabin boy, you amuse me. You should apologize for misbehaving not tell me my actions are inappropriate. And, come to think of it, I've yet to hear a promise."

"I'm sure Adelina would not mind scrubbing your back or any other part that suits your fancy," she tried that route again. "She has most likely done those things before."

"Adelina has booked passage. She is not being paid to provide services to this ship or me. I would never ask her to wash my back or anything else for that matter."

"Put me down."

"Another order, and all I ask of you is for one word. A simple promise that you will stay and do my bidding." He taunted her.

She couldn't.

"You don't seem to have much integrity or loyalty to your ship's captain. I would ask more of you. Perhaps I'll leave you at the next port and you can be another captain's worst nightmare."

"I'm not a nightmare and I've done everything you've asked, well almost everything." She tried and that attempt had to account for something. But this was unconscionable. Again, she reminded herself if she was truly a boy and at his service, she would accept this duty with no complaints.

"All this time my hot water is growing cold, and I'd thought to offer you the leftover water." He tempted her.

"I'd like that," she spoke too quickly before thinking better of giving him something to hold over her head.

"Then I could wash your back," he offered sweetly. "I believe I would enjoy that, reach all the places you can't."

"No, sir, I can wash my own, reach every place myself." Bloody eyes but he was obstinate and stubborn to a fault. Couldn't he just let this go?

"If you promise, I'll set you down." His hand settled tightly on her waist.

"Promise."

"Ah and now I know how to bend you to my wishes or make you behave. All I have to do is offer you a bath. It seems even cold water tempts you." He chuckled softly.

He pulled her off his shoulder before holding her against him, his hands cupping her derrière. She slowly slid down the length of him, feeling most every part of him, and she imagined he felt every part of her. Then in a deft move he turned her and he was in the tub, leaning over so she could wash his back.

He looked up and pointed to the washrag and the soap. "Bloody hell, you really do want me to wash your back." She didn't know why she half expected something else, perhaps she just hoped.

"That's what I told you. You thought something different?" His bland voice penetrated her thoughts, sending her emotions spiraling.

She soaped the rag, beginning with his shoulders, not daring to wash lower than his armpits. Several minutes dragged by. She soaped and washed then soaped and washed again.

"You going to stay in the same spot forever? If you do that, I might not have any skin left. Besides, I'm pretty sure my shoulders are clean and while I don't mind, your water is taking on a decided chill."

She ventured lower, suddenly beginning to enjoy the moment when his huge body shuddered. She could do that to him with her touch? "Is that good enough?" she asked.

"All the way to the bottom of the tub."

She did.

"Now my hair."

"Really, you're determined to make sure the water is cold for me?" she said indignantly but complied, soaping his hair, letting her fingers wind through the strands and massaging his scalp.

"There is a bucket of rinse water. You can pour it over my head."

"I'll do that," she smiled inwardly. Picking up the bucket, she let the contents rinse away the soap and roll down his face.

When she finished, he shook his head, water droplet spewing over the room then stood.

"Thank you." He grabbed a huge bath sheet and wrapped it around his hips before turning. "It's your bathwater now. If you change your mind, I really won't mind washing your back." He grinned.

"No, sir." If he found a way to make her comply to his question, then he would know she was a girl and she couldn't risk that.

"Very well," he crossed his arms over his chest, waiting all the while watching her. "Your water is colder every second you dally."

She cleared her throat, "I'd like some privacy, please." She spoke so softly she wasn't sure if he heard.

"What was that?" He leaned forward, closing the distance between them.

"I'd like privacy. I'd like to bathe without you standing over me. If I wanted that, I'd let you wash my back."

"I'll dress and go on deck."

A few minutes later she watched him leave. Closing the door to the bathing room, she slipped from her clothes as quickly as possible then her bindings. She'd never felt so vulnerable.

The water even though a bit cold was divine. She set her head on the rim of the tub and closed her eyes, soaking up the feel of the water as it caressed her skin, not wishing to ever leave.

"You done yet?" he called from the main room.

Nearly jumping out of her skin, "No," she cried out, "stay there," searching the room for another bath sheet she could put in front of her if he walked through the door.

"Hurry up then." He sounded impatient and annoyed.

She did just that, using the same soap and washrag to clean herself then her hair. She didn't have a bucket so holding her breath she ducked beneath the water.

The door opened and his used bath sheet flew through the air, landing on the floor beside the tub then it closed. She inhaled a long deep breath of relief before bolting from the water and drying herself. The bindings were not easy to put back on, but with a concerted effort, she finished then dressed.

Just in time the door opened and James stood between the frames. "You could have knocked," she said indignantly, once again forgetting her place in the pecking order of this man's ship.

"It's been on and off sunshine and rain all day. Right now, the sun is shining and I thought you might like to be outside. Seamus will make sure no one bothers you."

"Is Adelina outside?" She was eager to talk with the young woman again as well as feel the sun on her face. She wanted to tell Adelina about the bath and find out what she thought. Was one of the cabin boy's duties really washing the captain's back?

"She's speaking with Seamus," he said as he opened the door for her. "Is she telling any secrets about you? Anything you need to tell me?"

She stepped outside. "You know everything there is to know about me, I have no secrets you need to discern," she whispered softly, waiting for some type of acerbic reply.

"I must," his tone turned to ice, yet he stopped to gently brush a strand of hair from her face and behind her ear.

The wind picked up and undid what he'd done. She shivered from his touch, reminded of the feel of his flesh against her fingertips. The sensations he evoked in her never ceased to amaze and excite.

"There is Adelina," she pointed starting forward, yet his hand on the back of her neck stopped her. His thumbs moved gently there then across her shoulders. "Captain, sir," her voice cracked, "what are you doing."

"Making you feel good. Is it working?" he whispered close to her ear. Goosebumps rose on her arms. "A massage always eases tense muscles."

"No, sir," her shivery sigh whispered in the wind, her muscles now tenser than before.

"Liar." The tip of his tongue touched her ear lobe.

"Is this what you're supposed to do?" She moistened her lips, turning in his arms, and gazing at him, his mouth so close it briefly touched upon hers.

"Perhaps," he grinned wickedly at her. "Perhaps not, did you like it?" he queried softly, the steel glint of his eyes cast down upon her.

"I shouldn't," she said, "You shouldn't. I'm a boy," she persisted. "I don't believe it's right."

"James, Tommy, what are you doing?" Adelina stepped toward them, Seamus following. "Come watch the ocean with me." It seemed her new friend sought a diversion from James' hold upon her.

"Thank you, Adelina, I would love to." She left James, meeting her new acquaintance half way.

Adelina put her arm through hers, drawing her close. "What the devil do you think you were doing and on the deck for everyone to see? Never allow the captain to take liberties."

"I..." Tommy began then stopped, having no idea how to respond to the heated question.

"Never mind, I understand it's not your fault. I'm going to have a talk with that man and put a stop to this unseemly behavior."

"Nothing you say will change anything he does. He won't listen." James Macmurra would do exactly what he wanted whenever he wanted.

"But you enjoyed his attentions. Of course, you did, yet you can't let him know how he made you feel," she said, her tone adamant.

"Like I was melting?"

"That bad or is he that good? Tommy, you've got to be careful where that man is concerned. From what I just saw, if he makes you melt barely touching you, and with just the suggestion of a kiss, you'll never be able to say no if he takes it one step further."

"What am I supposed to do then?" she asked, tears welling in her eyes. "I saw him naked and he made me wash his back when he took a bath. I tried to tell him no, but he wouldn't allow me to disobey. Told me if I left the room, naked or not, he'd come after me."

"Why, the nerve of that man. You saw him naked? James Macmurra, I should have you skinned alive for your audacity." She sounded as if she couldn't believe what she heard. "The nerve of that man. Even a ship's captain should have a few limitations. Seamus knew what was happening and he wouldn't let me anywhere near the cabin. I had my suspicions." Adelina glared at James, tapping her foot angrily, deep creases furrowing her brow.

"Just from the back," Tavia murmured.

"That is still just so not appropriate."

"You should not get in the middle of this. We both know I'm a girl even though he doesn't. It's possible he treated me like he would every other cabin boy."

"Even if he knows you're a girl, that is no way to treat someone. He should have his ears boxed. Believe me he would never come close to kissing a boy," she said indignantly. "Despite his despicable behavior I have something for you. Here," she handed her a small bag. "This is everything you'll need for your private days. I don't know how you're going to keep it from him though."

"I'll deal with that when the time comes. He seems agreeable to giving me privacy when I ask." Yet the problem plagued her. With less than two weeks before her time, she had to find some resolution.

"So, what else has happened?" Adelina asked concern in her voice.

"I can't get into the hammock or out of it. This morning I found myself sprawled on top of him."

"How did you feel about that?"

"Convoluted. I liked the feel of him. Is that wrong?" The play of his muscles in opposition to her softness wreaked havoc within her. "I want to touch him, explore his body." She shuddered at the memories. "I really don't see how I'm going to continue to deceive him, but if I tell him I'm a girl, I'm going to have to tell him my name."

"This is your decision, of course. But if you want my opinion, the sooner you explain your actions the better for the both of you, he will be angry of course."

"Tommy, get back to the cabin." His curt voice interrupted their conversation.

She started to tell him no, but Adelina's elbow to her ribs stopped her. "Yes, sir, Captain sir."

"Your compliance, how unusual," he mocked her, his voice a sultry purr that rattled her nerves.

"Well, I haven't been out here very long. I was enjoying the feel of the sun against my face. Please, I'd like to stay on the deck a bit longer." She needed to tell him how she felt.

"And you will again soon, but I need to talk with your friend and find out what nonsense she is filling your head with."

"She only speaks of herself and tells me I should obey you. It's unseemly for me to defy a ship's captain, she says."

"Well, I believe I like her better all the time. Go on now, I'll be back before you can miss me."

"I won't do that, miss you." She shouldn't challenge him. If she did, who knew how he'd retaliate. He would always get the upper hand. Yet some devil inside her wanted to provoke him.

He roared with laughter, touching her face with a calloused fingertip and seeming to enjoy the trembling of her body. "See, you miss me already."

She turned and darted to the cabin. Her limbs quaking, she threw herself on the bed. His scent lingered on the pillows and sheets. She pulled a pillow to her face, and closing her eyes, recalled his hands upon her, the mercuric sensations of his touch. She was damned.

He would be back soon. She could never anticipate his demands on her and her body. She would never best him. Even now the sizzle of his silver-gray eyes cut a path into her soul.

She would have to harden her heart and learn to distance herself. Yet he would close the space between them whenever he wanted something, when he felt the urge to torment her.

Tavia put the bag Adelina gave her in a safe place, away, she hoped, from his inquisitive eyes. Now, she stood, searching the room for something to keep her occupied while he pried information from her friend.

The breakfast dishes had been cleared and the bed made. She straightened the few wrinkles she'd just put on the quilts. Searching through his things she found two shirts that needed mending. With further exploration, she discovered a needle and white thread.

She settled herself on a bench near the window, determined to do something that might garner his praise instead of his disdain.

~ * ~

"Adelina," James called out harshly as he approached the woman who now seemed to be Tavia's confidant. "A word with you."

She didn't seem to cringe or back down even with the gruffness of his voice. "A word? Whatever for? If you want to talk, I'd be more than happy to fill the boring spaces of the day on the ship. What do you want to know?"

"It seems my cabin boy has been spending quite a lot of time with you. I don't like it. You need to be accountable for what you tell him, and I need for you to tell me what has been spoken between both of you." This lady was no whore. She misrepresented herself to Tavia and now he wanted to know who she really was and why she told lies.

"No, sir, you need to be accountable. Your actions speak louder than any words I can say to you. I find them quite distasteful. What do you have in mind for that poor young boy?"

He ignored the insinuation she tossed at him. He would do what he pleased and it pleased him to tease his soon to be fiancée. He redirected the conversation to her. "You're not a whore and I doubt if you've been sold to anyone, let alone the highest bidder at a whore house. Who are you?"

"A whore, that is all. I've nothing to hide from anyone." Shrugging her slim shoulders, she persisted in her defense. "You have no reason to think otherwise."

The arrogance of her voice, her manners all spoke to higher breeding. Her language held no indication of guttersnipe dialect. She spoke impeccably well, sounding more as a member of the aristocracy than a woman who lived in a brothel or prostituted herself on the street. It would not take much to deceive an innocent such as Tavia.

"There is more about you than meets the eye. You are hiding something, and I will discover the truth even if you don't tell me." He stepped back, studying her with furrowed eyebrows, hoping to see her squirm.

Casually and seemingly unaffected by him, she leaned on the railing, her fingertips tracing the smoothness of the wood. "You and I both know Tommy is a girl, and I suspect you know her real name. It is not fair to treat her as if she is a whore. You abuse her trust and set the stage to hurt her deeply. She fancies herself in love with you."

"Tommy is his name and what I do with him is not your business," he said, his voice menacing, suddenly tired of defending his actions to both this woman as well as Seamus.

"Of course not, your business is your own, but it seems I've begun to care for the young lady," she agreed sweetly. "All you need to know about me is that I'm meeting my husband in Barcelona. He bought me just as Tommy most likely told you. I will do everything in my well-trained means to give the old man the heir that he wants with all his heart and soul."

"Logan and Drake," he spoke softly, suddenly understanding they were behind this woman and her destination in Barcelona. So many commoners in many countries were rebelling against the aristocracy, attempting to overthrow the governments. Adelina spied for them, for England and his friends were behind the ruse. Tavia could not become part of this scheme.

Her face paled suddenly and he heard the sudden swift intake of her breath. "I don't know them," she said too quickly, unmistakably giving herself away.

He smiled, now having the knowledge he wanted. "While that may be true in part, you work for them. All of this has been prearranged along with your story. Nothing about you is true. You're a made-up person. You, my dear, are a spy. Probably one of the best I've seen."

"What if I am? Would you give me away?" She spoke so softly he had to lean forward to hear.

"Not if you come clean, tell me who you really are and why you want to influence my cabin boy."

"Cabin girl," she amended for him. "I can't tell you my real name. It would be a breach of trust, and it could put my life in danger as well as you and your friends. I don't want to influence her. Tommy confides in me, and I simply tell her what I think."

"So, you believe Tommy's a girl..." he paused thoughtfully, leaning on the railing next to her. "That's an intriguing idea."

"Please," she told him, speaking softly, "it doesn't become you to continue this ruse. We both know the truth."

He considered her words for a moment. "I know Tommy's true identity but if you tell her that, I'll put you off the ship when we stop in

Bordeaux. I mean to find a suitable ship there, one I can book passage for her back to London. If I can do that, she'll be none the wiser."

"That is always a possibility and before I knew her better, I would believe it was the best possible scenario." It seemed she thought about what he said. "You should listen to what I think, yet I realize you will do whatever you want."

"I'm listening," he spoke gruffly. Her words would not sway him, he determined before she began.

"Tommy is a beautiful and an innocent young lady. Putting her on another ship might ease your conscious for a little while, but it won't solve your bigger problem. She knows who you are and exactly how you've treated her. She remembers the vow you made to The Duchess before you started this voyage. Unless you undo the damage, it will haunt you as well as your relationship with her for a long time."

"You sound like Seamus," he murmured, raking his hands through his hair while remembering the sensations her touch evoked and how he had a devil of a time keeping his hands to himself whenever she was close. "I hardly doubt anything I've done will haunt me."

"So, Seamus backs you up, hides your indiscretions from the world yet lectures you about your behavior." Adelina laughed softly. "I like the man, your first mate. What if Tommy refuses to let you put her on another ship sailing to London? I'm sure she is capable of creating a memorable scene."

"She can't refuse." Tavia would do as he ordered.

"Of course she can. She is capable of making your life a living hell while you are trying to put her aboard another vessel. In case you haven't noticed, she has a mind of her own and is not afraid of voicing her opinions."

The possibility existed that she would refuse. She did know who he was and that he meant to court her, but the best possible scenario would be for her to return to London.

"I will talk to Tommy about it and she will comply to my wishes," James said, understanding that if he hadn't made her so uncomfortable already, she would never do as he said. He also knew he wouldn't make her leave if she said no because he enjoyed her company.

"So, you're stopping in Bordeaux. That was not a prearranged stop, I take it," she said without hesitation. "My soon to be husband will be unhappy when my arrival is delayed."

"No, but a necessary one. It will be good for the crew to have a night away from the ship. And your fiancé will just have to understand." James had heard the rumors as the men grew restless for some of the pleasures they said he was partaking.

"Your crew, you understand, they bet on the sex of your cabin boy and some have gambled she will be with child before you arrive in London. There are others, only a handful, though who think Tommy is a boy. Perhaps it is safer for her if she leaves this ship and finds another one. You will have to buy things for her if you want her to sail with someone else; a couple of gowns, shoes, other things, perhaps a few accessories. If you like I can help with the purchases," she offered, seeming to know he would reject her offer.

"No need for that, I'll see to all of Tavia's needs." Only the most austere gowns for her, he'd make sure of that. No one would be able to imagine her sweet curves but him.

"Suit yourself," she smiled as if she knew things about Tavia that he did not. Then as if reading his mind, "A man can imagine the curves beneath even the most modest gowns imaginable. It would surprise me if she would wear something like that, but I suppose she will not have a choice if you have your way."

There were depths to this woman and contradictions too. Logan and Drake put their trust in her, yet he was wary of her intentions. One needed to be guarded when it came to dealing with any spy, especially a female, a woman who was willing to give sexual favors to do her job.

The ship should arrive in Bordeaux in a week's time. After docking he'd visit the harbormaster and locate a ship headed to London. Adelina could do whatever she wanted, go ashore or stay on board, send a message.

The crew could have leave to go ashore; two shifts, one on board the other with shore leave then the reverse. They would sail with the tide two days after. He had one more ploy to convince Tavia to leave willingly.

The sun was beginning to set, "Best you get below before night falls," he said. "Not safe up here."

"If you don't mind, I'd like to stop by and see Tommy for a few minutes." She turned to him, smiling sweetly.

He was sure she had something in mind he wouldn't like, and he didn't trust her. "I do mind. You can wait until tomorrow to see her."

"Very well then. Perhaps I'll see Tommy tomorrow." She left, her back rigid, clearly displeased with him.

Tavia's fate would be decided as soon as they made port, and he'd see if Logan was in residence at his vineyard. The more informed he was about the female spy on board his ship the better prepared he'd be to deal with her. He watched as Adelina strode to her room.

"Seamus," he yelled for his first mate.

"Aye, Captain."

"Were you standing there just waiting for me?" surprised by the quick appearance of the man.

"Anticipatin' your every command, Sir." He grinned, rubbing his bristly chin thoughtfully. "Didn't mean to eavesdrop, Captain, but she's not to be trusted. Tommy has confided in her and she has an agenda as God is my witness. That woman is a she devil."

"That's what I thought too. Think I'll go see Tommy and talk to her. See what she's up to." He looked warily at the cabin. He had never thought he'd fall in love with a woman. Had thought to wed for convenience and to have children just because he wanted some. When had he fallen in love with Tavia?

His steps slowed as he made his way to the cabin and another confrontation. Challenging her every step of the way had not been his intention, but he couldn't help but tease her. He wanted her in his arms and his bed. Every time he looked into her eyes, she tempted him. When he touched, even simple touches, she responded quickly and passionately.

If he were honest with himself, he didn't want her to leave the ship and his cabin in Bordeaux. He set his course and made his decisions. He wasn't going to change his mind. Before he had no control left and tossed her on the bed to make love to her, he was going to find passage for her on another ship.

This had to come to an end before he lost his mind and control of the vessel. He never believed anything like this could have happened to him. The men gambled on her sex, made bets about her, bloody eyes. By stealing on board in the disguise of a cabin boy she set events in motion, events that could have dire consequences for her.

Tension radiated from him, his usual calm vanishing under the weight of the decisions that needed making. He threw open the door and watched as her body jumped then quivered with surprise. Gut wrenching emotions shimmered to an inferno deep inside.

The light from the setting sun shone through the window painting her in a warm glow of color. Her beauty shone brighter than the incoming light highlighted by the colors from the setting sun. It seemed she made herself at home in his quarters.

Leaning against the door, his arms crossed in front of him, he tilted his head slightly. Not wanting to say anything and break the fragile peace of the moment, he watched her.

"You returned sooner than I expected," she told him, smiling beautifully.

It seemed she wanted the same thing he did, a moment's respite. He sat down and poured them both a glass of wine from his private reserve. Still wondering how long these precious seconds would last.

"Here," he handed her the glass.

Tavia let the shirt lay on her lap and accepted the glass. "Thank you." She sipped then set it on the table beside her, taking up her mending again as if he wasn't hovering over her. It seemed she could ignore him.

Watching her mending his shirt created a strange sensation and emotions he'd never known before. In that one moment, he felt as if he could see a home with children running wildly around the room, food on the table and a beautiful willing woman at his side. Nostalgia for a well-remembered childhood and his lost family hit him in the gut hard.

He'd gone to sea at fifteen. The same age Tavia had told him she was right now. He didn't know her real age, eighteen or nineteen he guessed, twenty at the oldest. Even then he was large for his age, his arms and legs gangly from his rapid growth. Until he stopped growing, he'd been an awkward boy, stumbling over his feet.

"I see you found something to do," he approached her carefully.

She shrugged her slim delicate shoulders as she made tiny neat stitches in his shirt. "I get bored easily, and since you seldom let me have a breath of fresh air..." she left the rest of the sentence for him to finish.

"It's strange for a boy to be so skilled in women's work." Now the calm had ended. He'd meant to keep his thoughts to himself for now. That didn't work out so well for him.

"Where I come from there is no such thing as women's work," she said, smiling sweetly.

"So, you come from a place not on the planet earth?" he challenged her, the boy named Tommy, to tell him more. Knowing she was Ella's sister, he remembered she came from the eastern part of England, close to the Scottish border. Earlier she'd told him that little bit of information.

Her body stiffened and she shuttered her expressio n, hiding behind lowered lashes. "You make too much of women's work versus men's. Sometimes a woman has to learn how to farm the land, and there are times when a man has to mend clothes. It is really not so strange."

Perhaps she was right about that. For weeks now, he intended to mend the shirt. Yet he knew the stitches he put in the fabric would not be as neat and precise as hers.

"Forgive me," he told her. Picking up his glass of wine he strode to his desk and sat down, unable to keep his gaze from her. He wanted to find a way to make her unbind her breasts. Tightly wrapped, she could not be comfortable. Short of unveiling his knowledge of her, he could not mandate it.

He opened his ledgers and began to write about the day's happenings, just as he'd done night after night. She tormented him beyond his endurance, his breath quickening with each stitch of her needle.

Seamus and Adelina were right about one thing. He should have told her the first time he saw her that he knew she was Tavia Hepburn. If he had though, she would no longer be a virgin, could never again claim her innocence. Her voice, the tilt of her chin and silken fire of her hair all gave her away. But her eyes, her eyes looked into his soul and left him on fire.

He'd never be able to put her on a ship in Bordeaux or any other port for that matter. He didn't want her to leave him, and he could never watch her sail away on someone else's ship with a captain that wasn't him. Yet somehow, someway he couldn't fathom this charade would have to come to an end. He would have to find the words and the courage to tell her the truth, damn the consequences.

"It makes me nervous when you stare at me," she murmured softly, keeping her gaze on the task at hand. "I wish you would go outside and steer the ship or do something captains do."

"Swab the deck maybe. Why?" Staring at her sent his blood thrumming through his body, his mind imagining the way her body would look when she was naked and how it would feel when she was in his arms and beneath him. He needed to see her eyes when he brought her to a climax. He wanted her now.

She set the shirt on the table and, for the first time since he sat down, looked at him. "This is the last one. It's finished."

"Why does my watching you make you nervous?" he rose, walking around the desk and sat beside her. The window bench was narrow, suitable for only one person so he pulled her onto his lap, damning himself and any attempt at good behavior. The feel of her in his arms was magical.

"Because you always surprise me and do things like this." To no avail, she squirmed, trying to dislodge herself.

He wrapped an arm around her waist. "Hold still, you have no idea what you are doing to me and the repercussions if you continue in this way." She was not responsible for his actions, yet with a smile, a gesture she could set his blood on fire.

She stiffened and stopped moving as if she knew what he talked about. "I'm sorry. I just want you to put me on the floor."

"In time," he whispered close to her ear then blew softly, reveling in her swift response, the rapid beating of her pulse. When she was finally his wife and in his bed, he knew she would respond sweetly and with more passion than he could imagine. "What was in the bag Adelina gave you?"

"I can't tell you." She turned to stare out the window.

"I see. She has given you a secret gift. Are you supposed to deliver it to someone? Tell me where. I don't want you involved in espionage."

His grip on her loosened.

"I'm not a spy. Why would you think something so preposterous?" she declared and taking advantage of his lost focus, she sprang from his lap, hands defiantly on her hips.

"But Adelina is," he told her. "The two of you are not plotting against me or England, but what is her purpose in Barcelona? You realize, of course, her story about her sale is not true."

"You would have to ask her. I'm sure I don't know. Why would she make up a story like that?"

She had not moved far enough from him. He easily reached out to her, placing his hand around her wrist and slowly drew her toward him. "This is where I want you, Tommy, on my lap. I have asked her why. She is evasive at best. People could be hurt if she is stopped and possibly if she is not stopped. What did she give you?"

"Something private, it is not for you in any way, nor is it some secret gift to another spy. Something I might need in a week."

His hand rested on her abdomen, suddenly realizing what she must be speaking of. This moment was not the one to pursue the truth. "Very well, you can have your secrets and your privacy. If she gives you anything else, I want to know. Promise me."

"I don't want to lie or disobey, but I can't promise anything like that. I won't betray her trust."

He ran his hands from her narrow waist up her ribcage, stopping just below the slight rise of her breasts. She inhaled sharply, stiffening then she did not move again. This façade had gone on too long. He had to put an end to it soon.

"Even if it could mean the lives of you, me and this crew, you would keep the information from me. ?"

"Captain," Seamus pounded on the door. "Captain, you in there? Need you on deck."

He let go of Tavia and rose to open the door. "What is it? If this can wait..."

"It can't, Captain. These two men were fighting about you know what," he nodded his head toward Tavia. "Can we talk outside? Their punishment needs to be decided."

~ * ~

One week later the Firtha docked in Bordeaux. A message was sent to Logan, but the return reply told James he was not in residence. With a heavy sigh and great reluctance, he visited the harbormaster, learning two ships were headed to London in the next couple of days.

He vowed to end the pretense but had been unable to reason with himself and accept the repercussions his silence had created. He kept telling himself the time was wrong and there would be a better day to tell her. Day by day his procrastination would cost more when the truth was finally revealed. The last two weeks he kept his distance and watched her with a brooding silence.

Now faced with her eminent departure, neither of the two ships was suitable. The first ship was old and barely sea worthy, and the second ship had a captain who was well known for his sexual debauchery. He would never book passage for Tavia on either ship.

Seamus agreed with him. Neither vessel was suitable. He didn't want to return to the ship and face Tavia. He wanted to get drunk and fight. A good brawl would make him feel better.

"Want a drink? It seems I'm parched and in need of a diversion," he turned to Seamus who nodded, seeming to understand the underlying emotions and questions.

"You're needin' to get drunk? Nothin' goin' your way today. Told you, you'd be tied up in knots before this was over. Shoulda told her the truth that first time you saw her smile sweetly at you," the first mate said a smirk on his face.

The man knew exactly what he needed. "Want to hit something," James muttered, pounding one fist into the palm of his other hand. "Need release before I take advantage of someone I care about."

"Might be easier to find your lady friend in Bordeaux," Seamus said. "You wouldn't have any cuts and bruises to deal with when you returned to the vessel. No explanin' to do either."

"Against my vows," he muttered, wishing for some relief from the tension plaguing him. "Can't find release with another woman, beside I don't want anyone but Tommy."

Seamus pointed in the direction of what seemed like a ribald establishment. "If not a willing woman in your bed, beer, women and brawls, what more could you ask for?"

"A willing woman named Tavia Hepburn," James whispered, clenching his fists tight, his strides lengthening as he headed toward the tavern, eager for a diversion.

Inside, the sailors and bar maids chattered and drank. Seamus and James found a place near the bar with their backs to the wall. After ordering a pint each, James sat back, legs crossed, content to watch and wait. Seamen staggered, clearly drunk, ready to brawl.

James sat back, drinking the ale, waiting for the action which was clearly part of the seaport tavern.

"Should I join you or help you find the way back to the ship when it's all over?" Seamus asked placidly.

"I'm sure together we can find the path to the ship."

"I'm in," Seamus said, grinning clearly just as ready for a fight as he was. "I'll guard your back if you guard mine."

When the first man crashed on top of the table, James let go a solid punch to the man's chin, sending him flailing into the main part of the room. The feeling amazing, the two men joined the fray. They fought whoever came close, sending punches that sent men reeling.

In between bouts, both James and Seamus downed their drinks, signaling for one more, eventually losing count. Lines began to blur. Where there was once one person now there were two, sometimes three. James blinked and sent a solid punch to a man's nose, reveling in the release it gave him. He took a punch to the side of his face, head jerking backwards. The pain ignited the simmering anger inside.

This was what he wanted, a good scuffle. He'd come home with black eyes and probably a broken nose, but it was nothing new to him. He tackled a man who had his eyes set on Seamus. They tumbled to the ground, wrestling on the floor until James hit the man's jaw.

"Thanks, didn't see that one coming," Seamus said, his lip bleeding and a cut over one eyebrow as he helped James from the floor.

"No problem," James' words seemed to slur. He grabbed another man by his britches and collar before tossing him out the door.

"Stop it! Stop it all of you."

James blinked several times. "Adelina?" She stood in the middle of the doorway, hands on her hips, tapping one foot. "What the devil are you doing here? It's no place for a lady."

"It's Tommy. She's in a lot of trouble. You have to come, *now.*" She didn't wait for them but whirled on one heel, marching from the tavern, clearly expecting him to follow.

He rose from his place on the floor and was met by a solid punch to his face, sending him back to the ground. Returning the favor, he sent his attacker to the floor. "Seamus!" he bellowed, "We're done here." Then he raced from the room toward the ship, catching Adelina before the gangplank.

"What's happened to Tommy?" He reached out to stop Adelina for an explanation, but she shook his hand off her shoulder and picked up the pace. "No time for explanations. Her life is in danger," she shot back, looking over her shoulder.

"Life in danger?" How the devil could that happen if she stayed in the cabin?

"No time, she's in trouble." Adelina repeated, "Tommy scurried up the mast to get away from some of your crew who were betting she was girl. She's hangin' on for dear life as we speak, and I don't know how much longer she can do that before she falls."

"Bloody hell, why didn't you say so sooner." He raced up the gangplank of the ship, his worst fears coming true.

Chapter Five

James had been gone for what seemed like hours and bored to tears, Tavia stepped outside, the sun sitting on the horizon and a crisp breeze blowing from the ocean. Only a few crewmembers were a top and they were working. She didn't see any harm in staying a few minutes.

Leaning on the railing, she watched the lights from the harbor town grow brighter as the sun slipped beneath the Atlantic Ocean. So, this was where Eveleen lived part of the year. She'd give anything to be able to see her cousin. It had been so long since Ella's wedding and almost all of them arrived in London for the festivities.

"Tommy, what's you doin' outside the captain's quarters?" one of the seamen stepped up close. "You plannin' on doing a little work for the crew. We could all use the help. We all know you've been shirkin' your duties."

She turned, surprised one of the crew addressed her. Usually no one spoke to her. "I needed some fresh air, that's all," she said simply, returning her gaze to the village. A shiver of fear raced up her spine when two more men suddenly surrounded her, shoving her from side to side.

"You a boy or a girl? Prove it now. We got money ridin' on the question." The man speaking rubbed his crotch.

"You been the captain's whore for a month now. Time we got some of what he's been gettin'" another said, pushing her to the deck.

She sprawled on the ground, realizing much of what James told her about men might come true. "I'm no one's whore," she said, rising and attempting to push through the men, but rough beefy hands held her back, touching her in places she'd rather not be touched, seeming to explore her body.

"Not goin' anywhere fast. We want to know the truth. Prove you're a boy," His fingers tightened around her arms, dragging her so close she smelled his breath.

She straightened, trying for bravado she didn't feel. "The captain will have you keelhauled for this. Let me go and I won't tell him what you're doing." She tried to pry the man's fingers from her arm.

"Maybe," another said. "But whatever punishment he doles out, will be worth it to know what you are, lass or lad."

"Prove it," a chant went up. "Prove it. Prove it. Prove it."

"One way or the other, ye ain't got nothin' we haven't seen already."

"Take off your clothes or we'll do it for you."

She trembled. From head to toe, she shook with terror. Surrounded on three sides, she saw no other option. The mast stood tall and straight in front of her. Quickly, before anyone could stop her, she scurried up the mast. At the top and breathing heavily, she stared down at the men who accosted her. They surrounded the pole, arguing.

They were all capable of following her, but short of falling to their deaths in an attempt to bring her down, she didn't believe any of them would be so bold.

"You can't get away from us. We can wait you out."

Most likely they could. James would return and rescue her but when? She'd heard talk of him going to one of the many women he had waiting in port. He might not be back until tomorrow morning. If that were the case, he'd have hell to pay when he learned her true identity. Even with the fear and the danger, a wave of jealousy swept inside, burned her core.

She glanced higher but the crow's nest was on a different mast. As time passed, her arms and legs trembled with fatigue. She could do it, could stay here until James arrived. Determined not to give into her fear and exhaustion, she clung tighter to the wood.

Escaping up the mast pole for the moment and to hang on for a rescue had been a good idea. If they discovered she was a girl, what would they have done? Surely not rape her? The sin was punishable by death in England, and they were English sailors.

She closed her eyes tight, wishing these men away, breathing deeply and praying for strength, knowing she could not hang on much longer. A man started up the mast toward her.

"No."

When he reached her, he grabbed her foot and she tried to pull herself higher, but the weight of the man kept her where she was.

"Come with me and no one will hurt you," he promised while he tugged and his grip around her ankle tightened.

She tried to kick his hand from her. "No." She pulled her foot higher, but the man persisted.

"I'm bringin' you down with me. Best you not fight it or we'll both plunge to the deck."

"I'm not going willingly with the likes of you." Again, she tried to shake off the hold he had upon her. All she had to do was hang on until James reached her.

From below, Adelina caught her attention and nodded toward the town, mouthing something Tavia couldn't understand, but her friend's gesture gave her hope and the courage to hold on longer despite the numbing of her hands.

Wherever you're going, please hurry. The man continued to tug at her. She fought him off, kicking him in the face and causing him to cling to the mast instead of her. She heard his cursing, but he didn't grab her foot again. When he backed down, she heaved a huge sigh of relief, praying no one else would come for her.

"It's a she devil for sure," the man said as he dropped the short distance to the deck, wiping the blood from his nose with his sleeve. "Any of you want to prove this point, you try to pry her down."

She watched, her heart in her throat as another man started up the mast. Sweat beaded and slipped beneath the bindings and between her breasts. She'd seem this man before. He was strong. He carried large barrels from the ship with ease. His muscled forearms bulged beneath the fabric of his shirt. What was she to do?"

Quickly, he reached her, his hand tightening around her leg. With a sharp tug, he loosened her hold. The next pull sent her flailing with a scream to the deck below. One moment she clung to the pole, the next she was on the deck, hard wood meeting her fall.

She landed on her side, pain rushing through her body. She

couldn't breathe, couldn't move. Pain froze her in place. She closed her eyes, trying to move away from the crowd surrounding her.

When hands reached toward her, "D-don't touch me," she whispered through the overwhelming pain.

"Hush, little darling, I'm here."

"James," she whispered his name before closing her eyes and knowing he had indeed come to her rescue.

James swept her into his strong arms, carrying her through the mass of people who now surrounded them. "Everything will be alright."

"Is she alive?" Seamus asked.

"She's going to be fine." James let Seamus open the door for him and close it behind them.

Gently he set her on the bed, but every tiny movement sent agony searing through her. She found if she didn't move there was no pain.

"Where does it hurt?" he asked, running his hands down each leg then arm. "Nothing broken there."

"My side," she told him, holding her breath against the searing agony. "My ribs, I think."

Taking his knife out he paused before cutting and turned toward Seamus.

"Leavin' now," the first mate backed from the room.

"Good, I'd have to kill you if you didn't," James muttered.

Before she could protest, he slit her shirt from hem to collar. "W-what are you doing?" But she knew. He meant to cut through her bindings to see how badly she'd been wounded. He would know now. He would see her body and know she was a girl.

"Need to see if you broke a rib or two. What were you doing outside?" he asked, sounding concerned. "I told you to stay in the cabin."

"Nothing broken," she whispered. But he was looking at the bindings and swearing softly.

"Damn fool girl." With expertise he cut the bindings off then sat back on his haunches watching her as her breasts were revealed to him. He couldn't stop looking at her, at them, then he saw the beginnings of a bruise and swelling which would get worse before it finally healed.

"You knew?" she asked then grit her teeth against the pain she incurred when she tried to cover herself with her hands. "D-don't look at me. It's not right. You shouldn't."

"Hell, everyone knew. Is that why you fell from the mast? Was it my crew who sent you scurrying skyward?" His fists tightened. "I will ask Adelina who the men were who provoked you, and I'll see them off this ship." He covered her with the shirt he cut from her body. "I have to look so I can see if anything is broken then I'll have to look again when I bind your ribs."

"Y-yes, your crew," she grimaced when his finger moved over her ribs. "I'm n-naked. You should..." She wasn't making any sense. "It hurts," a tiny cry escaped her.

"Would you rather my first mate do this? I can call him. He is the doc on the Firtha."

"No, but..."

"Tommy, I don't think you have any broken bones. I'm going to bind your ribs again and it will help ease the pain when you move, but unfortunately the wrap won't eliminate the pain. You have not taken good care of yourself. You have sores. I need to put salve on them and that will hurt too."

"When I saw Adelina leave, I knew she would find you and you would come for me." She could do nothing but lie on the bed, nearly naked with only the ripped shirt to cover her.

"Hush," he put a finger to her lips. "I'm going to help you sit and it's going to hurt, but if I'm going to wrap the ribs and put salve on your sores, I have to do it. This is my fault. I shouldn't have left the ship for my own purposes."

He gently placed his hands beneath her arms, lifting until she sat. Her breath stopped and she froze, holding herself still until the pain lessoned. Inside she screamed.

She was lucky she wasn't dead, she mused, trying to take her mind away from the fact he touched her, looked at her. For now, his back was turned to her while he searched for something, bandages, salve he'd said.

When he returned, "First, I'm going to put this on the sores." Carefully he administered to each one. If she didn't move or flinch when he touched her, what he did didn't hurt. "How do you feel?"

"Embarrassed, in agony when I move even the slightest." She knew he took great care with her and she was thankful for that.

"No need for embarrassment. I'm trying my best not to touch you anywhere inappropriate." As he worked, he moved the covering, maintaining her privacy yet still doing what was necessary.

She was grateful for that. "When you finish, I've another shirt in my bag, please. If you don't mind getting it."

"I'm going to bind your ribs." He told her.

She nodded and she knew what he didn't say. This would cause her pain. She closed her eyes, bracing herself. Nothing hurt unless she moved, and how could she not? When he finished, he helped her into the shirt.

She lay back against the headboard, her heart pounding. He came to her with a glass of brandy.

"This will help the pain. Should've given it to you before I wrapped your ribs up tight."

He strode to the door and hollered for Seamus then stepped back, walking to her and sitting by her side, holding her hand in his. "I'm sorry all this happened to you. You didn't deserve this."

A few minutes passed. Seamus walked inside with a tray of food and hot tea.

She held her arms tight to her sides, the brandy close to her lips and sipped. When she finished the brandy, he poured her a steaming cup of tea. "This will help too, and you won't get drunk."

"What is it?"

"Willow bark tea. Be careful, it's hot." He handed it to her.

She didn't want anything more to drink. "Where am I going to sleep? I can't get in there," she looked above her head to the hammock.

"I'll sleep there," he said. "Do you want anything to eat?"

Lips pursed, she shook her head, afraid eating would hurt, just as moving. "No, not now."

She watched him walk to his desk. He took his ledger out. His pen poised above the paper, he began writing. She wanted to know what he was thinking and what he was putting on that blank piece of parchment. He was probably telling the world about her foolishness.

In a few hours her life turned upside down and backwards. Now he knew she was a girl, yet from his earlier remark he'd known for a while. He'd tormented her, touched her in ways that made her heart pound, giving her sensations she'd never felt before.

Her growing anger at him escalated. She remembered the vow to The Duchess. In her mind, he broke that promise when he tried to seduce her. She heard him swear beneath his breath. Perhaps he realized the same thing. What he didn't know was that she was Tavia Hepburn, and she knew what his actions would cost him.

Still muttering words she couldn't understand, he strode to the window. Hands behind his back he watched for a while, rocking on the balls of his feet.

Then he turned quickly. "What made you go outside? I gave you a direct order to stay inside. You're supposed to obey. Don't you realize, I just meant to keep you safe from yourself?"

"I thought the command stupid. Truly, I didn't believe there was any danger on your ship." She realized her mistake within minutes of stepping outside. When the first man approached her, all she wanted was to race back to the cabin, but she was never given the chance.

"You were wrong," he told her yet his voice didn't seem to hold any recriminations.

"And you were right," she shot back only to grimace at the sudden stab of pain and wishing she hadn't been so impetuous in both her actions as well as her words.

He sat on the bed beside her, "And," he began, "I wish I had been wrong. You can't imagine just how much I wish I had been wrong." He brought his hand up to gently touch her cheek.

She shivered at his touch and wondered if she weren't in such pain, if he would take this further, her identity officially revealed to him. "How long before I don't hurt any more?"

He let his hand rest on her leg, "I don't know, a week maybe longer. I will have to change your bindings every day."

"Maybe Adelina could do that?" she asked, sure he would tell her no.

"If Adelina would like to help, I'd be more than willing to let her.

94

Keep in mind though, I will still have to help you sit," he told her, the steel glint in his eyes set an inferno penetrating her soul. She was lost to him, could never tell him no even though she might object.

"You would let her into this cabin," she asked.

"I would do whatever you asked. She is no threat to you or me at the moment," he told her.

"She is a spy. You told me to take care lest I get caught up in the intrigue of it all." She couldn't imagine he would change his mind about her. He'd spoken so strongly against her case.

"I don't believe she would hurt you. I'm sure Adelina was hired by Drake and Logan. I sent a message to Maxwell, but he's not at his vineyard," he said, his hand moving provocatively down her leg then up.

A wave of heat swept through her as her blood pounded beneath her chest. Even in her condition, the sensations generated a need she couldn't explain to herself. She wanted something more but didn't know what that would entail. "I'm glad you feel different about her now. Is it because she found you and brought you back? Will I see her tomorrow?" She wondered how far she should push this before his darker side shuttered his face and expressions.

"In the afternoon, I will see if she wants to come here. Does it hurt as much now?" he asked. "I'm hoping the brandy and the tea will ease the pain enough so you can sleep."

"The pain seems to have dulled a bit. It's turned to a dull yet incessant throbbing," she said as she turned a bit.

"Good, if you need anything tonight, all you have to do is ask me," he told her, glancing at the bathroom.

"I can walk there. I don't need help. There is nothing you can do that will ease that pain. I will have to live with it for the time being."

"Little darling, you are very courageous."

"Probably stupid is a more appropriate word for me. I should have believed you simply because I've never been on a ship or around sailors. I put my life at risk just to defy you and your order. I needed to prove to you that you didn't know what you spoke of, and that you are perhaps too protective of a boy." She had said too much so she closed her eyes in hopes he would ignore what she said.

He let out a roar of laughter before he tapped the tip of her nose with a fingertip. "You have a way about words I'll never understand. Will you obey me now?" he queried.

"I don't know. Perhaps obedience is too much to ask." She yawned, the intensity of the day's events taking over her body. Perhaps it was too much to expect that he sleep in the hammock. His presence next to her in his bed would not surprise her when she woke in the morning.

"Perhaps I shall have to beat obedience into you, at least while we are at sea," he told her. "I don't want to lose you. In the morning I'm going to buy you some new clothes."

"You plan to see me when we are not at sea?" she asked, praying he would tell her no.

"That all depends on how you feel about a dalliance or two."

~ * ~

His life passed in front of him when he saw her lying, unmoving, on the deck of his ship. Two weeks had passed since her fall, and the images in his brain haunted him still. Now he taunted her with the promise that seemed to plague him from the moment he woke to the time he closed his eyes at night. If he made love to her, would he break his vow?

"I wanted adventure, not this. I won't be one of your women waiting for you to see me in the port of convenience. There is more to life than that," Tommy said, a soft whisper to her heated words.

He arched a brow, inclining his head, taking his time because he really didn't know how to reply. He was doing his best to keep his hands to himself when all he longed for was to pull her into his arms and never let her go. "I don't want a mistress, and I've never thought to leave you somewhere so I can visit you when my cargo takes to that port."

"What do you want from me now?" Her voice trembled as she asked the question.

"I believe the most important question is what do you expect me to do with you now? There is still no room for you on this ship. The passenger's quarters are full. You still cannot stay with the crew."

"I couldn't say," she slipped beneath the quilt he covered her with.

She would feel the effects of her movement. Still he carried on a conversation with her. "Do you expect me to sleep in that hammock for the duration? I would have my bed back now that your pain is minimal," he warned, wondering himself if he dared crawl into bed with her.

She pushed the cover from her face seemingly determined to do something foolish. She tried to push herself to a sitting position, and a small cry of pain erupted from her, her brows creasing. Then she pushed away again with the same results.

"Help me into the hammock. I would not deny you your bed any longer. You are the captain after all," she said with an expression so determined he might laugh if the situation were not so dire.

"As much as I like my bed, you will not sleep up there again." He turned to the door and despite the fact he told her he would take the hammock instead of her, he had no intention of doing so now that she was healed.

"What?" she asked, brushing hair from her eyes and wincing again. "Where then?"

"Seamus!" James was at the door bellowing for his first mate. "Seamus," he yelled again when the man didn't instantly appear.

"Captain? What do you need?"

"Take that contraption off the wall. I no longer have need of it." James stepped away from the door making room for his first mate to enter but he remained outside.

"You sure, Captain? The little lady..."

"Is no concern of yours." James knew what Seamus thought of his actions. His first mate voiced his concerns many times.

"You're right, sir. Probably don't need or want it," he said as he walked into the room. "Really should wait until she's out of that bed. Wouldn't want to step on her."

"Then this evening. The lady will dress and take a walk with me on deck. It's really about time she got some fresh air." Frustrated, James ran his hands through his hair gazing at Tavia.

"Anything else I can get for you?"

James turned to Tavia who had once more slipped beneath the covers. "No, we're both fine. On second thought, send Adelina here if you can find her. Tommy will need help dressing, and I'm sure not the one to do that."

Seamus slipped out the door and once again, James was left with his musings and what his actions had cost him. He'd never waited for anyone or anything, and now he waited to bed her because of a promise made, one that no longer applied to their situation.

The knock brought him back to the present. "It's me, Adelina. Did you need me for something? Tommy? Is she alright?"

"We want to stroll and enjoy the evening now that the weather is more pleasant. Would you help her dress?"

"Yes," she eyed him suspiciously before turning to Tavia. "Is that what you would like?"

"I think we both want the same thing for a change. Yes, and I'm sure I cannot lace the corset by myself."

"Five minutes," James said, leaving the room and closing the door behind him. He leaned against the door, wishing for a future with Tavia, one that was open and honest.

"Let's see what we have for you to wear," Adelina said.

From outside the door James heard the rustling of packages and some of the conversation. He hoped they would choose the daffodil yellow walking dress he purchased and the stockings with the embroidered yellow flowers decorating the top.

If he stayed to help lace the corset, they would not be walking on the deck. Still he didn't know what would happen when he unlaced it. *Liar, you do know what you want to happen.* The memory of her breasts when he cut through the tight bindings haunted him since that day. As she healed, it had taken everything he had to call Adelina to check on her ribs.

Now she was well and the only thing that would stop him from making love to her was Tavia herself.

"You understand that tonight you can say no to him. He's going to take whatever you allow him."

"What do you mean?" Tavia asked.

"If my guess is right, he plans to seduce you tonight. He's wanted you for well over a month, and while he's been anything but a perfect gentleman, as of yet he's not compromised you. Tonight, if you let him, he will take your virginity. Make sure that is what you want before you let him make love to you."

"I will."

"Promise me."

"Yes."

He heard every word and all she said was correct. Adelina was right. Tavia's *no* was all that would stop him. He'd waited and now his patience was at an end. Tonight, she would be his.

"She's ready. Be a gentleman tonight, James Macmurra," Adelina warned. "If you're not, I'll personally..."

"Or what? I'll have you to contend with?"

Adelina smiled before she walked away without another word. He watched her go, back straight, hips swaying. So tight lipped, she must make one incredible spy. He wondered what exactly her mission was.

"The night is warm and beautiful, the wind calm," he told Tavia while he gave her an arm to hold. "I want you to enjoy the evening." He placed his hand over hers, feeling the delicate bones. How had she ever thought anyone would believe she was a boy?

"Are you planning on seducing me?" she looked up at him, moistening her lips with her small pink tongue.

He cleared his throat, "If you'd like for me to seduce you, I'd be happy to oblige," he smiled at her yet he didn't touch her except for her hand.

They stopped at the side of the Firtha, watching the water and the moonlight shimmer together. He wrapped an arm around her and drew her close. "Are you warm enough?" he watched her for a few seconds.

"I am, sir."

He turned her toward him and slowly pulled her into his arms. She should do as Adelina suggested. She should resist him, run as fast as she could, but it seemed she melted into him, her gaze meeting his.

Moonlight glistened on the blackness of her hair. He brought a lock to his cheek, inhaled the sweet scent. It seemed to him to be silken fire. He longed to wrap himself in its length. Too bad she cut it all off.

"Who are you, Tommy? None of your stories have rung true. Do you indeed have family somewhere who cares about you?" He drew a line with his fingertip around her earlobe then down her neck to her pulse point. The beat was rapid beneath his fingertip.

"I have no one who cares, which as I told you before, is why I wanted to have an adventure." She leaned into him.

He wondered if the rapid beating of her heart was caused by the lie she told or his slow seduction. "I don't believe you, Tommy no name, but something tells me I will never hear the truth from you. Do you run from an unwanted suitor? Or a horrible husband, perhaps. I would protect you with my life." When exactly had he fallen under her spell?

"No, none of those things," she moistened her lips, clearly distraught by his questioning.

Slowly he lowered his mouth to hers and swept his tongue across her lips, searing her, branding her as his. He'd never kissed her and if he had, she would have lost her virginity that first night she slept in his cabin. He pulled away, watching her, seeing the sweet essence of her bloom in front of him. Slowly, she opened her eyes, her hands set upon his chest, her fingers winding tightly into his shirt.

"A kiss," he murmured, a first kiss between them, he would remember until his dying day.

"A kiss," she repeated, her voice whisper thin seeming to float on the breeze off the ocean.

Once again, she moistened her lips. When their lips met again, her warm tongue met his, her breath whispered sweetly into him. He ran his hands from her narrow waist up her ribs to rest beneath her breasts.

"Do they still hurt, your ribs?" he kissed her again, before she could answer. Her warm tongue touched his, dueled and explored. She made a small sound of pleasure into his mouth.

When he pulled away, another tiny sound escaped her. "No, not much, only when I cough or move the wrong way."

His hands swept lower, resting on her derrière, pulling her closer. His need for her was all consuming, scorching him. Her delicate touch set an inferno burning inside.

He stopped, touching her chin and lifting her face so he could see into her eyes. "I don't want to hurt you," he whispered, swirling his tongue along the soft pink shell of her ear.

"You won't."

James needed her to burn as he did and want him just as much. His hand rested on the small of her back before he turned her. "See," he pointed to the ocean, "where the moonlight shimmers across the water. It's a pod of whales."

She relaxed into him, giving her trust to him and he hoped soon she would give him more, "They are beautiful."

"They are orcas," he massaged her neck, before running his finger along the neckline of her gown, wishing the cut of the gown was lower.

"They are beautiful."

He felt her shiver against him. "Are you cold?"

"Yes, no, strangely hot."

His laughter rolled over the Atlantic. "What am I supposed to make of an answer such as that?" he asked, placing a kiss on the top of her head. "Yes, no, strangely hot. Would you like to wear my jacket or return to the cabin?"

He watched her swallow and hesitate before she gave him an answer. "Jacket, please."

"Here it is." he placed it over her shoulders, remembering another time she wore his jacket, a time when the chance to kiss her was stolen from him. Whatever she would allow would happen tonight. There was no one here to interfere or play chaperone.

She shivered inside while he pulled her closer, enjoying holding her as well as the feel of her next to him. "Better."

Yet she still trembled. Nervous energy or genuinely cold, he wasn't sure. "Let's go back to the cabin where it's warm and I can make you hot. I want to set you on fire."

On the way back, they passed Adelina who was also returning to her room. James was sure the woman had been spying on them.

"Good evening," he said to her.

"Good evening."

Once inside she returned his jacket. "Thank you," she smiled.

"Brandy or wine?" He strode to his personal reserves and waited for an answer.

"Brandy," she told him sitting down at the small table and looking out the window.

He handed her the glass and poured each a drink. "What is it you're thinking, that has your mind so far away?"

"Adelina said you should act like a gentleman and I think you are." She traced the rim of her glass with a slender fingertip. "You're acting sweet and considerate."

"You don't know." He downed his drink and poured another before standing behind her.

"No," she was quick to say and he knew she lied.

Tavia knew exactly how a gentleman should act, and he was about to change the way he proceeded. He let his fingers feast at the base of her neck, slowly undoing the fastenings, one at a time, revealing more and more soft skin. "More brandy?" he asked.

"You want me drunk?" she asked, shuddering as his lips met the tender flesh on the back of her neck.

"Just relaxed," he murmured placing kisses along the column of her neck even while his fingers continued with the fastenings. A low cut gown with tiny sleeves would have been much easier.

"James..."

"Yes," he stopped holding his breath and praying she wasn't about to tell him to stop. "What is it?"

"I like what you're doing," she whispered softly while she bent her head forward as if to give him greater access.

A heavy pulse began in his groin. Her tender flesh was exposed to him, waited for him and he wanted to see more. He unbuttoned his shirt, pulling it loose from his britches.

"I like what I'm doing too. Do you want more? Tell me now if you don't." He pulled her from her chair and to him. Her hands on his chest, she smoothed her hands up then down to his waistband. He sucked air.

"Did I hurt you?" When she gazed up at him, her eyes were wide and such a beautiful color of green.

"You could never hurt me. You're small and delicate. I can wrap my fingers around your wrist almost twice. You're half my weight." He must take care not to hurt her, this beautiful tiny woman.

He let her explore his body, her hands moving to his back and drawing a line up his spine while he unfastened the rest of her dress. His hands ran across her shoulders sliding the sleeves down her arms, gazing hungrily at her. Beneath his fingers her body trembled. He turned her and with his lips he followed the earlier path.

She was in her corset and shift. Deftly, he unlaced the corset, letting it fall to the floor. She stood in front of him clad in only her shift and stockings. Her green eyes wide and filled with passion. The outline of her breasts was clear through the fabric still covering her.

He swept her into his arms, striding to the bed. Together they came down upon the mattress. He wanted to give her pleasure first, teach her how sweet lovemaking could be. Through the fabric of her shift he touched a finger to a nipple, felt the rise of her hips against him even as he did so then followed the touch with his mouth, tasting her, reveling in the intense rise of passion within her. Tavia's fingers wound into his hair, pulling him closer.

James felt sweat break out on his brow. He knew he should wait until the proper time, until they were wed, but he simply did not want to stop and it seemed Tavia wanted the same.

Tavia moaned softly as he shifted his position so he lay between her spread legs. He moved to give his attention to her mouth. "You are so incredibly beautiful," he said against her cheek. "So absolutely perfect."

"James," was all she said, and her voice broke on the word.

"Yes, my little darling." He kissed her again and as he did so, he used one hand to lift the fabric of her shift so he could touch the tender flesh of her leg. He could not bear to have anything between them, "Sit up and raise your arms." She did and he pulled the shift over her head.

"Too beautiful, exquisite. I thought so the first time I saw them." He whispered, unable to look away from the firm, milk-white globes tipped by pink buds that tilted up as if begging for his attention. His body shook with the need to make these moments perfect for her.

"Oh..." she let out a tiny cry as his hand moved higher, nearly to the apex of her legs, to the triangle that hid her femininity.

He gazed into her eyes then bowed to lick a nipple. Her small scream brought a smile to his lips and he returned to her mouth for an instant, silencing her, absorbing her passion. But soon he touched the tip of his tongue to the nipple again, flicked it back and forth until she moved slowly against him and pulled him closer. With more strength than she could have known she possessed, Tavia forced his mouth hard against her breast, and he answered her silent plea by sucking her nipple deep into his mouth, by biting gently that tip.

"James," she gasped, her heart beating hard against his hand that rested just beside her breast.

Smiling yet again, he moved to the other breast and worked diligently, producing soft little shrieks of pleasure even as he used his fingers on the nipple he had abandoned. She was so passionate and hot. She was sweet and made just for him.

"James, I feel...I feel so hot inside," she swallowed, her breathing heavy. "I ache, James. There is such...such I don't know what it is. I've never felt anything like this. Burning, and—" she suddenly froze, her eyes even wider than before.

Curious, he lifted his mouth a fraction but could not bring himself to leave the voluptuous flesh that caused his cock to bruise itself as it surged and surged against the confines of his clothing.

When she remained silent, he stopped, "You burn, my little darling? A good burning, I hope? Do you want it to go away?" He could help her in that.

"I am... Oh, my goodness, James, I am...I can't be. I don't understand." She ran her hands across his shoulders, pushing the sleeves of his shirt down. "Your arms are so huge."

"Tell me what you feel," he coaxed her. Her innocent honesty never ceased to amaze me.

"I believe I'm wet. How can that be? And there is the oddest of...sensations in a...certain part of me. I didn't know..." Her voice rose and weakened with every word.

James smiled again and returned to suckling her. While she pushed herself helplessly against him, he returned his hand to her leg and ran his palm over a silk stocking until he reached incredibly soft skin above.

She became still. "James, should you be doing what you're doing? Is it part of you seducing me?"

He didn't want to frighten her or have her say no. He must be very careful here. "Just a small thing to relieve the amazing sensations, little darling," he told her and deftly tucked his hand around the springy brush of hair at the apex of her thighs.

"James, I didn't know you could make me feel this way."

"It's only because you're an innocent." He delved into the wetness that had so amazed her, delved and parted the fattened, completely feminine folds shielding the tiny woman's bulb that could bring her to a place she had never dreamed of.

He raised his head, watching her heaving breasts, her pink tongue darting over moist lips. James rubbed that awakened nub until Tavia ground against him echoing tiny mews of pleasure. He watched her body spasm again and again as she reached the climax that had been building.

His lips parted, he drew back with the exultation of watching what he wrought in her. Wanting to see that other part of her aroused body reach its release he moved to her side so he could see her pale utterly perfectly shaped hips. Her thighs jerked and her wetness slicked his fingers. She was lost, carried away on the sea of need he had created. The tops of the embroidered yellow silk stockings had worked down to rest almost at her knees.

James bent over her, biting at her nipples once more, licking the fullness of her breasts, before driving her, with a last strong stroke to her shuddering climax. Her body shuddered against him. His lips found hers and he swept his tongue inside.

"James," was all she whispered before sagging in his arms.

James gathered her close, held her while her eyes remained closed, while her breathing calmed. Everything seemed to slow and stop throbbing, but not the jabbing need in his crotch. He needed to make her his own, enter into her and claim her innocence.

"Are you alright?" he asked, his hand resting on her chest, just beneath her breasts.

"James, I thought you would. Aren't you supposed to..." her breath slowed and the words she spoke were weak.

"Of course there is more, but I wanted to pleasure you first." He laughed as his fingers once again skimmed over her body and moved in perfect harmony while she responded with all the passion he knew she possessed and ached for. He rose from her and unfastening his britches, he slid them down his legs and kicked them away.

"I don't know if I can do this again. You've exhausted me. I feel very nearly boneless." She arched again and he laughed low and deep.

"Exhausted you say." As soon as they reached Barcelona, he was going to marry her.

"What about you?" With no hesitation and surprising him, her fingers closed around his cock.

"If you keep touching me that way, I'm going to explode without giving you pleasure," he said slipping two fingers inside her and finding more cream. "Are you ready for me? All of me? Tell me now if you want me inside you." Terrified of a reply of no, he waited cautiously. She nodded. His prayers had been answered.

Lost in the mystery and the magic surrounding Tavia, today she'd become his woman, his lady, The Duchess and her mandates be damned. The scent of her blended with the energy of the night and magic of the moonlight. She enchanted him.

"James..." His name floated in the heat of sultry night surrounding them.

His mouth slanted hungrily across hers. He nibbled on her lower lip, his teeth biting down gently and tugging. He stroked inside her mouth while he tried to hold himself still. His arms circled her back and pulled her tighter until they seemed to meld as one.

Unable to help himself, James pulled away from her, watching her, studying her face and the rhythm of her body, knowing he had to rely on patience. But her kiss-swollen lips held a mystery he couldn't resist.

Her nails raked down his chest across his nipples in a primal evocative dance. He held himself rigid in a futile attempt to keep the pace slow. It seemed she would have none of it. He shook with the need for her and to feel her move beneath him.

He kissed her eyes, her cheeks, the corners of her mouth, then depended the kiss. Nibbling on the tender flesh, playing chase with her tongue, he kissed her hard and she responded. He knew she wanted more and he would give her the world. He kissed her again and again.

"Little darling."

"James..."

He could wait no longer. His huge body flexed and she followed the rhythm he set. Slowly, he slipped inside her until he touched the fragile barrier claiming her innocence. Once he broke through, she would be his for the rest of eternity.

James stopped, hesitating. "This might hurt a little. There will be a tiny pain then only pleasure."

"Please... I need...you."

He didn't wait longer. He drove deep inside her then stopped, hearing her cry. Resting on his forearms and with patience he didn't realize he had, he waited, brushing the silken hair from her face, kissing away the teardrops.

When Tavia began to move beneath him, lifting her hips and pulling him deeper inside her walls, he said a silent prayer of thanks. He began to move again, setting the pace, waiting for her sweet passionate response. Feeling her cream and knowing she could accept his size, he drove inside her over and over again. With long deep strokes, he continued, until she cried out.

Pleasure exploded within him, liquid fire raged inside. "Tommy," he whispered her name even while he shook with the fever pitch she sent spiraling inside his body.

Slowly they calmed. She raked her fingernails over the taut muscles of his back as if exploring. Long quiet minutes passed. He settled her against him, her back to his front, holding tight to her, not wanting to ever let her go. She turned to face him, a lazy smile on her lips and he studied her and wondered what she was thinking.

James touched her collarbone then farther down. His light touch to her nipple brought it to an abrupt swift peak. He laughed softly and knew the sound of a man well satisfied and a woman who enjoyed the attentions he gave her body. His cock hardened and they made love again.

"Tell me what you feel." Tenderly he ran a finger along her chin. Understanding she might not want to talk about what just happened.

~ * ~

Swearing beneath her breath, Adelina paced the tiny room she called her own. This was not supposed to happen. James Macmurra was an experienced and reliable captain. His ships were always on time. The ship had been delayed in Bordeaux and her contact might not be in Barcelona when she arrived. It was imperative that she pass on the information Drake Montgomerie had given her in a timely fashion.

The envelope was sealed and it was to remain that way. She could not open it on penalty of death. So what was she to do if they were late to arrive? She would have to give herself to the wealthy Spaniard in order to maintain her cover. And she would have to wait for further orders. Her body shuddered at the thought of lying in bed with a man she'd never met. James was right when he told her she was no whore. In truth she was in love with one man and had been for quite some time.

Adelina shuddered again at the thought of the Spaniard's hands groping her body and touching her intimately. She thought of the young lovers in the captain's cabin and the one love she lost so long ago before their love could be consummated. She searched through her trunk for the small gun she always carried and made sure it was loaded. It was a precaution she always took. Adelina placed it in her reticule for safekeeping.

Startled by the knock on her door, she stuffed the reticule inside her trunk. "Who is it?"

"Seamus, may I come in for a bit?"

What on earth did he want? She was frustrated and angry. She really didn't want to chat with anyone. "Yes, yes, of course," Yet Adelina liked the older man and enjoyed his company. Impatiently tapping her foot, she opened the door for him.

"What is it?"

"Just curious. You weren't on the deck very long and I wondered if everything was all right." Seamus stepped through the open door, rubbing his chin as if in thought.

"Do you have time to sit down?" she asked, looking to the one chair she nodded in that direction and for herself she sat on the bed.

Perhaps she needed a short diversion.

"Don't need to be on duty for a few hours. Sure." He sat on the chair. His elbows resting on his legs, he watched her.

Adelina pulled a bottle of whiskey from her trunk and poured two glasses. Handing one to Seamus, she said, "Everything is fine, just a bit distressed by the delay in Bordeaux. Now I'm sounding selfish. Poor Tommy has recovered and I'm very glad about that, but I need to arrive in Barcelona on time and at this point I don't think it will happen."

Seamus was shaking his head, "We won't make it there when we were supposed to," he sipped as he talked. "Believe we might have another stop before that one."

She inhaled a sharp draw of breath, startled by the first mate's comment. "What makes you say that?" she asked, her heart pounding fear for her life very real. "I can't afford to be delayed much longer."

"Well," Seamus began, "let's just say I know James Macmurra better than most men, and I think he's going to stop at the next port. He's a man of loyalty and honor. Tonight he took something that wasn't his right to take, and I'm sure he will want to rectify that."

"Of course," the lump in her throat grew. "He's made love to Tommy. That doesn't come as a surprise."

"Don't jump to conclusions. Let's just say I'm guessing and it seems you're guessing too. Don't know for sure. I'll say something to him about your arrival time, but if he's made up his mind, it won't make a difference. Since we just sailed through the Strait of Gibraltar. I think we'll put it at the port of Malaga. Just waitin' for the order."

She saw her life flash in front of her, her mind searching for alternatives when she reached Barcelona. There was only one choice.

Chapter Six

Tavia woke in James' arms as sunlight filtered through the window. His hand rested on one breast and his leg was thrown over hers. She nestled into his large body feeling at ease and protected within his embrace. His warm lips along with his teeth and tongue touched upon her flesh down the back of her neck and across her spine. She shivered with the passion he ignited and wanted to return the desire.

Between his fingers, he touched her nipple, caressing, traced a path from one to the other, enticing her surrender. She couldn't suppress the tiny sounds erupting from her lungs. She would tell him how she felt later.

He had made love to Tommy and in doing so betrayed Tavia. To her it made no difference they were one and the same. The Duchess might think otherwise. James didn't know she was Tavia, and that was what infuriated her. Or did he know? What if he knew and he wasn't telling her? Yet a little voice in her head reminded her she was not truthful with him either. Perhaps he was just as stubborn and to what purpose? She made plans to say something as soon as the time was right. Still, with his touch she succumbed to the need to feel him deep within her again. He awoke feelings and sensations she never knew existed.

Yet she couldn't change anything that happened between them and she had no regrets. He had become a part of her, stormed his way into her heart. She wanted to touch him, run her hands along the hard angles and planes of his body, but he held her firmly in place, seducing, tempting, and burning her as he caressed, within and without. He ignited an inferno soaring through her veins. She clung to his arm, ran her hand on the only part of him he allowed her to touch while he had access to all of her.

She pushed against him and felt the pulse of his hard male flesh against her, the part that had given her so much pleasure for the last few nights. It seemed they spent the better part of most days and nights in bed. They ate, drank and made love.

"I want to touch you everywhere," she whispered softly into the silence of the room. "I need to kiss you, I..."

"Later you'll have your turn." His lips and warm tongue continued their assault upon her, across her shoulders and down her spine, and his hands played and toyed with her.

Without warning he was inside her, his fingers working their magic on the most feminine parts of her. He drove inside her while she pushed against him, taking all of him inside.

Within minutes she cried out, "James."

He turned her then, her breasts touching his chest while he pulled her close. "I've ordered a bath. I want you to dress in the evening gown I bought you. We're going ashore as soon as you are ready."

Gently holding both sides of her head, he kissed her, a long deep kiss that excited and seduced then he slanted his mouth across hers again and let his lips mold to hers. Yet when he drew away, he rose from the bed. He was naked and bronzed and when he turned, he looked upon her with an all-knowing smile. She trembled with the passion he created in her.

"Have we reached Barcelona then?" she asked, sitting up and letting the sheets fall to her waist, feeling comfortable with her nakedness. She pushed her hair behind her ears, moistening her lips with her tongue, hoping he would come back to bed.

"No, Malaga, another port city," he said seemingly unable to take his gaze from her. "If you stay that way, naked and inviting me, I'm not going to be able to resist you. I'll be deep inside you and our excursion will be delayed. I don't want that to happen."

"Are we supposed to stop there, Malaga? Adelina is impatient to reach Barcelona. She told me she must be on time. It's very important. Besides the man she is to wed there is another man she has to see." Tavia pulled the sheet around her.

"I'm sorry for her, but we're stopping. It's urgent, something I must take care of immediately. I cannot let any of this," he spread his arms wide, "go on any longer this way."

"Are you going to help me with my corset?" Provocatively, she rose naked from the bed, completely at ease now in front of him. She loved to watch his eyes rove the length of her even while she tried desperately to ignore the very real fact he thought she was Tommy.

"Of course, after your bath and mine. Although I'll have a devil of a time lacing it when I'd rather take the damn thing off."

"Water's here." The call from the door had Tavia bringing the sheet closer around her.

"Come in," wrapping a bath sheet around him, he strode to the door and let the men bring the water to the tub.

When they left, "Would you like to go first?" James politely asked.

"No, you go first. I'd like to take a few minutes to soak in the hot water. While I do you can do whatever it is you do and come back to help me dress." She sat back against the wall.

"We could bathe together," he grinned at her, enticing her to accept the invitation, but her muscles were sore and she wanted to let the healing powers of the hot water soothe them.

"Maybe another time." She watched the play of his muscles while he stepped into the tub and was reminded of another time. She rose from the bed. Beside the tub, she picked up the soap and the sponge, washing his back with long gentle strokes.

A deep low groan rumbled from his chest. He turned quickly and lifting her, set her in the tub with him. This was not what she expected when she decided to wash his back.

Now she straddled him, his hot male flesh pushing at her core, and before she could say yes or no, he was deep inside her.

"James..."

He kissed her hard and deep while she moved on his shaft. In seconds she climaxed and leaned against his chest. "James," she whispered his name again, "you unravel me to my very core."

"I'm sorry. I couldn't resist. You should have known better than to touch me when you're naked." He stroked her cheek while she lay against him. Her breaths were labored for a time as she fought to calm herself.

"I'm not sorry," she told him, placing her hands on either side of his head and kissing the corners of his mouth.

He set her aside and rose, water sluicing from him. His body fascinated her, the hard muscled legs and arms, the narrowness of his hips and his broad shoulders.

"We cannot do this again or we will never leave. Relax, in the water. I'll dress and return to help you with your things in ten minutes. By that time the water will be cold."

"Are you sure?" She rose to her knees in the tub with the clear intention of seducing him.

He bent over and gave her a quick kiss to the forehead. "I'm sure, my little darling."

She sat back, disappointed but not surprised. When he left, she turned and put her head on the rim of the tub, swirling the water around her with her hands, letting the warmth soothe her. She closed her eyes and forced thoughts of his perfidy from her head. She was just as much at fault. She could have told him who she was and she could have refused him. If she said no, he would've never made love to her, but he had to know who she was, the vow to The Duchess be damned.

Seconds turned to minutes and she realized he would return soon. She remembered that first bath when she'd been terrified of him walking into the room and seeing her as she was, a woman. If he had, so many things might have been different.

She soaped her hair, wishing for the long hair she chopped off with the words to Tira, "It will grow out." They had been so naïve. Was Tira now in Baltimore learning the trade of building ships? Had she cut her hair? Her twin could be in just as much trouble.

Here she was stopping at the port city of Malaga to do something with James. She was having her adventure but at what expense? Using the last bucket of water, she poured it over her head, rinsing the soap away.

"Are you done?" He stood in the doorway, hands on his hips and feet planted shoulder width, a smile on his devilishly handsome face.

"Yes, only because the water grows cold."

"I would that you could have more time, but the dinghy to takes us to land is here and waiting for us."

"You are so mysterious. What are we going to do?" Her curiosity was getting ahead of her patience.

"I want it to be a surprise." He toweled her off quickly, and set her clothes on the bed then left her to finish drying herself.

"I don't like surprises," she said with as much annoyance as she could muster.

Her irritation didn't faze him. He let out a roar of laughter. "You're going to like this one. At least I hope you will."

"How can you be so sure?" she shot back, grinning at him. "You don't know me all that well."

"I disagree. I know you very well, perhaps better than anyone else in your life."

"Not my twin."

"You have a twin."

"I did." It seemed he wanted to carry on this ruse, so be it. She would play his game and see what transpired. He knew she'd been lying. And once again, it seemed he wasn't going to confront her about this.

James stood in front of her, watching her then quickly turned away as if the sight of her burned him.

He shrugged, "I'm just hopeful but I'm also very confident you will appreciate my efforts."

"You never took me into Bordeaux so I'm glad you let me step foot on Spanish soil. It will feel good to touch down on solid ground."

When she stepped into the main room and dropped the towel, he groaned in the back of his throat. "Little hussy," he murmured. "And now you know how much the sight of you with nothing on tempts me."

"I didn't mean to tempt anyone." She stepped toward him before turning her back so he could wrap the corset around her and lace it.

"Of course you do," he said, laughing placing soft enticing kisses along her shoulders. "Just as I know how to make you want me."

"You said we have to go. No time to play in bed." She intentionally prompted him, now impatient to discover the surprise he had waiting for her.

"Good of you to remind me." He cleared his throat.

When he held up the gown, a tiny startled gasp emanated from her lungs.

"The gown is beautiful."

"It's the Macmurra tartan," he told her, his tone so low and gruff she could barely hear him. "I hoped you would like it and enjoy wearing it."

"It is made of such fine silk and so beautiful," she said, forgetting for a moment she shouldn't know something like that, but she didn't know how to cover her mistake so she hoped he didn't hear it. The tucker was made of crepe lisse folded *a la farinet*, confined in front, on each side, and on the shoulders by pearl loops. The sleeves, short and full, were set in a band of twisted satin and edged with a delicate Buckinghamshire lace.

"I'm glad you like it. After all the joy you've given me, I wanted you to have something that represented me." With his hands behind his back, he rocked on his heels, clearly pleased with himself and the dress he chose for her.

He held out an arm for her and she took it, excited by the prospect of touching her feet on solid ground as well as discovering the surprise. Once on land, she breathed in deeply, sweeping her gaze across the harbor building. Most were taverns and brothels. There were food carts selling an assortment of fresh food and drink.

They stopped and he bought a bouquet of flowers. Not only was she wearing fine clothing, but she finally noticed he was dressed in a black silk shirt, tight fitting breeches and a jacket made of the finest material. Perhaps he was taking her to the opera or a play, yet that did not seem urgent and a reason to stop at an unscheduled port.

She stopped him, taking his hand in hers, her heart pounding with happiness, "Whatever you have planned for this evening, thank you," she smiled at him before caressing his cheek.

He squeezed her hand as they walked farther into the town. Finally, he hailed a cab and helped her inside. He gave directions.

"Where are we going?" she asked again, sucking her bottom lip between her teeth, knowing she had asked the question multiple times and he never answered. He wasn't going to now.

He smiled and holding her head between his hands, let his mouth touch her. He drew a line across the seam of her lips with his tongue then his lips and tongue created a path to her ear then down.

He looked up, "Is it working?"

She tilted her head to the side, "I don't understand."

"Am I taking your attention away from the excursion?"

A tiny noise escaped that sounded something like "maybe," she held her hands on the sides of his face, enjoying the feel of his beard, wishing he'd let her explore him.

When he pulled away, "Every time you ask me that question, I'm going to kiss you," he dragged her into his arms, holding her close, his forehead resting against hers.

"Then I should keep questioning you," she moistened her lips, her fingers winding into the fabric of his shirt.

"Don't tempt me too much," he warned. "If you do that, you'll never find out what the surprise is because we'll stop and get a room."

She pushed away from him, crossing her arms in front of her chest. "James Macmurra, you're a tease. I know you won't do that."

He tapped on the top of the cab, and it slowed.

She sat still, holding her breath, wishing for what she wasn't sure. He was so mysterious yet debonair. One moment she believed she could guess what he thought, and the next she didn't have any idea. She certainly didn't know what he was about.

"Are we there?" She really didn't imagine he would stop what he planned, to find a room, to make love. He could do that at his ship, just about anywhere he pleased.

"No, there's a nice hotel across the street."

"But..." he helped her from the vehicle.

"But what?" He smiled and it seemed a bit wicked. He told the driver to stay, they'd be right out.

They walked inside. The foyer was opulent, with winding stairs and chandeliers gracing the interior. The décor was golds and reds. James got a room just as he said he would do, and they walked up the stairs, her heart pounding. Was this the surprise? She didn't think so. He would have told her this.

"James, what are we doing? I don't understand. This is not what I expected." She stepped inside the spacious room.

"Do you like it?" He asked, pulling her to him and kissing her.

When he was done, "Yes, but...you wouldn't stop in an unscheduled port to take me to a beautiful hotel room in the city. You have cargo and a passenger who is eager to reach Barcelona."

"You're right. I wouldn't. Come, I'm going to give you the rest of the surprise." He held out his hand waiting for her to accept it.

She tilted her head slightly, confused and suddenly wary. Swallowing her confusion and concern, she walked with him.

He dismissed the cab, telling the driver he changed his mind and they wanted to walk.

Outside the sun was high in the sky, casting long shadows. A warm breeze blew from the ocean inland. They passed restaurants and shops. People sauntered and chatted along the way. Still they strolled, his hand tighter around hers.

"Where are we going?" She stopped on the walkway, meaning to stand her ground until he told her what he planned.

"Hush, we're almost there. Close your eyes."

"No." She didn't want to close her eyes. She needed to see what was going to happen next.

"Ah, now you're disobeying orders again."

"I'm not the bloody cabin boy anymore. I don't have to obey your orders." She wasn't going anywhere with him until he told her what he had planned.

"I was going to do this before we got our room in the hotel, but you forced my hand," he said, "Just a few more minutes and you will have your surprise. Close your eyes. I insist. As a favor."

She complied with his wishes and let him lead her through the people to wherever. They turned.

"There's a step here, a few more."

His hand was on her back making sure she didn't fall.

"How much farther?" She was breathing hard and now more impatient than ever.

They stopped, "here we are."

When she opened her eyes, the magnificence of the cathedral stole her breath. "James, what are we doing in a church?" She twirled, gazing at everything, absorbing the beauty.

His hand on her arm, they continued walking until they stood just in front of the altar and a priest stepped through an arch in the back. "James Macmurra?" the man questioned.

"Yes, and Tommy..." he turned to her.

She stiffened, the color draining from her face, her body trembling. "Just Tommy. James..." she looked to him for answers. "What is happening here?"

"We are getting married." He smiled down at her.

"No," she was shaking her head and backing away from him. "No, it's not what I want. We can't do this, not now, not like this."

He bent low, "Of course it is and right. Now at this very moment you aren't thinking about all the possible scenarios and repercussions. You could be pregnant, or have you thought about that fact?" he said, his voice harsh for the first time since they left the ship.

He was supposed to return to London and court her, and now he wanted to wed Tommy. *How dare he.* Somewhere in the dark recesses of her mind, she believed she could have everything. She didn't want him to admit he knew she was Tavia Hepburn, and she didn't want to tell him the game was over. If she ignored everything that had not been said between them, she could be Tavia again when they were back in London. *I'm a fool.* "You need my consent. You can not force or coerce me into a marriage I don't want."

"I do want your consent and in doing this I trust you to know I've your best interest at heart. What is there to protest?" he asked, picking up her hands and holding them in his. "I thought we did well together. You never want to leave my bed. Isn't that enough for a marriage?"

"We do, I...you took me by surprise. I never expected this. You never gave me time to think about wedding you." She wanted to yell at him that she fancied a real wedding. One The Duchess could plan and her family could attend. If she did, it would be admitting the truth, a truth she wasn't willing to give up. The betrayal was so intense it nearly sent her to her knees. What had she done to create this horrific scenario where all her dreams were shattered, and now she didn't know how to undo it, but Adelina might?

Adelina was on board the Firtha waiting to get to Barcelona.

"Are you willing?" His eyes sizzled with blue fire.

She inhaled a deep breath, hoping for an answer. "Yes and no." She wanted to run, yet she wanted to say the words that would make her his wife. In his eyes, Tommy would be his wife not Tavia. She'd thought she had time to fix this retched situation.

His laugh was harsh. "What does that mean? Yes and no. The priest has provided two witnesses and is willing to marry us on this short notice, but you must make up your mind now."

"Now?" she breathed in deep. "Now..."

He smiled, "Now. Do you want to marry me or not? I only ask once," he encouraged her with a threat.

She looked at her feet, trying to decide if she should commit. "Alright then, we can do this." They could work through the inherent problems later.

"So enthusiastic," he laughed.

"Well, you could have given me a clue as to what you had planned." She still wasn't sure about this; the time and the place were all wrong.

"She's agreed," he told the priest.

Soft organ music began to play as they stood in front of the priest saying their vows. "Will you promise to love, honor and obey?" the priest asked.

She had been trying to obey him for over a month now and had not faired too well in that regard, but he didn't seem to mind when she didn't do what he asked. Except when she nearly fell to her death.

She cleared her throat and tried to say the words but they came out in a whisper. "I," she moistened her lips. "Y-yes."

The ceremony continued and finally the priest pronounced them man and wife and said, "You may kiss the bride."

James pulled her close and kissed her softly, his lips gentle against hers so unlike his usual seduction. This kiss promised the future. Then he picked her up and twirled her around. Finally, he set her down, "I was so afraid you'd say no."

"I almost refused. This was too big a surprise for me to deal with on such a short notice," she told him, wondering how he would explain this marriage to Tavia, to her when they reached London.

"You didn't refuse though," he said, "We have to sign the papers. Come," he told her, taking her hand in his again.

"Sign?" She couldn't put her signature on those papers. That would be giving up her quest because now she knew, she wanted James to admit to everything. "I can't write," she blurted.

He stared at her for several seconds. "You can use an X for your signature. It's common. I'm going to have to teach you to write your new name."

A man came with the papers. James signed and Tavia put an X for her name, knowing the lie for what it was, but this was something else she was going have to explain. Lies seemed to multiply around her.

All James did was remain silent when he should have told her he saw through her disguise. She told multiple lies, one after another then another, pretending she was someone she was not. How had she come to this?

"Any more surprises?" she asked, looking at her feet, unable to meet his gaze, sure he would start laughing and all the lies would be forgiven. He wanted to marry her and in a way had called her bluff, but she refused to lose this round.

"Hungry? I had Seamus go ahead and make reservations for us at one of the restaurants we passed on the way to the church."

She licked her lips, nervous, for the here and now as well as the future. Her stomach was sour. "I'm not sure I can eat anything. My stomach is rolling."

"A glass of wine will calm your nerves, and you don't have to eat anything if you don't want to."

"I'll try." She nodded, so unsure of what was happening. The speed of this adventure took her breath from her lungs.

Her hand on his arm they strolled to the restaurant and were ushered to their seats.

The wine poured, James lifted his glass to hers. "To you, Tommy no name Macmurra, and to our future. At least now you have a last name."

She gulped the wine. *I had one before.*

~ * ~

James understood Tavia nervousness. They both lied and he wasn't surprised when she told him she couldn't even write her name. Putting her signature on the papers would reveal her lie, and she obviously didn't want to risk that.

He was pretty sure from things she told him she could read and write two languages just as her sister Ella could, English and French.

Now he was happily sitting across from his new wife eating dinner in a beautiful restaurant in Spain. What more could he want in life? Stability. He wanted the lie to come to fruition. He needed to hear her say the words that would end this travesty. She started the ruse, now it was up to her to end it.

More than anything now, he needed truth from his beautiful wife, and he had been sure she would have revealed the fact she was Tavia Hepburn when they first made love. Yet she remained frustratingly silent. He knew she resented him and what he'd done, even while she allowed him to make love to her.

The young waiter brought cheese and tomatoes, followed by calamari and lobster. The meal was delicious, but Tavia only pushed her food from here to there on her plate, tasting little of the meal. Clearly distressed about the events of this evening.

He poured her more wine.

The wine on little to no food would make the evening interesting. The thought crossed his mind that if he got her drunk and gave her enough cues, she might reveal to him that she was Tavia Hepburn. Then the next phase of this nightmare would begin.

He'd never knowingly helped a woman let alone a wife get drunk so he could get what he wanted. He shrugged, watching as her fingers trembled. There was a first time for everything.

But this wasn't one of those times. He finished eating and paid the bill, lending her his arms as they strolled along the walkway. Still she held herself away from him, something she'd never done in the past. The night businesses were beginning to thrive and gaslights illuminated the area.

At the hotel room, he helped her from her pelisse then her bonnet,

"Something to drink?"

"Yes, please," she sat down, her hands folded in her lap, her eyes focused on her hands.

"What are you thinking, Tommy?" He handed her a glass of wine and watched while she traced the top of the glass with a finger before setting the crystal goblet on the table.

She looked up, a different expression on her face. "This all happened so fast. The wedding, why?"

"Why, you ask?" He grimaced wondering how to explain his reasons and searching for the right words. "Rumors and talk. I don't want people to think badly of you. As I said before, you could be carrying my child."

"That really doesn't explain anything. I was your cabin boy and now I'm just a girl with no last name. No one cares about me. We've been through that before and it's still true."

He walked behind her, his hands on her shoulders, gently massaging her neck. Tight muscles met his fingers. With tension radiating into his fingers, he shuddered at how he'd taken advantage of her. "If you recall, we, I, took no precautions. I did not treat you well."

"You didn't have to marry me, you know. You could have asked me to be your mistress or your whore. I'm nothing to you." She moved her shoulders, trying to stretch the muscles and ease the tension.

His fingers tightened into her flesh. "Perhaps not, but I did. Are you happy? You have a last name now." He wanted to shake her until she admitted who she was.

"Happy is not the right word. I don't know how I feel. You gave me a choice, but I really didn't feel as if I had one." Tavia stared into his eyes until hers seemed to cross.

"Why would you say no? I can give you everything you've ever dreamed of." He still didn't have a title, but she never seemed to care about that. He took the pins from her hair before running his fingers through the silken strands. It was still short and he remembered wishing he could do this when her hair had been long. He never wanted her to cut it again.

"You don't know what I've dreamed about."

"True, perhaps I only imagine certain things such as a roof over your head and food to eat. But then I could be wrong. That brings me back to the first question. Why would you say no?"

"Because you don't love me," she said, her voice barely a whisper.

"I don't love anyone," he lied, knowing he could never tell her his true feelings as long as she masqueraded as Tommy. "Love does not play a part in marriage. There's no room for such a foolish emotion. One must have a wife in order to have a legitimate family."

She stiffened at his words and beneath his fingers she shuddered. "I won't be a brood mare to give you an heir. I know of a woman who died because her husband forced himself on her so many times, trying for a son she had no strength left to live.

"I still want a family, children who are not bastards. Love means nothing to me."

"Then I feel sorry for you. I know people who are in love and they are happily married. Love is not foolish."

"Then," he paused as if in thought yet knowing her answer and bending so close to her his words whispered into her ear. "Do you love me, Tommy?" he meant to challenge her. "Tell me true."

"No, how could I love you when I barely know you?" she questioned him.

"Ah," he touched her lips with a fingertip, stroked softly. "We know each other quite well. I know how to make you sigh with pleasure and make those tiny sounds in the back of your throat. Who else can do that?" he queried, realizing he wanted her love more than anything. Perhaps one day soon he would hear her say the words.

"I don't feel comfortable with this conversation," she said, looking away before rising and walking to the window.

He followed her and let one hand settle around her waist. She was running from him, and he needed to make sure she did not get away. "Would you like to go to bed then and consummate this marriage?"

"I'm not tired." Yet she leaned into him, seeming to need the support his huge body could give her. When he wrapped his arm around her, his hands reached her abdomen and settled there.

"Me neither, but that isn't what I asked."

"What should we do then?" She hesitated a second, waving her hand in the air. "Never mind."

"You knew I'd want to seduce my beautiful wife, and you don't want that. It's because you didn't eat anything at dinner. You must be half starved. I'll send someone to a bakery."

"My stomach is not feeling well. I'm sure I couldn't eat a thing, especially something sweet. Sending someone would be a waste of time," she said with a heavy sigh as if to punctuate the statement.

"You've got to try. You'll waste away to nothing."

"What is going to happen when we are in London again?" She turned into his arms.

Weakness assaulted his limbs. James closed his eyes and saw hazy specks of color dance behind his eyelids. "You do not have to worry about that. I will take care of everything."

"I can not help but worry and wonder what will happen to me."

He lightly kissed her. *Little liar.* "You will come to my home." He'd imagined a home and a family for years. Now he had the promise of that very thing, although obstacles still lay in his path.

"And where is that? Do you have a home in London? It seems I heard you tell someone you do not. Was I wrong?"

"I don't recall saying anything about a home." He'd never said anything while on the ship. She must be remembering something from that first evening at the opera. "Before this ship sailed, I solicited someone to find a home in the countryside and perhaps a townhouse for the winter months." Not so far from Drake Montgomerie that she couldn't easily ride to see her sister.

"Who?" she asked, tilting her head slightly to one side, clearly interested in the answer. "Who is your solicitor?"

"Does it matter? You wouldn't know them, Tommy." He smiled, understanding how hard this must be for her to keep her questions from giving herself away.

She shrugged her delicately slim shoulders, her eyes sparkling where the moonlight glistened on them. "I suppose not. I'm just curious."

"What would you like in a home?" He pushed a few wayward strands of hair behind her ears.

"Nothing pretentious."

"Not pretentious?" he asked. "Who are you, Tommy, besides a person who has no one but me to care about you? I thought you grew up with few possessions, and yet you ask for a home that is not pretentious. I would have thought you would want more."

He watched her rub her temples before she spun away from him and started to pace. "I have a headache," she murmured.

Most likely he'd have a headache too if he was immersed in so many lies. At the moment he had only one to contend with. In everything else he told the truth, but with Tavia, one lie led to another. He needed for her to end this charade.

"It must be because you didn't eat today. I really should get you something." He turned to ring the bell that would bring a servant from downstairs to their assistance.

"I suppose I could eat something, but no pastry, nothing sweet. I don't think it would sit well in my stomach." She stopped in front of him before returning to chair where she'd sat earlier.

"Maybe some tea and honey or perhaps bread and cheese?" he asked, concerned now for her health.

"That would be good."

"Come in," he called.

The man stepped through the door. "Sir?"

"We would like a hot pot of tea with honey and bread and cheese. As soon as possible, please."

"Yes, sir." The man left.

He wanted to make this night perfect, but it seemed to go farther downhill with each passing moment. "Would you like to get comfortable? I picked up a few things for you including a nightdress and robe. Seamus brought items for the night." He pointed to the small bag in the corner of the room.

"Yes, maybe we can talk a little bit more." She searched through the small valise and found the nightclothes he spoke of then walked into the bedroom. A few minutes later she reappeared.

"Need help?" he asked, smiling. He prayed his patience would gain him some ground in this battle of lies or perhaps wills they fought.

"You know I do." She spoke softly, turning her back to him.

He wasn't about to let this small opportunity pass. He placed tender kisses along her neck and across her shoulders while he unfastened the gown, drawing the sleeves downward until he could unlace the corset. His gut tightened knowing he could take this to its logical conclusion, but he resisted.

"This should help and you should be able to finish." His words were smooth and soft, setting the stage for the night to come.

"Thank you." She disappeared inside the bedchamber just as the food was delivered.

"Set it on the table." James nodded to a small table near the window.

"Yes, sir."

James sampled a slice of cheese and broke off a bunch of grapes he envisioned feeding Tavia. Bloody hell, but he also envisioned calling her by her name. He wasn't going to get any more of Tommy's story because she didn't have one. And yet he wanted to try, to probe for answers and maybe come closer to getting her to disclose the truth she seemed to be still avoiding.

She appeared totally unaware of the revealing nightclothes she wore. He had found a small dress shop that must cater to men who had mistresses. Many of the items were revealing and meant to entice and seduce. The negligee she wore was made to do just that.

Beneath the fabric he could see suggestions of all of her curves, dark shadows indicating her nipples and the triangle at the apex of her thighs.

"You are truly beautiful, Tommy, a man's wildest dreams are embodied in your form." He truly couldn't breathe while looking at her.

She looked at the floor then met his gaze. "Are you going to eat too?"

Tavia intrigued him. He wanted to get to know Tavia, not Tommy. In London, he'd had very little time with her.

James watched her covertly, this complicated creature who had become his wife. His gaze returned to the pale yellow nightgown hiding very little, enticing all of him. She was the most beautiful woman he'd ever seen and the most distracting woman he'd ever met. Tonight her short-cropped hair was sticking out in different places in a very boyish way, enhancing her finely boned face. Her appearance was a deceivingly demure façade, captivating him.

James' fingers stole over Tavia's. He turned up her palm and held her hands. "I should have given these to you sooner. I wanted to when you first put on the evening gown." He reached into the pocket of his waistcoat and produced a handful of jewelry that caught the light and sent flashing prisms in every direction. "These go with your dress," he said, dumping a necklace, earrings and bracelets of emerald and gold into Tavia's lap.

Tavia gasped and tried to withdraw her hand. "You shouldn't."

"Of course I should."

James held her tightly and extricated another fabulous bauble, this time from his other pocket. "My bride should have this. It is only fitting. The ring will seal our vows and proclaim you, Tommy, as my wife." With that he slid a ring onto her finger.

The light in Tavia's eyes seemed to unravel his soul with the sudden frigid temperature emanating from them. When James released her, she wiped her palm on a napkin, never glancing at the huge diamond surrounded with emeralds that sparkled just as icily as her eyes from her hand.

"A diamond for my wife. You're mine, Tommy," he reminded her, studying her reaction and the stiffness of her spine. He thought he might have waited for a better time rather than rubbing it in her face that he married Tommy, not Tavia.

"Where did you get this? I thought you were just a captain of a ship."

One eyebrow rose in speculation. "Just? Is that what you think of my profession?"

"I didn't mean anything by that. I really don't know who you are and what you possess. What can a wife expect from you? There's more to you, James Macmurra, than you've shown me."

"I own a fleet of ships, not that I have to explain myself to a wife. I find your curiosity endearing but at times irritating. Money is of no consequences to me. I've plenty where that came from even though I don't have a title to my name. The ring, however, I won in a game of chance."

"I see." She stared at her hand. "Diamonds are my favorite stone. How did you know?" she said as if she were disappointed he didn't purchase it especially for her.

Well, he didn't know that tidbit of information. There had been no time for such a thing, and the ring had been in his possession for months now. The ring was convenient. When he decided to wed her, he retrieved it from his trunk. James stared at Tavia's bowed head, at her flyaway boyish hair cut, and the clear-cut bones of her face. Something odd stirred within him, a tightening of the gut, a long drawing in of breath he couldn't seem to release. His jaw clenched—and his fists tightened where they lay on the table.

He felt...possessive.

The next thing he heard was a glass falling to the floor. Red wine splattered the rug and table in tiny blood-red droplets. "Do you want more wine, Tommy. The food is ready and you really do need to eat something, keep your strength up for tonight."

Her lips trembled then tightened into a thin line. She whispered something he couldn't make out.

Possessive? Bloody hell, he would not allow himself to crumble before this woman who lied to him, still thought she deceived him. If she wasn't going to back down, neither was he.

"Tommy," he said clearly and speaking slowly, "kindly answer me. Do you want more wine, food?"

James knew he had pushed her too far. He was disquieted to feel his heart thud. Her hands were in her lap, and he covered them there.

"Tommy?"

She nodded her head.

A moment of confusion, his patience stretched thin, he provoked her even when he'd decided all this would come to an end when they returned to London.

Tears, one, and two, fell on the back of James' hand in Tavia's lap. Her shoulders began to shake. Her neck was white and childishly vulnerable. A single wisp of hair fell across her eyes. James had an overwhelming desire to touch it, run his fingers through all of it.

He didn't dare. "Please don't cry. I'm sorry. I'm not too sure what just happened here, but it would be best if we don't pursue whatever it is that has you in tears. It is our wedding night."

"I think I'd like some more wine and food. James, I like the ring. Thank you."

He poured another glass for both of them. The hour was late but he was not sleepy. "Eat. We'll return to the ship first thing in the morning."

She broke off a piece of bread and ate, chewing slowly, not taking her gaze from the food. She swallowed her glass of wine all at once.

The silence filled his soul with despair. Tonight he'd single handedly made their situation worse. If he could take back his words, he would. Although he knew, if he could do this over, he'd make no changes.

Slowly, Tavia stood up. She raised her chin and stared straight into his eyes. "I'm not at all sure what happened here tonight. I feel as if you know something I'm unaware of, or that you think I know something. You have stolen something precious from me, yet you have tried to make it right by marriage. I respect you for that."

James crossed his arms in front of him. He did not like the tightening of the muscles in his gut.

Picking up the jewelry he gave her, she swept from the room, her back straight and stiff. He was not welcome in the bedroom with his new wife. He could sense the ice in her veins.

Minutes passed and the stillness became unbearable. James caught up a decanter of brandy and a glass and sat in a chair by the fire regarding the flames.

The spirits burned his throat—at first. Soon he felt nothing but the dulling warmth seeping through his veins. He studied the glass as if it could give him answers. He wished he had the balls to bring this all to a crashing end. If he did, it couldn't be worse than it was now. Nothing could be worse. Tavia knew it was him, thought he broke his vows. How on earth could she believe he didn't recognize her? Perhaps she didn't.

This was his wedding night.

He filled his glass again, drank, and stared morosely into the fire. The flames leapt and danced, sending a warm message that didn't reach his heart.

It wasn't possible.

He rose. He wasn't going to spend his wedding night alone. A few minutes later he strode down the street, seeking a diversion of sorts. Once again he needed to hit something.

Seamus appeared at his side. "Wedding night not going as planned?" The old man spoke with a certain humor in his voice.

"You think this is funny?" He turned on his first mate, wishing Seamus could be his punching bat.

"Nah, I'd love to see you happy. Nothing would please me more. But I've told you before, you won't be happy until the truth comes out. Are we lookin' for a fight tonight, or do you just want to get drunk?"

"Last time we fought, Tavia nearly fell to her death. A few drinks then I better get home."

"Suit yourself, but I think you're itching for a fight."

~ * ~

The Duchess set the letter on the table and cackled with delight. "Married," she said. "My little Tavia has found a match for her need for adventure. But there will be hell to pay, either way before they reach London or on the return trip. Nothing good comes from lies." She ran her fingers through her graying hair, remembering fondly the times with her duke.

"What is it Auntie?" Larena swept into the room. Picking the letter off the table, "I see you've heard from Tavia. She stared at the note, reading while she sat down near.

"Not Tavia but James."

"No word from my cousin then?"

"No, but James writes that he wants me to find a home for him to buy. Somewhere in the country and close to the Montgomerie estate and if possible a townhouse too."

"He has money then," Larena mused. "I would have never thought. I doubt if Tavia does either."

"There is more to this tale. It seems James has known all along that it was Tavia masquerading as a cabin boy, but as of this letter, he has not told her. On the other hand, Tavia has not told him she is indeed Tavia."

"Oh my. What are the two of them thinking?"

The Duchess laughed softly. "They are not thinking at all. They are feeling. Emotions are running high. James did not see an alternative to his love making except marriage. He didn't want to take the chance of siring a child."

"Do you think he loves her?" Larena sighed softly.

"Of course he loves her, but the question remains has he realized it himself."

"Men are so obtuse. I know Gavin is thickheaded." Larena rose and walked from the room, suddenly whirling to face her.

"Things are not going smoothly between you and Gavin?" The Duchess bit into a lemon bar before sipping her afternoon tea.

"You know it's not. You have men following us wherever we go. It's not fair. I should do what my sister did and runaway with Gavin." She stiffened her back and stuck her chin in the air.

"But Gavin won't do that will he?"

"Of course not, he's all proper and etiquette and by the rules. He would faint if I suggested such a thing, and I would have to find some smelling salts to revive him."

"There is nothing wrong with etiquette and rules. Make no mistake he's more interested in you than you think. He's a man and will find the right time to seduce you. You must be ready and willing to tell the man no."

"What if I don't want to tell him no?" she asked.

The Duchess tapped the cane on the floor, a stern look on her face. "You will do what you wish, and if you do the wrong thing, you might live to regret that choice."

"My sisters and cousins have done exactly what they wanted, and they are all happy now and wed." Larena seemed to challenge.

"Yes, but they went through a lot of difficulties in achieving this happiness. Look at Tavia. There will be hell to pay for both of them when the fat hits the fire. Do you want that, the misery before the contentment?"

"Of course not." She folded her hands in her lap.

"So, tell me about your last escapade with your young man."

"Not so well. I was just watching a protest and he dragged me away as if I'm nothing more than a sac of potatoes. He doesn't understand that I want my life to have meaning."

"Ah, but if he didn't intervene, you could have been hauled off to Newgate prison or sent away to Australia or Tasmania on a prison ship. Would you want that?" The Duchess caught her breath and held it, feeling the pain and the fear for her dear charge. "It's a man's world. Never forget that. You can circumvent it but you can never best it."

"That's what he told me. He had no feelings though. He took me to his office and set me in a chair before proceeding to lecture me as if I were a small child."

"If you were wed, that would be his right."

She turned away, her brows drawn together. "He shouldn't be able to tell me what to do. It shouldn't be his right to control me. I'm not a child."

"Don't ever forget that whoever you marry, they will have that right. But if the two are in love, it will make it easier."

Chapter Seven

She woke in his arms. He was spooned tight against her, and while she still wore her nightclothes, he was naked. She'd gone to bed both angry and sad, crying herself to sleep. Another sob ripped through her body.

Waking up several times during the night, he had not been in bed. She even rose to check the main room, but he wasn't there. He had no moral values. He could have spent the night in someone else's bed and she would never know. Her trust for her new husband went about as far as she could toss the huge man. After all, as rumor had it, he had women in every port. Perhaps he had one here, in Malaga, and he went to the woman on his wedding night. Furious, she punched her pillow.

Now he lay next to her as if nothing was wrong. She felt his breath, smelled his scent, and she didn't want him touching her, making love to her. She should have never agreed to marry him. Staring at the diamond on her finger proclaiming his possession of her, she wanted to rip it from her hand and throw it at him. Thinking about his past actions, her anger escalated.

If she tossed it at him, he would duck and laugh before retrieving the bauble and putting it back on her hand. Bloody hell, he was awake and amorous. She felt his warm tongue and lips across her shoulders, felt him move her hair to one side so he could draw a path up her neck. *Not now, not this morning.*

She pushed away from him and stood on the opposite side of the bed. Her emotions seething, her fists clenched at her sides. "Isn't it time we return to the ship?"

He sat up, casually leaning on one elbow, a smile on his arrogant face. "We still have time." He patted the spot next to him. His intentions were anything but subtle. "The ship won't sail until after the noon meal.

What has you so angry, little darlin'?"

"You really don't know?" She turned her back on him and stole from the room only to find the small table in the main room decked with an array food and a hot pot of tea.

He stood behind her, once again touching her, possessively sliding his hands along her arms. "Don't do that," she said and whirled in his arms to be confronted by his nakedness. "James!"

"Don't do this?" He swept a fingertip across her lips before bending to touch her lips with his own, his warm tongue sliding against her mouth, his teeth biting gently, creating sensations she wanted to deny existed.

A tiny sound escaped from the back of her throat as she leaned into his body. "No." She pushed on his chest before she turned away from him. Tavia sat down at the table, trying to calm her ragged nerves and racing blood. She poured a cup of tea and added honey then dished up a plate of food for herself.

She heard the soft tread of bare feet as he walked to the bedroom. Trying to ignore him, she buttered a piece of bread. "I ordered a bath for you, if you'd like." He spoke from the bedroom.

A bath would be wonderful, but she didn't want to acknowledge his existence by speaking to him. Didn't want to admit to needing anything that came from him. The ice she felt when she thought of him lying in bed with another woman surged within.

"Would you like a bath?" He walked into the room and before sitting down at the table, he set a dress on the divan then he leaned forward and rested his forearms on the table. His silver blue gaze focused on her. She tried to breathe but the air caught in the back of her throat.

She closed her eyes, gritting her teeth before answering him. "I would like a bath, but I won't share one with you."

"I didn't think you would. I don't seem to be your favorite person at the moment. I'm not sure why though. I did the honorable thing last night and married you. You should be thrilled to finally have a last name." He spooned jam on his bread and sipped from the cup of tea he poured. "What has you so angry this morning?"

"You were gone all night." She choked on the bread. "I don't understand why you think I should be thrilled."

"I didn't think you cared what I did." He smiled at her, waving the butter knife in the air. "I'm not taking a bath. You can have it all to yourself. I'm meeting Seamus downstairs. When you're finished bathing and dressing, you can meet us and we will head for the ship. Feel free to take your time."

"Did you meet one of the women you're known to have in every port?" She couldn't help herself or the words spilling from her mouth. She only wanted to hear his answer if it was no.

One eyebrow rose in question. "Jealous?"

"Of course not. You've made it perfectly clear you married me because you didn't want complications. It wouldn't surprise me if you cried out for an annulment if I'm not with child."

The icy blue sizzle of his eyes was the only indication he might be furious with her. He cleared his throat before answering. "Not that I have to explain my actions to my wife or any one else, I spent the night drinking with Seamus because you made it perfectly clear you didn't want me in our bed."

"No, of course you don't have to explain anything to me. I'm just a woman," she bit out sarcastically.

"The water will be here in a few minutes and when it comes, I'll leave. Is there anything I can get for you?"

"Where did you get the dresses and the jewelry?" He'd had no time to shop in Bordeaux and certainly not here in Malaga. Did he always have spare women's clothing in his trunk?

He leaned back in his chair, crossing his arms in front of him, a dark brooding expression on his face. "If you must pry into my past life, I bought them in London?"

"Whatever for? Were you planning on a dalliance?" His answer brought her curiosity to the forefront.

He smiled. "There was a certain debutante I was courting in London and when I was passing a dress shop, I saw the evening gown made out of my clan's tartan. I thought at the moment it would make a wonderful gift for her. While I was in the shop, I bought a few other items."

She felt the blood drain from her face. "For the debutante?" Anger and frustration eating at her, her hand tightened around the handle of her teacup, her fury increasing. She wanted to throw it at him.

"Yes," he said and to Tavia it didn't appear he felt even one tiny bit of remorse. "Your coloring and size is the same as hers, so I knew the gowns would do well. Am I right? You must like them. They are perfect for you."

She smashed her napkin on the table, rising to her feet. Leaning towards him, her anger beyond anything she'd ever felt before. "You're wrong. I won't wear anything you bought for your debutant." Her annoyance had no logic to her. He bought them for her, gave them to her and all she needed to do was admit to him all she'd done and why.

He shrugged, "Suit yourself but then you'll have nothing to wear, including that negligee." He seemed pleased with himself.

"I have my britches and shirt. I will wear those."

"Even if I hadn't thrown them out, they would have been on the ship. Would you walk naked as Lady Godiva did through the streets of Malaga?" He smiled pleasantly at her, seeming to enjoy this conversation.

"You threw away my clothes? You had no right." Her breath caught in her throat and her eyes seemed to cross. The room swirled in a red haze around her, and she had to sit back down before she fell on the floor.

"I'm your husband. I had every right," he said, smoothly tapping his fingers on the tabletop.

"That's just not right. You don't own me or my possessions," she protested to no avail.

"I do own you. The moment you became my wife. But you must understand it is the way of the world, a man's world. Eat now, you'll need your strength for tonight. After all you didn't eat anything yesterday. Enjoy your bath. I don't plan to stay out of our bed tonight," he told her as he strode to the door to let the servants carrying the hot water into the room.

Her breath and her blood raced, an inferno boiling within. "A man's world," she muttered as he walked from the room. With everyone gone, she let her head fall into her hands and tried desperately to keep the tears at bay. "You cried too many tears last night. You don't have the energy for more. Your bed is made and now you must sleep in it." She talked to herself, wondering what Adelina would tell her.

But she knew. Adelina would say, tell him the truth and all of your problems will be over sooner than later.

She looked at the dress and the under things he left for her to wear. There was no corset so he really didn't intend to come back and taunt her with the debutant, and how he bought these things for her, for Tavia Hepburn not Tommy no name Macmurra. She was Tavia and she was sure he knew it, had known it from the moment she first entered the captain's cabin.

She brought the new yellow walking dress into the bathing room as well as the new underclothing. Taking the robe and nightgown off, she suddenly realized just how sheer they were. He could see everything, all of her. Folding each piece, she set them aside.

Once in the tub, the water was hot and soothing. She closed her eyes, trying to relax and form words to go forward into the future with her great bear of a husband. She soaped and rinsed then toweled herself dry, unable to reach conclusions of any sort.

He was right, the gown fit her perfectly; the fasteners were in the front so she didn't need help. Bloody hell, but he'd thought of everything. She had no makeup and no comb so she ran her fingers through it trying to manage the fly away strands.

She put the negligee and robe in the bag James left then grabbing a chunk of bread and some fruit, she started for the stairs. In the lobby, both Seamus and James waited for her. Seamus sprawled in one of the chairs, but James leaned against a pillar watching her, his expression shuttered.

When he saw her, he straightened and strode toward her, taking the bag and lending him his arm. "That did not take long," he said pleasantly. "I half expected you to bolt and I would have to search all of Malaga for you. I would not have liked that at all."

She took his arm, remembering the other times when she walked with him, when she wasn't so furious with the man and the moments she enjoyed with him. "I knew you wanted to get to your ship. I wouldn't bolt.

Where would I go? I've no money and only the dress you so graciously gave me."

"I did, I do, and Tommy, sarcasm doesn't become you." He smiled but it wasn't a joyous smile. It looked forced.

The silence between them seemed frigid, and it remained that way throughout the cab ride, up the gangplank and into the cabin. Sometime since they arrived in Malaga, the Firtha must have been granted a dock slip.

"Stay put, I will see you tonight," he told her when he closed the door to the cabin and left her sitting by herself, fuming.

"Is that an order?" she murmured to no one but herself. "I suppose it is. Now what do I do?"

Adelina poked her head inside the cabin. "Talk to me." She sat down at the table next to her. "Tell me all about last night."

Tavia shrugged, hesitant to tell her what happened yet knowing if anyone understood how she felt, Adelina would. "It was a disaster from the beginning to this moment," but she held up her hand, the ring still on the finger.

"A disaster you say? But the ring, does it mean you are married to the sea captain, James Macmurra?" Adelina held Tavia's hand and examined the huge diamond. "That must have set him back monetarily. It's a real beauty and huge."

"No, the ring cost him nothing. He told me he won it in a game of chance."

"Really? Then he is skilled at hiding his emotions. That should tell you something about your man. Perhaps he knows more about you than he has let on."

"He didn't school his feelings at all well last night or this morning. His irritation was obvious and he made no attempt to hide it."

"What did you do to make him so angry?" Adelina rose and walked around the room, picking up various objects then setting them down.

"My reaction to the wedding." She smoothed her skirt with her hands, loving the cut and color but not wanting to admit it to James.

"And what was that?"

"He wed me, not Tavia. He knows who I am but he won't admit it. He made me believe he married Tommy. I can't believe he married another woman just because he made love to her."

"So, Tavia is your real name. I recognize it. The Duchess is in charge of you. There could be hell to pay when you reach London. It was probably his best decision to wed you before we dock again. He could not stay out of your bed," Adelina mused.

"The decision might be the best one he's made, but he needs to admit he knows who I am. He still wants me to believe that he thinks I'm Tommy, and he didn't have any trouble staying away last night. He went out drinking with Seamus and didn't return until this morning. Then he had the nerve to strip and crawl into bed with me."

"With his wife." Adelina reminded her. "He has every right to do that. The fact he didn't force you speaks to his character."

"He," she sobbed, "bought dresses for the debutant he courted before he left. The dress I wore last night when we were married was of his clan's tartans. It was so beautiful, but the gown was meant for Tavia."

"Tommy, or Tavia, so you are the debutant? And you are Tavia so you should appreciate his generosity and thoughtfulness."

"Yes," she whispered softly.

"You have dug yourself deeper into a hole than even I believed was possible." Adelina was shaking her head. "You are far too young to understand the repercussions, but your man does not have that excuse."

Tears started to flow and Tavia wiped them away with the backs of her hands. "I thought he was with one of his other women. I thought..."

"You think too much. Would you like to go for a stroll on the deck? Let the wind caress your face and dry your tears?"

"He told me to stay put."

"And just now you are going to start obeying his orders?" Adelina questioned with a little laugh. "If you disobey, what will he do? Lecture you? Perhaps, but from what I've seen he indulges you even when he is angry.

"I believe I should obey him. I overheard them talking about loading cargo and how dangerous it is for people on deck, particularly those who are doing nothing. Crates could land on them and kill them."

"Like us?"

"Like us," Tavia parroted.

"You should understand they are not loading cargo. The crew is preparing to sail. Remember this was not a scheduled stop."

"You must be furious with him. Your arrival in Barcelona is almost a week late." Tavia meant to change the subject from herself.

"No, this mission will either succeed or not. I cannot be angry over something I've no control over. I decided last night to stop worrying."

"You still have to sleep with an old man, one you don't even know." At the thought, Tavia shuddered. "I could never do such a thing. How can you summon the courage?"

"Well," she sat down and took Tavia's hands in hers, "I've a sleeping potion that I plan on giving him in the evenings. I'm not intending to sleep with him ever. If he's counting on me to give him an heir, he won't have one."

"You can do that?"

"I have to. I'm there for information, nothing else. Now I understand you're curious but that is all I can say. Perhaps I'll see you in London sometime in the future. If my new husband dies, I'll be sent home. I'm sure his younger brother is not interested in his heir. As it stands, the younger one stands to gain all the property."

"I might see you in London?" For the first time since the wedding, she felt eager to return home.

"If all goes well. My boss will have the last say in this. Enough for now, I've already said more than I should. Let's go for a walk on the deck and defy your new husband."

"He will be furious with me."

"Why, Tommy, that never bothered you before. In fact I believe you took great delight in tormenting him with that fact. Don't change now that the two of you are wed. He loves you just the way you are." Adelina laughed delightedly. "You are so precious. You've no idea what your youthful enthusiasm and naiveté does for me."

"I suppose you're right. Let me grab my pelisse then we will stroll the deck and watch Malaga disappear from sight."

Arm in arm, they strode on deck, settling at a spot where they could watch the port city disappear from their vision. Tavia thought this was the second best part of traveling, the best part was watching the new destination come into view.

She heard him clear his throat, his hand settling possessively on her waist. He leaned toward her, his breath whispering on her face. "I thought I told you to stay in the cabin."

She whirled, grinning at him, trying to retrieve the gutsy Tommy to her character, and smiled at him. "No, you told me to stay put and I'm doing that. I'm staying put right here."

To her surprise he didn't appear angry. Then, after a couple of seconds, he laughed. "I suppose I did. Touché."

"I intend to breathe in the fresh air and watch the ship pull away from Malaga, the city where we were married. I hope I don't need your permission to do that."

"Acting as your captain and your husband, Tommy, you do need my permission in all that you do."

"That's outrageous." She fisted her hands, tilting her head sideways and squinting her eyes.

"Don't get too upset. I'm going to stay with you here so you have my permission." He ran his hand up her back then down, clearly broadcasting his ownership of her.

"I will leave the newlyweds to whatever newlyweds do and go to my cabin. It's a wee bit chilly now that the ship is picking up speed. Have a good evening, Tommy and James. I'm sure if you can solve your differences you will enjoy the rest of the journey."

That was the key, solve their differences and put aside the wrongs he'd done to her. She didn't think she could do that, put aside his wrongs. What about what she did to him, was still doing to him?

"So, you confided in Adelina? Is nothing sacred between husband and wife?" His hand settled on her neck, his thumb rubbing tiny evocative circles there.

"I did." She acknowledged, moving away from him. Yet he followed and she knew her defiance was a lost cause.

~ * ~

James would never force Tavia. Every night when he came to her, she turned her back on him. When he tried to seduce her, she pretended to be asleep. By the time they reached Barcelona and she said goodbye to Adelina, he had Seamus put the hammock back in the room. The nights were long and cold.

Two months in the hammock had him reeling with annoyed frustration and ready to confront her, but he'd waited this long, he could wait longer. He meant to expose her when The Duchess showed up at the docks to take them to their new home.

He no longer cared if her fury kept her from his bed and his arms. She had denied him for two months now. Tonight he would sleep with his wife.

Excitement grew within him as the ship turned into the Thames and they sailed toward London. They were almost home. He would make arrangements for another captain for the Firtha. Seamus didn't want to captain a ship, but he'd remain first mate as long as he wanted the position.

"You've been more grumpy than usual. I suppose that comes from not being able to bed one's wife. You should have told her the first day." Seamus cackled, seeming to enjoy his situation.

"You told me and I know you're right. Your advice was sound, but unfortunately I didn't take it. You have my permission to remind me daily." He sighed heavily, watching the buildings of London slowly come into view. "Our reckoning is coming, and I wonder how much longer she'll make me pay for not telling her I knew who she was from the first moment I saw her."

"I'm sure it won't do your cause any good to remind her she is just as much at fault here," Seamus said. "You should have a reply ready for her, some excuse. Remember, if you keep her happy, you'll be happy."

"Do you think she loves me?" He turned on his first mate, his heart pounding in his chest.

"Now I can't say anything about love. Been a long time for me, don't know if I've ever been in love myself. She married you, that must count for something. Do you love her?"

"Don't know if love exists. I'm not as jaded as some. I've bedded a lot of women and have never felt that emotion. Tavia is different. I don't want to live without her." He closed his eyes, remembering how she felt in his arms and how he loved the conversations with her, how his gut tightened when he was close to her. She would never obey, but he didn't want that in a wife.

"Of course you do, but like everything else you're going to have to figure it out for yourself. Anyone ever tell you you're a slow learner?"

"I suppose so, but she isn't making this easy."

"Too stubborn, both of you are just too damned stubborn. This won't be the first time the two of you butt heads. Mark my words. Always have a second plan figured out. Don't forget to tell her she's right."

"Tavia's the stubborn one. I was ready to end this the night we wed."

"Why didn't you?"

"Because she was so angry that I married her, she was an ice queen in my arms. I wasn't about to give in to her ploy. It would put her in charge for the rest of our lives." He remembered the silver ice emanating from her eyes, the coldness of her stance.

"Too damn stubborn," Seamus muttered again. "Both of you."

"Where is she? Probably hiding in the room. She knows there's going to be a reckoning. Sure she's trying for courage, just as I am. The moment The Duchess appears, her ruse will be disclosed."

"Those two cabs, they yours?" Seamus asked. "I'll go get her, if it pleases you."

He looked to the heaven above as if trying for courage he would need today. "Go get her. Better you than me. She might bite my head off."

A few minutes later. "James," she was by his side, her body stiff and her voice cold just as it had been since they left Malaga.

"Tavia, Tavia, there you are," Larena raced up the gangplank her arms extended wide for an embrace. "I've missed you so much. You've got to tell me everything you've done. What have you seen? I'm so jealous. Tira left for Baltimore."

James tried to hide the smile when he watched the horror cross over Tavia's face. She shot a quick look his way before she was bowled over by her cousin. "Larena," she whispered softly, trying to keep her balance, "what are you doing here?"

"Why, taking you and James, your husband, to your brand new townhouse. He asked The Duchess to find a place for the two of you to live."

"James did that."

"Yes, he sent us a note several months ago, telling us about your marriage. I think maybe from Malaga."

"Why would he ask The Duchess to do that? It's not as if he can afford all that," Tavia said.

"Of course it does. Are you daft?"

"No, it doesn't. He didn't marry Tavia Hepburn. He wed Tommy no name, the girl who was masquerading as his cabin boy," she stubbornly kept up the lie.

"He doesn't know he married you? Is that what you think?" Larena asked. "But he does. He used your name in the letter he sent Auntie Charlotte. He sounded so pleased with himself."

"I didn't ever want to admit that he knew."

"Go on," James said, wishing he could see inside her head and read her mind. "Take the first cab. I'll meet you at the townhouse. Need to talk to The Duchess about a few things."

"Fat's in the fire," Seamus said walking up to James. "Wish I could ride along and see how this all turns out."

"You have work to do here. Too bad. You won't be by my side to gloat."

"Now I wouldn't do that, Captain."

"Of course you would." James sauntered down the gangplank, watching the cab Tavia rode in pick up its pace. "Nice to see you, Duchess. It's a beautiful day." He gave her his arm.

"And since you married my niece and my charge, I've no recriminations. We can plan a reception when the two of you have reconciled."

"That might be a while. I'm sure she's going to continue to turn a cold shoulder to my advances when she finds out I knew from the first day who she was."

"But you took every means you had to protect her. Am I right?" The Duchess looked into his eyes.

"And I did a horrible job at that. I couldn't keep her in the cabin, and she had the infuriating need to disobey my orders. Here we are."

He helped her inside then climbed in and settled on a seat across from her, his forearms resting on his thighs.

"So besides you not being able to keep your hands off her, what happened?" The Duchess asked.

"You don't hold anything back, do you?" He said his voice so deep and rough he didn't recognize it. His gut clenched, remembering Tavia lying on the deck, unmoving.

He recounted the events of the voyage to the best of his ability, including the fall and the disastrous wedding. The Duchess needed to know everything that happened to Tavia.

"I see then, you've done all a man can do with a stubborn, willful girl who is hell bent on getting her way in all things. I've been run ragged by all twelve of my nieces. Now you can understand how I've felt the last few years. Amorica and Ella were much the same. Tira and Aiden have run off to Baltimore; one to escape her beau, and the other to learn how to build a ship."

"That doesn't make me feel any better. Are we on our way to the townhouse and were you able to find a country home?" He would feel better once he could begin a new life with Tavia.

"Yes, to both. Right now I want to know what your plans are concerning my niece, Tavia."

"I'm not sure I understand what you're asking." He grew still. "I'm not sure that my intentions are any of your business. Tavia is my wife and my responsibility now."

"You're right, of course. I don't know you well enough. Your character and how you will treat your wife is in question."

"Not by me."

"Well, I suppose you are trying to make a point, and if I didn't know men so well, I wouldn't question your priorities where Tavia is concerned. She is really very naïve."

"You question my priorities? You question when I slept in a

hammock for two solid months because she didn't want me in my bed. You question my priorities when she put an X on the marriage certificate where she should have written her name." His anger grew with each question The Duchess posed.

She waved her hand in the air, a smile growing on her lined face. "That is good to hear. That means she is not carrying a child. You have done well, James Macmurra, very well. You must have had a devil of a time. No wonder you're angry."

"I'm not angry," he protested heatedly then paused. "Just a little. I'm more worried about the nights to come and how long her ice cold anger at me will continue."

"I would be too. There are a lot of lies between the both of you, and you should not be the only one who suffers, but unfortunately you will be the only one." She smiled. "You will have to find a way to stay strong and bring her over to your side and into your arms. I'm sure part of her is relieved you didn't break your promises to me."

"That broken vow was the crux of our disagreement as well as her anger after the wedding. She did find a way to forgive me for sleeping with her before the wedding. I guess that wasn't as large of a problem as the marriage.

"She tried to refuse the clothing I bought for Tavia, but she would have been naked for two months if she did." That thought did bring a smile to his face. Even though it had been months of celibacy, he remembered how perfectly her breasts filled his hands, the scent of her and the feel of her skin beneath his fingers. He needed her more than ever.

"You convinced her wearing her clothing was best for both of you." She laughed, tapping her cane on the floor of the carriage.

"I wish I hadn't been so convincing," he muttered, thinking of making love with his wife again. "Perhaps if she'd been naked, she would have come to me for warmth."

"It seems we've reached our destination. Now keep in mind there is only a minimal amount of furniture in the house. It will have to do for tonight. You can purchase more tomorrow."

"A bed?" he asked, his heart racing even while he knew he might not get her into it tonight.

"Yes, I thought a bed was a necessity. One bed, one kitchen table and two kitchen chairs. After that Tavia will have to shop for the rest of the furnishings. Of course I will help, but this is her house to decorate. Can I assume you will give her the needed funds?"

"Whatever she wants she can have." It was late and she could be damned sure he wasn't going to sleep on the floor despite her wishes. A hammock was one thing, the floor something else entirely.

"Good, she will need permission from you and it will have to be taken care of tomorrow."

"Should I give her an allowance?"

"By all means, but she shouldn't be expected to spend her allowance on furnishings for your homes. This money needs to be separate. I will go with her tomorrow to help pick out the new furnishings. It will be fun."

"Yes, fun. Perhaps I will take your place. I would like to have a say in our home." He would go and perhaps the more time he spent with her on mundane, everyday things, she would come to accept him in her life.

"Men don't do that," The Duchess said, looking him squarely in the face.

He shrugged, stretching his muscles as he did so, "I want to spend time with Tavia. Together we have created a chasm between us. If we don't see each other and believe in each other, we will have a very lonely lifetime. Besides, I think it would be fun, and I could pay for everything as we go. I need to see her in a different setting."

"Good luck then. I have a feeling you're going to need it for the following days and nights."

He helped her from the carriage, and before entering, he studied his new home and made a mental note to lease his apartment.

"What do you think?" The Duchess asked.

"From the outside it's everything I could want." He started for the steps, eager to see the inside.

The Duchess followed but entered first when he held the door for her. Larena and Tavia were chatting in the kitchen, sitting in the only two chairs existing in the home.

"There you are," Larena said happily. "We waited for you both before we toured the home. She rose, "Come on Tavia. Aren't you eager to see your new home?"

"Yes, yes I am very eager." Her eyes were cold when she looked at him and her shoulders stiff. By the look on her face, her anger must be simmering deep inside, ready to explode.

The tour was brief. Upstairs there were three bedrooms plus a large master chamber with an adjoining room. In the middle of the master room there was a large bed.

"You thought of me." Surprised, he turned to address The Duchess.

"I had it made special for you. Don't give me all the credit. Drake suggested it, saying you would be much happier if your feet and half your legs didn't hang over the end of the bed," The Duchess offered.

"Thank you." He gazed at Tavia, her face pale. She seemed to be seething despite the fact she knew he wouldn't force her. They really needed to empty the house of well-wishers so they could be alone.

"I'll meet you all in the kitchen," Tavia said, turning and walking stiffly from the bedchamber.

He grimaced, his heart in his throat, needing to find a way to soothe her ruffled feathers. "Maybe you could cook us something to eat." *That was stupid. When you should be making everything perfect, you challenge her.*

The icy look she shot him over her shoulder gave him reason to rethink everything he knew about her.

"You shouldn't have said that to her," Larena told him, her hands on her hips, one toe tapping. "I don't know what's going on between the two of you, but you best make it right. Dinner is a mute point. I had Scarlett and cook bring a meal fit for a king, a queen and their court. The two should be here by now. I also told them to bring a few more chairs. I am looking forward to hearing more about your adventures. This time from Tavia's mind."

"Best way to hear it. I'd like to know what she is thinking also," James said, roughing his hands through his hair. Perhaps if he heard a recounting of events by Tavia then he might be able to form a plan to regain her acceptance of their marriage and him.

In the kitchen an amazing amount of food had been placed on the kitchen counters as well as the table. James held up a bottle of wine. "From Logan and Eveleen?"

"A wedding gift. They like to give everyone several cases of his wine. Did you know he now owns a winery in Tuscany? My son, Richard, won it in a game of chance and he didn't want it. Logan sent a case of Chianti for the two of you also. I do hope you like wine."

James wanted to see Tavia's joy again, needed to know if she didn't love him, at least she cared for him. She'd given her innocence to him and now because of his actions, she withheld herself from him.

Silence seemed to creep into the room at a snail's pace, but The Duchess still wore a smile, seeming to enjoy the discomfort surrounding her. No, perhaps she suspected they would patch up their relationship. They had to. At the thought of Tavia pushing him away for the rest of his life, his gut tightened and the breath that was stealing into his lungs stopped.

Larena broke the silence. "Tell us about your wedding."

Tavia sat down and traced the rim of the wine glass James poured for her. "I'd rather not. There is not much to tell. James surprised me. We had no one there we cared about. I would have liked to have Adelina and Seamus as witness but..." Before they could ask, "Adelina was a passenger on his ship as well as a friend and Seamus is his first mate."

"So, no one knew about the wedding?" The Duchess pried.

"Maybe Seamus but I don't know." She looked to James.

"What did you wear? Did you have a wedding dress?" Larena asked questions James was sure Tavia didn't want to answer.

Tavia seemed to be fascinated with her hands, which rested on her lap. When she looked up, moisture filled her eyes.

"With the help of The Duchess and her seamstress, I bought several gowns before I left London. I didn't know Tavia would be one of my passengers at the time. It was a beautiful silk evening gown made from my clan's tartan. She looked beautiful wearing it."

"It was truly quite beautiful," The Duchess said in an attempt to take everyone's attention from Tavia until she got her emotions under control.

"After the wedding we walked the streets of Malaga and ate a nice dinner, although my beautiful bride just seemed to push her food around her plate."

"She was nervous," Larena sighed, "the wedding night and all. I know I'll be nervous too."

"Let's hope that is true. I'm praying you will still be a virgin when you are married," The Duchess told her niece, patting her on the hand while she spoke. Her smile seemed to erase some of the age lines.

"By the way, how is Gavin?" Tavia asked in a seeming attempt to switch the conversation from herself.

Larena's smile changed to a frown. "He is so busy. I hardly ever see him, but we do have an outing planned for this weekend. Last time I saw him he pulled me away from a lamppost I climbed so I could see the protesters."

"He didn't," Tavia said laughing, "You climbed up a lamppost. If you were caught with the protesters, you could have been arrested."

"That's what Gavin told me when he pulled me down," Larena said, still seeming indignant.

"Much better than a mast and much safer," James cut in, immediately regretting his words when he saw the blood drain from Tavia's face.

"You climbed up a mast?" Larena asked, her eyes wide. "Why on earth? What happened?"

"And I fell from it and bruised my ribs. I think my lucky angel was on my shoulder because Seamus told me I could have died." Tavia looked to James, her lips thinning as if she remembered that night and the ones following.

He prayed she'd remember their good times and the emotions between them. They were deeper and more poignant than just the sex. He needed her in ways he was hard pressed to explain to himself.

"How high?" Larena questioned.

"Too high," James waved his hand dismissing the questions. "You've touched on a subject neither one of us would like to talk about. Perhaps with time it won't create such pain for both of us."

"Perhaps it is time for us to say goodbye." The Duchess looked to Larena and nodded. "There will be time for more questions later when Tavia knows how she feels."

~ * ~

"Addle, I didn't expect to see you so soon." Hamilton Winthrop the third held Adelina's hand and pulled her into a small alcove. The ball was to celebrate some holiday Adelina had never heard of. Her husband of one week sat in a corner chair, his head hanging down sound asleep and drooling. She cringed at the thought of marriage to this man until he died.

"Hamilton..." she breathed as he lowered his head to mold his lips to hers. She felt the rush of blood and the fierce longing that flowed within when he held her in his arms. His hand rested on her breast as if he wanted to touch her bare flesh.

"Please..."

"Addie," his breath whispered across her face. "I've missed you so much, little imp."

"Don't call me that. I don't like that nickname. Hamilton, we can't be found here together. We shouldn't." But she felt the rush of energy, and the fierce need for him.

"Your husband is sound asleep. He'll never know what you do here with me. Bloody hell, but I never thought I'd feel jealous of a man such as that one. You are not sleeping with him." The harshness in his voice chilled her, sent goose bumps up her arms.

"No, I have my sleeping potion, but I've only used it once. He sleeps most of the day and all of the night. His brother has made a point of telling me if I ever carry his child, he'll kill me." She vowed she'd never let that happen. The thought of him possessing her made her shudder with revulsion.

"If what you say is true, that won't be a problem. Have you heard anything you can pass on?"

"No, although the liberal ideas of the French Revolution are prevalent among many, the political climate doesn't seem to be quite so tumultuous as a year ago. There are still a good number who disagree on how the government should be run." She wished she'd never volunteered for this mission. At the time she'd thought it would be simple and over before it began.

"Do not take notes, save in your head. Do not pen anything to paper. You cannot risk anyone discovering what you are about. Ruthless and cruel men who believe in the liberal cause abound, and they will stop at nothing to topple the existing government. You not only have the brother to fear but the men we spy on."

"Neither can you," Adelina said, moistening her lips in hopes another kiss was forthcoming.

"My life is not at risk." He bent to kiss her again, his tongue drawing a path across her lips as she allowed him entrance.

When he pulled away, "We are always at risk and you know it. Don't deceive yourself. One mistake, a slip of the tongue, could give you away." They had been in this position so many times, too many to count. It seemed they pushed their luck. Perhaps it was time to end the games they played and the thrill of each new adventure.

"At least I don't have a younger brother looking for an excuse to kill me. He will stop at nothing to keep his inheritance."

"Should I tell him I'm not interested in anything his family owns." She tapped her fan on his shoulder. As she tried to turn from Hamilton, he held her back, his fingers tightening around her waist, his hold upon her possessive.

"You must promise me you'll be careful."

"I always take care. You know me, one of little courage." She ran her hands beneath his waistcoat, enjoying the play of his muscles beneath her fingers and the low groan in the back of his throat.

"You wear too much makeup," he told her, trying to fix the smear of color on her mouth where he kissed her.

"I'm a whore who has become the wife of a wealthy man. I have to stay in character."

"You are no whore," he growled. "I don't see how Montgomerie convinced you to masquerade as one. The idea was preposterous."

"It was for the good of our country and you know it. Why else do you still do this when you should settle down and marry the love of your life?" She laughed, hoping she was that woman, but he'd never pretended to love her. He wanted sex from her and little else. They worked well together. This was the first time he ever showed a hint of possessiveness.

"We are getting to old for these adventures. You should find a good man, settle down, have children of your own."

She moistened her lips while his eyes smoldered with passion. There was no love between them, just passion... There was an abundance of hunger. In bed together they were well suited.

"I'm too old, on the shelf I believe would be used to describe me. Hamilton, I've seen so much pain and suffering, settling down would be wonderful. But there is no one who would have me."

"You are twenty-five, hardly past your prime. You are a beautiful woman," Gently he pushed strands of hair behind her ears. His tenderness unraveled her every time they were together.

"Why do you think Montgomerie sent both of us to Barcelona. There were so many other places. I don't think it was a coincidence." She let her cheek rest in the palm of his hand. The security he offered overwhelmed her. This was the first assignment where she felt uncomfortable, her life possibly at risk. Knowing Hamilton was here for her gave her more confidence than she should have. Closing her eyes, she inhaled deeply.

"I want you to check in with me everyday," he told her, studying her, his eyes focused on her as if he thought she might lie.

"Of course I will. Whenever I can."

"That's not good enough. You have to promise me. Everyday."

"I promise." She knew Hamilton and understood he would not stop asking her until she delivered on the promise.

"Tomorrow, two o'clock then at my lodgings."

~ * ~

Hamilton paced the tavern beneath the apartment he rented for the duration of his stay in Barcelona. She was a half hour late, but she promised to meet him. Addie would not break her promise. He ran his hands through his hair as he strode to the door to look out, searching for her.

He held his breath, his fists clenching at his sides. From a distance he watched her riding a horse, pushing the horse to its limit. She was a good horsewoman. Today, she rode astride, just like a man. Despite what she told him, she was courageous and fearless, too much for his taste. Those two characteristics were what made her so good at espionage. And she could lie convincingly without even a blink to give herself away. He was never sure until he looked into her eyes. Last night was the first time he'd ever seen fear.

In an easy fluid motion, she dismounted and handed the reins to the stable boy. "Wipe him down please. I'll be ready to ride in a couple of hours." Then she strode toward him, a beautiful smile on her face.

So, she had some extra time to spend with him. He hoped for that last night when she melted into his arms at the ball. The kiss had been bittersweet yet stole his breath from his lungs. Their last parting back in Paris had not been congenial. She left him angry about something he couldn't even remember. He cared deeply for her.

"Hamilton," she wore no hat, her hair coming lose from its pins and falling in beautiful disarray around her fine boned face. "You see, I kept my promise to you."

"Addie, you came. Until this moment, I wasn't sure," he said, smiling and walking toward the tavern. "You hungry?"

"You made me promise. I can only stay a short time. I must get back in time for a party in my husband's honor."

"And from what I witnessed last night, my guess is that he will sleep through the festivities." Hamilton laughed placing a possessive hand on her waist as they walked up the stairs.

"He will stay awake long enough to eat and drink his fill. Then his head will drop until someone brings him upstairs to his bed. I will follow and go to my chamber next to his."

His insides clenched at what she told him. He needed her, wanted to feel her breath and know at least for this moment she was his. Once inside, he shut the door behind them, leaning against it as he watched her. Addie's cheeks were a beautiful pink from the exertion of riding. She wore no face paint and her face was lightly dusted with adorable freckles. Her dark brown eyes glowed with passion.

As if they couldn't wait a moment longer, they came together. Frantically, she pulled his shirt from his breeches, while with nimble fingers he unfastened her riding habit. In a few seconds they were naked, his hands cupping her derrière and reveling in the feel of her lush breasts flush against his chest. He swept her into his arms and came down on the bed. She was on top of him. Their lovemaking was urgent and primal. It had been so long since they'd been together.

"Addie," he moaned in a deep growl. "How do you do this to me every time I see you, touch you, feel you against my body?"

A tiny sound came from her that sounded like his name as he turned her over and she spread her legs, giving him access to her very core. Once a long time ago, she gave him her innocence, and he didn't believe she'd been with any other man since then. He couldn't say the same, but no one else created this gut wrenching longing inside him.

She cried out his name as they reached a climax and he spent his seed inside her. He knew instantly this was a huge mistake. She might pay with her life. But he could not stop himself, and this time they made love slowly, enjoying every sensuous caress between them.

Addie lay in his arms, her hand resting on his chest, drawing tiny circles. She didn't say anything. There was nothing between them but sex and yet...

"Addie, if you find you're with child or even think you might be, come to me. Don't waste even a second in thought. Don't pack, don't take anything with you. Race the wind to me and we'll leave. Nothing is worth your life."

"You really think he might kill me?" she sounded incredulous to him. "I think he's bluffing."

"No, the man is ruthless."

Chapter Eight

"Why didn't you tell me?" Tavia sat on one of the kitchen chairs, her hands in her lap. She didn't want to look at him, didn't want to admit that perhaps she'd been wrong, and that she longed for him to take her into his arms. Last night, she'd thought he would make love to her and everything between them would change, but he only held her.

He did everything in his power to protect her, and she still managed to find trouble. If Adelina had not run for help the evening she fell from the mast, she didn't really want to think about what might have happened. She'd already spent more hours than she could count doing that very thing.

"Why didn't you tell me?" he countered, sitting down across from her, breakfast on the table. "Once I knew you were a woman, you should have told the truth."

"It was nice of The Duchess to send food again." She paused, tapping her fingers on the tabletop and recalling last night. She'd slept in his arms, longing for more. She didn't want to talk about the past.

"Yes," he said through a bite of eggs. "You're ignoring my question."

"I didn't think you recognized me when you called me to your cabin, and I wanted an adventure. I believed I could get away with it, and I was afraid you'd send me home if you knew." She recalled that first exciting day when she actually was a cabin boy. She climbed the mast and did some of the jobs that were expected from her and she'd never forget the thrill of looking at the world below her from the crow's nest.

"Cutting your hair and binding your breasts did not make you look like a boy. Every time you bent over..." he cleared his throat, looking away from her for a moment. "Every time you bent over, I could see the curve of your hips. Those were not boy's hips, but even that didn't matter. Your

156

face gave you away. I had a moment of doubt when I thought you might be your twin, but as soon as you spoke, I knew it was you."

"Why didn't you tell me?" she repeated the question, not understanding his purpose. She'd spent so many nights silently condemning him for breaking his vows to The Duchess then for condemning herself.

"The facts are pretty simple when I stop to think. You wanted an adventure on your own terms, and I needed to give it to you. I would give you the world if I could."

"By keeping me in your cabin you pretty much ended my escapade." She had wanted to see and do so much more but he'd been adamant.

"I kept you alive and your innocence intact, if you recall. Yes, I should have told you, but I also knew that if I did, you would be carrying my child by the time we reached London again. I didn't want that for you."

"You have no restraint then." She tilted her head slightly, staring at him. She would never forget the sensations he evoked within her when he made love to her. He was so gentle and seeing to her needs before his.

"Not where you're concerned I don't."

"You haven't touched me since we were married." She needed to remind him. "Why?"

"And that took more willpower than I ever thought I possessed. I would never force you, and you obviously didn't want my attentions. Recalling that night, are you going to sign the wedding papers?"

Embarrassed, she nodded, "I'm sorry about that. I should have told you then who I was."

"Are you forgiving me then?" He held her hands in his.

"Yes, I'm trying. I know we both acted stupidly and with our own interest in mind. The Duchess said you want to go furniture shopping with me. I wager you'll grow tired of it by noon and plead a headache." She smiled at him, before she rose to put her dishes in the sink. She would wash them later.

"Never," he smiled, appearing eager to begin this new project. "What should we purchase first?"

"Food for the cupboard. While it's nice to have already prepared food sent to us, we can't continue to impose."

"If we get food, we have to have pots and pans, plates and silverware. Do you know how to cook? I don't. I'm not sure I could boil water. Well, I take that back. I think I can do that."

"Rest easy, I can prepare just about anything you would like," she lied. "We didn't have servants when I was growing up. My father wastes away mourning for our mother, his wife, who was killed by smugglers when I was a very little girl. Amorica and Ella did most of the cooking, at least until they left for London. Tira and I never really had to learn cooking skills."

"Perhaps we should hire a cook."

"If we want to eat, that would be a splendid idea."

"I'd like to have something to sit on in the parlor and a few side tables," he added thoughtfully.

"Two armchairs and a settee with end tables to go with the chairs. Then I'd like to purchase fabric for curtains. The bedroom and the parlor to start." She paused. "That will take a while. Could we purchase the fabric and have someone else make them? Do we have the money?"

"Within reason you can have anything you like." He sat back, casually folding his hands in his lap.

"Within reason has many different meanings, but as long as you are with me, I'm sure you'll tell me if I over spend." She moistened her lips and sipped tepid tea to ease her parched throat. He gently touched her hand. She suddenly imagined that love might be a grand and magical thing. He did not touch her then to enflame her, but to just idly feel her flesh and to soothe her. There was something honest and true between them she had never known before.

"I suppose I would stop you if you meant to bankrupt me, but that would be very hard to do."

"So, no time to waste."

"The list is long. Let's go then." He held out his arm for her, a crooked grin on his face.

The markets were open and they bought as much food and cooking utensils as they could carry.

"I'm hungry," she said as they passed a vendor selling bread. "And exhausted. We've only finished half the list."

They stopped, buying a loaf of bread they could share. "We need to take these home, perhaps a nap then back to work." He laughed. "We need to ask The Duchess about hiring that cook and some other help."

"I really can cook," she said indignantly.

"But you don't want to spend half the day shopping every day then go home to cook meals. Do you? What else would you like to do with your time?" he asked.

"No, I suppose not and I never really gave my spare time any thought. Ella is teaching children at an orphanage to read and write. I could probably help her."

By the evening meal, Tavia could say the day had been productive. They accomplished everything on the list. She was washing dishes, thinking about the day and the man she wed when his hands were around her waist and his lips on the back of her neck.

"Will you come to bed with me?" he continued his seduction. "We can make love tonight if you're agreeable."

"Will you dry the dishes?" she countered, leaning into him and deciding their feud was officially at an end.

"If it gets you in my bed sooner."

"Our bed." She handed him a newly purchased dishtowel. "Besides it's too early for that."

"Not for me?"

"Seamus here," the knock on the door surprised her. His first mate was poking his head around the opened door. "You didn't hear me knocking or I wouldn't have come in."

James set the towel down, striding into the foyer. "What the devil?"

"Think I found a captain for the Firtha. If it's alright with you, I brought him along for you to meet and give your approval." Seamus took his hat off and held it with both hands against his chest.

The man in question stood behind Seamus. "Let him in. We even have chairs to sit in tonight. We can talk."

Tavia stood half way to the front door, a towel in her hand. "Seamus? What are you doing here?"

"Mrs. Macmurra," Seamus acknowledged with a quick nod. "Just business with the captain."

"Is it alright with you?" James asked Tavia. "It's only going to take a few minutes. I trust Seamus' judgment."

"It's fine with me. It seems Larena has come to visit also. We'll stay in the kitchen so you can have your privacy."

Larena waltzed in behind Seamus, skipping as she went. "Tavia, you cooked dinner. Did you burn it all?"

"Bite your tongue or I won't offer you a drink. What will it be tea, or wine? It seems that's all we have, and if you pick wine it will have to be served in a cup since I have no glasses."

Larena wandered around the kitchen, looking in cupboards and under placemats. "You really did some major shopping today. I'm amazed. Was it fun? Did James go with you like he told Auntie Charlotte he would?"

"I was exhausted. I never realized how time consuming it would be. James and I've decided to hire someone to help with the shopping and cooking. Admittedly, I lied to him when I told him I could cook most anything. He's going to get tired of the same things day in and day out. He thinks I should help Ella with the orphans if she'd like.

"It was first Amorica who cooked then Ella until she left. I was only in the way when I spent time in the kitchen, so I visited my friends instead. They really should have given me lessons and prepared me for marriage."

Larena sighed deeply. "I've the same problem. Ravyn then Storm did most of the kitchen duties. Fayth a little, but I was rarely in the kitchen."

"I thought it was great at the time," Tavia said.

"Have you two resolved your differences?" Larena asked, stealing a bite of leftover food. "It's good. Maybe you'll learn. I can have Scarlett get some recipes from cook. Only if you want."

"Go ahead, I'd love some recipes. Couldn't be too hard. I don't know how much money James really has, and I don't want to overspend when I can do it myself. I'm a Hepburn after all, Macmurra now."

"He bought two homes and by the look of things he's not denying you anything you want. I wouldn't worry about his money. That's the man's job," Larena said with a lopsided grin.

"Larena, I can't believe you said such a thing. It's goes against your very character."

"I was just joking. The man I marry will have to have a lot of tolerance because I'm going to do exactly what I want."

"Well, I do worry about money. This has all happened so fast. I thought I would go on my mini journey, return then hopefully he would court me and we would get to know each other. Somehow I got things backwards. We barely know each other at all."

"I need to go home. Was just checking on you to see if everything was alright." Larena hugged her cousin. "I'll stop by tomorrow sometime. Have a wonderful night."

Tavia watched as her happy-go-lucky cousin slipped out the backdoor and made her way around the corner of the house. She clasped her hands in front of her, gazing at a strange movement in the yard. Stepping from the house she waited and watched.

"Edwin McMasters, what are you doing at my home?" she asked, her heart in her throat. "Go home. You have no place here."

He waved a pistol in the air, his face contorted into a sneer. "I told you that you'd regret snubbing me and dancing away with that ship's captain. I've had to wait months. Where have you been?"

She straightened her shoulder, pushing her fear to the back of her mind. He was nothing but a bully. She stepped back, intending to run and lock the door behind her.

"I know what you're thinking. If you run inside, I'll shoot you where you stand," he threatened, waving the gun in the air, moving quickly toward her.

He was beside her before she could move her feet, grabbing her and pulling her against him.

"You thought your man would come find you if you yelled. Of course he would then I would have shot him dead. You don't want him dead do you? Best you stay quiet." His voice was a gravelly sneer.

His breath smelled worse than she remembered. "No, I don't want him dead. You won't get away with this, you know." Sweat broke out on her forehead, slipping down her face. She struggled against him, but he tightened his grip, yanking her inside the house.

"Oh, I believe I will get away with everything. Got it all planned out. Sit down."

"I won't ever sleep with you."

"Don't want used goods," he said. "Just revenge."

She let out a sigh of relief. "I'm glad of that."

They stood inside the kitchen now. Edwin loosened the ropes he brought with him. He tied her hands behind her back as well as her feet. "I'm going to enjoy this."

"What are you doing?"

"Gag you and wait for Macmurra. That's when the real fun is going to start. You just wait and see what I've got planned for the two of you."

He placed her so she was looking at the door to the kitchen and would be able to see James when he walked inside. She closed her eyes, praying the slimy man would not best James, but she didn't hold out much chance for him. Edwin stood by the entrance, a fireplace poker in hand. Edwin was a tall man, almost as tall as her husband. She reminded herself to keep her wits about herself and continued to tell herself James would best the horrible man, and James wouldn't let him hurt her.

Minutes ticked by, silence seemed to surround her even as the room began to swirl, and she felt her senses unravel with each tick of the clock. Nausea filled her and she worked to keep from vomiting. She would suffocate if she allowed that to happen.

"Tavia?" James strode into the kitchen then stopped midstride. "Tavia?" he started forward before Edwin hit his head then his back with the iron poker. James crumpled to the floor.

She was terrified Edwin had killed him. He touched a finger at the pulse point of James' neck. "Still alive," he mumbled, grinning while he bound James' hands and feet before gagging him. "If you're wondering what is going to happen next, the two of you are going for a little swim in the Thames. All this and for what, to die by drowning? You could have been my wife, you know, but as I said before I never take anyone's leavings. Since you are no longer a virgin, I no longer want you."

A swim in the Thames, tied up? She could swim and she knew she would have to do all in her power to stay afloat. If James remained unconscious, she would have to save him. She inhaled long and deep as if this was her last breath, but now she was focused and ready.

Edwin muttered something she didn't understand while he drug James through the kitchen. A few minutes later he was back for her. "Before the swim, we're going for a ride in my carriage. Had to make sure there was no blood trail." He laughed, seeming to enjoy himself.

He picked her up and carried her to the waiting carriage, tossing her inside with little care to her well-being. Tears flowed, running down her cheeks. She wiggled her way to James and tried to touch him, to see if he lived, if he regained consciousness.

James, wake up. You have to open your eyes.

Nothing, but she felt his breath on her cheek. She placed her head on his chest and heard the steady beat of his heart.

The carriage rumbled along a winding road, bouncing mercilessly on the rutted lane and swerving as it rounded corners. By the time they rolled to a stop her body was bruised her muscles sore from trying to keep herself from bouncing around the vehicle.

"We're here? You ready for a little swim?" He poked his head through the door, dragging her to the edge of the river. "This is going to be the end for the both of you. Here's to your death. Rest in Peace."

He left her on the bank while he drug James to her side. There was a slight embankment, between them and the rushing water. She struggled to spit out the gag, to break free of the bindings. Tavia tried to call out to him through the gag, searching for the means to change his mind. She would do anything.

With James in front of her, he pushed the two of them down the embankment. Their bodies plunged into the frigid water. Holding her breath, she moved her body toward the surface, seeking air. She couldn't think of anything but saving herself, couldn't think about James and what was happening to him. She had to keep her head above the water. Rolling onto her back, she floated and tried to kick her feet pointing her head toward the side of the river and praying a beach of some sort would come into view.

When she turned to look for James, it seemed he did the same. Momentary relief swept through her. He was awake and struggling to stay alive then he was pushing her toward the bank. Fighting exhaustion, dry land seemed a long ways a way.

Her back hit solid ground and she wriggled snake like to move away from the water then she felt James nudge her forward with his head. She lay on the earth, water washing at her feet and watched James make his way toward a large rock. Closing her eyes, she tried to breathe, tried to slow her racing heart. They might freeze to death but they weren't going to drown.

He turned, rubbing the back of his hands against the rock. The edge must have been sharp. He broke free of his bindings and quickly removed the gag.

"Are you alright? You're alive. My God the man is mad, crazy as hell to think he could get away with this." His words rambled while he rid himself of the ropes on his ankles before rushing to her side.

He pulled her gag from her mouth. "I'm fine, just very cold," she said while she shivered her body trembling.

Quickly he undid her bindings and helped her to her feet. He pulled her close in a tight embrace, his hands roaming down her back then to her face. He kissed her quickly, "We have to get out of here. Find some place to spend the night. Can you walk?"

"I think so." But her feet felt numb from the water and the tight bindings. She stepped forward but stumbled, reaching out for James.

"Let me help you." He wrapped an arm around her waist while they stumbled forward.

"Do you have any idea where to go, or where we are?" She peered into the darkness and saw nothing but trees.

"No. What I do know is that we have to find shelter or we'll freeze to death."

Even now the skies let loose with a torrent of water. The dampness made no difference but the wind did. It chilled every part of her. Still, they stumbled forward into the blackness of the night.

Minutes turned into hours. No moon brightened the darkness of the night. She collapsed to the ground. "I need a breath of air. I have to stop and rest."

"We'll stop a few minutes." He pulled her onto his lap, putting his back to the wind and shielding her from the ever-present gale tormenting them. "You can wear my jacket. I don't know if it will make you any warmer. We have to keep moving. I'll carry you if you can't walk."

"Why? There is nothing out there." She didn't want to give up, but she was so horribly tired.

He pulled her close, resting the base of his chin on her head. "Because we might find an old house or a new house with a barn somewhere we can shelter. I'm not going to lose you tonight."

"Help me up. I can do this," she said, determined to show him how resilient and adept she was. "I refuse to give Edwin any satisfaction."

"Are you sure?" he questioned even while he helped her to her feet. "I can carry you," he repeated.

She was shaking her head in denial, determined to carry her own weight. "Not unless I collapse and can move no further. I'm going to walk."

They strode in silence, her body's ability to move beginning to shut down. She was ready to give up and let him save himself. Perhaps the sun would come out with the dawn and would warm the earth. Perhaps it wouldn't.

With no words said between them, he swept her into his arms and continued on. A barely perceptible lighting of the sky showed her a pinprick of light. "James, look over there."

He turned then kissed her cheek. "A light, hopefully it will be friendly." Still it seemed to take at least another hour before they reached the small cottage and barn.

Instead of knocking on the door and risk a volatile owner, James entered the barn. The animals greeted them as if they were expecting their early morning meals. In a far corner, he sat down, still cradling her in his arms and rocking her, crooning nonsense words.

"At least it's dry. I was getting very tired of the rain," she said as she snuggled into his warmth.

"Hush, little darlin'. Sleep now," he said, "I wish I had a blanket or warm clothing for you. With a little luck these people will help us."

"Do you think we're safe?" She placed her hand on his chest, feeling the beating of his heart.

"For now. What happened at the house?"

"Edwin was there in our backyard, watching me, us. When Larena left, I saw something moving so I stepped onto the porch. He could have just shot us there. Why would he go to such length?"

"And be convicted of murder? If he shot us in our home, there would have been no doubts of his perfidy. His problem now is that he underestimated us. He had no idea we would survive."

"But we did survive." She yawned and once more, and he tried to shelter her from the cold of the night, pulling her tighter into his arms.

"We did indeed, but I don't think we will get sleep anytime soon." James pointed toward the barn door.

She sat up, pushing hair from her face and squinting towards the opening. A boy of about twelve walked through the door, heading for the feed, humming a tune and talking to himself as he walked.

"Don't scare him," she whispered, her breathing ragged as she tried to pull his jacket closer to her. "He's so young."

"I wouldn't dream of it," he cleared his throat. "But I won't be surprised that if I stand up and say hello, he'll bolt for the house."

She giggled softly. "You have to do something to introduce yourself and not scare him to death."

"I understand. Just not sure what that would be." He set her aside and stood, groaning softly from last night's exertions.

"Be careful." She smoothed her damp dress, wondering what would happen next and finding she was holding her breath.

"Hello there," James called out. "Was wondering if you could help us? We don't know where we are."

The boy dropped the bag of feed and fled, crying out for his father. "Papa, papa..."

"What would you bet the boy's father shows up with a gun of some sort?" He sat down on a bale of hay to wait for the father to appear.

She nudged him in the side and whispered with a small giggle, "You're wrong. He's got a pitchfork."

One more time he stood, his hands in the air. "Hello, sir, we could use some help. Don't mean you and your family any harm. Someone tried to drown us last night. After we swam from the river, we found your barn. I hope it's alright that we spent a few hours here."

"Who are you?" The man pointed the weapon at him. "How do I know if you're tellin' me the truth? You scared my boy."

James held out his hand, slowly approaching the farmer, "James Macmurra. I own a few ships. I'm a merchant. Can you tell us where we are? We could be on our way and no more bother to you and your family."

She didn't think she had the strength or the will to leave and continue walking until they found what? They had no idea where they were. She didn't think she could walk all the way back to London.

"You said someone tried to drown you? Do you know who?" He set the weapon down and leaned on the handle. "A couple months back two bodies washed ashore. They were bound hand and foot with gags on their mouths. No one took much interest in them. I doubt if the murders were ever solved."

She gasped, hearing what he told James. It couldn't be...

~ * ~

"Really," James stepped forward. "That's exactly what happened to us, but we were able to float ashore and save ourselves. I used a rock to slice through the ropes binding my hands. After that I freed myself and my wife then we walked here. Don't know where we are though. Don't know where he tossed us in the river. Would like to go home." Exhaustion filled him and he knew Tavia was worse. He feared for her condition, for her life.

"You're on the outskirts of the Montgomerie estate. I own a small farm here and give some of my produce to the Duke, well, usually the heir apparent, and he lets me sell the rest for a tidy profit."

"Drake Montgomerie." James murmured relieved that he found someone who wouldn't put a pitchfork through him and ask questions later. "I've been there, to his estate. How far?"

Tavia rose, smoothing her skirts and trying to straighten her hair, her arms wrapped around her to ward off the horrible chill that seemed to encompass her. "Did we really just find someone we can trust," she whispered to James.

"I'm glad to hear you work for the duke. Drake is married to my wife's sister, Ella. If you could send them a message, I'd be eternally grateful as will Drake. I'm sure he'll reward you and come for us." James prayed this man would do his bidding.

"When you tell him we're here, can you ask him to send me something to wear? I'm freezing and I'd really like to get into something dry and warm."

"I'll send my son. In the meantime, I can give you blankets and food. Are you hungry?"

"More cold than famished." Tavia shivered. "A blanket would be absolutely wonderful."

"Jacob," the boy appeared immediately as if he'd been listening. "Get two blankets and bring them some bacon and hot cups of coffee. You might need some help so you can ask your sister. Then I want you to ride to the Montgomerie estate as fast as you can with this message." He told the boy what to say, that James Macmurra and Tavia were waiting at his barn and are in dire need of help.

The boy nodded and sprang into action.

"Thank you," James said, taking stock of the barn and anything the family might need to help them out. "My wife and I appreciate your help more than you can know. Someone tried to kill us last night, but I don't think you and your family are in any danger. I can understand if you'd rather we didn't remain in the barn. We could wait on the outskirts."

The man seemed to ignore that statement before speaking, "You have any idea who did this to you," he asked again. "I know the bodies that were found have all the people in this area terrified of this unknown killer. Two more were found just three days ago."

"Know exactly who tried to kill us. A trip to the constables will be the first place I go once we are cleaned up and warm," James said, determined to see Edwin in Newgate Prison.

So Edwin had taken action against other people. He'd been at sea too long. He would have heard rumors, perhaps heard about missing people.

"I suppose you would go to the police. He wanted you to drown. That's a horrible death," the farmer said. "Can't imagine why anyone would want to do something like that to other people.

"Or he thought we were dead before he dumped us," James seemed to shudder as he thought about what he said.

"He knew I wasn't dead." Tavia said softly. "He knew and he wanted me to suffer, wanted both of us to suffer."

"The bastard," James muttered before turning to her. "Where did you learn to swim? We are both lucky you knew how to float. I could have never retrieved you from the bottom of the river."

"At home when I was little. Mother taught me," She never felt more thankful for the constant lessons her mother had given her before she died. She was slow to learn and her sisters teased her mercilessly.

The boy returned along with his sister and set the food on a bale of hay before handing the blankets to them.

Tavia quickly wrapped herself in the warmth while James grabbed two pieces of bacon, handing her one then the coffee.

"Take the stallion," the father told his son. Then to James, "I have chores. Can I assume the two of you will be alright until your people arrive?"

"We'll be fine," Tavia said, wrapping her hands around the hot coffee cup and slowly chewing on the bacon. She smiled and it stole his heart. "This is heavenly, a hand warmer."

They sat cross-legged on the floor, eating and drinking the steaming coffee. "Do you want to sleep while we wait?"

"Only if you hold me. I don't think I've ever been so exhausted and cold. We could have died last night." She snuggled into his arms.

"Hush, everything is going to be fine, sleep now," he murmured, stroking her hair. The truth of her words whirled in his head. If it was the last thing he did, he would see Edwin prosecuted for this crime.

He was left with his thoughts and the repercussions of what happened to them last night. Montgomerie would help him find Edwin McMasters and they would see him hang or shipped off to Australia. He squeezed his eyes shut, clenching and unclenching his fists.

Her breathing was easy and soft, her head resting on his chest, her hand just below her head. Gently, he stroked her hair, wishing they were safe at home and in their bed. When he confronted the evil man the first night he met Tavia, he could have never guessed that slight would come to this. Edwin was crazy and dangerous.

"James."

She caught at him with a slender hand, peered up into his eyes, in the light reflected from the sun shining through the rafters. She moistened her lips, preparing to speak.

"Everything is fine, Tavia," he told her, shifting her head from his chest where she had slept since a few minutes after the farmer and his boy left. "Drake will be here soon then we'll be home. Just rest the best you can."

"I'm still so cold." She hugged the blanket in which he'd wrapped her tightly to her chin. In the shifting light as the morning turned to noon, her eyes were huge and her hair still a tangled mess but a glorious mess.

He tried to pull the blanket closer to her. When that failed, he covered her with his, fear for her life becoming more real with each second. He had to get her warm.

"They'll be here soon and I'm sure Ella will be more than happy to order you a warm bath." She had slept so quickly and he no longer suffered from the chill of last night's adventure, he'd thought nothing of letting Tavia sleep. Now he feared for her life.

"I thought we were going home," she told him. "I want to go home and sleep in our bed."

"First things first," he trailed his finger along her chin. "You have to get warm before we can go anywhere."

"They won't take us home? Why not?"

"We must have floated a long ways if we are close to the Montgomerie estate. I would feel much better if you got warm as soon as possible. The closest place is where I intend to have Drake take us."

"I had wished," she sighed, her hand resting on his chest. "You are really not cold?"

"Listen," he grinned and kissed her. "Stay put."

"You're always telling me that. Do you really think I'm going to obey this time?" she asked as she extended her hand for James to help her stand.

"I suppose not," he told her, resigned, knowing she was going to look no matter what he said. "What if it's Edwin?"

Her eyes closed for a moment. "Perhaps I'll just sit on this hay bale."

Tavia's words made him smile. She was learning his main concern was for her safety. They would do well together. "Thank you," he told her before he strode to the barn door opening.

The carriage rounded the corner, kicking up dust as it slowed to a stop. Drake jumped from vehicle, racing inside. He stopped when he saw James standing in the doorway. "Good God, I was terrified. The boy said you were in dire need of help."

Ella stepped from the vehicle with the assistance of the driver. "Where is she? Where is my sister?" She strode past the men into the barn. "What has happened to the two of you?"

Tavia ran to meet Ella, tears rolling down her face as the sisters hugged. "He tried to kill us," she whispered. "That horrible, crazy, insane man tried to kill us and he almost succeeded."

"Who?" Drake asked. "What happened?"

"In a minute. Tavia nearly froze to death after we were tossed into the Thames. She needs a hot bath to take away the chill. Can we go to your home instead of London?"

"Of course, you can tell us what happened on the way," Ella said, giving her sister another hug.

"Let me return the blankets and cups. I'll just put them by the back door," Drake said, picking up the items. "Get in the carriage, I'll join you in a minute."

James would not let Tavia walk. He'd almost lost her twice, and he wasn't going to take another chance. His actions and his alone had put her life in jeopardy both times. Where Tavia was concerned there were a great deal of things he should have done differently and would if he could. He swept her into arms and carried her through the barn and to the carriage, gently placing her inside before jumping in behind.

Ella and Drake followed them, sitting on the opposite side, watching him as he cleared his throat, preparing to enlist Montgomerie's help. Drake Montgomerie had contacts, just as The Duchess did, that could be used to find the man who tried to kill them. Yet Edwin didn't know they were alive, and he wouldn't go into hiding unless he somehow found out.

He inhaled a long breath of air, thinking over everything he needed to say. "Edwin McMasters," he began, his emotions intense and all consuming. "Edwin McMasters tried to kill us, and I'm sure he'll try again if he knows we're alive."

"Do you have proof?" Drake asked, leaning forward, clearly interested in what he had to say.

James shrugged his shoulders. "Our word against his, I suppose, but I can take you to the spot on the river where we left the restraints. If I can find the place," he added. "The night was dark and rainy. I know the general direction. If we scour the beach, we will find them."

"I know I couldn't find my way back. I have no idea from which direction we came," Tavia spoke softly, her arms still wrapped around herself while her body trembled violently.

"You still cold? I would have thought..." James asked, concerned. He pulled her into his lap, hoping his body warmth would heat her. With the passing seconds his fear for her escalated.

"I feel as if I'm cold inside as well as out. I can't stop shivering." She closed her eyes. "The coffee helped while it was hot but now..." she let the sentence end prematurely.

"The farmer told us two bodies were found a few days ago by the river, bound hand and foot and gagged just as we were. Do you think Edwin is their killer also?" James ran his hands along Tavia's arms. Her body felt cold on the outside too.

"First thing, after we get Tavia into a hot bath, you two are going to find that place he left you and collect the evidence," Ella said seeming determined to make someone pay for this crime against her sister. "I suspect you want to see to the bath, James."

He nodded, "Just until I see that she's warm and I know she'll recover."

"I won't let her out of my sight. I'll stay with her and after her bath make sure she is put to bed with plenty of food and a warm nightgown,"

Ella said, taking her sister's hand in hers.

James didn't want to leave her but understood Ella would take care of her. He clenched his jaw, agreeing to leave even though he didn't want to be separated from his wife. He understood it was imperative they collect all the evidence they could.

"I'll trust you to her care," he said. Reluctantly unwilling to let go of Tavia, he carried her up the stairs and to the room. She leaned into him, her strength seeming to fade before his eyes.

"While you and Ella take care of your wife, I'll get the horses ready." Drake left them.

Ella appeared a few minutes later followed by servants carrying steaming water.

When the water was filled, Ella said, "If you want you can undress her and help her into the bath, but if you want to go now, I'll do it."

"No, I'm not sure you have the strength. For that matter how will you get her out of the tub when the water turns cold?"

Ella smiled, "Don't worry, I've my ladies' maid. She saved my life when... Anyway, she saved my life and I stole her from the whorehouse she was living in and gave her a job as my most trusted servant. Together we will see to Tavia. I won't let anything happen to my baby sister."

"I can't thank you enough," he turned on a heel and made his way to the stables.

"There you are."

"I was going to lend you a pair of buckskins and a shirt to wear until I realized you'd split the seams of anything I own."

"My clothes, while they'll never live another day, they are dry." Unlike Tavia who had so many different layers, nothing underneath the gown was dry. In truth her dress had still been damp when he carried her up the steps. No wonder she was chilled to the bone.

"Let's start at the farmer's barn and go from there." Drake suggested as he kicked his horse into a gallop.

James didn't have a chance to answer. Hard pressed to keep up with the more experienced rider, he hung on and let the horse do what it was supposed to do. Bloody hell, he'd spent his time at sea not on a horse.

His expertise was in dire need of lessons.

If the situation had not been so dreadful, he would have enjoyed the moment as his huge body began to relax in the saddle and join the rhythm of his horse. Unlike the day before, the sun shone down and began to dry the ground.

Drake reigned in his horse and James followed suit, breathing hard from the exertion of the ride as well as the terrors of the night before. "Should we walk our horses from here?"

"Not until we get closer to the river. Do you know which direction you came from?"

James pointed. "Tavia saw the light from over there. I was carrying her. If there are any prints, they'll be deeper than normal. I suspect though that with all the natural debris on the ground, there might not be prints until we reach the edge of the river."

Through the field they rode slowly, studying the ground for tracks or signs of human passage. "Look over there," Drake pointed to the ground. "I believe those are your prints."

"I'm not much of a tracker, but they are prints and they appear to be about the size of my feet." James leaned over to see more clearly what Drake pointed out.

Drake put a marker where they saw the first print. James looked at him, questioning.

"So we can bring the constables back here then with the marker we can show them where you've been. It might be a good idea for you to bring whatever it is you use aboard your ships to see in the distance."

James laughed for the first time in quite a while, "A telescope, most would call a spyglass?"

"That, yes," Drake said, picking up his speed to an easy trot.

For at least an hour they followed the prints. "We headed inland. I don't remember following the river at all. I suspected we'd find help quicker if we left the river."

The sun was sitting low on the horizon when they finally reached the Thames and dismounted. "You go upriver and I'll go down. Whistle if you find anything," Drake said.

They had to be close to the spot where they managed to find dry land. He felt it in his gut, deep down inside. Carefully, he searched along the bank, recalling the large rock where he cut the bindings. It was growing darker, the sun nearly descending when he heard a loud whistle.

He turned and headed upstream. Drake was waving his hand, a grim expression on his face.

From where James stood it seemed Drake stood by another victim. When he reached the spot, he cringed, his body shuddering at the terrible sight in front of him. The woman lay face down, her hair splayed around her head, hands and feet bound.

"My friend, we've stumbled on more than we've bargained for. It's another possible murder by Edwin. If you stay here, I'm going to ride to the farmer's home and have him send a message to my estate for the constables. We can't leave the body here, but I don't know..." he paused. "I don't want to demolish any evidence they could find."

"Stay here, I'll find or make a litter and we can bring this poor woman to a safe place."

When Drake turned her over, he inhaled a swift sharp breath. "I've seen this woman before." He looked up as if thinking. "I can't seem to place her though."

"Where could you have seen her? This has to be another one of Edwin's victims."

"I don't remember. Any number of places, perhaps Ella would know. We should leave her here until the police can take a look."

James' thoughts turned to Tavia and fear for her paramount, but he had no options tonight. He paced as he waited, time creeping by while all he wanted was to rush to Tavia's side. Sleep deprived, he could barely keep his eyes open as his stomach growled hungrily. At least the night was clear with the moon lighting the earth and very little wind.

He sat down, leaning against a boulder and closing his eyes. Tavia cried out for him, her body burning, seemingly on fire. She moaned and called his name. Startled, he bolted upright. He was alone, the night dark, stars and the moon still filling the sky with their light. He was by himself, no one around, his body shaking with fear for his wife.

He rose warding off the sleep which threatened giving him nightmares, pacing along the beach, wishing someone would come.

Tonight the moon was bright and clear, the weather cold and dry. Staying put here went against all his instincts, and still he feared for Tavia's life. A myriad of scenarios swept through his mind. Visions of Edwin finding her and Ella alone at the summer home, where they were so very vulnerable, flitted through his head.

The sound of horses' hooves gave him a modicum of relief. He stopped and watched as three men approached. His heart in his throat, he stood frozen to the spot.

"As it turned out the farmer left his chores and went into town to find a constable. He'll take over here and you're free to go. If you want to return tomorrow and search out the place where you and Tavia found the shore, we can ride together. I've informed these two men what you told me as well as the farmer's account of the other bodies."

"Let's go home." James mounted his horse. His need to see his wife driving him beyond his endurance, he raced through the fields.

~ * ~

Addie stopped at the mirror in the hallway, pretending to preen while she listened to the couple speaking in muted tones in the parlor. Her husband's brother and her maid spoke to each other in hushed voices.

"No, she has not bled, they were wed weeks ago so..."

Hearing that, Addie turned and quietly and as quickly as possible fled to her chambers. She picked up the satchel she'd packed two weeks prior when she spoke to Hamilton in his room. Stuffing her satchel under her pelisse, she made her way through the house to the stables.

The young man who managed the horses must have seen her coming. By the time she stepped through the doors, her horse was being saddled. In another few seconds, he helped her mount.

"I'm riding to the ocean. I want to run this little mare on the beach and feel the breeze on my face," she told him. Leaving the stables, she began her journey in the directions she told him. A half mile later she turned and raced the horse as quickly as she dared to the tavern where Hamilton was staying, praying too that he was there.

Reaching the tavern, she quickly dismounted and tied the mare to one of the posts provided.

Addie grabbed the satchel from the horse and raced up the steps to Hamilton's room. Her hand raised to knock, the door swung open.

"I saw your horse," Hamilton said, casting a cautious gaze her way before pulling her into his arms for a quick kiss, then setting her back on her feet. "Something happen?"

She tried to catch her breath, inhaling deeply. "I think I'm pregnant."

The following pause stretched into seconds. "My child?"

"Yes, I'm sorry, but I have to leave. If you don't want to go with me, I'll go alone. They are watching me, and my bed sheets. They will kill me if they believe I'm carrying a child. You said so yourself."

"We're leaving now." He strode to an armoire, grabbing a satchel before he took her by the hand.

Stopping downstairs, he grabbed some bread and cheese, stuffing them into the bag he carried.

Outside he untied her horse and gave the mare a slap on the rear to send the horse on her way. He paid the stableman for two horses and bedrolls and they began their journey.

"You had this planned," she said as she rode alongside him. "Just as I did, but I didn't believe it would be this soon.

"I knew within a few weeks of seeing you we would have to leave. I've been checking the ships in the harbor. There is a ship bound for London, but it doesn't leave until tomorrow morning, and we can't wait that long. If they come after you, they'll find you and make sure you don't leave with the vessel."

"We can't risk that," she said. "I don't think his brother really cares enough to chase me, but I don't want to take that chance. There could be other factors we know nothing about that could influence him."

"Me neither," he told her. "In any case, we're going to stay off the main roads, so we can't be seen at least until we're sure no one is following us. There is a safe house down the road about three hours away, but we can't stay there. It's too close."

"There is nothing else? Nowhere to stay?" she had never had to abort a mission in this fashion, and she never spent the night on a bedroll in the woods. Her body shuddered at the thought.

"Nowhere safe," he said. "I'll make sure everything is alright and protect you from whatever stirs at night."

"You have survival skills?" She didn't know why she asked? He'd been in the army, served in India and various other places.

He smiled at her, "You know I do," he said softly. "I wish our trip didn't have to be this way."

"It's just that I'm so terrified I can't think straight. My heart is in my throat and pounding so hard it feels as if it's going to jump right out of my chest. I don't like bugs and things that crawl around in the night. Then there are the human vermin."

"I'm scared too, frightened that we're doing something that will harm our baby. I'm humbled by the fact you carry my child, and I've a great need to protect both of you at any cost. This is the only night we won't have a roof over our head."

"Promise?"

He slanted a crooked smile a bit wistful in its appearance. "I wish I could, but you and I both understand one can't predict what will happen in the next second let alone something that might be two months away."

"I never thought you were capable of feeling fear." Her voice was whisper thin as she swallowed trying to form words over a parched throat. "You are always so calm. You seem calm now but you tell me..." her voice trailed off. "You tell me you're scared."

"Where you're concerned, your missions have always frightened me, but this one has hit me in the gut from the first time I heard about it. I asked Drake to have me assigned here in case you needed me and now you do. It wasn't fortuitous," he told her.

"I'm glad you did. I thought this assignment would last a year or more then I'd be able to return home no harm done. I never believed there would be any danger here."

"Here," he pointed to a small opening on the side of the road. "We turn off here. There is an animal trail we'll follow. We need to stay off the roads the rest of today and probably tomorrow. We should reach a small inn by the end of the day tomorrow."

She peered through the dense trail. There was barely room for the horses and their pace slowed. She dodged branches and was hit by spider webs. As the day passed, darkness began to fall. They would not be able to travel much longer in the waning light.

"How much farther?" She rubbed her shoulders before pressing a hand to her back. "I'm not sure I can stay on the horse another minute. Every muscle seems to ache.

"Tired?" he asked, turning in his saddle to look at her, concern etched in his steel blue eyes.

"I'm not used to riding for hours. Not sure if I'll be able to walk when I get off this animal." She laughed softly just as her legs seemed to cramp and she cried out in pain.

"We'll stop as soon as I find a suitable place to camp. A place protected on all four sides would be nice, but three would work. We've been following a small stream so there will be water."

It seemed to Addie he was too meticulous by far. They passed several places she thought would be wonderful to lay out their bedrolls, but they weren't protected on three sides let alone four.

Finally, he stopped. "We'll make camp here."

"In this copse of trees? It's so dark I can barely see my hand in front of my face."

"That's the reason we're making camp here. You can't see out and no one can see in. We'll hear anyone before they see us."

"Oh," she said. "I never thought of that."

"I don't suppose a city girl would." He laughed, dismounting quickly before helping her from her mount. "Can you walk?"

She nodded, taking a few hesitant steps, her legs cramping with fatigue. "If I can lay out my bedroll right here, I'll be just fine."

"Stay put," he said, grabbing the blanket and marching to what appeared to be a flat site.

"Why is it men always tell women to stay put?" she asked, remembering James would constantly tell Tavia those very words.

"Because you'll do something stupid if we don't. Like right now, you're walking and I would have carried you."

"You still may have to." She stopped holding out her hands to him as she began to crumple where she stood.

"Addie." He swept her into his arms before she hit the ground. Striding to the bedroll, he set her down. "Stay put," he told her with a lopsided grin.

"You don't have to tell me a third time and are you grinning at me?" she smiled and leaned against a nearby tree. "Are there bugs on the tree? I told you I'm terrified of bugs."

"I suppose, but you didn't tell me you were terrified, just that you didn't like them," he said.

He rummaged through his satchel and brought out a small bag. Sitting down next to her, he broke off a hunk of bread then handed her a large slice of cheese.

"You think of everything." She had not thought to bring food. "It was everything for me to get away without anyone knowing."

"Eat, you did the right thing," he told her, striding to the river with two cups and brought water for each of them.

"Can we start a fire?" She pulled the sides of her pelisse closer together for warmth, shivering as a breeze found its way through the branches and leaves sheltering them.

"Not tonight. We'll have to rely on body heat to stay warm. Now where do you hurt?" He began to gently massage her shoulders.

"That's heavenly," she said leaning into him, her head falling forward in order to absorb the soothing of her muscles. "I hurt practically everywhere, and it seems I'm drained of all energy."

His hands continued their journey down her back, then her arms. "Lie down so I can work my magic on your legs."

She did as he told her. He lifted her skirt and massaged the sore muscles of her legs, one then the other. She closed her eyes, enjoying the feel of his hands. "You can't imagine how good that feels."

"I hope you brought something more appropriate for riding." He smoothed her skirt back, covering her.

"I brought two pairs of pants and two shirts. I was pretty sure the journey would be difficult. I've no intention of masquerading as a boy though," she said almost as an afterthought.

"You could never masquerade as a boy even if you cut your hair short and bound your breasts. Anyone who looked at you would know immediately you are a woman."

"Hmm... Thank you for the massage." She rolled over, thinking, just like Tavia could not convincingly pretend she was a boy.

He pulled her into his arms and covered them with the blanket. He held her close, his hand resting on her stomach as if he meant to protect the child growing there. "I really wish you didn't have to flee for your life," he murmured, placing small kisses on the back of her neck. "I wish we dared make love."

The sound of men approaching sent her heart to a rapid staccato. He tossed her the satchel with her gun and he pulled a pistol. He didn't have to tell her to be quiet.

Chapter Nine

When James returned home, Tavia was curled up in bed, her face heated. She was wearing next to nothing. Ella sat by the bed, bathing her arms and legs with cool water. She had a cool compress on her forehead.

"She has a fever. She was extremely cold for too long," Ella said. "Now she's too warm."

"I'll take over for you." James couldn't bear seeing Tavia suffer. He needed to make everything perfect for her.

"If you don't rest, you'll also take sick. Tavia doesn't need that. You have to sleep and eat. How long has it been? When were you abducted? My maid will take over in an hour. I'll rest then she'll wake me and I'll do the same until you are well enough to see to your wife."

"No," he said, slowly shaking head, unwilling to give in to his needs. "No one is taking care of her except me. I caused this to happen."

"You did not cause anything. You must do as I say. There is no other choice and you did not make this man go insane enough to kill people," Ella told him intensely, waving the damp washcloth for emphasis. "You have to take care of yourself or you'll do Tavia absolutely no good. I won't let you stay here. If I have to, I'll get Drake and his men to haul you off to your bed."

"Wouldn't want that," he mumbled, backing away from her still reluctant to leave, he acknowledged the truth of her speech. "This time your words make some sense."

"Of course they do. I never talk nonsense." She turned her back on him as he reluctantly left the bedchamber.

"What has you looking so stern?" Drake met him in the hallway, grinning as if he knew the answer. "You have words with Ella? I'm afraid of her too. When she gets that way, best you do as she bids."

"You guessed my problem. Says I have to sleep and eat or she'll have you see to it that I do. It would be a daunting task and one you couldn't win." James began to see the humor in all this and the reality of a truly loving married couple.

Drake let his head back and roared with laughter. "She does the same thing to me all of the time. I never get a moment of peace around here. Come, let's see what's leftover in the kitchen. We'll eat first and if nothing happens that we're needed for, we can sleep although I'd rather not sleep without my wife beside me."

James meekly followed his brother in law through the house. In the kitchen they found a hearty venison stew, fresh baked bread and an array of vegetables to choose from.

Between bites, "What's the time frame tomorrow?" James asked, washing the food down with a glass of Maxwell's fine Bordeaux.

"We're going after McMasters tomorrow unless something happens tonight that changes the time frame. I've set my men watching his house in case he decides to leave. They're going to report to me any movements, and if he goes after another woman, they'll stop him and ask questions later."

"I believe it would be best if The Duchess and Larena move in here until the man is caught. I'm worried about them, and I don't need their safety on my mind as well as Tavia's. A man such as Edwin is not predictable. If he thought he was wronged, he could do anything," James said between bites.

"I've been thinking the same thing and weighing the pros and cons. I'll send for them first thing tomorrow morning. The Duchess is going to protest, of course. She didn't like it when I made her move here when we worried about Ella's safety. She's not going to like it any better now."

"Good, if you keep the house guarded, they'll all be safe as long as they don't go anywhere. I won't have to worry any more than normal." Lord, but this was hard and he prayed life with Tavia would become easier and less fearful.

"Montgomerie, sir." One of Drake's men strode into the kitchen and stopped.

James wasn't at all certain he liked the expression on the man's face.

"What is it?" Drake rose, striding toward the man, seemingly ready to ride this minute.

James set his fork on the table and followed suit.

"McMasters left his house and is on his way into the city. He's riding in his carriage. I've sent two men after him. Three are still watching the house. Don't know where he's going."

"We'll have to wait for news. How long since he left?" James asked, interested in the time frame.

"Took me about twenty minutes to ride here, sir. About that much time."

"Set up a patrol along the river. I'll send a message to the runners who are working the case and tell them what we're doing."

"It could be nothing," James said, terribly afraid someone else would be murdered tonight. "Or he could be searching for his next victim."

"Are there any balls or parties tonight that he might attend?" Drake asked.

"If you don't know, I'm hardly the guy to be questioning about it." Yet James felt sure Drake was thinking in the right direction. Who would snub him tonight and inadvertently put her life in danger?

"Ella might know," Drake said. "I should check."

"I might know what?" Ella asked as she walked into the room. Gazing in James' direction, "Shouldn't you be in bed?"

"Don't think I'm going to make it there tonight. We all want to know if there's anything going on in town tonight, a ball or a party that Edwin might be invited to attend?" Drake asked, pulling his wife into his lap and holding her.

"Let me think," she turned to Drake. He drew her hand into his, watching her. "The Lady Talbot is having a small fete. She did not invite that many and was sorely disappointed when I turned her down. I know how much you detest gatherings of that sort, not that I like them much better. I always prefer to spend the evening alone with you and our child."

"You are a dear for remembering my distastes. I'll remember that gesture." He brought her hand to his lips to kiss the back before turning her hand over to run his tongue along her palm.

Watching the loving couple, James felt a swift urge to be with Tavia. He longed for the type of relationship Drake and Ella had.

Drake turned back to his employee. "Go to the Talbot's. I'll have another of my men accompany you so there will four of you. Don't go inside and by all means don't confront Edwin. Just watch the house and keep him in sight if he goes anywhere. If he does, send one of the men to report then make sure you follow him."

He called out and another man appeared. After giving him the orders, the two men left the house to join with the other two.

"Under the circumstances aren't you leaving the house vulnerable?" Ella asked, moving to a chair and tracing the rim of her wine glass with a slender finger.

"Not at all," Drake reassured, "both James and I are here, and we've both learned to sleep with one eye open."

"Speaking of sleep," Ella said, smiling. "If you are satisfied, isn't it about time you went to bed? I'm going to retire now and get up to take over for my maid in about six hours."

"You're right," James rose, striding from the room, leaving Ella and Drake chatting. He headed for Tavia's room. Inside, he sat on her bed and told the maid. "I just want to check on her for a moment."

The maid walked to the window, turning her back on them. James leaned close and kissed her cheek before tracing the line of her jaw with his finger. She didn't seem to be as hot. "I love you," he whispered to her. "You have to get well so I can tell you. I'll see you tomorrow." With that said, he left, wishing he could lie down beside her and hold her throughout the night.

In another room, he disrobed and settled into a hot bath Ella must have ordered for him. The steamy water was bliss. He ducked beneath the water before soaping his hair and beard. With both arms on the rim of the tub, he rested his head on the back.

Closing his eyes, he tried to unravel the events of the last two days. The hard metal had hit his head and he fell to the floor. He was groggy, not unconscious, which was what he supposed saved his life and Tavia's, although she'd done an amazing job of rescuing herself.

Bound hand and foot, he'd never found himself in such an untenable position. He'd fought pirates on the high seas and commanded naval ships, firing on the enemy. The vulnerability of that moment transcended anything he'd ever experienced.

He'd heard the flow of the river and feared the worst. Before he hit the water, he managed to fill his lungs with air, and holding his breath, he used his legs to kick his way to the surface. His relief at seeing Tavia had done the same thing gave him reason to believe they might find their way out of this predicament and live to see another day.

The thunder of horses' hooves reverberating through him set him to a standing position, water sluicing from his body. He reached for a bath sheet and wrapping it around his waist, he strode to the window. Sounds of horses and men talking echoed into the room, but he understood little of what was said. He could see no one.

He reached for his used clothing and found a set of fresh clean buckskins and a white shirt. Drake had sent men to his house for new garments. He prayed no one had seen. Edwin didn't have the means to have men watching his home. After all he was supposed to be dead.

He didn't know how long it had been, but he hadn't slept. Still, while he didn't feel refreshed, he was ready to lend a hand. Dressed, he raced down the stairs, finding his way to the parlor where one man had news.

"Edwin left the ball with a young woman. She stepped into the carriage with him. I rode here and Jonesy followed McMasters, sir. Jonesy heard them talking about going to his house."

"If my other man followed the carriage and we presume it is going to Edwin's home, then we should go to the river," Drake said.

"I remembered an embankment, a drop of about three yards before I hit the water." James said, rubbing his beard and thinking briefly he needed to trim it. "Do you know anywhere about a mile upstream from the farmer's land where there is an embankment of some sort?"

Drake thoughtfully shook his head then looked to his man who also told him no. "We know where the girl's body was found. Let's ride to a point about a mile upstream from there. We can search out the area. The sun's about to rise, and by the time we reach the river, it should be above the horizon."

James strode toward the front door, intending to reach the stables quickly, but he was stopped short by Drake's hand on his shoulder.

"Did you get enough rest?"

"I want to catch the bastard." James shook off the hand and kept going, hearing Drake behind him. "I can sleep later."

"I'd feel the same way if he tried to kill Ella."

The sun rose and seemed to shed light on the search party. They followed a path upriver for about a mile, finding nothing that remotely appeared like an embankment.

"I've an idea," Drake said, spurring his horse forward the others following. They rode for about five minutes and reached a place where water had been diverted from the Thames by a small levee.

"Bloody hell, carriage wheel tracks and drag marks. This is where he dumps the people. Where he dumped us." James' heart raced, his fists clenched, needing to bring McMasters to a swift justice.

"Now, if we follow the river downstream from here, we should be able to find the ropes and gags that bound you and Tavia." Drake looked to his man. "Go get the Bow Street Runners working this case and bring them here. Stay away from the tracks," he warned.

"We are so spread out trying to get ahead of this man, I don't know if we'll ever catch him. If he keeps everyone alive until he dumps them, we could save a life if it gets this far."

"I'm sure the runners will put men here," Drake said thoughtfully. "If they don't, I will. It will be easier to catch him here. This is where we know he goes. In that case it won't be yours and Tavia's word against his."

The peace and serenity of the river belied the horror that surrounded it and this spot. They rode for nearly thirty minutes before James spotted the place where he and Tavia washed ashore.

He closed his eyes, wishing the nightmare away, clearly seeing her lying on her back, the gag in her mouth unable to move or speak. He wanted to go to her and reassure her, but he could not until he rid himself of his bindings. Since he'd been with Tavia, there had been no normalcy to their lives. They'd gone from extreme to extreme, but they seemed to have weathered each part.

He didn't know if she returned his love, he prayed she did. "We are done here then," James said gruffly.

Drake marked the spot. "When the runners arrive at the embankment, we'll tell them your story, and it will be up to them whether they believe your story or not."

"I don't want to leave this up to people who are not personally involved," James said. "If you are done with this investigation, I have a ship in port, and I'll enlist my crew to keep an eye out for anything else that might happen."

"Your men can help, but with Ella being Tavia's sister and Larena her cousin, I'm not taking anything for granted. We can use all the help possible. The man is insane and with that comes surprises. He could change how he kills or escalate. We don't know what will happen next, but I'm pretty sure he won't stop murdering people until he is apprehended. Until we catch him, we're his enemy and everyone we hold dear are in danger."

When they reached the dumping area, the runners had arrived. Their concern seemed sincere, but once again James wasn't going to leave anything to chance. They recounted the story, and by the time they finished, the sun was descending on a long day.

"Let's go home," Drake said, sounding frustrated and exhausted. "Hopefully my men will have brought everyone we care for to the estate and they will be comfortable and safe for the duration."

For several miles they rode in silence, each seeming to be immersed in their personal thoughts. James' feelings now focused on Tavia, remembering the chill that seemed to encompass her and affect her wellbeing. If he closed his eyes, he saw her lying on the deck, her body limp and unmoving then he saw her on the riverbank.

She was so small and fragile. Her need to be treated as a man, as an equal astounded him. In many ways she surpassed him in her abilities, but in strength and stamina she would never be his equal. He had to find a way to convince her of this and curtail some of her activities. What happened to her the other night though, it had nothing to do with strength or stamina.

He had been so in fear for her life too many times and never wanted to feel this way again. How did he convince his incredible wife she was not invincible and never would be?

"The same way I did," Drake muttered as he rode next to him. "The same way I did."

"You reading my thoughts?" James didn't understand how this man he barely knew understood what was in his head.

"Ella acts just the same as Tavia. I don't understand how they were brought up. She is courageous beyond her strength and believes with her entire heart that she can do anything a man can. I thought I convinced her she could not, but discovered I'd done nothing of the sort. Instead of waiting to be rescued, she saved herself."

"What would have happened if she waited for you to find her?" James was suddenly curious to know more about his wife's sister. He'd heard part of the story but decided the tale was most likely gossip.

"They are cut from the same cloth," Drake muttered. "I don't know what could have happened. She might have found herself in a harem in Turkey or some wealthy man's concubine. As it was, she nearly died waiting for me at my father's townhouse. Perhaps she did what she had to, but my fear for her took over my soul."

"Montgomerie," the shout came from behind them. "Is that you, Drake Montgomerie?"

Both James and Drake turned their horses, hands on their pistols ready to confront this new foe.

"Adelina and Hamilton, what the devil are you doing here? I thought you were in Spain," Drake said, waiting for the pair to meet them.

"Adelina," James breathed, confirming his guess that this woman was connected to the heir apparent, Drake Montgomerie. He'd heard stories that swirled around Drake about espionage, but he never believed rumors until proven true. "Your marriage to the old man in Spain didn't work out?"

"It was never a real marriage. The priest was as fake as the vows," Hamilton said before Adelina could speak.

"So, your gut instinct was right?" Drake asked Hamilton. "Adelina was in grave danger."

"Never more right. If you hadn't allowed me to go in as back up, she might be dead now. Addie and I, well, we're done with the covert missions you send us on."

"I will miss the two of you," Drake murmured, "But I believe there is more to this story that needs telling."

"We plan on explaining everything," Hamilton said.

"Including what made you decide to abort the mission." Drake addressed Hamilton, sounding harsh.

James was surprised by the dark brooding look suddenly shuttering Drake's features. This was a man of many depths he had yet to discover, and he wondered if Ella knew he was still involved deeply with the espionage game in England.

"Everything. Perhaps we could have a spot of tea, a brandy, a bath and maybe something to eat as well as the fine Bordeaux Maxwell gives you. We've been on the road for more than two months now, fleeing for our lives, dirty, hungry and sleeping on the ground."

"I'm sure there is some exaggeration in your story," Drake said, humor lacing his words.

"There always is," Hamilton said with a deep sigh, "and you always find a way to call me out. But that's what makes us good spies. Isn't it?" There was a challenge in what he said.

"Really, Hamilton, you don't need to argue with Drake. He knew from the beginning there was a chance we would abort. He cautioned me from the start to leave if I had an inkling of danger."

"Nothing new here. He always knows there is a chance of danger and loss of life."

"The brother meant to kill me whether I gave my husband an heir or not. He told me as much the first time I spoke to him. There was no way he was going to let my husband have an heir to claim the inheritance. The brother believed it was his and meant for his oldest son to eventually inherit."

"You didn't take a ship? Seems as if it would have been much safer. Looks like the two of you haven't had a bath in months." Drake looked them up and down. "We can probably oblige you with hot water, if you want to tell me the real reasons why you fled and so soon. You must have been there only a few weeks. You promised me you had a sleeping potion and he would never get you pregnant." Drake was too blunt.

James cleared his throat, watching the blush heat Adelina's cheeks. He wondered why Drake was acting so obtuse. It was clear to anyone looking at her she was pregnant, but it wasn't his place to say anything. He rode easily, watching the interplay of words between the trio.

"Don't really want to tell you anything, old man. It's private and when she's ready to share, I'm sure she will," Hamilton said, urging his horse to a faster clip then looking over his shoulder as Adelina slowed the pace.

Adelina smiled an all-knowing smile as if she enjoyed the banter between the two men, one extremely protective the other insufferable. She winked at James, and he returned the gesture, understanding what she was saying.

She slowed her horse so she rode beside him, "You have to understand how protective he is of me."

"I believe I appreciate that emotion," James said laughing.

"Of course you do, you have Tavia."

"You two in love?"

She shrugged slim delicate shoulders. "I don't know. We haven't figured it out yet."

"Since you carry his child, perhaps it would be prudent to figure it out," James challenged her.

"You're a fine one to talk. Where Tavia is concerned, have you figured it out? I don't believe your marriage is valid, correct me if I'm wrong. Tavia never signed her name to the papers. It seems you should correct that error as soon as humanly possible."

"You're having Hamilton's child but you don't know if you love him?" he asked, trying to solve the puzzle of her words.

"Again, I don't know if I love him or if love even exists. It seems we can't keep our hands to ourselves when we're alone. I believe one would call that lust."

"Thought about the signatures once we returned to London and she knew what everyone else including you knew. Your life isn't the only one that has been threatened."

"Tavia?"

"And myself. A man we slighted before we set sail took it as an insult and tried to drown us. Almost succeeded too."

"Is Tavia alright? I need to see her. We've so much to talk about."

"We are hiding at the Montgomerie estate along with her cousin, Larena, and The Duchess. Since we are headed in that direction, you will see her. When I left, she was chilled to the bone and had a fever. I could do nothing more there. Her sister attended her. I opted to search for our would be killer."

"Bloody hell, I hope she's like a cat and has nine lives. It seems she's used up two already."

"And all of them when she was in my care, my protection."

"Don't worry too much about that. Hamilton feels much the same about me. He thinks he has to be there for me. I would have managed on my own without him, although I'm truly glad he was there to help. James, don't tell him I said that. His ego," she scrunched her face. "It will go to his head."

~ * ~

Tavia and Ella sat on the veranda facing the gardens watching Ella's baby boy play with his toys. Tea and scones with marmalade had been set out for a midday snack.

Tavia loved watching the small boy play. They named him Ashcroft; much too big of a name for this tiny little man.

"He is so adorable," Tavia said, wishing she had the strength to get down to his level and play.

"Don't you ever tell Ash that," Ella warned laughing. "He'll be just like his father and will let the compliment go to his head. In short he'll be insufferable."

Tavia laughed with her sister. "Aren't all men just like that? You compliment them and they strut like peacocks around the room."

"On a more serious note, do you think they've found out anything? They've been absent all day. I'm beginning to worry," Ella said.

Tavia clenched her jaw, understanding the gut reaction to the fear surrounding all of them.

"Well, just look at little Ashcroft. He's so cute with his pudgy little cheeks. Don't you just want to pinch them?" The Duchess strode onto the veranda, Larena and Scarlett following, breaking the tension with her comment.

Tavia and Ella gave each other a knowing look, but Ella didn't repeat her response to Tavia's statement about her little boy, even though she was pretty sure The Duchess would agree with the statement.

"I see you had my lemon bars made," The Duchess sat down and poured a cup of tea. "Would've preferred brandy though." She picked up her favorite snack.

"We have brandy. I'll go get it, Aunty," Ella said.

The Duchess tapped her cane. "Of course you won't do that. Tea is fine. Besides we've a wedding to plan. It needs to be just as nice as Ella's without all the drama."

"Who's?" All three girls responded, staring at The Duchess then Larena. "We're both married."

"Yours of course, Tavia. We can have it here if Drake is amenable. I've written to the families and I've given everyone enough time to find their way to London for the nuptials. However, Amorica and Damian are already on their way. They thought it was a fine time to visit. Their two adorable children are a bit older now, and they feel the trip will be easier. Tira and Aidan won't be coming for reasons we can easily guess. Ravyn says she will stay at home also."

"My wedding?" Tavia asked, surprised that was The Duchess' intent. "We were wed in Malaga." Tavia had thought all along all she had to do was change the X to Tavia Hepburn to make this legal.

The Duchess leaned toward Tavia, holding her hand in hers and patting it as if she was a small child. "That was no wedding. You must have something nice with your family and friends in attendance to make sure you sign the proper documents. You need all the frills, and I need to do this for all of my charges if I can."

"I agree with Aunty," Ella said smiling. "You must have a proper wedding gown you can hand down to a girl child if you have one and the memories to share. The recollections are everything. Although I pray your memories will be much nicer than mine and that no one poisons the wine."

Tavia remembered James and how tall and handsome he was at Ella's wedding. She wished the first time she saw him that he was to be the one ushering her down the aisle at her sister's wedding and she hoped she could dance with him.

But Drake's brother cut the dancing short. He was the man who had not been invited and who had threatened them all.

"Really I don't need all that. It pleases me though you would take my feelings into consideration. I'm sure James doesn't want to marry me again. Honestly, I'm not sure he wanted to marry me the first time."

Larena tilted her head slightly, "Of course he wanted to marry you in Malaga. He's not the kind of man who does something he doesn't want to do. You really should have a proper wedding. I agree with Aunty and Ella. You are outvoted."

"James will not be pleased. He doesn't like things like that," Tavia told them, wondering if she was right about what James liked and didn't like and that perhaps she protested a bit too much.

"You don't understand your husband at all. He loves you so he would want you to be happy, and if a wedding would make you happy, then..." Ella let the sentence end itself.

She didn't know if he loved her, he'd never said so. "He's already spent so much money on the townhouse and furnishings. I would have to have a wedding dress and flowers and a cake and food...the list will go on and on."

"Pshaw," Aunt Charlotte said, waving her hand in the air. "He has more than enough funds to pay for all of that and more with enough left over to purchase another fleet of ships, cargo included. Child, there is nothing to worry about except that madman Edwin McMasters. Once he is put to rest, there will only be smooth sailing ahead for the two of you"

"So we're all agreed there will be a beautiful wedding, and we're all planning it," Larena said, clapping her hands together in apparent delight.

"Who's wedding?" Eveleen McLellan stepped onto the veranda, her voice filled with curiosity.

"Tavia's!" Larena and Ella exclaimed as they raced to hug their cousin. "Tavia and James are going to have a real wedding," Ella said. "Isn't that just grand?"

"And yours. You and Logan should also have a proper wedding," Aunty Charlotte, said a crooked grin on her face.

"Mine?" Eveleen questioned, "I've been married over a year and I'm pregnant. I don't need to walk down the aisle again. It was horrid the first time, and I don't want to take a chance on a second time."

"Another child. I can hardly wait. When are you due? The baby can play with little Ash," Ella said.

"October, I believe." Eveleen appeared confused, looking between her cousins and The Duchess. "I had a wedding at McLellan castle, in case you all forgot that fact."

"Yes you did but you were traumatized before and it lasted approximately twenty minutes, maybe less if the accounts I've heard are correct." Charlotte bit into a lemon bar, powdered sugar coating her lips. "Am I correct?" Aunt Charlotte appeared pleased to her core.

"You're right. But... But Logan won't like it."

"He has no say besides, as I just told Tavia, if it makes you happy it will please him too."

"So," Ella clapped her hands together. "We have a double wedding to plan. Much more to do in any case. We'll have to go to the dressmakers tomorrow and the florist to order the flowers, yellows and greens. We need to have two cakes, smaller ones of course."

Tavia exchanged a panicked look with her cousin and mouthed, "What have we gotten ourselves into?"

"While we could probably say no to Logan and James, it seems The Duchess and Larena are a bit more obstinate."

"Ladies," Tavia said, clapping her hands to garner their attention. "We cannot do anything outside of this home until Edwin is captured. We have to stay put and stay where we are safe, as James would say."

Larena turned to Ella, "Do you have any fashion plates here? We could begin to look at dresses. I'm sure I would have fun."

"I don't need to do that. I want one that looks as close to Ella's dress as possible. I know I shouldn't copy it, but I loved it and with perhaps a few tweaks here and there to make it mine, that's the dress I want," Tavia said.

"I see you're slowly giving into our plans." Ella said happily. "What about you, Eveleen?"

Tavia glanced at Eveleen once again and shrugging her shoulders Tavia said, "I don't think we have a choice. The two of you will go forward with or without our permission."

"I don't want another wedding," Eveleen tried to protest. "I don't want the extravagance."

"Do you want different memories of that day?" Larena asked pointedly. "We've all heard stories about what transpired on the island the day of the wedding as well as your terrible hangover the next morning. Logan practically dragged you out of the castle on the morning after. I doubt if you even had an appropriate wedding night. Now you can do everything properly."

"You shouldn't listen to gossip," Eveleen said, staring at her feet. "It wasn't all that bad, and I really don't want to talk about that day and night or the next morning."

"True enough but you and I both know there is fact in the rumors and now we have a chance to give you and Logan the wedding the two of you should have had in the first place. Your flight to the McLellan land to hide from Logan kept us from planning a ceremony and reception you deserved."

"I told you," Tavia said softly, "It's best to just give in and pretend it's what you want."

"My dear nieces, I—we only want the best for both of you. If you truly don't want us to celebrate your commitment to the men you love, then stop us now and there will be no weddings."

"I'm fine with the wedding," Tavia said, looking to Eveleen, "It will be easier if it's a double wedding."

"I'm fine then, too, if Aunty will tell my husband. We've brought Chianti from Tuscany so the wine will not be tainted. We won't even open the crates until it's ready to be served."

"Coward," Charlotte laughed. "My sister raised a woman who's afraid to ask her husband for a proper wedding. I'm only teasing. I completely understand why you don't want to ask your young man."

"Well, it was your idea not mine," Eveleen shot back clearly miffed. "And you're right. If I want a proper wedding, Logan will stand beside me and I do believe he's regretted the hasty marriage as well as the lack of a wedding night. We finally worked through the events on the island, and our relationship is stronger because of it."

"Where is Logan?" Tavia asked, expecting to see him walk through the door at any time.

"He heard James and Drake were looking for someone, and he rode out to meet them," Eveleen said, sitting down and pouring herself a cup of tea. "What's that all about?"

"Edwin McMasters tried to kill Tavia and James the night before last. He nearly succeeded with Tavia. She's just recovering from a severe chill and fever. That's why she's sitting in the chair all wrapped up in a blanket when the sun is shining and it's warm."

"Franco." Eveleen murmured, her face turning white. "He tried to kill me and Logan.

"Franco?" They all chorused.

With a huge sigh Eveleen began her story. "Before the revolution, Franco's family owned the vineyard in Bordeaux that Logan bought. He held a grudge, believing he could own the land again, thinking it was rightfully his."

"I'm assuming Logan wasn't about to give up his property," Larena said, leaning forward seemingly eager to hear the recounting of this story.

"You are right. Of course, the land was his, but the new French government wasn't about to sell it to a man who was once a noble," Eveleen said. "In any case, he pursued us from Bordeaux to Paris overland and before that he pirated two of Logan's ships, stealing the wine in hopes of bankrupting him."

"My dear nieces, why do all of you have to make your lives so difficult? I would that you all could settle down, have children to torment you as you all have tormented me and let me spoil them all just as your mother's would have done if they'd lived."

Larena rose and hugged her aunt, "You don't have to worry about me. I don't want all that excitement. I don't like excitement at all. And you won't have to fight me for you to plan a wedding for me. I'm already looking at fashion plates. That should please you, Aunty."

"It does, except you have no real beau yet. From what I've heard, you're too political for Gavin, and he doesn't like extricating you from lampposts."

"Pshaw," Larena waved her hand in the air, grinning. "That is nothing. Actually, I think he enjoyed it."

The girls cut her off, laughing at her mimic of Aunt Charlotte.

Larena began again. "He likes the excitement. And when he pulls me down, he doesn't hesitate to let his fingers linger in certain places," Larena said before covering her mouth with her hands and staring red-faced at The Duchess. "I didn't mean to say that."

"You know my thoughts and my history." The Duchess tapped her cane on the veranda floor as if emphasizing her point. "That young man appreciates your body, but he must also appreciate your mind as well as your character. I won't ever judge you, but don't let that man take liberties you don't want him to take. It is your body, remember that. You can always say no."

"He disagrees with everything I do and how I feel about those people who just want decent wages for their grueling day of work." Larena crossed her arms in front of her, appearing to pout. "I will not let him change my mind."

"Are you sure he disagrees?" Tavia asked, "He might just be concerned for your safety. I realize now that was James' motivation when we were on his ship. Every time I defied his orders, he moved heaven and earth to keep me safe."

"Truly, he doesn't understand the plight of the poor, but I'm not sure he disagrees with me. I don't know what he thinks. He just doesn't want me in the middle of the fray. He says I'll end up in Newgate Prison."

"Perhaps you should ask him what he thinks," Ella said softly.

"He's so busy litigating some case he won't talk about that he barely has time to see me. He keeps telling me it will be over soon, and he will lavish his attention on me." She paused to look at all her cousins sitting in the warmth and enjoying the sunshine. "I'm not sure I believe him. I think there will always be a case that comes before me."

"Some men put work before their ladies, but most will lavish attention on them whenever they can. What has he done with you?"

Larena squirmed in her chair as if there was something more she didn't want to tell her cousins. "He might if he loved me, but we really have spent very little time together."

"Hopefully, he is speaking the truth, and when this litigation is over, he'll change his ways." Tavia said, trying to reassure her cousin. "Then you should be prepared for a myriad of difficult decisions. You have to learn to think with your head because as The Duchess has told you, your beau will not."

"Men don't change their ways, but you can improve them, and perhaps sway them a tiny bit to your way of thinking," Adelina said, waking onto the veranda.

"Adelina! You're here." Tavia wanted to race to her, but Ella sensing what she wanted put a hand out to restrain her. "Why?"

"I was in trouble and a friend of mine helped me out," she said, "May I sit down and have some tea? I'm truly exhausted."

"Of course, but it seems you might want food then a bath. I'll have Alma show you to a room and bring you hot water as soon as you've eaten." She paused, "You seem to be a friend of Tavia's, but I doubt if that's why you're here."

"I am Tavia's friend. At least I hope I am. As to why I am here you need to ask your husband, Drake. He will either tell you or not. I have no idea. And thank you for your hospitality. I'm Adelina."

"You were my friend and talked to me, gave me advice when I had no one else. You saved my life by finding James and bringing him to the ship. Thank you. But I was worried about you when you left."

"All that, when I wanted to ask why I had to defer to my husband as to why she was here," Ella said, looking between the two ladies.

"I work for him," Adelina said.

"How so? And why are you here?" Ella pursued.

"Because I work for him and needed to tell him that I quit." It seemed Adelina tried to hide her emotions.

James, Drake, Logan and another man no one save Adelina

seemed to know strode into the room. They were all in dire need of a bath and clean clothes. The fourth man seemed as filthy as Adelina. James strode to Tavia and easily lifting her in his arms, he sat down in her chair and set her on his lap.

"How are you doing?" he whispered.

"Much better" She felt his gentle kiss on her cheek and leaned into him content to watch the drama unfold in front of her.

"Perhaps you and I should discuss this in private," Drake looked to his wife.

"I don't think so. Everyone here will discover what you want to tell me sooner or later."

"What if I tell you it is a matter of national security. The information is secret."

"Well, it is no longer," Adelina said. "We quit so you can tell them what we did if you want to. Of course that will be divulging, it seems, a secret you are keeping from your wife."

"The secret is for her safety. The less she knows about what I do for the government the safer she is."

Ella stood, hands on hips. "Drake Montgomerie, how dare you tell me you are no longer a spy when you are obviously lying to me."

"I'm not lying, my *petite rayon de soleil*. I'm not a spy."

"He just tells the rest of us where to go and what to do. He's the boss," Adelina laughed. "And a damn good one."

"Until he sent her into a lion's den where she almost lost her life," Hamilton added. "I'm Hamilton Winthrop the third, if anyone wants to know."

"It was not that close. I left before they knew," Adelina said. "I'm good at what I do and you know that."

"Knew what?"

"Thought they knew," Adelina corrected, seeming to delight in the men's confusion.

"Semantics," Drake gritted out.

"Darling," Ella stood by him, bringing his head close to her then whispered, "Adelina is obviously pregnant."

"Pregnant. Why didn't you tell me?" Drake glanced from Adelina to Hamilton then back, clearly distressed by the news. "You need to get married."

"He doesn't love me, Drake," Adelina said.

"Addie, Drake is right. You carry my child. We've been on the run so I haven't had time to rectify this situation and marry the mother of my child. I wanted to propose to you when we reached my home and give you my grandmother's ring, but it seems I should propose now."

"You don't love me." Adelina said, stubbornly folding her hands in her lap.

"And you don't love me, but I certainly could spend the rest of my life with you and my child. I wouldn't mind having more than one. I adore the process needed to create one," he winked at Addie.

Adelina set her cup of tea on the table before rising. "Is my bath ready? I need to go somewhere that has fresh air."

"Alma, would you take Adelina to her room."

No," Hamilton cut in and taking Addie's hand in his, got down on one knee. "Addie, will you marry me?"

A hush settled around the room as everyone waited for the answer.

Addie looked to Tavia who nodded then whispered, "If it's what you want."

"Yes," Addie said.

A cheer went up around the courtyard.

"You've made me the happiest man in the world," he rose, "and I promise you a ring as soon as I can get it."

"I don't need a ring. I'll be very happy to marry you with or without one." Addie said.

"Come with me," Alma motioned for Adelina to follow her.

"Men," Adelina mumbled. "They are so obtuse."

"He loves you," Alma murmured as Tavia watched them leave the room, her heart pounding.

"It seems we have three couples to wed. In one month all of you will find your happiness and pray to God your lives will be at peace," The Duchess said. "In two days if Edwin is caught, we'll meet at the dressmakers."

~ * ~

"Bloody, bloody, what the...how dare..." Edwin mumbled to himself and pushed the horses harnessed to the carriage harder. "Lights, lights everywhere, I don't know where...got to get rid of her. Don't have time to stay here."

The moan in the back of the carriage sent him searching the river for a place to go but there was nothing. His heart seemed to pound in his throat. He turned the carriage inland, remembering the cottage on the outskirts of his land and the escape route to his home.

"What to do, what..." His heart raced, the thrill of the moment sending his emotions to an escalating peak. He'd have to think of something else, outsmart the oppositions. Bow Street Runners were imbeciles.

He grinned, thinking of what else he could do with the woman in the back, things he didn't have time for with the others. "Such a hurry, always such a hurry, take my time with her.

"There it is. Haven't been here since I took my first debutant on the dirty floor. Should have had the Hepburn girl. Would have it wasn't for Macmurra. I took care of them. Drowned them in the river, I did."

All he could see in front of him was the dark outline and shadow of the small hut. The distance didn't appear to be all that far, but it seemed to take him forever to get there. When he turned his head, he could still see tiny dots of lights bouncing around in the darkness.

Eventually, he pulled to a stop in front of the tiny cottage. He jumped from the driver's seat and rounded the vehicle.

"We're here," he said before grabbing the girl by the shoulders and hauling her from the carriage. Her tiny groan gave him a pleasure he couldn't describe, but it was all-consuming and sent his emotions spinning in too many directions. It was a feeling he only got when he killed.

"We can talk here," he pulled the gag from her mouth before he drug her over his shoulder and strode inside. He let her down roughly on the hard floor then searched for something to brighten the room before thinking better of it. If he lit candles the searchers by the river might see the light and come looking to satisfy any curiosity they might have.

"Don't want to talk? Maybe it's the gag?" he asked, noticing her silence and pale features. "Maybe you will later. Going to put the carriage in the barn. I'll be back before you can miss me. I promise." He left, enjoying this slight diversion. He could leave her here as long as he wanted. Even if he didn't get back to her because of the runners, she'd die.

But that wouldn't give him the rush he liked to feel when he watched his victim's heads disappear beneath the water.

He hummed softly as he led the horses and the carriage inside the barn. Taking his time, he cared for the horses, stroking them and making sure they had water. Then he returned.

The girl had scooted next to the fireplace and was trying to cut through the ropes binding her wrists. He pushed her with his foot, laughing as she toppled to the floor, landing face first before moving away from him, her eyes wide with terror.

He bent close to her, "I'm not going to let you get away no matter how hard you try. You're mine for as long as you live." Gently he stroked her cheek, pushing errant strands of hair behind her ears. "You're going to die tomorrow if not today." He removed the gag, needing to hear her plead.

"Please," she whispered so quiet he could barely hear her one word.

"Please myself? I just might do that. Would you like me to make love to you before I kill you?"

She had pushed herself against a chair and could not move farther away. She was shaking her head in seeming denial, "No, I wouldn't like that," she moistened her lips, "what have I done to you?"

"Nothing, darling, absolutely nothing. You were just in the wrong place at the right time. I wanted someone else, someone who snubbed me but you were there instead. Would you snub me?"

"No."

"Ah, you're a pretty little liar. Your eyes tell me a different story. If you let me fuck you, I might let you live. Is it worth the gamble? A night of pleasure in exchange for your life?" he asked her, wondering why he would give her a chance to live. But the ploy suited him. He would have his way with her before he taught her how to swim.

She nodded, her breaths coming in short little gasps. "Yes," she breathed in a lungful of air. "I would take that gamble."

He smiled at her, bending to settle his lips on hers, sweeping his tongue across her mouth. He felt the terror well up inside her, smelled the fear emanating from her. She was far from willing, still...

"You don't seem to want me. You're going to have to try better than this if you're going to win your life back." He sat back on his haunches, watching her. Rape had never been his thing. He wanted to have sex with her, but he needed her to be a willing party. "No, this just won't do at all. You may tell me yes, but your body is telling me no."

"I want you," she told him, "really I do. I want you to make love to me. I want to live."

"Ah but there's the problem. You just want to live. You don't want me deep inside you. Tell me, sweetheart. Are you a virgin? I can find out easy enough so don't lie to me."

Her eyes widened further and her breaths coming in short tiny pants. "Yes." she barely whispered.

"Such a shame. You will die before you have a lover. You see, it won't be me, simply because you don't really want me. You don't even like me."

"You can kill but not rape? I will let you have your way with me if you let me live, and I won't tell anyone about you. I promise."

She seemed to gain courage when she thought he would give her the gift of life. He liked that in her.

"Show me," he said and moved close enough to her she could touch him with her mouth. "Let me feel how much you want me."

"I, I don't know what to do. I've never..."

"You will have to be a fast learner. If you convince me you want me, I might untie you. Kiss me like you want me."

She leaned closer to him, placing her lips on his for a second before moving away. "Will that do?"

"Such a chaste kiss. I suppose you are truly an innocent. Touch my lips with your tongue and I will give you a surprise."

She did and he sucked it into his mouth, biting her with his teeth, enjoying her tiny cry of pain. He didn't give her a chance to withdraw from him, holding her head close he drove his tongue inside her mouth, touched her, and breathed in her essence.

"I like you," he said, moving away from her. "Perhaps I can train you and in time you might want me. Right now you don't. You're not a good actress."

He decided to keep her with him instead of leaving her here. After all she was a needed diversion to the men searching for him. Retrieving the gag, he put it on, "Now, don't worry. I'm going to take you to my home. I've changed my mind. You're not going to die tonight." He swept her over his shoulder and striding to the barn, he found the entrance to the tunnel that led to his home. It was an old escape tunnel used in case of fire or intruders from times past. Lined with cobwebs, it had not been used in decades. As he walked, he batted the spider webs from his face.

Chapter Ten

Dinner was served; venison, salmon, beans, asparagus and more servings than anyone could possibly eat. Logan provided the Chianti from his new vineyard in Tuscany. The vineyard had been a gift from Eveleen. Richard, Charlotte's son, better known as Roc, won the winery in a game of chance but didn't want it. Charlotte sold the deed to Eveleen for a meager sum and she gifted Logan with the winery.

"There are to be three weddings at once. How is that going to work?" James asked, sitting back in chair and watching his wife who seemed to only pick at her food. He didn't know how he felt about a second wedding, but if Tavia wanted one he'd stand beside her.

"I don't know. It depends on what the girls want. Everything is up to them," Aunt Charlotte grinned at them as she smiled benevolently at her nieces. "It's hard to say if something like this has ever been done before." She helped herself to salmon and more asparagus before holding her glass, silently asking Logan to pour her more. "This is very good."

"We'll have to figure it out," Ella said, looking from couple to couple, finally stopping at Addie and Hamilton. "I suppose the best thing would be to have all three couples go down the aisle at once. They can speak their vows at the same time."

"Who thought of this strange extravaganza?" Logan asked, sipping the Chianti as he gazed at Eveleen with adoring eyes. "How do you feel about a second wedding," he asked his wife.

"It certainly wasn't me," Addie said indignantly. "I'm not sure I want a wedding even now."

"Or me," Tavia said, placing her hand on James'. "I think we should discuss this instead of letting Auntie Charlotte, even though we all know she has the best intentions, make us all wed in a single ceremony.

"I can not make anyone wed, nor do I want to." The Duchess

defended herself and her intentions.

"Do any of us want to have a triple wedding?" Eveleen asked, searching the room for answers. "I'm not sure how all of this happened. Seemed we arrived separately, and I think Tavia was the first because Aunty wants to make sure her marriage to James is legal, but I think all she has to do is put her name to the paper and get rid of the X ."

"That's the problem. We don't really know if it will be legal," Drake said.

"You're all wrong. The only real wedding Aunt Charlotte got to plan was mine, and it was a disaster from the beginning to the end. Ravyn's doesn't count since it was in the parlor and an accident. She would like to have the chance to help plan a wedding that goes ahead without a hitch. Well, maybe not the wedding night," Ella looked at Drake lovingly. "The very end was nice."

"Is that all you can say about the wedding night, nice? I would think there are better words to describe what happened in our bed," Drake asked his wife, sounding piqued. yet grinning from ear to ear as is he was remembering every detail fondly.

"In public, yes. Nice is the only word I plan on using." Ella patted the top of his hand. "You already know how I felt. You shouldn't need your ego propped up. Now, no more talk about our wedding night until we go to bed this evening and you can show me."

Drake puffed up his chest. James was sure Drake didn't realize how obvious this was, and he was pretty sure what was going to happen tonight in their bedroom would be more than nice. Hopefully, the same would happen in his. It had been a long time since he'd made love to his wife.

"You need to eat more food," he spoke to Tavia, hoping she was the only one who heard what he had to say. "You need your strength." One eyebrow rose for only Tavia to see.

He was sure she understood by the blush growing on her cheeks.

"I've eaten all my stomach will hold. You don't want me to get sick, do you?" Tavia asked.

"No, of course not." James smiled at his wife's words, still hoping Tavia would want to renew their lovemaking.

"Thank you." Shyly, she looked at her hands then at him, her eyes seeming to shine with passion.

"Perhaps you'd like some wine from Tuscany, a little Chianti?" James placed a gentle hand on her shoulder.

"All of you are talking as if I'm not in the room," The Duchess said. impatiently tapping her cane. "I'm here and we all know who had the idea for the three weddings. I did," she acknowledged without hesitation. "I agree that they should happen at the same time. Any other way would not make an iota of sense. We will go to the dressmakers tomorrow," she said, moving the timeline up, "if Edwin is found. If not, then the dressmaker will come to us."

"She will do that?" Larena asked, obviously not understanding the power The Duchess held in this town. "In any case it would be much nicer for her to come here. Since two of the brides involved are in a family way," she said, smiling prettily.

"Offered enough money, she will do most anything for me. It will not be much work for her. Drake will make sure she has safe passage to and from the house."

"Three dresses, not much work?" Eveleen asked as if anticipating the fittings. "I would like a nice dress. I don't even remember what I wore during my wedding at the castle. Everything was done so hastily. I believe my maid picked out my best dress."

"I remember vividly. You were so beautiful, you stole my heart even before that day and have kept it ever since. Indeed, I believe you stole my heart the first time I saw you at the ball where Drake and I had to make a hasty exit in order to save a friend's life. If The Duchess had found him, he would have been keelhauled on his own ship."

"Yes, when you rushed away to save Jarrett?" Eveleen seemed to recall that night.

"That's the time." Logan said, crossing his arms across his chest, grinning. "The night was really quite fun, exhilarating."

"What about you, Drake? When did I steal your heart?" Ella asked, tilting her head in a flirtatious manner, seeming to know she put him on the spot. "Was it that night too?"

"You've caught me in a place I'm not sure I want to be. If pressed,

I was too worried about Jarrett that first time I saw you, but I know for a fact when you first put on the pants and shirt, you totally stole my heart. I was yours from that day forward." He paused. "No, I'm wrong. It was the day I saw the drawings. No, when we talked about different types of love..."

Ella put her hand over his mouth. "Hush, Larena is sitting here. Besides you can't talk about things like that in public."

He let his head back and roared with laughter, the others joining with them. Even The Duchess chortled with glee.

"You, Ella, are precious, my *petite rayon de soleil*. Never change, promise me," he said, bending over and planting what appeared to be a soul stealing kiss on her lips. "Every time you do something outrageous, you bind my heart and soul to you even more."

Ella looked down for a moment before she graced him with one of the most beautiful smiles James had ever seen. Only Tavia's smile was more beautiful, touching his heart deeply every time she favored him with one.

"Back to the dressmaker and the business at hand," The Duchess started in again then turned to Addie. "We will have to get your measurements, my dear, unless of course our dressmaker has them on record." She slanted Hamilton a glance.

"I don't need anything special," Addie said, also looking to Hamilton as if she wanted him to kidnap her and take her away from this strange situation. "I'm sure anything will do."

Hamilton stepped forward saying, "I have her measurements with my dressmaker. I've bought her some things over the last few years. In fact, I believe it's the same shop as yours. Drake recommended it to me when I found myself in need of one." He placed Addie's hand in his. "Just as Eveleen and Tavia, you need a dress of your dreams."

"What about you, Hamilton? When did Addie steal your heart? We've all confessed. It's your turn now." Drake nodded to Hamilton.

"I would guess the first time she drew a gun on me. She didn't know I was there to help if she needed me. I guess she thought I was the enemy."

"It was no mistake. At the time you were my enemy." Addie took her hand from his, slanting him a frown. "You've always known I can take care of myself, as Drake has known since he recruited me."

"Masquerading as your foe, and I explained myself several times afterwards. You almost shot me," he accused. "I could have died and where would you be if I had."

She shot him a look that said *you'll answer for that when we have some privacy*. Then she told him bluntly, "I wouldn't be pregnant, and we wouldn't be planning a triple wedding."

Immediately, he looked contrite, his dark brows drawing together. "I thought you were happy. Was I wrong?"

She looked away before returning his gaze. "I'm not unhappy. It's just so much has happened in the last few months that have spiraled out of my control. This all has turned out to be a nightmare, and I can barely wait until it is over and we can find some peace."

"As soon as Edwin is..."

She stood up, hand on the table. "I've heard that for almost two days now. *As Soon as Edwin*. When is this going to end? We've been on the run from a crazy Spaniard, slept on the ground too many nights to count and I'm so exhausted I can barely keep my eyes open. I'm going to bed if no one minds." She started for the door, but she stopped, her hand on her head, placing a hand on Hamilton's chair, seeming to steady herself.

"I'm going with you." Hamilton rose and wrapping his arm around Addie's waist, "We'll see you in the morning. Have a good evening and hopefully we will wake to good news."

The Duchess tapped her cane on the floor to get everyone's attention. "That's normal. It seems she has had a bit of a dizzy spell. Of course Addie is tired and I'm guessing you are too, Eveleen. We should all retire to the parlor to finish the discussions about the wedding or go to bed."

Charlotte rose, but instead of the parlor she headed for her bedchamber. Over her shoulder, she said, "I'm going to bed. I don't have as much energy as I used to have."

"I think we've overwhelmed even your aunt," Drake said. "Should we go to the parlor and continue this conversation?"

"I'm not tired." Ella accepted Drake's hand. The couples left and Larena joined them in the parlor.

Drake stood at the sideboard, "Whiskey or brandy?" he asked.

"I'd like brandy," Tavia said.

"Even though it will put you to sleep," James said, taking two glasses, one for himself and one for Tavia. "I would like my wife awake this evening."

"It might make me more relaxed," she said, moistening her lips, a silent invitation he hoped for him.

He wasn't sure what to make of her comment though. It had been so long since he dared touch her he was afraid he was reading this wrong. "Me too," he raised his glass to her, standing behind the chair she sat in, his knuckles touching the back of her neck.

Everyone seemed to stare at them. He cleared his throat before speaking. "Do you think they have Edwin in custody yet? Have you heard anything?" he turned to Drake.

"Nothing so far. I'd like to think the runners would contact us as soon as they have them. I still have men with the investigation."

"So, we haven't heard anything yet." James was unwilling to go to bed and sleep when that man still eluded the law, yet if he had to rest and to make sure his wife slept and regained the energy she lost during the trauma of the last few days, he would.

"No." Drake sipped his whiskey, confirming the fact Edwin was still at large and a threat to all of them.

Yet, for a moment, it seemed their wishes had been heard. "Sir," one of Drake's men stood in the hallway. "We have news or perhaps no news."

"What is it?" Drake asked.

"We think McMasters escaped our surveillance tonight, and there are numerous rumors that a young debutant has been abducted. But the man neither left his house nor returned to it. We were at the dumpsite all day and night. He didn't come. Men are still positioned there to capture him if he shows up, but I believe he saw us."

"How obvious are they?" Drake asked, knowing the answer before his man said anything. He'd expected this investigation to be conducted with the same expertise the missions he set his spies on were conducted. Alas, it didn't seem the runners were experienced in intrigue.

"Well, it wasn't well done. Anyone would have seen the activity had they been nearby, and if they had nefarious purposes, they would have raced the other way. I'm not at all surprised he didn't show up at the embankment. What I am surprised about is how he got out of his house without anyone seeing him. He must have an alternate entrance."

Drake took another sip of his drink. "We have an escape route through a tunnel from this house to a cottage on the outskirts of my property. I wonder if McMasters has the same type of tunnel. This one was built eons ago when there were invading armies."

To his man, "Don't speak to the runners unless you have to. They have bungled this and Edwin should be in custody by now. I don't want to waste any more time. Check the surrounding property and see if there is some kind of barn or small home that could be used for the purpose of escape. Report back to me when you find it. We'll figure out a way to seal the tunnel so he has no recourse but to use his front door."

The man nodded and stepped from the room.

"You really think he used something like that to getaway and kidnap another girl? "Ella asked, leaning into her husband for comfort. "I can hardly believe this horrible man has not been stopped yet."

"I do suppose there is another woman at risk, but this time we'll be ready for him. I don't want to believe the runners bungled this operation, but somehow Edwin knew where they were. He's going to need a new place to leave his victims, and I don't want to even think about what he's done or is doing to this young woman he took. He would have to go upriver."

"Is there anything we can do right now?" James asked, willing to confront the man at his home if necessary, his fists clenching at his sides. "I want Edwin McMasters to pay for what he did to Tavia."

"We brought the authorities into this, and now we have to wait and pray the runners do whatever is necessary to save his new victim. We can't take over the hunt for Edwin until the runners withdraw," Drake spoke up.

"So we need to stay here and wait." It seemed Logan needed

reassurances just as much as he did. "I've never been someone who could sit and wait. This is preposterous. Can't you use your influence with the government to rectify this?"

"None of us are the kind of men who like to wait, but in this case we have no other options."

"It's really too bad we brought the authorities into this. If we hadn't, I think together we could bring this to an end tonight." Drake nodded to Ella, "I'm going to bed and hope the rest of you will do the same. If there is no news in the morning, we'll make plans of our own."

James stood and, stretching his hand to Tavia, he gave a silent invitation. "Would you like to go to our bedchamber?" His hopes for tonight hinged on Tavia's health, and if she was strong enough for lovemaking. Some color had returned to her cheeks and her smile seemed sincere rather than forced.

"I'm ready," she placed her hand in his, the smile he just thought of appearing on her face.

Thinking better of his proposal and not wanting her to spend energy walking to the room, he swept her into his arms, placing a chaste kiss on the cheek. "How are you feeling?"

It seemed she chose to ignore his question. Instead, she turned to look at him and touch his beard then drew her finger across his mouth. He touched the tip of her finger with his tongue and delighted in the tiny sound coming from her throat. "I think I've forgiven you everything. What about you? Will you ever admit that you should have told me all you knew?"

"There was nothing to forgive where you are concerned." He paused, leaning on the banister to catch her lips with his. She opened for him and responded with the passion he remembered and longed for. He pulled away, wishing they were in the bedroom. Then taking the rest of the steps two at a time, he reached the room. Inside, he couldn't wait, seemed to need her now. Her hands wound into his hair and pulled him closer.

He pressed her against the wall, his kisses trailing down her neck then back to whisper across her ear, his tongue darting inside.

"I need you, James. It's been too long. Why did we waste the time?"

"I don't know. We were foolish. Wrap your legs around my waist." James trailed kisses across her collarbone then lower to her cleavage, enticing and encouraging.

"Why?"

"Because you'll like what I'm going to do." He ran his fingers through her hair, dislodging the pins and watching the dark length fall in beautiful disarray across the top of her shoulders.

Her throaty purr of encouragement gave him undeniable pleasures. With his hands free, he slowly pulled the tiny sleeves of her gown down her arms, watching as her breasts were finally exposed.

"So exquisite," he murmured.

James lowered his mouth to her breasts still covered by her chemise. His lips drew circles where ivory satin skin became a rosy enticement he was trying to resist for a few seconds longer. He stared at her beauty for several moments then looked to her passion filled eyes. She was ready for him, needed him as much as he did her.

"Do you want me?" His words meant to reassure himself that her needs were as great as his. Recriminations afterwards were not acceptable.

"No, I need you, James."

He moved away from the wall and quickly walked to the bed. They landed gently on the mattress, James bracing them with his arms. Rising above her, he slipped out of his shirt, her hands at the fastening of his buckskins.

"Oh, God, Tavia. You're so beautiful." He turned her, unfastening her dress and pulling it off. He placed tender kisses down her back and the dimples at the base of her spine as he slowly unlaced her corset revealing every inch of her to his gaze.

Her body responded to his attentions as she moved with each touch a soft moan vibrating from her lungs. Finally, she wore nothing but her stockings embellished with embroidered flowers at the top. She turned in his arms, naked to his gaze. He could resist no longer and settled his mouth on the tip of one breast, his fingers touching the other. He sucked and nibbled then very slowly he released her captive breast and admired the high ruby crown his mouth had created, before turning his attention to her other breast.

Her hands wound into his hair and tugged as her hips arced and enticed his pulsing rod. With her head thrown back, she pulled him tighter against her. He had not believed she was so strong. His hand rested near her heart and he felt the rapid beating.

Wanting more, his palm skimmed down her body and across her abdomen, pausing a moment to think about a child who might grow within her soon. Then he continued to glide over the dark curls he longed to comb with his fingertips, looking for the fragrant passion and the small bud he knew ached for his caress.

Gently, he pressed his hand between her legs. His fingers cupped around her softest flesh as his palm brushed languidly over the dark curls that no longer concealed Tavia's sultry core.

He continued, enjoying the cream spilling from her and the tiny sounds of pleasure she made with each new caress of his fingers. Finding the tiny nubbin between her feminine folds, he caressed until her body seemed to mindlessly respond.

His hand moved again, slowly, and her response spilled over, burning both of them with the sweetest type of flames. She made a sound deep in her throat as she lifted against his hand. He stroked again, needing to feel the sweet movement within her. He inserted one finger then two, bringing her higher with each new touch. He withdrew his fingers from her and quickly rising from the bed, he kicked off his boots and the r est of his clothing. Settling between her legs, he entered her slowly, enjoying each moment as well as the velvet sheath that now surrounded him. For more than two long months he'd wanted to feel her embracing him more than he wanted to breathe.

Need clenched savagely in James, making him groan as he withdrew then drove into her. With unleashed urgency, he increased the mounting pleasure, smoothing the heat of her response over her most sensitive flesh. When he caressed the nub of desire he had ca lled from her, she cried out with surprise and violent pleasure. His fingertips circled her aroused sensitive flesh, tugging at her, holding her captive for the hungry testing of his stimulated shaft.

He let out a deep primal cry of pleasure as he spilled his seed deep inside his wife. He held her for the moments they needed to calm from the tempestuous ride they just embarked upon. Rolling off her, he pulled her into his arms, wishing he risked telling her he loved her. Yet he didn't dare gamble it all, not now, not until he was sure she returned the sentiment.

"Tavia," he pulled away so he could look into her eyes and see the real feelings she could hide if he allowed her, "how do you feel?"

She closed her eyes and he spent a second fearing she would tell him to go away that they had resolved nothing between them. "I don't know. My heart beats so fast, almost out of control and you gave me such incredible pleasure. I feel boneless, unable to stand if I had to."

He grinned at her, her returning smile stealing his heart once again. Her body was perfect as was her mind. "You are amazing to me," he whispered. "Are you tired?"

"Exhausted," she told him "but..."

Footsteps thundered up the steps to their room. He pulled a cover over her and quickly slipped on his clothes. "It seems we are about to be disturbed. I hope it is good news or perhaps a call to action."

"What is it?" He opened the door, stepping into the hallway. He turned to Tavia. "Get some sleep. I've a feeling I won't be sharing the bed with you tonight."

"We've a lead on Edwin." Drake stood in the doorway. "Sorry to interrupt the two of you."

~ * ~

Tavia slept fitfully that night, waking to pound her pillow into shape every few hours. Nothing seemed to work. Sleep so very illusive. Every sound, every little movement of the curtains had her sitting up, listening and waiting for some sign of James. Eventually, as the sky began to lighten, she felt the dip of the bed and his strong arms pulling her close. She let a soft sigh escape her lips.

One large hand settled on her breast, teasing, exciting, giving her the pleasure she knew so well. "You need to sleep," she whispered. "This cannot be good for you."

"Not yet and no more than you," he gently swirled his tongue in her ear then let his lips and teeth work their magic.

"James," was all she could manage as he pulled her on top of him and she felt his hard length beneath her.

"Straddle me," he told her, his hands resting on her hips, lifting her so she understood what he wanted.

They made love and several minutes later, she lay next to him, his long slow breathing telling her perhaps he slept. She was cuddled in his arms and every time she attempted to move away, his arm would tighten around her. She needed to discover what happened, why he'd been called away.

She knew he didn't sleep, just rested. Every instinct she possessed told her she should let him sleep, but she wanted to know why Drake called him away when they'd just gone to bed after an exhausting day. What news about Edwin had sent the men from the house to some unknown meeting in the middle of the night?

"You're not sleeping," she spoke softly in case he really was, letting her fingertip draw a line along his arm.

"Neither are you." His hand rested possessively on her stomach. "You must take care of yourself."

"But I slept all night." She protested vehemently, knowing she lied. "Unlike you who was pulled from our bed and had no chance for slumber," she paused, "Did you catch him? Is it safe now?"

"No, to both," he sighed heavily.

She understood his frustration because she felt it too. Edwin had eluded so many for what seemed an eternity when only a few days had passed since their abduction.

"Did you find a home on the property? Did it have a tunnel?" She had been so sure that when he'd been called away in the middle of the night the news would be good.

"We did and sealed the entrance from the cottage then we stormed the house. There was no one there."

"Nothing? He wasn't there? What about the missing girl?"

"Ropes, a cold bath, a soiled dress, nothing more," he said, "but it was eerily strange. I felt as if someone watched me."

"I believe Edwin probably was spying on you. He will know you're alive. That won't make him happy. A lot of the older homes have secret panels with just as secret openings and passages within the home. If you go back and check the rooms for hidden openings, you will probably find something."

"I will pass that on to Drake," he said, running his hand along her bare thigh before traveling higher.

She felt his lips, teeth and tongue on her shoulder. Shivering with the surreal sensations he evoked and mercuric rise of heat within, she whispered softly. "You've not had enough of me?" she queried.

"Never get enough of you, Tavia," he murmured, his nimble fingers seducing, creating the magical enchantment that always existed between them. "Every time I look at you, I want you."

"I would suspect Edwin has moved on. He'd be really stupid if he remained in the house after the runners and Drake's men invaded it." She wanted to turn in his arms and touch him and explore every part of him. She needed to feel his strength and the corded muscles that were so much a part of him beneath her fingers.

"Everyone has left; Drake's men, the Bow Street Runners. There is no surveillance at his home or the cottage," he murmured, his finger roaming close to her core.

She couldn't suppress the tiny sound emerging from her or the movements of her hips against him. "If I were him, I would have left. I would find somewhere else to live. I'd run to a different country."

"You're right. When we left, the carriage was still at the cottage along with a horse. I've got to admit though, I don't have the energy to chase after that man right now."

"You need to sleep, not make love to me," she told him, understanding at this point in time sleep for him was not an option, not while she lay in bed with him. She would have to leave.

"You don't want me to love you?" he said through a yawn.

"Of course I do, but..." She couldn't talk, could only breathe and feel. Her pulse beat out of control while he made sure she was satisfied with his masculine endeavors. She closed her eyes and let the pleasure he gave rush through her as her body responded to his seduction, her hips arching upward beyond her control.

"Sweet, sweet Tavia. I have no power over myself when I'm naked and in bed with you."

"You unravel me one tiny thread at a time. I could never tell you no, nor would I want to, but James, you must rest, sleep. What if you fall asleep on our wedding day and can't say the vows?" She punched him gently on his shoulder. "Then we still won't have a legal marriage contract. All of our children will be born bastards, or we'll have to have a third wedding. Would you want that?"

She suddenly found herself pulled a top him again. "Tavia? What are you saying?"

She was shaking her head, unsure what he meant by the question, yet ready to laugh at his seeming naiveté when she finally understoo d the gist of his question.

"Of course I'm not saying that. You can't even mean to ask such a thing."

For a short time he looked a bit contrite, some of his ego vanishing with reality. "I would like children," he told her, tracing the line of her neck with a calloused fingertip. If she stayed here, he would never sleep.

"Well, I would too and perhaps we've started one. We won't know for a while though." She laughed, loving the feel of her breasts against the course hair of his chest.

"How many do you want?" he asked her, allowing her to roll off his chest and lay on her back beside him.

She stared at the ceiling. "Two, maybe three at the most. As long as there are no complications with our first two children. I'm not really sure what to do with a child. I wish there was a book."

"You never watched the younger children around your home?" he asked, sounding a tiny bit incredulous.

"No, there weren't any. Tira and I were the babies. I'm sure Amorica and Ella took their fair share of time watching us, but I have no experience."

"Then I suppose I'll have to teach you all there is to learn. I was the second of eight children."

"Oh my, so many. You don't want to have that many, do you?"

Panic at the thought swept through her.

"My mother was worn out all of the time. Father didn't seem to care about his wife or his children. In her last years she did all she could to keep him from her bed. There was really nothing she could do though. When he wanted her, he took her, and yet she seemed to accept him."

"Did he force her?"

"Yes and no. I do believe she loved him, but she truly didn't want to have more children, and father was too callous to take precautions. I think mother finally just gave up on life."

"Exhaustion. Just watching Ella and Ash makes me tired. He has so many needs and every other moment she's jumping up to get something for him, or to keep him out of trouble."

A crash from below had both of them bolting upright then thundering footsteps racing up the stairs created more noise.

"Edwin?"

"He wouldn't dare invade Drake's home. No..." they listened to the sounds.

"Jessie, stop!" Amorica cried out just as the little boy bolted into their room, his eyes seeming to bulge with curiosity.

Tongue-tied, Tavia pulled the quilt up to cover her, but not before the little boy saw her naked from the waist up.

"Mommy, they're naked just like you and Da," Jessie said, continuing into the room. "Why do adults always have to be naked in bed? You make me and Lyssa wear nightgowns.

All Tavia saw was a hand grabbing little Jessie's collar and pulling him from the room. Then, from outside the door, "Tavia, James, my sincere apologies for my son and his glib tongue. He got away from Damien, of course he did. My husband was supposed to be watching him, while I spoke to Ella. Somehow that just didn't work out very well."

Tavia couldn't help herself. She lay back on the bed, laughing. "I think it's time to rise and see what the day has in store for us. Seems as if the wedding party has begun to arrive. Wait until Storm and Fayth come with their children. It will make Jessie's antics seem like nothing."

"Maybe we don't want children after all. Not sure I'm ready for the little ones and the unexpected. Don't want them barging into our bedchamber all the time and seeing things they shouldn't."

"You said you had experience," she challenged him. "Besides, most everything has a logical explanation."

"I did, I thought I did. It might be too late to change our minds." He laughed. "I wouldn't trade the experience of little ones of our own for anything, and I'm sure you will be able to think of a logical explanation. I'm sure I can't. I'd probably blurt out the truth."

"Are you ready to get up or should I leave you here for some much needed sleep?" She rose comfortable with her nudity, something she never thought would happen. James had touched and kissed pretty much all of her. As she walked away from the bed, she felt the heat of his gaze rest upon her.

In the other room, a bath had been drawn. It was beyond her how Ella's maid almost always knew when she was going to get up. The water no longer steamed but it was warm. She settled in and let the heat soothe her but understood her oldest sister waited for her downstairs. They had a lot to talk about. Amorica had been away for so long it seemed an eternity.

She heard James dressing and knew he would be joining the other men to search out Edwin's property. It was foolish of her to think he would take time out to rest.

Later, dressed and presentable, she found Amorica and Ella in the kitchen, chatting and eating. "Oh, the bacon smells so good. I'm famished after too many days of no food or just broth."

Amorica rose and Tavia rushed into her arms for a much needed hug. "I'm truly sorry for what happened this morning."

"Don't worry about it. I'm sure Damian will have an answer," Tavia laughed, "And he's just a little boy."

When Ella saw her she poured her a cup of tea then she motioned for her to help herself to the eggs and bacon. Tavia sat down to a full plate and a cup of tea, hungrily eyeing everything.

"The Duchess is still in bed. She'll be down around ten. The dressmakers will arrive at one o'clock. I've sent Alma to the baker's to order the cake. The wedding will be one week from today." Ella finished reciting the list then inhaled a deep breath.

"One week from today?" Tavia put her hand to her chest, unable to believe she was going to have a real wedding and in seven days. "Oh, my, so soon? Where are Eveleen and Addie? Oh, and Larena? Are they still in bed?"

"They are walking in the gardens, getting to know each other I suppose. Addie is so unconventional. I like her," Ella said. "I believe they wanted to give me some alone time with Amorica."

"Where is your little girl? I don't think I ever learned her name and I haven't seen her. We both know I met Jessie," Tavia said, laughing at Amorica's distressed face.

"Her name is Lyssa and both my children are outside tormenting Damian and testing his limits. Jessie will try to get away with anything and everything he can. Of course he's used to having the property to run around on. He's been confined to the deck of the ship and it seems he's ready to explode." She laughed, "Damian really is very good and patient with them, but sometimes they get away from him. You just wait and see. The men are all so proud of themselves and their abilities to slay dragons, but given a pint size ball of energy, they tend to be out of their element."

"Is it safe for them outside in the gardens?" Tavia asked. "No one knows where Edwin is."

"To date I don't think he knows you and James are still alive. With the law pressing him, I doubt if he'll come here, but Drake left several men here to guard us. Nothing will happen," Ella said.

"I wish I could be so sure. I still remember how he marched into my house and took both of us captive as if he apprehended a tiny animal. We were both helpless and James had the distinct feeling when they searched Edwin's home someone was watching him. If that's true, Edwin knows James still lives and might jump to the conclusion I'm alive too."

The kitchen door crashed against the wall. Shrieks of delight swept through the tiny room. "Wait for me," Lyssa called out to her brother. "Stop right where you are. Da's going to be furious with you."

Jessie and Lyssa ran through the kitchen, both grabbing bacon before heading out the backdoor. Damian followed at a slower pace, also grabbing bacon. "Good morning, ladies. I do believe I heard a carriage arrive. Could it be your dressmakers? The children seem as if they're out of control, but I've got them handled," he said as he disappeared, chuckling to himself.

Larena poked her head through the door, "I can barely breathe. Alma must have laced my corset too tight. By the way, a carriage pulled up and it looks like the dressmaker." She sat down, grabbing a plate and heaping it with her favorite foods.

"They weren't supposed to come until one. Should we wake Aunty?" Tavia asked.

"No, don't get her up, let her sleep. They will be here all afternoon, I'm sure. Cook has been baking little cakes and things to feed them this morning," Ella said.

"Is anyone letting them in?" Addie strode into the room. "Hamilton said he'd pay for anything I want. The trouble is I don't want anything but he insists. Just give me the simplest gown they have."

"You should at least find out what they have to offer. You, hopefully, and unlike Eveleen and myself, will only get married one time. I'm going to find something that will truly make me feel beautiful," Eveleen said wistfully as if she remembered her first wedding and wedding night which ended in a disaster for the newlyweds.

"I certainly will look for something beautiful," Tavia said, "but I don't know what James can afford. I don't want to spend too much money."

"I'm sure The Duchess will pay for whatever he can't," Larena said through a mouthful of food.

"Your James has more money than you could imagine. He's worked hard and built his fortunes," Ella said, turning to her sister. "Drake told me the extent of James holdings, and we all know Logan has more than he could ever spend in a lifetime. Neither of you need worry about your husband's finances."

"Alma will see that our seamstresses are comfortable until we get there. They will set up in the dining room where we have a large table and where we can spread out the plates and make our choices. They told The Duchess they would bring plenty of sample fabrics, and trims for us to make our decisions. Personally, I'm going to find a beautiful bridesmaids dress," she looked to the others. "We are all going to be bridesmaids?"

"Of course you are," Tavia said. "Everyone, the cousins and the sisters will have a role to play."

The tapping of the cane on the kitchen floor stopped the chatter. "Why didn't anyone tell me they were here? Pour me a cup of tea. I can bring a plate of food into the dining room while I watch all of you. This will be so much fun."

"Go on, I'll bring you tea and breakfast, Aunty," Larena said. "Can I get a new dress too?"

"Yes, dear, anything you want."

Everyone except the Hepburn girls left. "I don't have a good feeling about this wedding ceremony. It's kind of the way I felt when Drake and I were married. I'm going to have Drake set out more guards that day. Nothing is going to go wrong," Ella promised.

"You don't think..." Tavia didn't want to believe Edwin would show up at the wedding. That would be suicide. Yet any man who could drown people for excitement or a thrill had to be insane enough to crash a wedding and cause trouble.

"No one is to speak of this around Aunty. I don't want her to worry just because of a gut feeling I have. Now let's go and make the planning and the day the best day of Aunt Charlotte's life. For what she's put up with over the years, she deserves the best."

In the dining room, chaos seemed to be the order of the day. Jessie and Lyssa swept through the room just after the seamstress stacked the materials, sending everything crashing to the floor.

The owner of the shop, Madame Chantel, stood in the middle of the dining room, her hands at her temples, shaking her head and mumbling something Tavia didn't understand.

When Amorica looked up, she shot Damian a fierce glare but didn't say a word for a few moments. Her sister seemed to be holding her breath.

"You must keep those children where they belong, under lock and key," she said, her voice cross as she shook her finger at the door the children had disappeared through.

Nothing she said seemed to faze Damian. He smiled, his hands resting on the back of a dining room chair. "Jessie, Lyssa, come back here and pick everything up. You've made a mess of the room and you must apologize," his voice loud enough to be heard a great distance away.

Seconds later as if listening for the call from their Da, Jessie and Lyssa appeared in the doorway, "Yes, Da, we're here," they said in unison and moved toward the fabrics.

"No!" Madame Chantel waved them away. "Shoo, don't touch a thing. An apology and a promise to stay out of this room is enough. I don't want those urchins touching anything in here. They have dirty little hands."

Tavia had an urge to laugh at the slight blush rising to cover Damian's darkly shuttered features. Everything Madame Chantel was true. The pair did have dirty hands. They must have been digging in the garden.

"Jessie, Lyssa stop where you are and apologize." Drake's voice was a command the children didn't dare defy.

"I'm sorry for making such a mess. The things you brought are really beautiful," Lyssa said sweetly.

When the silence lasted longer than it should. "Jessie!" Damian said, rocking on the balls of his feet as he studied his son.

"I'm sorry," the little boy said then turned to leave.

"The lady wants a promise to stay away," Damian reminded them.

"Can I stay and watch? I promise I won't touch anything, and if I do, you can give me to the pirates," Lyssa said solemnly.

Amorica, who had stayed quiet throughout the duration, held out her arm to her little girl laughing. "Of course you can as long as you stay on my lap. We'll both watch what transpires, and if anyone asks for our opinion we'll tell them how much we love their choices. The pirate thing is a tiny joke in our household as well as a reminder for them to stay close to the house since I was abducted by pirates."

"Would you want me to lie if I don't like something?" Lyssa asked, clearly appearing shocked at her mother's request. "You've always told me I have to tell the truth."

"You can give your honest opinion to me," Tavia laughed. "I'll feel much better with an honest opinion rather than showing up to my wedding in something that might look ridiculous."

"You are such a dear," Addie said. "I would like to know your opinion too. You have beautiful eyes, just like your mother's."

"Thank you," Lyssa said politely, seeming to smile at the sincere compliment. "I like you, and I'd rather be here than getting into trouble with my big brother. This will be so much more fun."

"Very well, you can stay as long as you behave. But go wash your hands then you can come back," Madame Chantel said. "Shall we begin?"

"Not quite yet," Alma entered with a tray of little cakes and tea. "This is for all of you." She set everything on the sideboard. "I will also bring in some fruit later. Please enjoy."

The fashion plates were spread on the table before they were passed around to the brides. Larena and Amorica looked at fashion plates for evening gowns.

"First things first, if you find one you like, hold on to it. We don't want anyone with the same dress. Once the patterns are chosen, you can decide on the fabric and the trims."

"Can I have a cake?" Lyssa asked.

The loud crash of the front door sent all the ladies to their feet. Amorica set Lyssa on the chair she vacated and headed for the front of the house.

"It's nothing I can't handle," Damian held out his hands to stop Amorica. "Jessie found the banister."

~ * ~

Edwin pulled up in front of a rustic cottage buried deep in the woods. He'd run across it quite by accident. The little home was perfect for his immediate needs, not doubting for a second he would have to move on very soon. Nan would appreciate a roof over her head for the night, one night at least. He couldn't stay in one place for more than an evening or two.

Nan lay in the back, bound and gagged. A tiny wave of guilt swept through him. She professed her loyalty to him many times, but years of abuse taught him he couldn't trust what people said, particularly women who had something to gain by lying.

Looking inside the carriage, he told her, "Be back in a minute,

Nan. Have to take care of the horse first." He led the carriage into the barn before unhooking his horse. Finding feed and water, he gave the animal food.

Quickly thinking this morning, he had piled a basket high with the food he had left in the house. It wasn't much but would take care of them for a couple of days. Maybe more, Nan didn't eat much.

Instead of tossing her on the floor of the vehicle, he gave himself a pat on shoulder for resisting temptation. He propped her on the seat so she could sit and told her she was lucky today. He was going to keep her with him for a while. The company was nice. He was so tired of living alone with no one to talk with about his problems.

Before he helped her out of the vehicle, he untied her feet and guided her inside the cottage. "Nice and comfortable," he said. "What do you think?" He finished untying her.

"Are we going to stay here?" she collapsed to the rug beside the fireplace, slumping at the waist. "It's cold and my legs are numb. Do you have to keep tying me?"

"Maybe I can find a blanket. I'm sorry your bath today had to be cut short. Your hair is still damp. No wonder you're chilled." He strode through the small cottage, searching for a blanket.

Lord, but he recalled the way Nan looked when she stepped into the bath this morning. Her breasts were small but perfectly formed and the curve of her hips beckoned his touch. He'd had an urgent need to taste her essence and feel her sweet movements beneath him.

She's still afraid of you, fool. You threatened to kill her. She kept her back to him when she shed her clothing but once in the tub he walked around so he could watch her and admire her beauty.

A fleeting thought of pushing her head beneath the water and watching her struggle for air passed through his head. It wasn't right. He'd given his word. Besides, where Nan was concerned, those images didn't excite him.

When she looked at him, she blushed prettily before lowering her lashes. He imagined making love to this innocent young virgin, a debutante. It was the end of the season so he surmised she must not have caught the attention of a man.

Perhaps no gentleman sought her out because she was too thin or had the personality of a shrew. She would have blended into the curtains. Although she was thin, her curves enticed him. Tonight he would see if she no longer feared him or his touch.

She'd heard the sounds first, even before he did, the runners barging into his home to search for him. He'd been able to grab a robe from a nearby chair and get them both into a hidden passage behind the wall in his bedchamber where he could observe through a pinhole.

He almost gave them away when he sucked air at the site of James Macmurra appearing in the room.

If Macmurra lived, did Tavia? He couldn't leave until she died. She had to die. She had snubbed him and he'd never forgive her for that.

He returned from a small room off the main one and tossed the nearly new covering to her. "Nan, you hungry? Maybe in the mood for a picnic with wine and cheese."

"Could you start a fire?" She pulled the cover around her, her teeth chattering. "I can't stop myself from shaking."

"Can't take the chance of anyone seeing the smoke from the chimney. I'm sorry," he told her sincerely. "If you're cold, I could keep you warm."

"Let's eat first," she smiled shyly, batting her lashes at him. "We haven't eaten all day."

When she looked away briefly before looking at him and smiling, he understood the game she played. Flirt then act shy, entice then refuse, he could play her game too.

When the runners and Drake's men left, he'd gathered her small clothes and the dress she'd been wearing. He gave her time to don her corset and underthings. Cautiously making his way with Nan by his side, he walked through the escape tunnel to the barn where he kept his horse and the carriage. It was blocked so he had to risk returning and leaving through the back door. Each second set his nerves on edge, expecting to be caught but everyone had vacated the area, leaving everything intact. "Stupid fools."

She finished dressing while he got the carriage ready, hoping no one would see it and report to Montgomerie. Before he left the area for good, he'd make them all pay. James and Tavia would die. He didn't know how they saved themselves, but he wouldn't fail again.

"We need to ration the food. I'm sorry." He set out a few small portions for each of them.

"That's alright. I don't eat very much. Everyone says I'm nothing but skin and bones and not very attractive." She shrugged her tiny delicate shoulders. "But I eat everything I want. It's just the way I am."

"I wish you had something nicer to wear. All I had were men's clothing. I put in a few things for me before we left but nothing would fit you. Maybe when we leave here, I'll find some ready made clothing for you."

"You would do that for me? My clothes are fine, you know. I don't need much, never have."

He drank from the bottle of wine he stashed in the basket before handing it to her. Her eyes wide she looked at him as if she were about to refuse before taking the bottle and holding it to her lips. "I've never had wine before. My sponsor wouldn't let me drink."

"Try it then," he urged.

She drank then coughed, holding her hand to her mouth. When she looked at him, she moistened her lips, and he had the urge to taste the tiny pink tongue she just showed him.

"Do you like the taste?"

"It's nice." She moved from the floor to the hearth, handing the bottle back to him. "I don't like the gag and the bindings. I wish you would trust me." Her voice was whisper soft, a siren's song.

She tempted him. "Nice," he mused thoughtfully. "It's all we have so why do I have the notion you're lying to me. If I'm going to trust you, you must always tell me the truth, promise me."

"I've never had wine before," she told him. "I thought the taste a bit harsh, but I believe I might like to try some more."

He handed her the bottle, watching as she tipped it up and drank a bit longer this time before wiping her mouth with the back of her hand.

"Not even at the debutant balls and parties? Didn't some young man courting you offer you wine so he could seduce you?" Edwin asked, curious about her past and eager to learn more about her.

"My chaperone wouldn't let me drink, afraid of what you just said, but no one courted me either. I was never even asked to dance. Instead, my chaperone forced me to eat until I threw up. She always said I was too skinny and no man would ever love me unless I had more curves for a man to hold onto." Tears slid from her cheeks, leaving paths as they trailed to her chin.

A wave of empathy swept through Edwin as he gently touched the drop of moisture with his fingertip. "I'm sorry for you," he said, his voice tender and filled with compassion he didn't understand, a different emotion for him. "I suppose we are two of a kind; both rejected by the beautiful people of the ton."

"I never wanted to be a debutant. All I wanted was to be left alone with my books and my dogs. My parents threatened me with a marriage to an old man in our village if I didn't go and find someone who would wed me. I don't want to go back there."

Edwin was overwhelmed with compassionate feelings for Nan, sentiments he'd never known before and didn't grasp now. His hand at the back of her head, he drew her close for a slow tender kiss. When their tongues met, he tasted the essence of her.

He picked her up and carried her to the tiny bedroom. Gently setting her on the bed, he came down beside her. "Let me make love to you, Nan. Will you let me?"

"I trust you," she murmured. "Yes."

Chapter Eleven

The day of the triple wedding arrived with the weather doing its best to send warm rays of sunshine to the earth, only a few clouds dotting a cerulean blue sky.

The Grahams arrived as did the McLellans and the Greys, and of course, the Hepburns, all but Tira, Ravyn, and Aidan who were still in the United States. Much to the surprise of the Hepburn ladies, even Tavia's father, Charles, arrived at the Montgomerie estate in time for the wedding.

The night before, the men celebrated drinking at Almacks, and the women had a few bottles of Chianti and Bordeaux at home.

When James returned to the estate and to his bed, it was to find it empty and a note from The Duchess.

James,

To honor your new bride and to make the wedding night more exciting, you will not sleep with Tavia this evening. She is in my chamber and if you want to risk the wrath of the dragon lady, come retrieve her if you dare. On the other hand, you could accept my wishes and sleep well by yourself, of course. The other ladies are sleeping alone tonight also, so be it known I've not singled you out. In any case all the grooms will sleep alone tonight.

Love,

Aunt Charlotte

PS. I've hired Drake's men to guard the door. You will stay away from your beautiful bride soon to be your wife.

James laughed when he read the letter then started for Tavia's room before he noticed the postscript. *The Duchess thinks of everything. Suppose I'll follow her wishes tonight.*

In the morning, James lay on his bed, hands tucked behind his head, thinking about the upcoming nuptials. He was blessed, more fortunate than he'd ever deemed possible.

A bath had been drawn and clothes befitting the ceremony were laid out in the dressing room. He took a few minutes to trim his beard and mustache before he strode down the steps to discover he was the last man to arrive on the veranda.

An array of food was laid out on a table near the terrace. Flowers of varying colors decorated the walkway to the gazebo as well as around the structure. His heart raced with anticipation. He supposed The Duchess' decision to keep Tavia from him enhanced the excitement of the day as well the coming evening. Sometimes Aunty Charlotte knew a few things.

Guests were arriving nonstop, and he wondered if Aunt Charlotte invited all of London. Gifts were piled high on three tables near the foyer, each marked with a couples' name.

James had not thought to invite anyone in his family. When he left home, he left for good, never looking back. Yet it seemed The Duchess had thought of everything, and how she discovered who his family was and where they lived went beyond his imagination. Tavia always said The Duchess had at least a million favors to call in from the ton when she needed something.

Cameron Macmurra, his older brother, stood in front of him, hand extended in friendship. When their hands clasped, Cameron pulled him forward for an embrace. "James, it's been a long time. You haven't written but I'm glad this fine lady found me and invited me to your wedding." He turned to the woman by his side, "My wife, Lara."

"Children?" James asked, trying to maintain a flow of conversation, yet his mind was focused on the others in the room as well as the guests. He was curious about his brother and had a few questions to ask about the rest of the family.

"Two," Cameron said. "We'll let you attend to things and Lara and I will find a seat. We left the children at home. Didn't want the chaos that comes with their attendance."

"You sleep well?" Logan slapped him on the shoulder, grinning and searching the room.

"'Bout as well as you did, I suppose. Didn't much like sleeping alone, felt as if I'd done something wrong," James laughed, vowing to keep Tavia happy. "And Hamilton, how was your lonely night?"

Before Hamilton could answer, more guests arrived, some stopping to chat and find a snack and something to drink, others walking into the garden to find a place to sit. Logan had spared nothing where the wine was concerned. Glasses of his Chianti and Bordeaux were set out for their guests.

Drake had guards placed around the house just as he'd done at his wedding. This was more crucial, however. No one knew if Edwin had moved on or was nearby planning revenge.

"Any of you want to run the opposite direction?" Hamilton asked with one eyebrow cocked upward. "Not only did I miss my Addie, I'm terrified of what is about to happen. Always thought I'd remain single, never believed I'd want to settle down with one woman. Never expected to have children either and now one is due in about six months. I've the feeling as bad as my sleep was last night, it was better than what's in store for me."

"James and I have nowhere to run. We're already married, shackled for life. You, on the other hand could escape right now." Logan grinned and gestured towards the door. "It's now or never."

Hamilton seemed exceedingly uncomfortable, rocking on the balls of his feet and gazing at the stairway as if he expected Addie to appear. "Just never made a commitment like this before. This isn't for a month or two, it's for life. Takes some thinking about."

"Do you love her?" Drake asked, prying into his friend's thoughts and feelings. "It's an emotion some are loathe to admit to. I know I was. To Ella I was adamant that I cared for her but maintained for months that love didn't exist. She finally heard the words from me, and now I tell her every morning when we wake up and every night when we go to bed."

"Loved her from the moment I saw her, just didn't know it at the time. Didn't know there was such a thing as love," Hamilton said.

"Have you told her how you feel?" Drake persisted in his line of questioning. "You really should."

"Not yet," Hamilton admitted. "Been looking for the right time. These last few days I've barely seen her."

"You've had some nights. What are you waiting for?" Logan asked. "I know I waited too long, and we would have done much better had I said the words sooner. It wasn't until I almost lost her that I had the courage to tell Eveleen how much she means to me and that I love her."

"How about you, James?" Drake asked again.

"Not yet," James admitted, rubbing his chin.

"You've been married over two months. Don't you think it's about time?" Drake asked, laughing.

"Time to start." The Duchess swept into the male dominated room, head held high, her cane tapping as she walked, appearing as if she meant business. "No time to waste."

"Now, who are our best men?" She looked at the males who were huddled together near the entrance. She breathed in a deep and very long breath, creating an air of apprehension in James. "I don't think we need to do anything in order. There are so few of us here. Amorica is the matron of honor, so Damian will be the first to walk to the gazebo. Dear me it seems we are going in order again."

"We can just line up the way you want us. Call out our names. I don't think anyone cares," Drake said.

"Very well, but I will have to do some thinking. There is a certain pecking order in this," The Duchess said and with the aid of her cane sat down.

"None of us care about any of that," James said, running his hands through his red hair, sending the carefully groomed hair standing on end. We can just line up and walk."

"Of course you don't. If I have to guess, you all want this over with as soon as possible so you can have an unforgettable wedding night," she sighed, yet a small wistful smile graced her lips. "I do miss the Duke. Men. So, Hunter, Ryder, Hadden, and Jarret, that is the order. They only care about one thing."

"That's truly not fair," Drake protested in defense of all the males present. "I, for one, think about other things."

"Pshaw," she waved her hands in the air. "You of all people know just how true my words are. I will never forget I let you take Ella to your hunting lodge. Yet I've no regrets."

She turned to Hamilton. "You look terrified. Do you have anyone to stand up for you? It's not that important but it would be nice."

"I've my brother who will be here. You've seen to that, thank you, but Addie has no one. She has pretty much spent her life alone."

"Ah, since Gavin cannot be here, why don't we put your brother with Larena? She will be happy. Larena had a dress made special in hopes of impressing her beau. What's your brother's name?"

"Carson," Hamilton said.

"Then after Jarret comes Carson." The Duchess appeared pleased with herself. She clapped her hands together, smiling happily. "The flower girl is little Lyssa and the ring bearer is Jessie. They will be down soon. I so hope they can stay out of trouble long enough to do their jobs."

"Expect the unexpected and pray for the best," Damian said chuckling. "As they walk down the aisle, I'll give them my sternest look."

"If yesterday was an example of your stern looks, then they don't exactly work too well," James said, trying to keep his escalating emotions in check and see a little humor in Damian's children.

"I'll try to do better."

If possible, James' heart beat faster with each passing second. He inhaled a long deep breath, wishing the events of today were done. This pomp and circumstance was not something he felt comfortable with, and it seemed the other men were just as uncomfortable. He ran a finger around the inside of his collar as if it was choking him.

A few seconds later, the organist began to play, the music creating the desired atmosphere. The priest appeared from the shadows of the gazebo and stood with a bible held in front of him.

James understood the differences in the two weddings, feeling more committed to Tavia than ever before. Her family and friends plus most of London would witness the saying of their vows. He would love, honor and protect her in sickness and in health for the rest of their lives. He realized the first wedding was a travesty, a mockery of the true meaning of marriage and the promises that go with the institution. No wonder Tavia was angry.

"This is it, men. Run now or forever hold your peace. This is your last chance," Drake laughed. "I truly like being a groomsman much better than the groom, not nervous at all this time."

The men slowly proceeded to their places in front of the gazebo and waited patiently for the brides to make their way to them. James swallowed the huge lump in his throat before rubbing the back of his neck. They had practiced last night. Everything had gone well. There was nothing to worry about as far as he could see, yet he carried his knife in his boot. He knew Drake carried a pistol beneath his waistcoat as well as a knife as did Logan. Thoughts of Edwin were constantly on his mind.

The hair on the back of his neck stood on end. Rubbing the back of his neck he shifted his feet, taking his attention from the direction the girls would walk to the gardens and surrounding land. He saw nothing but the feeling of being watched didn't pass.

Hunter, Allura's husband, stood next to him. "Do you feel it too?" he asked in a hushed tone.

James stiffened before he nodded his head. "Someone or something is watching us, I'd swear. My instincts have never been wrong."

"Neither have mine. I've a wicked hunting knife stashed in my boot. Allura told me some of what happened to you and Tavia. I'd think this man should have been apprehended by now or left the country if he was smart." He spoke in whispered words.

"I've men stationed inside and out, guarding the house and the grounds. It would be terribly difficult for anyone to get inside the home or these gardens although anything is possible," Drake whispered, joining the discussion as they waited and remembering his wedding as well.

"Gives us something else to think about," Damian said. "If there's time, I could take a look around and return before anyone knows I'm missing."

The music changed to a different song.

"Too late for that," Drake said. "My men surround the house and the gardens. No one is getting inside. Enjoy the wedding."

All attention focused on the little girl, trying to walk slowly down the aisle, dropping flower petals on her way, a cherubic smile on her tiny face. When she reached the front, The Duchess took her by the hand and let her sit beside her.

"You did beautifully, absolutely perfect, Lyssa. See, your mother and father are smiling at you," The Duchess said.

"Thank you, Aunty Charlotte," Lyssa said, looking adorable and waving at her parents.

It seemed all who knew the little boy held their breath as Jessie began his stoic march toward the gazebo. He carried the pillow holding three rings in front of him, looking serious and dark just as his father did at times when he concentrated on something.

When he was close, Damian reached out his hand to his little boy, bringing him to stand in front of him, and placing his hands on his little boy's shoulders as if he meant to hold him in place. Then lowering his head, "Fine job little man. Very well done. We haven't lost the rings and you stayed on the path. It would be incredibly bad luck if we did anything wrong, and you don't want Auntie Tavia and James to have bad luck," he whispered.

Little Jessie beamed under the praise of his father. "No bad luck," he was shaking his head. "Not for my auntie. She was very pretty without her clothes on, just like mama."

"Hush," Damian said.

Tavia, the first to walk, stood at the doorway, her arm linked with her father's. Charles had still been in deep mourning a year ago and had not attended Ella's and Drake's wedding. With time he had slowly begun to recover, leaving his home to embrace his precious family. His appearance at this event had meant everything to Tavia.

Tavia, James' wife to be, was so beautiful. His heart skipped a beat. James didn't know much about dresses and what they were made of, but this one hugged her curves and highlighted her breasts. Her dark hair was woven in an intricate pattern with small diamonds sparkling through the strands. While she walked toward him, he held his breath. She handed her bouquet of yellow chrysanthemums to Amorica then stepped next to him.

Eveleen appeared next with the Laird McLellan accompanying her. James heard Logan suck in a deep breath of air when he saw her.

Eveleen's gown was as simple and beautiful as Tavia's, her bouquet was made of white lilies. At the gazebo, he handed her flowers to Allura and stepped beside Logan.

Addie stood stiffly by herself in the doorway, holding a bouquet of dark purple carnations. James' heart went out to her, yet he knew she didn't want anyone's sympathy. Both the McLellan and Charles had offered to walk her down the aisle, but she chose to walk alone. She'd said that was pretty much the story of her life until she met Hamilton.

When Adelina told James some of her story, his heart had gone out to her, but the real story of her life until she met Hamilton was heartbreaking. She'd lived in a whorehouse until she was twelve and Drake somehow rescued her. He kept her safe and enlisted her in several missions. They were missions that did not put her life in jeopardy but tested her abilities.

Addie smiled at Hamilton and regally, her head held high, began her walk toward the man who was going to make Addie his own. The couple was so very different. Hamilton had been born into nobility and was a wealthy man who loved to gamble and womanize. At least he wanted people to believe he enjoyed many women. The last thing Hamilton needed to do was to spy for his country, but he was bored living the life he was born into. Much the same as Drake and Logan, he sought excitement away from the balls and fetes hosted by other wealthy aristocrats.

When she reached the dais, she handed her flowers to Larena then stood next to Hamilton.

The priest cleared his voice before opening the bible. "Will the couples please face each other and hold hands?" the priest asked, his voice solemn, befitting the occasion.

With the others, James turned and held Tavia's trembling hands in his own. She was just as terrified as he was. He smiled at her, hoping to reassure. She clasped her bottom lip between her teeth.

The priest began, "Do you solemnly vow..." the priest continued, each person saying the required words together.

James felt as if he was in a hazy dream. He didn't remember anything as the ceremony continued. All he could do was gaze at Tavia and blindly repeat the words he was expected to say.

When the priest asked for the rings, little Jessie, helped by his father, Damian, first gave the pillow to James who took his ring for Tavia and placed it on her finger. When he handed the pillow back to Jessie, he repeated the process with Logan then Hamilton.

After what seemed an eternity of words that seemed to run together into one sentence, the priest said, "I now pronounce you husbands and wives. You may all kiss your brides."

James moistened his lips before he bent to take Tavia's lips with his. Her taste was sweet Tavia. He lingered for a moment, drawing his tongue along the seam of her lips in hopes of suggesting things to come during the wedding night ahead. His body hardened in anticipation. He looked up just as the Logan and Hamilton did.

A round of cheers and applause greeted them as well as a few ribald comments. He wanted to place his hands over Tavia's ears, but after spending months on his ship, he was sure she'd heard everything.

The priest had agreed to announce them one couple at a time. The guests rose, still celebrating.

"I give you, Mister and Misses, James Macmurra."

Smiling, his heart filled with happiness and pride, he gave his arm to Tavia. After she placed her hand on his arm, he placed his hand over hers. "Misses Macmurra, shall we meet our guests?" They walked slowly away from the gazebo, looking back and forth and nodding hellos at their guests as they proceeded.

When they reached the doors, they turned to watch the others follow.

The priest repeated his words with each couple.

"I give you Mister and Misses, Logan Maxwell."

Then, I give you Mister and Misses, Hamilton Winthrop."

After what seemed like hours in a receiving line greeting the guests and thanking them for coming and after hugs and well wishes, they were finally done. With a soft sight Tavia leaned into him. He wrapped a comforting arm around her.

"Now we can relax. Are you up to dancing?" James asked, relieved this part was done.

"My feet hurt," Tavia laughed "and I need a couple maybe more glasses of Logan's special Chianti. Then I want to watch everyone. Maybe later we can find time for a dance."

"You should probably eat something too. I want you wide awake and alert when we start our wedding night. I've something special to give you, but it's more for me."

"More for you?" she questioned as they started up the stairway to the ballroom on the third floor. "Then why is it a gift for me?"

He chuckled, remembering Drakes suggestion and the reasons for it. "You will understand when you see it."

Tavia punched him in the arm. "You're going to make me wait to see it, aren't you?"

"That's my plan." The garment wasn't appropriate to pull out anywhere but in the privacy of their bedchamber.

In the ballroom, the head table was set, and the plates heaped with food as were all the tables. Bottles of wine were also set on the counters. James picked up two glasses before pouring the wine and handing a glass to Tavia.

"Can we sit down?"

James pulled out a chair for Tavia. She sat, and closing her eyes, sipped the wine. He was suddenly concerned for her health. It had been little more than a week since she almost drowned. Her face was pale, her eyes too dark for his liking. She appeared beyond tired.

"You look exhausted." He held her hand in his, wishing they could leave. In that respect, their first wedding had been perfect. No one expected anything from either of them.

"I'm tired, but nothing that serious." She smiled him as if she were trying to reassure him and maybe herself.

Eveleen and Logan arrived and behind them were Hamilton and Addie. Addie sat next to her.

"Are you happy," Addie asked as she accepted wine from Hamilton who now sat down.

"It took us a while to tell the truth and forgive each other, but now that we have, I love him."

"Have you told him?"

~ * ~

"No." Tavia turned to look at James who was engaged in a lively conversation with Logan. "No, I haven't." She had wanted to speak the words so many times but something always held her back.

"Why ever not?" Addie asked sounding genuinely concerned. "You've had time haven't you?"

"So much has happened to us, so much trauma. I've wanted to tell him, but I need for him to say the words first. Shouldn't the man be the first to tell his wife he loves her?" Those words were ridiculous and she knew it. Even though men were supposed to be supreme, she'd never been raised to believe that for one second. And even though the world didn't think of her as an equal, she believed she was.

"You should both tell each other. What I'm seeing is the stubborn young woman I met on board James' ship. Perhaps you should try not to be so pigheaded. He loves you so you shouldn't fear that he won't return the sentiment. Sometimes it's up to the woman to take matters into her hands."

"He's just as bad," Tavia protested, glancing quickly at James and hoping he wasn't overhearing this conversation. "He's inflexible and headstrong to a fault. He has an ego that surpasses anyone's. Those are some of the reasons why we were angry with each other for so long."

Addie was shaking her head and smiling indulgently. "What you say is all true, but you should take a lesson from the past. I've never thought you were a slow learner. Tell the poor man you love him and take the pressure away from him."

"You're right," Tavia admitted, noticing people were beginning to eat. "But that admission doesn't mean I'll say the words first. Even though you believe he loves me, I'm still afraid he cannot say them back. What about you? Have you told Hamilton you're in love with him?"

"That's different." Addie looked down, smoothing her napkin in her lap before she faced Tavia. "He felt he had to marry me because of the baby. He is an honorable man. Hamilton has never mentioned love."

"Part of what you're telling me is probably true. I don't know him, but he doesn't strike me as the type of man who would marry a woman he didn't love because of a baby. No, he would support the child, smother the babe with love, but he'd never marry a woman he didn't want to wed."

"And that would be true of James also," Addie said. "I watched the two of you dance around each other for months. No one who saw the two of you together would ever doubt the love you hold for each other. Even Seamus saw through the antics."

Tavia held Addie's hand in hers, "I suppose all situations are different. If you're happy, I'm sure he is also. We'll figure this out, but we might have to do it the hard way. Who's to say one person should say the words before another? We have to act on what is in our hearts."

"You need to eat more food," James whispered to her. "Did you have a nice conversation with Addie?"

"I did but it was more like an argument about men and who should do or say what first, the husband or the wife." Tavia told him elusively. She knew she made him curious by her words and smiled at the thought.

James' brows drew together in concentration. "I'm not real sure I understood anything you said."

She smiled prettily at him, "When you do it first, I'll explain. Until then you will have to be patient."

Tavia pushed the food around on her plate, taking a few bites but enjoying the wine more than the food. She closed her eyes, thinking of all the nights she would have with James and wished this one could be in their townhouse. She was tired of fearing for her life and looking over her shoulder afraid she would find Edwin leering behind her.

Damian held his glass aloft, asking for toasts. "To Tavia and James," he said. "May they have happiness, love and lots of children, well as many as they want," he amended quickly, slanting Amorica an impressive smile.

The toasts went on for some time, stories of Logan more prevalent than anyone else. Few people in the room knew James all that well. Hamilton was the butt of jokes and stories as well. This went on until the three cakes were carried into the room.

The couples stood by their wedding cake, a knife in hand.

"Don't you dare smear cake on my face," Tavia said watching

James' wicked grin. "That wouldn't be nice of you or honorable."

"And what would happen if I did?"

"I would not sleep with you tonight," she challenged even while she knew if he kissed her, she wouldn't be able to resist him. One seductive look from him and she would melt into his arms. "You will have to sleep alone on the couch in the dressing room."

"Ah, but what if I refuse to do that. I'm bigger and stronger and..."

She interrupted him. "You would never force me."

In an instant his cockiness vanished. "I would not," he smiled again, "There is always seduction."

Given the signal they cut the first piece and fed each other. Their cake was white with lemon icing. James carefully used his fork and fed her.

"Did I pass the test?" James asked, bending close to whisper in her ear and touch the shell with the tip of his tongue.

"Very well." Tavia, on the other hand, swept the icing with her finger and drew a line across his lips with it, but he surprised her and sucked her finger into his mouth when she lingered a moment longer than she should have. The gesture was met with cheers and applause from the guests.

"The icing is good. You chose well," James said, placing a chaste icing kiss on her nose.

"James," she backed up. His grin purely masculine filled with ownership. "You're cheating."

"I think I won that one," he told her. "Our bed waits for us."

"Best you behave or you'll be on the couch," she reminded him, poking him in the chest as a reminder.

"I don't think so," he spoke with confidence. "Behaving just isn't any fun and as long as we stay here, there really is no couch."

"You're way too confidant," she told him.

With all the cakes cut the music began and the tables were cleared and hauled away, the chairs placed along the walls of the room. Alma finished cutting pieces from each of the three cakes for them to take home and preserve.

"Shall we dance?" he asked, holding his hand out for her to take.

"I'd like that. Dancing is the best part of any wedding."

Gallantly, James swept Tavia into his arms and twirled her around the room, ending up in an alcove near the back of the ballroom and away from the majority of people. She remembered the night she met James and how he rescued her from Edwin's horrible advances.

I've waited hours to do this." He lowered his head, tilting it slightly so he could reach her lips.

"James," she breathed into his mouth. His warm lips found hers and she opened for him, needing the comfort his closeness brought. His hand at her waist pulled her close. She felt him hard against her stomach, understanding his need was just as strong as hers grew. He was right. She'd never deny him because she wanted him and the love they shared.

For a moment he pulled away to search her face, the steel glint of his eyes, holding her gaze. She moistened her lips and his found her again, his hands on either side of her head, holding her still. She ran her hands through his hair, pulling him closer.

"Tavia," he whispered close to her, "you are so sweet. I cannot get enough of you. Kiss me slow."

Her eyes wide she looked into his, "I..." she began then hesitated. She had almost told him she loved him.

He pulled away from her, chuckling, "We need to get back to the main room before someone comes looking for us. The Duchess would beat me with her cane if she found me kissing you in a tiny alcove. I've heard reports of such a thing."

"From who?" She grinned at him, knowing the answer. Ella had told her more than once how Drake had tried to seduce her but was met by their auntie's cane. Of course it wasn't Aunty who wielded the cane. It was The Duchess. The Duchess and their aunty were two entirely different souls. Ella had also told her she was more than willing to be seduced by Drake even before they were wed. There had never been any question in her mind that she loved him.

"They wouldn't dare come for us. We're married and can do whatever we want," she murmured sweetly, trying to pull him close again. She wondered if she could seduce him.

"Of course they would and they would know what we've been

doing. Your lips are kiss swollen. You will have to keep your head turned to me, so I'm the only one who will see what we just did."

She touched a fingertip to her lips then looked to him. "And yours are not kiss swollen? Why not?"

"My beard conceals many flaws or truths in this case." And puffing up his chest, he told her laughing, "Besides the men here would be patting me on my shoulder, silently congratulating me on my manly prowess."

"Then everyone will think I was kissing someone else," she challenged him, grabbing the front of his waistcoat and pulling him closer. "Would you want them to think that?"

"Touché," he said. "And before I do something we'll both regret," he whirled her back to the floor, "we will behave ourselves until we can say goodnight and leave the ballroom."

If they had stayed a few seconds more in the private alcove, she thought to tell him she loved him but knew the idea for an excuse, nothing more. She had begun to say the words but he interrupted her.

"How long do we have to stay?" she asked, enjoying the dance as well as the music that touched her heart.

"You're asking me that question? A ship's captain?" he sounded incredulous. "I would think you know more about these things than I do. Ah, but you're eager to seduce me, have your wicked way with me. The sooner we can say our goodbyes the better."

"No," she protested too quickly, wondering if he'd read her mind. "I've only been to a few weddings, village weddings, none of this magnitude. Ella's was interrupted at the beginning of the dancing, so everyone pretty much left early. I have no idea what the protocol is."

"You have no more experience than I do then?" he chuckled softly, pulling her closer. "Perhaps we can spend more time in the darker recesses of the ballroom and I could explore other possibilities."

Suddenly, the music stopped and she heard the sound of pipes tuning. It had been so long since she heard anything so sweet and poignant. "What is happening?"

They stopped and looked in the direction of the musician. "It's Cameron and the McLellan. They're going to give us a bit of my Scottish heritage."

"To my brother, giving us a small portion of our legacy in this English house. I've seen that many of you are Scottish."

The bittersweet sound of the pipes filled his heart with memories and his soul with a time long past, a place where he'd never return. The nostalgia of the tune made him homesick. The two men played as one, the haunting beauty of the pipes echoing in the ballroom.

"Are the Hepburns English or Scottish?" he asked, watching her with amazing tenderness in his eyes.

"All of our mothers were Scottish, as is Aunt Charlotte. So we all have Scottish blood flowing in our veins. The unique music calls to me just as it does to you. Whenever we visited the McLellan castle, we would hear the pipes." Her lashes fluttered downward, moisture filling her eyes. "I barely knew my mother and I wondered what she would think of you."

She felt the tap on her shoulder. "May I have this dance?" Charles, her father stood beside her with a smile on his face. "A father should dance with his daughter on her wedding day. Don't you think?"

"I would love to dance with my father. I'm so happy you came. If it doesn't hurt you too much, I was just thinking of mother and how little I knew her. I wish I would have had more time with her."

"It hurts every time I hear her name or look into the valley surrounding our home. I go over all of the events of that day and wonder what I could have done differently to change what happened. If only I had been there, but I chose to work instead of playing with her and my children. I regret so much about my choices that day, but someone very wise convinced me I still had my life to live and a family to cherish. They told me my wife would not want me pining away for her and missing out on all the important events of my daughters' lives. I've met my three adorable grandchildren and two are boys. It would have made your mother very happy to have a male grandchild."

"The Duchess? She told you. When did she go see you?" Tavia asked, sure she knew the person responsible for finally shaking Charles from his mourning. He would have died soon had he stayed sequestered in his home refusing to see or acknowledge anyone including his daughters and grandchildren.

"Yes, Charlotte came to see me, and she told me about my grandchildren and how they needed everyone in their lives. I'm beholden to her in so many ways," he said, wiping a tear from his face.

"I'm thankful and grateful for Auntie. You really surprised me and walking me down the aisle was wonderful? I would have never thought you would be here. The only thing that would make me happier would be to have Tira beside me today."

"I would have loved seeing Tira also. I've missed all of you so much. I will regret to my dying day my selfish refusal to attend Ella's wedding."

"You should have no regrets. Your choices were not what we all wanted, but they were necessary at the time. Perhaps you can dance with Ella too. I know she would love it if you asked."

"I will make sure I do just that," he said, extending his hand to her, and holding her in his arms, they danced.

Time seemed to pass quickly as they whirled around the dance floor. "I wish Tira would write," she looked into her father's eyes. "We haven't heard from her in a few months.

"I would love to see Tira and tell her I'm through mourning. It's been a long time since I've paid attention to either of my two little girls. You were both so mischievous, playing tricks on the villagers, pretending to be the other one. There were a few times even I could not tell the two of you apart."

"You knew about the pranks?" she asked, realizing he must have cared more than any of them thought.

Lovingly Charles smiled at her, "I did. It's just that after your mother passed on, I didn't have the energy to deal with the two of you. It was easier to let you have your way."

"We only did those things to get your attention. We wanted your love and always thought we'd done something wrong." She would never understand the dynamics between her father and his children. Even though she loved James more than life itself, she didn't believe she would ever abandon her children to mourn his passing if such a horrible thing happened.

"I'm sorry. I cannot apologize enough. I was so lost without her I didn't know how to deal with the emptiness in my life. Come, no more tears and remembering the sadness of the past. You should dance with your husband." They whirled towards James then stopped. He bowed. "Thank you for the dance and letting me be part of your life again. Take care of her and protect her or you will have me to answer to."

"You have tears in your eyes. Was it so bad?" James asked, touching the moisture on her cheek.

"It was not bad at all. The moments with him were amazing. We talked about mother and her passing. He has changed and all for the good. I was sure he would die if he didn't come out of mourning. It was Aunty who finally brought him to his senses."

"Of course it was The Duchess. She seems to have this way about her that forces people to do the right thing."

"She always has. We used to be terrified when she came for a visit."

Tenderly James touched her cheek, watching her. "How are you feeling? Do you need to rest?" he asked.

"Only if you do, however, I would like a sip or two of wine. My throat is parched"

"Wine and a piece of cake. One bite was not enough if we are going to dance the night away. It doesn't appear if anyone is leaving yet. Look, even The Duchess is still here."

"Charles?" Tavia asked as she watched her father stride toward Charlotte. "Is he going to ask her to dance? I can't believe my eyes. Do you think he could follow in the Duke's footsteps and be everything to her?"

"No," James was laughing and shaking his head as they watched Charles offer his hand to Charlotte and was even more amazed when she accepted and he pulled her into his arms for a dance. "No, from what you've told me the two of them had one love and I doubt if either of them searches for another one, but perhaps they can keep each other company every now and then."

"One could only hope," Tavia mused, thinking they would be good for each other. They had both lost the only love they thought they would have in this life, but by some miracle, Charlotte had reached him and found a way for him to come out of the blackness where he lived when no one else could.

James placed a piece of cake on a plate and grabbed two forks. "Eat and I'll let you have another dance with me."

"You'll let me? Perhaps I'll let you." She devoured a small bite. "It's good." Then she ate another one but wasn't oblivious of the fact James wasn't eating. Her stomach had been tied in knots all day and until now, food did not appeal to her. She knew he was letting her eat the entire slice.

"Finish, please. Would you excuse me for a moment to speak to Drake." He kissed her on the cheek. "I'll be back before you can finish this lovely dessert."

"Of course," she started for one of the chairs, watching James stride purposefully through the ballroom to speak with Drake, disappearing behind the guests.

"You're alive. How droll."

She felt the butt of the gun on her back, dropping the cake and the fork, ice cold fear sliding down her spine. She knew the terrifying sound of the man's voice. "Edwin? You should have left the country."

"Not before I kill you. You're supposed to be dead," behind her his voice was a low growl.

"You won't get away with this," she told him, wishing her words were true. Drake had the place guarded. What had happened? Edwin should not have been able to find his way inside.

"Maybe, maybe not. You see I don't really care anymore if I live or die. There is Nan though." He cleared his throat. "As long as you die, I'll die a happy man. How did you get out of the river?"

"I can swim, Edwin, since I was five. Kicking my way to the surface even with my legs tied together was not a problem; getting out of the bindings was, however." Bloody hell, she searched the room for James. His back was turned to her then he disappeared again behind dancing couples.

"Macmurra saved you," he said with a sneer. "If I kill you and leave him alive, it will be a better revenge. Macmurra will suffer more and all this on your wedding day. What a delight. I couldn't have planned it better."

"What happened to the missing debutant? Is that Nan you just spoke of?" she asked, hoping he would shed some light on her whereabouts since her body had not been found.

"Nothing, she is no concern of yours."

"She is alive then?"

"Nan, yes," he told her, the gun no longer pressed on her back but touching her head.

Closing her eyes, she willed James to see her, to find some way to rescue her before he could kill her. He would shoot her, probably enjoying the moment when the bullet went through her head. "James," she whispered, silently trying to call to him. *I love you and I wish I'd had the courage to tell you. Now I'll never get the chance.*

"I suppose James kicked his way to the surface too. Why would that surprise me?"

"He did." She tried to think of questions to ask, of ways to divert his attention until someone would come to her rescue. She needed time. "Then he used a rock to slice through the bindings. Once that was accomplished and he freed me, we found a farmhouse and a warm barn to spend the night."

"No one has done that before, saved themselves."

"Why did you want me to die, Edwin?"

"You snubbed me, Tavia. At the ball you openly sneered at me. You deserved to die."

"You took liberties I wasn't willing to give," she defended herself. "I didn't want to kiss anyone but you persisted. I barely knew you. Perhaps if you had waited and courted me, I would have liked you."

"But you gave liberties to that giant Scotsman," he said.

"Not until we were wed," she lied. "I love him, Edwin. What do you know about love?" she questioned, wishing she could think of more to say, but her breaths came in short terrified pants and her body shook so hard she was sure she would crumple to the ground.

"More than you would know. Nan, she's..." he spoke so softly she could barely hear him. "Nan is nice and sweet, and she doesn't look at me as if I'm dirt beneath her feet."

"Where is Nan?" She swallowed the lump in her throat, but it was back before she could take another breath.

"Nan is no concern of yours. She is safe. We're going to take a little walk. Head for the door."

She was dead as soon as she left the protection of the ballroom. "How did you get past the guards Drake set around the house and gardens?" She began to walk as he bid but as slowly as possible. If he captured her, he would take greater pains to make sure she could not kick her legs and find her way to the top and breathe air.

"Keep moving."

"No, really how did you get past them?" she stopped. "Shoot me here if you must. I'm not going to let you take me from the ballroom. I'd rather a quick death than a slow painful one."

"They are incompetent fools. Montgomerie forgot about something. Once the ceremony was complete, a couple of his esteemed guards decided they needed to celebrate. All it would have taken was one man, but when there were two empty spaces. Maneuvering my way to the ballroom was easy and before that, getting into the house was easier still."

"Really, you should drop the gun and leave before anyone knows you are here. You can save yourself and go back to Nan. I'll stall for as long as I can. You can leave the country." She was grasping for words, her pulse racing as a fine sheen of sweat beaded on her forehead. She could no longer see James. All hope seemed to vanish as the seconds passed.

"Not before you die."

"Are you really that arrogant to think you can shoot me at my wedding and get away with murder? You are the fool here." She realized that was the worst thing she could say. He needed to be reassured and coddled, yet she couldn't find the words.

"I'm not arrogant. I know the runners have had my house watched as well as the riverbank and the cottage near my home, but they're gone now. I know they searched my house and found nothing. They believe I've left this country, just as you've said. You're wasting time. Now get moving." He prodded the gun at the back of her head.

"As I just told you, I'm not going anywhere with you. I know you will kill me. The question is whether it will be here where they will catch you or in the darkness of the night. I don't want to die by drowning. I'd rather take my chances with a bullet to my head," she told him again. She didn't want to die at all. There had to be a way to escape this man. So many people here would do everything in their power to see she lived.

Keeping the pistol on her head, he wrapped his arm around her waist and tried to drag her to the entrance. She fought him the best she could, praying the gun wouldn't accidentally discharge.

The gunshot behind her echoed in the room. She felt the vibrations from her head to her spine and was sure he shot her. Yet she felt no pain, nothing. She fell to her knees, her gaze focused on James as well as her father running toward her. Pain shot through her head.

The scene in front of her unfolded in slow motion as she slid to the floor. She closed her eyes as James' strong hands pulled her upwards and close to him. He held her so tight as if he'd never let her go.

"You are fine. Addie saved you, saved us all."

"How," she whispered, as his lips met hers in a searing life reaffirming kiss.

"Addie shot Edwin in the head. He's gone now. He can't do anyone harm," he said as Drake's men gathered around him. Drake bent to check the man's pulse.

"Addie did that? Edwin held his gun to my head. She could have killed me." Tavia turned to her friend. Addie held the gun in her trembling hand, her gaze still focused on the man she just killed.

Hamilton set his hand on Addie's shoulder and slowly took the gun from her before looking at Tavia. "Addie is the best shot I've ever seen. She never misses. You were lucky she was here. She's the only one who could have taken that shot."

Addie seemed to recover, tears sliding down her face. "I'm sorry I frightened you. I didn't have a choice. He was going to kill you. I've seen that expression too many times to count. He was evil and now he can no longer hurt anyone."

Tavia stared wide-eyed at Addie, still unable to believe what had just happened. When she looked down, blood stained her beautiful wedding dress. She felt the wetness on her face. Trembling she tried to wipe it off, but the blood wouldn't leave, yet she kept trying.

"Here," James handed her a cloth from the only table left in the room. "Use this."

She looked at him before trying to wipe the blood from her dress. "It won't go away," her voice was a shaky whisper. "I can't get it out."

"Let me," James dabbed the cloth on Tavia face.

Ella stood by her sister, her hand beneath Tavia's chin, "Look at me. Don't look at that man."

Drake's men were moving his body from the room, but a pool of blood remained.

Tavia moved slowly, looking around the room. She saw the concern etched in everyone's eyes as well as the fear. Her father's usually ruddy complexion was milk white.

"Tavia," Ella said with a stern voice, "I've asked Alma to run you a bath. James will take you downstairs to your room. Even though you are free to go to your townhouse, Drake and I both think it would be best if you stay here and move back tomorrow. You're in no condition to spend an hour riding in a carriage."

She looked to James who still held her. Closing her eyes for a second, she waited. "You have blood on you too."

"I suppose I do." He placed a tender kiss on her forehead. "Not the wedding night I would have liked or even dreamed of, but Ella is right. It's already late and by the time we bathe...we should stay here."

"It's a horrible way to end our weddings," Eveleen said. "Take care. Logan and I decided to leave now, go to our townhouse. Can we all meet here tomorrow morning?" She looked to Addie and Hamilton also.

"We're going home too, but we'll come back in the morning and we can all talk. There's a lot Edwin can't tell us that we need to know. Hamilton and I believe there is a woman, the missing debutant. If that's so we need to find her before she becomes another one of Edwin's victims."

"So it's not over." Tavia leaned into James as his arms tightened around her, reassuring her. "He told me her name was Nan and she cared for him."

"Edwin held a lace handkerchief in his hand. The initials

embroidered there are an L and an F, the same as the debutant who disappeared. Lucy Fields," Hamilton said. "If this is the same lady, Nan must be his own name for her."

"If she's still alive, she'll be in trouble. He would never leave her unbound," Addie said.

"I think she is alive," Tavia said. "The way he spoke of her. It was in the present."

"How did Edwin get inside?" Logan asked, "He should have never been able to get through your guards," he'd turned to Drake, accusation in his eyes. "He could have killed Tavia."

Tavia moistened her lips then breathing deeply before speaking. "He said you forgot about something and that it was easy to get inside. I didn't know what he was talking about."

"Tunnel to the barn and the old cottage. We were stupid," Drake said.

Tavia's breath caught in her throat. "I don't want to think what could happen to Nan."

James spoke up, pulling Tavia closer, "We should leave. This discussion is doing nothing to alleviate your terror."

"I apologize," Logan said to Tavia. "But these things need to be talked about."

"I have two unconscious men near the entrance to the tunnel. He got past them. They will be fired tomorrow, pending their explanation."

~ * ~

Drake waited until the newlyweds retired to their bedrooms or their homes before he pulled Jarret, Damian and the other men in the wedding party aside. Noticing Charles hovering nearby with Ella, he motioned for them to join them.

"Good you're all here. We've got to see if Lucy or Nan as Edwin called her was left in the cottage. She could need help." He turned to his wife, "Ella," then "Charles, I need for the two of you to make sure the guests are reassured. I've spoken with some of them and explained the situation. Keep the music going as well as the food."

"You're not going to take any chances," Ella said, her face etched with anxiety.

"There is no danger. Edwin is gone and he had no one helping him. Somehow he became attached to his latest victim."

"Still, take care."

He bent to kiss her before he turned to leave. "You will wait up for me?" he asked turning to look at her over his shoulder. He wished he could spend the night with her.

At the stables they mounted and rode through the night. He'd been this route so many times he was sure he could find the cottage with his eyes closed. Before they left, he packed bandages and willow bark. He prayed now they would find her alive and would be able to return her to her family.

Tonight, few clouds dotted the sky. It was a bright night as they rode past the small lake on his property. Thoughts of past memories with Ella crept through his mind. The time she was shot because he didn't take necessary precautions.

"We're almost here." He saw the dark outline of the building. Edwin had left no candle burning and no smoke flowed from the chimney. His gut tightened as he thought of the horrific things Edwin must have put this young woman through.

Jarret rode beside him. "Do you think the girl will be alive?"

"I've been praying she is."

"Me too," Jarret said, falling back as they entered the forest and followed the short path to the cottage.

They stopped in front of the door, "Damian, stand guard and call out if you see anything that looks at all strange. Jarret come with me." They strode inside.

"Anyone here," Jarret called as they stepped through the door.

He heard her labored breaths.

"Edwin, is that you?" a small voice came from a distance and seemed to haunt the tiny room.

"No, he's not here. It's Drake Montgomerie. I've come to take you home." He turned, motioning to Jarret and in a whisper, "Send one of my men to get the police. Tell them Lucy Fields will be at my summer home."

"Go away."

He stepped into the small bedroom. She was tied to the bedpost. "I'm going to untie you. I don't mean you harm." He approached her slowly, recognizing the panic in her eyes.

"Where is Edwin?" She struggled, backing as close to the bedpost as she could go, her eyes filled with terror.

"He's not coming for you," Drake's hands rested on the binding. "You'll be free in a minute."

"I don't want to go home," she said, seeming to recognize the fact Edwin wasn't going to return for her.

"Is he in jail?" Now untied, she brought her hands to her lap, massaging her swollen wrists.

"No, no, he's not. Edwin isn't coming back."

"You killed him," she said, her eyes even wider. "Why would you do that?"

"I didn't kill him, but he is dead because he held a young woman at gunpoint, threatening to kill her. Lucy, he tried to drown her."

Terrified sobs rent the air and Drake's heart went out to her. "He wanted to throw me in the river too but people were there and he couldn't."

"He kept you alive and seemed to care something for you?"

"I don't know about that, but he's the only person who ever listened to me," she sobbed, her face in her hands. "I don't want to go home, and I don't want to go back to my chaperone. She was awful to me."

"Where would you like to go?" Drake asked, concern for her paramount.

"I have money, a trust fund, but I can't access it until I'm twenty. I just want to be left alone."

"How old are you now?"

"Eighteen," she said as Drake helped her to her feet.

"Can you ride a horse?" He searched for an answer to her problems, noting he should ask Ella for some ideas.

Moisture from her tears lined her face while she was shaking her head in an effort to answer him.

"I'll have someone drive you in the carriage then. You'll have to go with the authorities."

"They will take me back to my chaperone. I can't go there. I'll run away."

"Perhaps he could enlist her as his newest spy. It was a possibility if she would agree."

Chapter Twelve

James wanted to sweep Tavia into his arms and carry her down the steps to their room, but when he tried, she protested. "I can walk."

"If you insist." With his arm wrapped around her waist and her head against his chest, they walked together.

In the dressing room, true to Ella's word, Alma had a hot bath waiting for Tavia.

"Lady Tavia, leave your dress outside the door and I'll see if I can remove the blood stains. I'll leave the two of you now. If you need anything, ring the bell." Alma backed from the room. "Have a good night."

"Would you like me to help with your dress?" James said, so unsure of what he should do or how he should act. In the short time he'd known Tavia, she had defied death three times now. He couldn't imagine a life without her, and he prayed the rest of their lives would be devoid of this type of excitement. He wasn't even counting the carriage accident.

Her small laugh held little humor. "Since Alma left, I do need you to help." She turned her back to him as he deftly unfastened all of her clothing, letting each piece slip to the floor so she could step out of the garments. "Do you have that gift for me?"

"You think of that now." He chuckled, hoping to lighten the moment." I'm going to wait until tomorrow night. The evening has been ruined for what I had planned. I'm curious, how did Addie conceal the gun all night? She must have had it the whole time."

"Addie had pockets in her gown. They were just big enough to carry the small gun she used. We all knew she planned to keep the weapon in her pocket, but she wouldn't tell us why. I don't think she trusts anyone save the people closest to her."

"She's a spy, Tavia. She probably always carries a weapon. We all had weapons with us."

"You did?" she asked, her eyes wide as she watched him take off his waistcoat to show her the huge knife he wore. She put a hand to her cheek, steadying herself with a hand on his chest, "The room is spinning, and I can't seem to stop this horrible feeling."

She wore only her shift, one arm wrapped around her and leaning into him to stop the shaking. He didn't think anything except time would end the fear from this night. Her face so pale, he worried over her. "Come, let me help you into the bath."

She nodded, "Fine."

"Arms up and I'll free you of this last piece of clothing."

She did as he asked then stepped into the water with a small sigh. With her hands, she swirled the water around her but made no attempt to wash the blood away. "It will stain the water red you know."

Without speaking, he soaped a sponge and gently began washing her face and shoulders. "We'll wash the blood away tonight, and with time the memories will fade. We'll make new pleasant memories." Carefully, he removed the strands of diamonds from her hair.

"They were Aunt Charlotte's diamonds. She loaned them to me and told me when she passed they would be mine. But I don't care about things like that, although they are beautiful."

"We need to wash your hair," he told her, unpinning the dark strands and letting them fall down her back.

"More blood, just get it out. Get it all out." Tears slid down her cheeks and more than anything he needed to make sure he held her through the night.

He washed and rinsed her hair then lifted her from the water. Reaching for one of the large bath sheets Alma left for their use, he wrapped the towel around her. "Wait here," he told her as he strode to the armoire and retrieved a warm flannel nightgown for her.

She dried herself, letting the towel fall to the floor. "Thank you." She held her arms over her head, letting him help her into the gown.

"Warm yourself. Sit by the fire. I'm going to take a quick bath then I'll comb and dry your hair."

She nodded and without saying anything, she walked into the main room and sat down on the hearth her hands folded in her lap.

He watched her from a distance, hoping she would be all right while he washed. Quickly, he slipped out of his clothing and into the water. It had grown tepid, but the liquid still felt good around his body. With the sponge he washed himself, hoping all the blood would be gone. He ducked under the water, running his finger through his hair.

Rising, he scooped up the second towel, drying himself as he walked into the room then securing it around his waist. She had poured them both a glass of wine and sat with her legs curled beside her on the fur rug.

"It was too hot so close to the fire," she whispered. "I feel better. The bath, the wine, is helping me forget. Now you can help me."

While he was in the tub, she had found his gift to her. She no longer wore the flannel nightgown but a sheer daffodil yellow negligée with a matching robe. He could see all of her. She had no idea what the sight of her did to him.

He wasn't sure what she was asking, but his heart leapt at her words. She had set the comb on the rug. He picked it up and sitting beside her, began to comb the dark silken strands he'd rather be running his finger through. They burned his fingers as if they soaked in the heat from the flames.

"You're hair has to be dry before we go to bed," he told her as he combed her hair, needing to see her without the robe. The straps tied and he could easily undo them.

"What about yours? Your hair should be dry too." She turned the tips of her breasts, subtly thrusting against the fabric of her gown, taunting and teasing him with their beauty.

This sheer negligée was one Drake had encouraged him to purchase for this wedding night, a night that had turned into a nightmare yet seemed to be taking a turn for the better.

"My hair?" He'd never thought about his hair before. "It doesn't matter."

She touched his beard before threading her fingers into his hair. "It's still damp. Should I comb it for you?"

His gut tightened and his body hardened with desire. "You don't

260

know what you're asking. Not tonight but perhaps some other time."

"I'd like to comb it for you." She began to finger comb the reddish blond hair.

"James," she spoke softly, "I'm not a delicate flower as you like to think. I need you in the most elemental and primal way as a reassurance of life. Please don't deny me, us, the pleasures of this night, our wedding night."

She was wrong, she was fragile and he needed to make sure nothing like this ever happened again, needed to make sure he protected her better from now on.

"I don't think so," he murmured. "You're not ready. You need to rest and eat. You're still recovering from the near drowning and the chilling night in the barn."

"Maybe you're not ready," she said, her expression filled with longing and her beautiful green eyes with passion. "Are you afraid?" Her hand rested on his chest.

He sucked air, his belly tightening as her fingers drifted lower. "You don't know what you're asking." It seemed he couldn't think, could only feel.

"I do but right now I'm not going to argue with you. If I can't convince you to make love to me, then I'll have no recourse but to seduce you." She slipped the robe from her arms and let it fall around her.

He couldn't help the smile. Her nipples beckoned for his attention. He settled his hands around her tiny waist then explored her small ribcage to her breasts then back to her waist. "I'd love for you to seduce me. My seduction would not be all that difficult but not tonight, not until I'm sure making love won't be detrimental to your health."

She watched him over the rim of her wine glass before tracing the top with a delicate fingertip, her green eyes seeming to sparkle. She was seducing him as they spoke, and he had to applaud her and concentrate on not succumbing to her ploy.

"You are the most stubborn man," she sighed softly then sipped the wine, catching a small drop with her tongue.

"You are just as stubborn, perhaps more," he told her, unable to take his gaze from her lips.

"Do you believe there is a young woman bound and gagged somewhere?"

It seemed she meant to change the subject and he was relieved. She didn't know it, but he was on the verge of carrying her to their bed. "There could be. If so, we need to find her soon."

But he was wrong about her changing the subject.

He shivered with need as she traced a path from one nipple to the other across his chest. The shifting of ideas was over before it had barely begun. Suddenly, all rational thoughts slipped from his head. All his primal male instincts kicked in. Taking her hand in his, he set it back on her lap. She pouted, tilting her head sideways, seeming to study him.

He wanted to get his mind on something else. "If Edwin didn't trust her not to run, he would have left her tied up. She would be cold and hungry."

"Hush, there is nothing we can do about it now. He didn't have a chance to talk or tell us anything; not that he would have. Perhaps she is alive but understanding this man is driven to murder, the body hasn't been found. If it didn't wash up on the bank of the Thames, it could be in the ocean by now."

"But what if she's still alive?" She touched his nipple again, slowly and gently raking her tiny nails down his chest, sending shivers of desire racing within.

"If she's alive, we'll find her. I promise." Perhaps the conversation had taken a wrong turn. "We should speak of things more pleasant."

"James, all this brings back the nightmare we went through. Hold me, make me forget." She clung to him.

He couldn't refuse her, but he had to find away to convince her tonight was not for lovemaking it was for recovering.

"Do you want to go to bed?" he asked, hoping she was so exhausted she would fall asleep.

"Not yet," she smiled prettily at him, bringing her hand to his face. "Have you always worn a beard?"

He needed to laugh at her question. "Not when I was a lad."

"Well, you know I didn't mean that." She ran her finger down his neck and across his collarbone before touching his nipples again. She picked up her glass of wine, sipping, but she spilled some on his chest. She bent to lick the moisture from his body.

He cleared his throat, his heart pounding beneath his ribs. He didn't know how to respond to the innocent yet erotic gesture. "Since I was twenty and could grow a beard that didn't look scraggly." Sometime when he wasn't paying attention, she unfastened the towel he wore. Her fingers touched his belly softly, sending molten fire through his veins.

"You want me," she said, softly reaching to touch his shaft. She ran a finger from tip to base then back. His body jerked with longing. As if proud of herself a small smile on her face, she sat back, gazing at him with her passion filled eyes.

"We can't," his voice wavered and she touched him again, teased and explored him.

"I need you, James. I'm not going to let you deny me." She pulled the silken negligee up her hips and slowly straddled him.

"The night has been..." he couldn't speak, couldn't find the words as her hot core met the tip of his pulsing shaft and she very slowly lowered herself on him.

She smiled again. "Do you like this, James? I thought you might. I've been dreaming of doing this for a while now."

She didn't move but he felt her clench against him, felt each tiny pulse of desire sweep through her and entice him. She was silken fire, her hair flowing around her, just touching her shoulders now. Picking up her glass of wine, she poured a tiny amount across his chest. Once more she licked the moisture from him, stopping at each nipple to tease and taste with her warm lips and hot tongue.

She slowly rose then moved downward again, hesitating, teasing him with her sultry heat.

"Ah hell." With her legs wrapped around him, he stood and carried her to the bed.

Hours later he lay in bed, staring at the ceiling and smiling. It had been a wedding night to remember and still Edwin even in his death haunted them.

Beside him, Tavia rose, her breasts brushing softly against his chest. "Tavia?"

"James," she hesitated.

"What is it?"

She moistened her lips, gazing at him, "I should have told you sooner."

"Tell me..." she had his curiosity clearly engaged.

"I love you, James. I've loved you for so long I can't remember when I first knew it. I didn't want to say the words though. I was afraid you didn't love me back."

"Ah, Tavia, I love you more than words could describe. I think I've loved you since the first day I saw you."

"Should we try to create a child?" she asked. "Would you like a baby? James II maybe?"

"I'd rather have a little girl who looks just like you," he said.

They made love again and prayed their lives would be long and peaceful.

"I love you, James," she said again as she watched him sleep. "I love you so very much. Thank you for coming into my life."

Coming from the Author
May 2019
from
Rogue Phoenix Press

Larena's Fascination
Twelve Dancing Princesses Book Ten

Chapter One
1821

Standing atop the base of the lamppost, Larena strained to see over the heads of the milling people while trying to shimmer higher. The day, notarized by people in the streets protesting repression by the English government. The citizens, in Larena's mind, had every right to want more from their government. They weren't asking for something they didn't work for. The citizens were proud and honorable people.

Over the years since the Napoleonic wars, food prices soared and wages fell. Fewer jobs existed because of industrialization and heads of families found it difficult to feed their children.

"What do you see up there?" Tyna, Larena's friend asked peering up at her, one hand shielding her eyes from the setting sun. "It's got to be very interesting to have you so focused."

"Soldiers are lining up with guns pointing at the protestors. Give me a boost higher," Larena said, wishing either she was taller or the lamppost was easier to climb. "I can't see very much."

For a moment she was pushed higher. Without warning, the friendly hands disappeared and she found herself hauled from the post and into hostile masculine arms. She struggled against the force taking her away from her vantage point.

"Put me down. You've no right to be so upper handed," Larena said, furiously trying to punch the horrible man, hitting only air.

"Little fool, what are you doing here? You're coming with me." Gavin Broon wrapped his arms tightly around her and pushed her through the rapidly growing crowds to a doorway. "You take chances with your life, and I won't have you doing that."

Bumped and battered from all sides by the throngs of bystanders, "No," she protested, struggling against him. She pushed at his arms yet they didn't budge from around her waist. "You... you can't leave me for weeks then show up one day telling me what I can and can't do."

Crowds swarmed past her. Somewhere shots were fired and screams filled the air. "Little fool," he bit out again with a hot whisper close to her ear. "What the bloody hell were you thinking? You could be shot or hurt by the stampeding herds of people."

"These people have a right to be heard. Those laws keeping them earning a decent living should be repealed and you know it. Only the wealthy who want to make more and more money at everyone's expense are for that law. They don't care about the people. What do you believe? What do you stand for?"

"Are you finished?" Gavin asked, sounding exasperated and frustrated. It seemed he was totally out of patience. "You know what I think."

"Do you want to hear more?" Larena didn't care how impatient he was and no, she didn't know what he thought. She had the right to her own pursuits of knowledge. She wanted to make a difference in the world.

"I'm sure you could recite all the laws and acts that have been passed since the Napoleonic wars, but we have something more pressing to do right now." His hands tightened around her, sending strange evocative sensations through her.

"What could be more important than the pursuit of free speech?" She still meant to protest his Neanderthal behavior, but she was fresh out of new arguments, at least ones she thought he might listen to.

"The extenuation of your life," he whispered close to her ear, sending more curious shivers within. She remembered their first kiss, but this was far more provocative and mercuric.

Up two steps to a small protective space, Gavin stopped, turning her. His lips descended on hers while he ran his fingers through her hair, pins clattering to the earth. Then with his hands around her waist, he pulled her close, running his hands up her ribcage, stopping below her breasts.

Then his hands framed her face as he kissed her, using his tongue and his teeth to punctuate his caresses. He stopped to look at her, the steel glint of his blue-gray eyes searing her. An inferno simmered deep inside, a sensation she fought to deny. As much as she loved the kiss, had even yearned for it, she didn't want to give into his mandates, and she was afraid that was exactly what she was doing here.

Her breaths came in short bouts, her blood pulsing heatedly. She brought her hand up to slap him. "How..."

He easily caught her wrist and brought it down, holding it tight against his chest where she felt the thundering of his heart. "How dare I?" he finished her sentence for her. "Where your safety is concerned, milady, I will dare anything. You have pushed past the limitations of my patience. The last thing I want for you is to see you on the gallows, a prison ship or in Newgate."

His huge body blocked her view to the street. Yet she was sure chaos seemed to encompass the thoroughfare. Shouts and cries of pain reverberated through the narrow thoroughfare.

"My safety was not in jeopardy until you showed up," she protested, struggling slightly in protest yet understanding he held the upper hand in this matter, brute strength. "What is happening out there? I need to see."

As if to deny her statement, his mouth descended upon hers again, his hand on her derrière pulled her flush with his body.

He pulled her shirt from the waistband of her skirt, his hand rising against her back until his fingers found her bare skin. "You should not be here," he whispered, his warm breath caressing her cheek.

It seemed at the moment he had no control, but she had longed for this for months now and she didn't want him to stop. Still, she objected. "Where I am is not your con..."

Stopping her protest, his lips met hers again, his tongue drawing a line across her lips. Once more she tried to speak. When she opened her mouth, he filled hers with his tongue. A tiny sound emanated from her as she wilted into him, wishing she didn't make this so easy. Too many months had passed since she felt the heat of his kisses. She'd thought he forgot about her. She braced herself, her hands against his chest in a feeble attempt to push him away. Something she hoped she couldn't accomplish.

He kissed her again and again, her lips swelling from the intense actions. She clung to his shoulders, barely able to stand and still his lips remained on hers, enticing in everyway.

"Master Broon, you shouldn't be here." The voice seemed to echo around her in a hazy void.

Gavin turned, keeping her behind him and pressing her against the door. "Constable. Sorry, I got carried away for a moment. We'll be going on our way as soon as you think it's safe."

"It's safe now, wont' be in another few minutes. This gathering is getting out of hand. We have orders to arrest everyone involved. You and your lady friend need to leave before it's too late. Find a place that's a bit more private for what you're doing."

Gavin cleared his throat. "As you can see, we are not involved in the protests. My lady friend and I just want to find a way out of here so we can be alone. My office is a block from here. Could you see us there?"

"Lady friend," she repeated, hitting him on his back, furious with his audacity even though that was almost what she wanted to be. "I'm not your lady friend."

Over his shoulder he stared at her, once more his glare shook her to the core. "Pretend."

"I'd be happy to help you," the constable said. "Follow me." He set off for Gavin's office at a quick pace.

"I don't want to go." She held back, refusing to move her feet to help him with this pretense. She was not going to pretend to be his whore even if it meant her safety.

"You want to see the inside of Newgate prison? If you don't move your feet, I'll carry you."

"Of course not. I would never get arrested and if I did, Aunty would call in some favors," Still she fought him, denying his words and his threats.

"Best you hurry," the man said. "The soldiers are heading this way. It's not the time to dally. If the two of you are having a lover's spat, wait till your safe and sound," he chuckled.

"Don't push this any farther, Larena. If you make me, I'll haul you over my shoulder."

As if to give credence to his relationship with her, he wrapped his arm around her shoulder, letting his fingers rest over one breast. She inhaled a swift deep breath. "Gavin." She recalled The Duchess' words, kisses are fine but anything else you need to tell him no. This, she supposed, was something else.

"Behave yourself then."

For a minute or two she pretended compliance. When she saw a small escape route, she jerked out of his arms. Freedom was close; she ran two steps before she found herself caught and unceremoniously slung over his shoulder. "No," she pounded him on the back, trying to wiggle herself from his shoulder. "You can't do this to me. I don't want to go with you."

His hand came down possessively on her rear and stayed there, his fingers moving on her as if he claimed her. "I already have done this to you and while I would normally indulge you in anything you want, I can't tolerate this defiance to the law."

"Hurry up," the constable encouraged. "You're almost there. You and your lady friend will be nice and safe at your office until it's all over. It won't be long before everyone is put in the wagons the soldiers have brought. You don't want to be rounded up with the hoards."

"What's going to happen to these folks?" Gavin asked pleasantly, waving his arm, indicating those who were racing through the street. "Will they be released?"

"The wagons are lined up and ready to take everyone who doesn't get away to jail. They'll be tried and sentenced." The constable seemed eager to get them away from the crowds.

"What then?" Gavin continued with his questioning, seeming to need to make a point that was directed at her.

Larena was sure Gavin knew the answer. He was asking for her benefit, but she wasn't about to listen. Hanging head down she closed her eyes and tried to close her ears as well.

"Off to a penal colony, either Australia or Tasmania," he said as if that was an everyday occurrence.

She gulped air, telling herself the lack of oxygen was due to her lungs pressed against his shoulder. Were the two of them in cahoots? She knew he would do anything to convince her he was always right.

"Long time to spend in the bowls of a ship with little food or water and no where to relieve yourself. Are the women raped?" Gavin queried.

"Horrible trip, I've heard. The pretty ones don't fare very well. Here you go." Seemingly intrigued, he stared at her as she lifted her head high enough to see where they were.

"Thanks, you're help is much appreciated." Not setting her on her feet, Gavin stepped into the building and taking the stairs two at a time, made his way upstairs.

"Put me down," she bit out, furious with him and unwilling to let him dictate her life. "I can't breathe."

"You should have thought about that before you tried to run into more trouble." Ignoring her, he strode through the rooms upstairs. She saw what looked like a living room but he didn't stop there. Instead, he strode into a separate room and before she could take another breath, she landed on a bed.

He came down beside her, his hand resting domineeringly on her stomach. "Did you hear what the man said?" The frigid glint of his eyes and voice chilled her. She'd never seen him like this.

She tried to scoot to a sitting position, but his body weight stopped her. "I didn't listen to him, so no." He had taken liberties she didn't know yet if she wanted to give him. His absence from her life had shaken her confidence, and now he suddenly reappeared. A stubborn streak settled in, and she knew she would not agree with him just on principle.

His eyes shimmered his mouth drawn thin. "I worry about you." He pushed tangled hair from her face. "You're too beautiful. I don't want anything to happen to you, and you do things you shouldn't. As formidable as she is, The Duchess might not have been able to pull in favors soon enough to get you out of that predicament you were so eager to get yourself into."

"What do you care? I haven't even seen you in weeks." She was determined not to let him touch her heart until he proved himself to her. A few kisses every now and then were not enough incentive for that.

When he looked at her, it seemed he gazed past her. She'd never seen him so severe and hard, unyielding would perhaps be descriptive. This time when his lips found hers, they were gentle yet still demanding a response she was unsure of. This was Gavin and she'd wanted his attention for so long. He was doing this to her, making her want him, ready to give up everything. She steeled herself against his seduction.

And yet...

Gavin touched her in ways she couldn't fathom. His hands moved on her and a molten inferno of his making rushed through her. His lips and warm moist tongue touched upon her neck and the curve of her shoulder, the line of her collarbone. She shivered in response, creating tiny noises in the back of her throat that he seemed to take pleasure in hearing.

Eyes half-closed, she watched him doing things to her she'd wanted for such a long time. She had given up on him, assuming she didn't interest him. Six months ago, two months, she would have given all of herself to this man who stole her heart the first moment she looked upon him. Now she held herself back, wishing for things that could have been. She looked to her future now and was unsure he held a place in it.

Coming to her senses and trying desperately to escape the sweet seduction of his lips and tongue where they met her flesh, "No, Gavin, not now. This can't happen." She pushed on his shoulders, her eyes wide open now. "You have to stop."

"This milady is our present and out future. In time I will have nothing but your sweet compliance," he murmured softly, the whisper of his breath against her still seducing. Yet he obeyed her request.

He rose from her, his gaze locked with hers. She would battle him with all her heart and strength. Here in London while he'd been gone, she found a purpose to her life and he must have found something somewhere else. He'd been away for so long.

She sat up, to no avail trying to readjust her clothing and hair. "Gavin?"

Shoulders rigid, he strode into the main sitting room. She heard voices and while she recognized the man's as Drake Montgomerie, her cousin's husband, she could not make out anything they said. When she drew closer to the door, she could finally make out some of their words.

"I found her," Gavin said. "Little hellion that she is, she's very special to me and I wouldn't want to see her hurt, her life changed irrevocably. She can't continue to run free with no guidance."

Her heart felt as if he slashed it with a knife. Little hellion, that was all he thought of her. For a fleeting moment, she'd thought he cared enough about her to find her. That his concern for her safety was sincere, but obviously she was wrong. He would not find a way into her heart.

Quickly, she rose from the bed, tucking in her blouse and finding a mirror, trying to put her hair in order. Nothing could be done about her kiss-swollen lips and the total disarray he'd created in her appearance. A lone tear slid from her eye. Furiously, she wiped it away with the back of her hand. Setting her hands on a table in front of the mirror, she drew in a long deep breath in an attempt to settle her nerves.

Drake would surmise what Gavin did to her and how would she explain her appearance to Ella. her cousin? Then she would have to explain to The Duchess what had happened. Clenching her fists, she strode into the room, back as stiff as she could make it, remembering The Duchess' advice: men think with their cock. It seemed she was right about Gavin.

Slowly, Drake looked from Gavin to her then back, his gaze held no questions. He knew very well what Gavin had done. She swallowed hard, thinking to stride from his apartment and hail a cab, but she doubted if either man would allow that to happen.

"It's not what it looks like," Larena said, still trying to put her blouse into her skirt and unable to meet his gaze.

Gavin strode to her, blocking Drakes view. "You should have looked in the mirror before you presented yourself half naked in the sitting room." His hands fell upon her blouse, fastening buttons that he'd skillfully undone, sifting his fingers through her hair as if he could replace the pins he removed.

She gasped at his words, looking down and feeling blood rush to her face. "You did this to me."

His arrogant smile left her breathless. Then he whispered, "I'm certainly glad it was me and not some other scoundrel. You could have told me no and rest assured, I would have stopped."

"What will he think?" She truly didn't understand herself. Of course Drake would believe the worst, and he would tell Ella who would tell The Duchess. No, Ella would say nothing, but she would undoubtedly have a nice long talk with her.

"I need to get you home. You do know you cannot have anymore contact with these people." He ran his finger down her cheek, a strange tender look in his eyes. "You need to stay away from them. They mean you harm and are taking advantage of your naiveté."

"Says you. I don't believe for a minute. Tyna would take advantage of anyone, especially not me." She challenged him in everyway she could think of. Obeying this man was not possible. He had no hold on her life nor did she want him to command her obedience, and she was not naive.

"You will regret it if you disobey. The Duchess, your guardian, would demand the same things." The silver steel of his eyes sliced through her heart.

It seemed Drake had watched their interchange. "Gavin is right, Larena. There are elements in play here that could be dangerous. We both understand this is not about obedience, it's about your safety. I'm sure Gavin would never command you do anything you wished unless he was serious about it."

"Probably not. Where I'm concerned, he sees danger in the sunbeam slanting across a window. At least today he does, tomorrow I won't see him," she replied, wondering if she was just being foolish and defying these men because she was angry with Gavin for abandoning her for months.

"Take heed, Larena. This is not a game to be played." It seemed Gavin couldn't stop himself from playing the autocrat.

"What ever you wish," she said, smiling sweetly. She'd been so bored and frustrated with her life. She'd tried to find something useful to do that would make her feel good about herself. Then she met Tyna, who gave her new purpose and direction.

"Yes," Drake said, stepping in to the conversation once more. "No one knows for sure what their future will bring, but you dabble in politics you know little about. I don't understand the argument between the two of you, but both parties should figure out what is really bothering you before it's too late."

"I'm not ignorant and I understand the politics. If I were a man, this conversation would not be happening." She fisted her hands, anger growing inside. Feelings of helplessness swept through her before she pushed them back, just as she tried to push her hair from her face.

"You don't have all the facts, either," Gavin said. "Here, let me help." Somehow he managed with the few pins left in her hair, to arrange it so she didn't look as if she just rose from his bed. "I don't mean to make you angry, Larena. I care about you."

"The people of London are incensed and some of them are using you," Drake told her as he paced the room. "You've got to understand the laws and that you must not be seen meeting with these people. That in itself could be construed as a crime."

"I don't believe you. Who is taking advantage of me?" She wanted answers. No one she knew played her. She made all her decisions from facts and what she understood to be right.

"Your friend Tyna, for one," Drake told her. "She is part of the resistance to the laws that have been voted on by parliament. She not only fights to see the laws repealed but the throne abolished as in France. Obviously, the government does not want that to happen and will use all its power to see it doesn't."

She stiffened, inhaling a quick deep breath at his words. "Tyna wouldn't do that. She has not expected me to do anything. In fact, she's counseled against some of my actions." Yet the girl found her one day when she was riding in the park and befriended her, telling her stories of her childhood and the suffering she'd seen around her. She had believed everything the young woman told her. Suddenly, Larena wasn't so sure about her new friend.

"All you know about this woman is what she's told you," Gavin pointed out, his expression changing to one Larena didn't understand. "You are innocent and believe in the good of all. She is not who you think she is and yes, she is using you to her own ends as well as her brother's."

"I'm not naïve," she said, realizing in this she most likely was too trusting. Thinking back she desperately tried to recall everything Tyna said to her, but very little came to mind.

Gavin looked away for a moment, and truly she wanted to know what he was thinking. She could not read his thoughts. What did he know she didn't, and why wouldn't he tell her?

"How you think of yourself makes no difference at this point. You're life is at stake here. I need your promise you will stay away from her," Drake said, seeming to step in where Gavin left off.

Perhaps it was a good thing the request was made by Drake. At this point, if Gavin had asked her to promise this, she would have promptly and without thought said no. Instead she decided to somewhat agree, "I will take your advice under consideration."

"I'm glad," Drake said, his hands behind his back, a dark shuttered look on his face.

"I'm supposed to meet her tomorrow for tea. I don't have anyway to contact her. She always sends messages to me." Her body quivered, wondering if Tyna befriended her so she could gain something from her.

"Where? I'll see that Addie meets the two of you. You can tell Tyna that Addie's your friend. In a way she is. You did attend her wedding," Drake said. His words seemed to give her some encouragement.

"I barely know the woman. What I do know is that she was one of your spies, Drake," Larena protested. "How will I convince Tyna she's a friend?" This had taken on a new dimension. "I'm not going to spy for you and she's there to spy on me, I'll..."

"What Larena? Dig yourself a hole so deep you can't climb out of?" Gavin spoke up, clearly finding it difficult to control his anger.

Drake broke into the conversation with a heavy sigh, "No one wants you to do that, especially not me. Addie will be there to protect you just as she protected Tavia at her wedding. I'm sure I don't need to remind you how she used her pistol to shoot the man who meant to murder your cousin. Addie is a good person and a better friend. You couldn't have a better person at your side."

"Do I have a choice?" She didn't believe for one second she needed protection from Tyna. The girl had been honest with her about everything. She'd always told her there was danger in what she did.

"No choice," Gavin said, "It's either Addie or myself."

"I'll take Addie any day over you," she said and was cheered for a moment by the slight flicker of insecurity in his eyes then it vanished, replaced by the hard visage she had become used to in the last few hours, realizing what she saw was not insecurity but annoyance.

He watched her for what seemed an eternity and with a shrug, he said, "Have it your way."

"You should get her home," Drake said with a tinge of laughter in his voice. "Do you need help, Gavin?"

"I can handle this one," Gavin said with a raised eyebrow, seeming to search her for some reason she might have to refuse. His eyes raked her with a careless disdain. A sizzle of mockery touched his eyes then vanished with something seeming a tiny bit softer.

"The Duchess will be waiting for the two of you. She has important news. I will see the two of you later. I hope you work out this problem between the two of you before you have to speak with Charlotte. Use the time in the cab to hash things out. A united front is always the best course." Drake turned on a heel and strode from the small apartment.

"Well," Gavin said, gallantly holding out his arm and smiling as if they were off to a picnic and had not spent the better part of the day at odds with each other.

She marched past him, head held high, her back stiff. There was no way she would talk anything out with the infuriating man.

~ * ~

By the time they hailed a cab and reached The Duchess' townhouse, the sun had set and streetlights were beginning to light the darkness. Gavin helped her from the cab despite her reluctance. He wished he'd handled the last few hours differently, but Larena had a way of getting under his skin, making him say things he didn't mean.

"Do you know this important news Drake spoke of?" Larena asked before they entered the house, having refused to speak to him for the duration of the ride. She suddenly needed to understand what was about to happen. "I probably should know."

"Come, she's waiting for us in the parlor." It seemed both The Duchess and her companion, Scarlett, waited for them. Larena was correct, however, he had ignored her for months but not because he didn't want to see her and court her properly. He understood the simple fact that he had to reassure her and instill in her a reason to believe in him.

"You're not going to answer me," she said, her words clipped.

"The Duchess will respond to all your questions." He opened the door for her. They walked into the parlor.

"Finally," The Duchess said, tapping her cane, a plate of lemon bars available. "What held you up? I thought you would be here hours ago."

"An altercation that couldn't be avoided," Gavin chose to reply before Larena could weave a believable story out of falsehoods. Then there was absolute silence while he watched The Duchess' riveted her gaze on Larena and back to him seeming to search for answers.

"What say you to that, Larena? The Duchess asked impatiently, narrowing her eyes at her wayward charge. "Can you tell me about this confrontation Mister Broon speaks of?"

Larena did not meet her aunt's gaze, seeming to like the looks of the floor and rug better. "I'd rather not talk about our altercation. In any case, the dispute between us was really nothing." Her gaze shifted from the floor to Gavin.

"You probably don't want my rendition," Gavin said pleasantly, "but if Larena doesn't want to tell her story, I'll be happy to explain our tardiness. May I take a seat?" He needed to tell all the truth, but he didn't want The Duchess to judge Larena too harshly or worse, keep him from seeing her. Now that his business was finished, he planned on spending every accessible moment with her, changing her mind about him.

"Of course, I'm waiting with baited breath for the story." The Duchess waved her hand, "Would you like something to drink or a lemon bar?" she pointed to the plate.

"Both," Gavin said, laughing, "A brandy if I may." He always enjoyed his sessions with The Duchess. In so many ways the conversations were always refreshing.

"Scarlett, see to their needs. I'm sure my niece needs a brandy too. The girls seem to have a penchant for the stuff. I'd prefer a fresh pot of tea today. Then we'll hear what they have to say."

Gavin sat down on a sofa next to Larena, lazily letting his leg touch her skirts, watching her as she turned to stare at him but made no attempt to move away. What was she up to?

Insinuating himself as far and as deep into her life as he could was his immediate intention. He didn't mean to give her a chance to run away from him, simply because he was pretty sure this was an act of defiance.

"Larena, do you care to tell me what made the two of you tardy by a couple of hours?" Once more she tapped her cane on the floor. "I'm not getting any younger."

Larena cleared her throat, "As I told you previously, I'd rather not. It was nothing to concern yourself about. Just something I was interested in. Nothing important. Nothing..."

"If it were nothing, you'd tell me." The Duchess turned to Gavin. "If you don't mind, I'd like to hear what happened."

"That's alright, Auntie," Larena hastily said. "I was watching a peaceful protest and Gavin, for no reason what so ever, kidnapped me and held me hostage until it suited him to bring me home." Clearly agitated, her breaths were shallow and deep.

Charlotte tipped her head to one side, her brows coming together in concentration, "You've never lied to me before. Why now? Perhaps I do need some brandy. This might be a long night."

Larena shrugged her tiny delicate shoulders, sipping the drink she'd been given. "Everything I told you is true."

The Duchess waved her hand in the air, "Pshaw...a lie of omission is a lie. You've left much from your fairytale." She turned, her attention now focused in another direction. "Gavin?"

"Duchess," he smiled politely.

"This is between the two of you. I understand that. I have to hear the truth, but for now I'll be patient." Turning to Larena, "I'm leaving for a few months. You will move to the Montgomerie estate while I'm gone. Ella and Drake will be your chaperones."

Larena rose quickly, "No. I won't go. I need to stay here, close to the city and my..."

The Duchess looked sternly at her charge then to Gavin as if asking him for help. "You don't have a choice or a say in this, darling."

"If it's a chaperone you want for me, Ella will not be able to fulfill those duties very well. Larena strode to the sideboard and after pouring another brandy, she downed it swiftly. "I won't go there."

"You need to stay away from the elements that are influencing your hasty and at times very bad decisions. I know Ella is no chaperone, but if you are out of the city, I'll feel you are safe." She turned to glare at Gavin again as if asking him for answers or another choice.

He didn't care and thoroughly enjoyed this altercation, which seemed to play into his hands. If he could get her away from the city, he could continue with his plans, without worrying about Larena's life.

"If you send me away, I'll return here," Larena said defiantly. "You know I will. I will go where I please."

"Your father left you alone too much. I suppose you can do that, but then I'll be forced to ask Gavin to take charge of your life. If you defy my orders, I'll hand you over to your young beau. I've done worse for my charges. Your life and safety is more important to me than your reputation."

Shocked by The Duchess' words, he looked to Larena for a reaction. He wasn't surprised. Larena's body shook with anger, he supposed. Her fists were clenched as was her jaw. Fury emanated from her so hard she quivered.

"And what does that mean?" she asked defiantly. "Do I live with him in his tiny apartment or does he come here? You do understand he has only one bed."

The Duchess leaned back in her chair, her hands resting on the top of her cane, a smile curving her lips. "I don't care. You and Gavin will have to work that out. I'm sure Gavin will have the last say. He doesn't strike me as the same type of man as your father."

"I'm meeting Tyna tomorrow. I won't miss it." Her eyes sizzled with a ferocity he'd never seen before. "Drake has arranged for Addie to be there, so I assume you'll agree to that."

His soon to be fiancée had a temper that he hoped he could turn to passion. Gavin sat back, settling an arm around her, touching her and to his delight, she didn't flinch away from him. Instead, it seemed she inadvertently leaned into him as if asking him for his support.

"The last person you should be seeing is this Tyna woman. She is at the root of all your bad decisions." The Duchess turned to Gavin, again seeming to implore him to do something.

"I will see that Addie meets them. I'm sure the trained spy will be able to take charge of the meeting if it turns in an awkward direction." The shimmer in Larena's aqua eyes could melt glass. Yet he took advantage of the rare moment and trailed his finger down her arm then back up, enjoying the slight trembling and wondered if the response was her fury speaking or passion.

"Addie must have better things to do than babysit me," Larena pointed out. "It's supposed too be a private conversation. She's my friend and she doesn't mean any harm."

"Private conversations are against the law," The Duchess told her. "More trouble is brewing and I don't want you in the middle of it."

"Ah, you forget that if you refuse to go to the Montgomerie's residence, I suddenly become your chaperone, an intriguing idea." The Duchess' judgment seemed to have deteriorated. She would know Larena would never remain a virgin if he was alone with her for very long. Maybe that's what she wanted.

"How on earth can a cad and a womanizer become my chaperone?" Larena turned to The Duchess, fists clenched at her sides. "You're going crazy in your old age. I thought you had more common sense that that." She suddenly stopped, her hand over her mouth.

Taken aback by her statement, Gavin cleared his throat. Despite what she thought about him, he was pleased with the new situation the two of them were just now thrown into. This way he could keep Larena from finding too much trouble. "While I'm hardly a suitable chaperone for a young lady such as yourself, I've never been a cad or a womanizer." He didn't like that his intended thought the worst of him.

"It is the wisest choice of all those presented to me as well as all the ones you refused," The Duchess said, the strange smile remaining. "Gavin will make a fine chaperone."

"Well, I don't like any of the choices. I'm perfectly capable of living here by myself. I've no need of a guardian," Larena declared heatedly. "Especially not Gavin Broon."

"I think you protest too much, sweet one." Gavin pulled her closer, wrapping both arms around her and for the moment declaring his possession of her. In his mind, she would always be his to protect and cherish. He did regret his too aggressive display of affection earlier today. She needed to be wooed gently, and he meant to do just that now that he was handed a golden opportunity.

"How well will this role work for you when all you want is to get me into your bed?" she shook his arms from around her and moved away.

"Hmm..." he paused then laughed softly, pleased with himself and the new opportunity. "In my bed would be a dream come true for me, but not until we're married. I planned to hold to tradition in this matter unless of course you manage to seduce me."

"Seduce you? Marry you? What makes you think I'd marry you or would want to seduce you? If you haven't figured it out yet, you haven't asked." She turned on him.

"Consider this a proposal," he said, watching her intensely, his heart beating furiously.

The Duchess clapped her hands together. "Perfect! I was hoping something like this would happen. Perhaps the two of you can wed this evening. I'll call in a favor."

"Stop right there," Larena said. "I'm not getting married tonight or tomorrow. I don't care a fig about a grand wedding any longer, but Gavin has paid no attention to me for months now. He can't just saunter into my life and think to marry me."

"Saunter into your life?" he repeated with sarcasm. "I was tied up in litigation then Scotland to attend to my mother's estate. I can assure you I thought of you every single day." He was disappointed she didn't understand the messages he sent her or the urgent necessity. What he hadn't thought was that she would act out because she thought he ignored her and put her life in danger.

"See, there you go," The Duchess seemed pleased with herself. "We have a match made in heaven."

"My answer is still no." She stood swiftly, her skirts flying around her so he was graced with a peek at her tiny ankles. Larena turned back to the room. "I'm going to bed now."

"If you don't intend to wed Gavin tonight, I insist you stay here until the carriage is loaded and I'm on my way." The Duchess tapped her cane. "I'd like the two of you to see me off."

With a heavy sigh, Larena returned. "You are leaving tonight? Is that safe? It couldn't possibly be safe."

"I prefer to travel at night, and I've enlisted several men to guard the carriage. I have found that in my old age I sleep while traveling. I sleep like a baby, makes the journey go so much faster." The Duchess turned to

Scarlett. "Are the bags and snacks ready to go?"

"I'll check with the butler and the cook," Scarlett said and left the room.

"Good, then the two of you need to find a way to cohabitate. I really have great expectations for the two of you. Gavin, you need to keep Larena safe from herself. I fear for her impetuous behavior. She doesn't ever think of the repercussion. Promise me that if you have to, you'll haul her off to Gretna Green and wed her before she does harm to herself."

"Duchess..."

"Promise me," she tapped her cane once.

"It won't come to that but I promise. One never knows exactly what the future will bring. However, Larena will have to agree to a marriage. In any case I would make sure to get her out of town." The trap The Duchess seemed to be laying was deep and intricate. But the trap was for Larena not him. This was exactly what he wanted, only he needed to figure out a way to stop Larena's irritation with him.

"I'm not going along with anything so absurd," Larena protested. "I don't know what has happened to The Duchess but I'd like her back, please. Where is my aunty?" She clasped her hands beneath her chin her eyes wide, regarding her Aunt Charlotte.

"The facts are simple, dear child. I'm a woman who learns from her mistakes. Every precaution I took with your sisters and cousins were to no avail. They and their beaus did exactly what they wanted despite my wishes and objections as well as all the care I took as a chaperone. I'm leaving the two of you with a clean slate. You can do whatever you want with it, paint any picture that suits the two of you. I'm exhausted and so I'm leaving for a bit of relaxation in the Highlands."

"The carriage is ready."

The Duchess rose, "Come, give me a hug, darling. I'm truly sorry for any inconvenience I've caused you. I do think this is for the best."

While Gavin leaned casually against the doorframe, Larena ran to her aunt and gave her a huge hug. "Don't forget to write, Aunty. I will miss you and I really don't think you're making a prudent decision here."

"I'll return each of your letters with one of my own," The Duchess told her. "Now, the two of you take care and don't do anything I wouldn't do."

"But...you and the duke," Larena said.

"Of course, dear, and if he's the one for you and you're the one for him, I expect no less. Just as it was with most of my darling charges, I did manage to get the ring on Ravyn's finger before Aric took her virginity, but she was the only one to my knowledge. No, I think Eveleen also had her virginity intact."

Gavin heard every word and smiled, his heart enjoying every second. The Duchess turned over Larena's future to him, and he'd have it no other way. Larena was his. She just didn't know it yet or accept the idea. He followed the ladies from the house and with Larena watched the carriage and her guards disappeared.

He heard the muffled sob from Larena and moving closer offered comfort in his arms. "I won't be a demanding chaperone. I promise." This was something new. He didn't know what to do with a crying woman.

"I won't come to your bed willingly," she protested as he wiped a few tears away with his thumb.

"I haven't asked," he laughed.

"You had me on your bed this afternoon," she told him, a tinge of defiance in his tone.

"Of course I did. I can have you on your bed tonight if I wish and you won't say no, but I'm not going to." He tilted his head slightly, studying this fragile determined woman he was trying to understand.

"Oh," she picked up her skirts, whirling then stepped into the house. "Arrogant... Infuriating... Annoying..."

Rocking on his heels, he looked at the moon, which cast soft tendrils of light on the ground. He wished he'd finished the renovations to the home in Scotland before he felt an urgent need to return home. It was something The Duchess had written that prompted him. His office and established clients waited for his arrival. Convincing Larena she belonged with him might take a few months as well as a great deal of patience. At this moment, time was precious and he intended to make the most of minutes and hours he'd been allotted.

Slowly he turned, walking up the steps to find Larena sipping brandy in the parlor. He'd been sure she would have fled to the safety of her bedroom, yet she stayed.

When he strode into the room, she looked up and held up her glass.

"Would you like another brandy?"

"Don't mind if I do." Before he poured a drink for himself he topped off Larena's. "You like to drink?"

"Only when I'm so angry I can't think straight," she told him sweetly. "Lately, you have a tendency to make me that way."

"So, what makes you angry?" he baited her, unsure of his reasons yet he loved to see her passion, wanted to feel it first hand and he needed to know more about her.

"You." She held her glass so tightly her knuckles were turning white. "You make me so furious I can't think."

"Me?"

"You arrogant man. Don't play innocent with me." She swirled the amber liquid before sipping. "You do what you want, take what you want..."

"I've only tried to do everything The Duchess and you as well wanted. My sacrifices make you mad. Now, I'm going to have to sleep in a strange bed." For a moment he thought she might toss the brandy in his face, instead she downed the liquor then held her glass out for more.

Reluctantly, he poured more brandy into her glass, understanding if he refused she'd get it herself and be even angrier with him. To hell with it all, if she got herself drunk, he'd be there to help. "If you get tipsy, it will be easier for me to take advantage of you."

Regarding him over the rim of her glass, her eyes narrowing, "I don't think you would do that."

"Do what?"

"You know, what you said. Take advantage of me."

That seemed to be an about face to Gavin. "Would you even know what I'm talking about?" He set his glass on the table and striding toward her, he took her glass from her and placed it on another table. Pulling her into his arms, "I've wanted to do this all night." His lips found hers while he held her still, his hands on either side of her face.

To his surprise she responded to his advance. Her tongue swept his mouth and he let her inside, allowed her the offense. Her teeth closed on his lips, biting gently then eliciting a groan.

She ran her small fingers through his hair, pulling him closer. He let her lead, enjoying her passion derived, he supposed, from her anger.

Pulling away, she said with an angelic smile, "I like the way you taste, brandy and something different...you."

His heart stopped momentarily. "It's the brandy you savor." If he let this go on much longer, she would be in his bed tonight. That was not part of his master plan.

"Maybe, but I believe it's more than that," she told him, her innocence staggering to him.

"Part imagination, I suppose." His laughter was quick and easy, enjoying her weakness for brandy. It seemed to serve him well. She was relaxed and so unlike the temperament she'd been in most of the day. This was the Larena he'd come to know months ago.

"No, I taste you, something beyond the brandy. It was the same this afternoon when you kissed me." Her hands were on his chest, tiny fingers grasping the cloth of his shirt.

"Perhaps we should table this discussion for another time," he murmured softly, his voice trailing away in a haunting sigh. His knuckles brushed over her cheek and his fingers whispered against the length of her throat. She gazed at him, unmoving, not protesting.

She stepped back, seeming to realize all she said and the implications. "I despise you."

He laughed, catching her wrist and pulling her toward him so their bodies met. "Despise? That's a very strong word when we barely know each other. But, my dear one, I promise you there will come a time when you don't loathe me. Just as I believe you're lying right now."

"Bastard!"

"Ummm... Perhaps I am in some ways but I can assure you my mother would take issue with your claim." He agreed and the touch of his free hand traveled lower, teasing the mound of her breast. She stiffened in his arms while his fingers continued their exploration, touching her breast, grazing her nipple through the fabric of her gown. Then once again he laughed and his touch vanished.

He handed her the brandy she set on the table then picked up his glass. "You were right. We should talk," she said.

Sipping his brandy, "Are you sure you haven't had too much to drink." His gaze ran her length then settled on her mouth. "You tasted of brandy but you smelled of the sweetest flowers."

"You may sleep in the room down the hall." She sat down, smoothing her skirts, keeping her gaze focused on her hands.

"No."

"There must be some sign of propriety." she looked at him, her face flushed and her eyes blazing once more but it seemed they burned with passion not fury.

He knew she wanted him. "Why?" He strode through the parlor, picking up items and regarding them before placing them into their proper positions, waiting for her reasoning.

"Because."

He shrugged his shoulders, anticipating an answer she didn't seem to be able to form into words. "Yes." One eyebrow rose in speculation.

She fidgeted. "You don't want to ruin my reputation. You said so yourself. Said you'd marry me before that happened."

"As long as I'm the man ruining you, I don't care a fig about your reputation. When the ton discovers I'm living in this house alone with you well..." He wanted her to finish the sentence.

"They will assume so many things that aren't true."

"And if you continue to play games with these protestors, you will find your reputation also ruined. You will have to choose, but I intend to do everything in my power to keep you from falling."

"I don't understand."

"Your well being is my only concern right now."

"That's hard to believe after you've..."

"Kissed you, touched you and came very close to ravishing you? Is that what you mean? And I thought I acted the perfect gentleman."

"Gentleman?" she was on her feet, her body shaking with fierce emotion.

Once again he touched a spark. "True, you've had the opportunity to feel my kiss and my touch against your flesh, but there was so much more I could have done. I believe I've tremendous restraint." Bloody hell, but in his mind he was a saint.

She stood, "Restraint? You call that restraint. "I'm going to bed."

"And I will be right behind you. I'm sure the room next to yours will be very acceptable."

"Do you think that was wise?" Scarlett asked. "Leaving the two of them alone with each other?"

"I don't know what to think any longer. You know as well as I do the young folks will do whatever they wish regardless of what people will think of them." Of course she had regrets about this, but the trip to the McLellan castle was necessary. "I need to see David. I've missed him and it seems to have been so long since Tavia's wedding and we were together."

"But to leave the two of them alone together?" Scarlett repeated her question, removing her gloves. "That just wasn't wise."

"I know they might explode. I saw the fire simmering between them. All it will take is the smallest trigger."

Scarlett leaned over and patted Charlotte's hand. "Remember, Larena was seen with an insurgent and as far as we can tell this Tyna is his girlfriend. The pair is dangerous and they will jeopardize Larena anyway they can just to get what they want."

"Gavin understands what is at stake here, and it's more than Larena's reputation. It could very well have repercussions on her life. He will do all that is necessary to stop anything that might happen. Drake was called in to help, but he can't possibly spend the needed time with her. Gavin can."

"Charlotte, we are getting too old for all this subterfuge. I say my heart goes out to the young ones. Life is so difficult now, not like it was when we were young." Scarlett wiped a tear from her cheek.

"I still worry about Tira and Aidan, Aidan especially. The two of them are totally alone. Ravyn and Amorica live miles away. If Blade finds Aidan, the fire between Gavin and Larena will be nothing compared to the explosion waiting to happen with Blade and Aiden."

"Those two girls were not with us long enough." Sniffles overtook Scarlett. "I miss all of them. Why did they have to move away?"

"No, perhaps if they stayed Larena would not have become involved with the social protestors. Until Larena got tangled with these people, I'd forgotten about the Peterloo Massacre. Half-a-dozen people were killed and so many more injured. I know Gavin returned sooner than he planned simply because I summoned him, needing his help."

"Gavin won't let anything happen to our sweet Larena."

Charlotte pulled a newspaper from a large bag sitting next to her, handing it to her companion. "Take a look at this."

Scarlett's gasp didn't surprise Charlotte. "This can't be. Say it didn't happen. No, no, no..."

"I wish I could. No, Gavin's going to have his hands full, already does. She's just as stubborn and impetuous as the rest of the girls." The Duchess wasn't sure what else could be done. She pulled open the basket of snacks cooked for them. "At least they will have good food while we are gone. Cook loves to have men to feed."

"Cook isn't eager to be the only one supervising those two as if she could, but she does love her job so she'll do her duty as best she can. I certainly hope the McLellan has an exceptional cook."

Charlotte gazed at the front page of the London Times for a bit before sighing and placing the horrible reminder that Larena needed a lot of looking after into her bag. "The butler didn't much like the job either, even though I told them they should just look the other way unless something occurred that might be life threatening." The Duchess tucked the bag into a corner, wishing she could tuck her fears away just as easily.

"I'm certainly relieved you wanted me to travel with you."

"You're my companion. I will always want you to be by my side. Oh look, Cook packed us a couple bottles of Logan's Chianti, my favorite. I'm sure the McLellan will have crates of both the Bordeaux as well as Chianti in his cellar, especially since Logan Maxwell is his son in law."

"A wonderful trip, relaxing, just what I need. I might just remain in my room every night with a bottle of each," Scarlett laughed, casting her blue eyes dramatically heavenward.

"I'm looking forward to spending time with David and reminiscing. I'm hoping he'll take me to this island the girls all rave about so I can see the danger and the draw." Charlotte continued to probe the basket, finding glasses for the wine and ham sandwiches for both of them. "I do hope you're hungry, Scarlett."

"Famished," she said as the carriage rolled to a halt.

Charlotte poked her head out the window. "What are we stopping for?"

Books by Christine Young
Available at Rogue Phoenix Press

Catching Meara
Book One in the McKenna Clan Series

Meara Thorton was a feisty, world-class computer hacker—cornered by the FBI and shockingly given the chance to be their newly acquired technical analyst. Brilliant and intuitive, yet aching with the loss of everyone she has cared about, her restless heart led her to discover a love she fought and a world she didn't know could possibly exist.

Sweet Sexy Sadie
Book Two in the McKenna Clan Series

From the first time Sadie's eyes met those of Brody McKenna in the hot Sierra Madre Mountains, theirs was a potent attraction—not gentle, slow, and easy, but hot, hard, and all-consuming. The daughter of a dysfunctional family, Sadie had dreams no man could wrench from her with hot sex and an all-consuming passion. She'd challenge this alpha male with all the strength she possessed. But her red hair, fiery temperament, and indomitable spirit obsessed Brody...and he knew he had to find a way to show her he was more than he appeared and convince her to make a life with him.

Sweet Misbehavin'
Book Three in the McKenna Clan Series

Cast adrift after fleeing the home of Jokul, the ice demon, Atantsi, a firestarter, grew to womanhood as she moved through time to keep the demon from finding her. Though stubborn and courageous, she was ill prepared to use powers she had not been taught. Her first sight of the intoxicating Carr McKenna left her breathless, and her second encounter gave her hope for a future she never thought she had.

A playboy, a second son and a shifter, a man who thought his life would be carefree, Carr McKenna was shocked to discover the woman he'd paid as an escort is a firestarter who is running for her life. He is the leader of all the McKennas around the world and that he has multiple powers. His passion for Margo and the need to defend her might cost him his life as well as hers.

Sweet Talkin' Sugar
Book Four in the McKenna Clan Series

Lyonesse McKenna, was dreaming or was she? From the instant Lyn saw Deacon McClain across a black jack table in a crowed Las Vegas casino the unmistakable attraction sent Lyn's senses flying into overdrive. Her family of shapeshifters believed in soul mates. She'd always been skeptical yet she couldn't help but question the way her heart sped when he looked at her.

When Deacon appeared in Las Vegas he knew his first job was to save Lyn from a Sea Demon, but the next order of business was to convince her he would someday mean more to her than she'd ever expected. But her stubborn nature and unbendable spirit consumed Deacon...and he had to chase away all the demons real and imagined in order to win her heart.

Sweet Surrender
Book Five in the McKenna Clan Series

Ripped from her family at the top of Infinity Cliff, Kimi McKenna finds herself thrust somewhere into the future. Dark elements threaten to destroy the earth unless Kimi can work together with the white witch to stop the destruction. Confused by her mate's role in the conspiracy, she refuses to acknowledge the connection. But amidst raging fire and attacks on the people she is coming to hold dear, she allows Maska O'keefe into her heart.

Maska O'keefe has loved the beautiful shapeshifter for years. Unable to save her life years ago, he vows to watch over her as he is given a second chance to convince her that even though he is a witch and not a shifter, they are indeed soul mates. Kimi's divided loyalties between her family and the cause she is now a part of will determine their relationship. Only the part she plays as the messiah can bring this to a conclusion in the final battle.

Dakota's Bride
The first book in the Lakota/Pinkerton Series

When Emma St. John received her brother's letter imploring her to escape her stepfather's vengeful scheme and to trust Dakota Barringer with her life, she was willing to chance it. But the handsome, brooding riverboat owner Emma found in Natchez a danger of another kind. For Emma soon found herself surrendering to an unrelenting desire.
Raised by the Sioux when his parents were killed, Dakota had been betrayed once before by a white woman. He wasn't about to trust another, especially one claiming that her stepfather, a powerful U.S. senator, had framed her as a murderess. But he couldn't let Emma's intoxicating effect on him. Now Dakota would risk his very life to protect the innocent beauty who had seduced him with her tender love.

My Angel
The second book in the Lakota/Pinkerton Series

A BEAUTY IN BUCKSKINS
When her father decided to send her to a finishing school back East, Angela Chamberlain refused to be confined to stuffy drawing rooms. Instead, the daring spitfire who could shoot like a man and ride like the wind longed for a life of adventure and romance—and she knew exactly who could give it to her. Devil Blackmoor was a hired gun with a dangerous reputation. But Angela was willing to go to the ends of the

earth to capture the handsome devil's heart.

A DEVIL IN DISGUISE
He'd come to America looking for excitement, but Devil Blackmoor got more than he bargained for when he encountered a beautiful rebel who answered his kisses with a wild innocence that touched his very soul. Yet standing between them were more obstacles than either ever dreamed. For Devil had strapped on a gun for the wrong man. And that made Angela his enemy. Now he'll have to choose between his duty and the woman he loves more than life.

The Locket
The third book in the Lakota/Pinkerton Series

The year is 1894. Seeking revenge for crimes against his family, Misha Petrovich follows a path that leads straight to Ariel Cameron's boarding house in Mist Harbor, Oregon. A family heirloom in Ariel's possession leads Misha to believe she is guilty. The locket has been handed down to the oldest girl in the Petrovich family for generations. Ariel is innocent of wrong doing, but her father is not. Misha is torn by his feelings for Ariel and his need for restitution against her father. Knowing that the relationship between them is fragile, Misha does everything in his power to protect Ariel's father. His efforts are to no avail when her father is shot. Ariel comes to realize Misha's steadfast courage and determination to protect her and her father despite what has happened to his family. Ariel's love and devotion heals Misha's heart.

The Talisman
The fourth book in the Lakota/Pinkerton Series

Running from a marriage that lasted one night, Dr. Moriah McKeown discovers the land she has settled on is coveted by determined and lawless men. Yet the proud young woman who once vowed never to abandon her home has second thoughts when her adopted children are threatened. Her only recourse is to enlist the aid of a dark, dangerous gun for hire.
Haunted by the past and a betrayal he will never forgive, Ian Civanovich uses his fast gun and his reckless courage to forget the faithlessness of a

woman in his past. He will trust no female—nor will he rest until the threat hovering over Moriah McKeown is put to rest.

Forever His
The fifth book in the Lakota/Pinkerton Series

Struggling to come to terms with the part she played in Jacob St. John's death, Etta Barringer resigns from Pinkerton Agency and seeks peace and solace in a Rocky Mountain Cabin.
Jacob has vowed to discover the reason Etta has betrayed him, sold him out to his enemy and left him for dead.
Isolated in their cabin, they discover their love for each other and learn to trust. But the trust is shattered when Jacob learns she is married to his sworn enemy; the man who left him in the desert to die.

Allura's Secret
Twelve Dancing Princesses Book One

Allura McClellan is horrified by her father's decision to take out an ad in the Times awarding her to the man strong enough and smart enough to win her hand and uncover her secrets. She's an intelligent young woman who takes great delight in the freedom allotted to her by her father. She's well aware that marriage would effectively curtail the adventures she's shared with her sisters and cousins.
Hunter Gray is nothing like the other men who've arrived to vie for Allura's hand in marriage and everything that goes along with it. However, he is the first to refuse to concede defeat and pursue her despite her attempts to disguise her true appearance. It's her temperament that is of more concern to him than her looks. Hunter has worked all his life with the hope of someday owning his own land. Now that it looks like there's a very real possibility that everything he's ever wanted is within reach nothing is going to deter him – including Miss Allura's disagreeable disposition.

Amorica's Wager
Twelve Dancing Princesses Book Two

Amorica Hepburn was sent to London to find a husband. Finding a man was the last item on her agenda. With her two cousins, Amorica wagers she can dissuade her suitor before the others. Despite her efforts she discovers a chemistry that cannot be denied. Suddenly she is the arrogant man's wife, pledged to a marriage neither desire. But swept off to his ancestral home above the Dover cliffs and into his strong embrace, Amorica is soon possessed by a raging passion for the husband she had vowed to despise...

Damian Andrews couldn't afford to trust the emerald-eyed spitfire who happened upon his secret. Amorica's hatred of all men of his kind only inflames the war that rages between them. Still, he can not control the intense desire his stubborn bride inspires, or make her surrender to his will until he has conquered the headstrong beauty on the battlefield of love...

Ravyn's Marriage of Inconvenience
Twelve Dancing Princesses Book Three

A REGAL BEAUTY
When the duchess decides to wed her to a wastrel and a fop, Ravyn Grahm takes matters into her own hands and declares her engagement to another man. Instead of fessing up and telling her great aunt what she has done, she goes through with the pretense. Aric Lakeland is the bastard son of an earl and has a dangerous reputation. But Ravyn is willing to do most anything to keep the duchess from discovering the lie.

A DEVIL-MAY-CARE SMUGGLER
He'd bought land in America, looking to put down roots and end his life of adventure, but Aric Lakeland got more than he bargained for when he encountered a beautiful heiress who made a promise she didn't want to keep. But the promise could not be undone and standing between them were more obstacles than either ever dreamed. Aric had made plans to spend the rest of his life in America and that was at odds with Ravyn's plan of living in England and running her father's estate. Now, he'll have

to choose between his dreams and the woman he loves more than life.

Christel's Sunrise
Twelve Dancing Princesses Book Four

He Made Her An Offer...

Life has thrown Christel McClellan some experiences that could have devastated a less determined woman. Beautiful, self-assured and fiercely independent, she is trying to forget the loss of her stillborn child. But is the child alive?

She Couldn't Deny...

Life is carefree for Ryder MacLaren who loves to see what is on the other side of the sunrise. Laird of Clan MacLaren, he is wealthy, handsome and happily unencumbered...until stunning Christel McClellan enters his life. When he hears her story, he believes the child she thought dead has been sold to a wealthy buyer.

Storm's Passion
Twelve Dancing Princesses Book Five

SHE MADE A PROPOSAL...

Life strikes Storm Graham a shattering blow when she learns her father has bartered her to a man she detests. Storm is beautiful, self-assured and fiercely independent, and refuses to be a pawn in her father's schemes, yet she can find no way out of this bargain made in hell. Going on the offensive she asks the wealthiest man on the eastern coast of England to marry her, never believing she might fall in love.

HE TRIED TO REFUSE...

For Hadden Johnston life has provided everything he ever wanted, including a sanctuary for homeless children. He is wealthy, handsome and happily unencumbered...until stunning Storm Graham marches into his life and proposes a marriage of convenience. Yet this type of marriage to a woman who inflames his senses is far from acceptable. If he's going to be tied down, he will move heaven and earth to have this woman warming his bed.

Gotta Have Fayth
Twelve Dancing Princesses Book Six

A regal beauty with raven hair and piercing blue eyes, Fayth Graham is unwilling to parade herself in front of the wealthy Lords of England during the season. Seeking a means to dissuade any man wishing to wed her, she seeks a way to ruin herself for marriage. When she unexpectedly meets a man with sparkling gray eyes and an infectious grin, she decides this is the man who will keep her from agreeing to obey.

He returned from six months at sea, looking for a few nights of pleasure with a willing lass, but Jarret Kinsley got more than he bargained for when he met a beautiful debutant who responded to his kisses with a wild innocence that touched his heart. Yet the obstacles looming between them might rip them apart. Both had vowed never to marry, so when consequences of their dalliances got in the way, Jarret would have to choose between the life he's always desired and the woman he loves more than life.

Ella's Pleasure
Twelve Dancing Princesses Book Seven

A WHISPER OF PLEASURE

Ella Hepburn was an auburn haired debutant from the harsh Scottish coastline—a wild innocent to be seduced and tamed. A spirited beauty, she captivated Drake Montgomerie's jaded heart—while succumbing to the smoldering desire she felt for her unyielding suitor.

A WHISPER OF DANGER

In Drake Montgomerie's glittering world of money and privilege, young Ella discovered passion and desire could overcome everything she'd been taught to resist—entangling Drake, the heir apparent, in a lethal coil of aristocratic family intrigue. But grave peril would only nurse the sparks of a love that knew no limits and a magnificent ecstasy that would not be denied.

Eveleen's Seduction
Twelve Dancing Princesses Book Eight

A WHISPER OF SEDUCTION

A brutal attack on Eveleen Hepburn's cherished island off the Scottish coastline leaves her shattered and bewildered. Learning a man she once trusted can kill as easily as he can breathe even though the deed saves her life, creates questions that need answers. An innocent beauty, she enchants Logan Maxwell's cynical heart—giving in to the raging passion she feels for her mysterious suitor.

A WHISPER OF INTRIGUE

In Logan's Maxwell's world of espionage and privilege, young Eveleen discovers truths about herself she never expected, and a need for passion and love can overcome all her fears if she learns to accept certain truths. She finds herself entangled in a lethal battle for land that was once owned by French nobility, taken from them during the revolution and sold to Maxwell. But grave peril would unleash the flames of love that simmers, creating a magical union that cannot be refuted.

Tavia's Deception
Twelve Dancing Princesses Book Nine

WHISPERS OF DECEPTION

When her father decides to send her to London for her season, Tavia Hepburn resolves to see the world instead. The raven haired beauty decides to disguise herself as a lad and find employment on a ship bound for Barcelona as a cabin boy. But she never bargains on finding passion and love to a red haired sea captain who rescues her from certain death.

WHISPERS OF MURDER

For James Macmurra, the world is black and white until he meets a young debutante, who turns his world upside down. He's unable to deny Tavia's intoxicating effect on him. In a match tense with obstacles, unwillingness to divulge secrets, and unforeseen peril, irresistible desire and passion grows into undeniable love. James would risk his life to shelter and protect the innocent debutante who seduces him with her sweet love.

Twelve Days to Love

When Archer Steele shows up at Calanthe Durand's failing plantation with an alligator over his shoulder, Cali thinks she's never seen a more handsome man. During the war she had to defend herself and her servants from both union and confederate soldiers. Independent and self-sufficient, she vows to never marry.

But Archer Steele has different ideas. The first time Archer sees Cali in town, he feels an instant attraction. He decides he will do everything and anything to convince the beautiful Miss Durand he is worthy of her love. During the weeks leading up to Christmas, he gives her twelve gifts in hopes she will fall in love with him. Yet they are faced with challenges they must overcome before Cali can commit to a marriage.

Door to Heaven

Jessica Lawrence is the stepdaughter of a woman born in the twentieth century transported back in time to the year 1868. An acclaimed suffragette, she raises Jessica to believe in the equality of women. Jess Law believes everything she was taught, and when the time is right she becomes a private investigator. Courageous and impetuous, Jess finds danger in her quest to save all women from white slavery. Her passionate mission results in a wedding to Roc Newman, a man she knows can steal her heart...

Roc can't trust the sapphire-eyed spitfire who invades his home in search of secret papers and knocks him flat with her karate moves. Jessica's refusal to obey his wishes serves to inflame the war between them. Still, he cannot control the intense desire his reluctant bride inspires, or make her surrender her independence, until he has conquered the headstrong beauty on the battlefield of love...

Rebel Heart

HER REBEL SPIRIT DEFIED HIS OUTSIDERS SOUL... She was velvet and silk, eyes the color of a summer storm and amber hair. Victoria DeMontville, because of a promise and a codicil to her father's will, was forced to marry one man to protect her from another. She hated Cameron Savage with a fierce passion. But to hold on to her genetic research and find a cure for the deadly Signe virus, she must pretend to love the enemy at her door, come with weapons of fire to melt her icy heart...

HIS OUTSIDERS TOUCH IGNITED RAGING PASSIONS... He wore a mask, disguised as the Phantom, a true legend come to life. Even as war and debate over new genetic research engulfed them all, he would find his greatest adversary in the beauty who'd branded him an outsider and barbarian, the woman he was born to possess, his soul mate.

Safari Moon

Solo St. John, a wildlife photographer, is preparing for a trip to Alaska. Suddenly, Solo finds women of all sorts invading his privacy, his home and his office, all cooing nonsense words and blatantly throwing themselves at him. Solo doesn't know why, and he has no idea how to rid himself of the persistent women. He finally decides to beg a favor of his best buddy Nyssa Harrington.

In love with Solo for the past ten years and knowing he doesn't return her feelings Nyssa doesn't want to talk to Solo. She knows if she accepts his phone call, she will not be able to resist the temptation to hope again.

Straight to Heaven

Running from demons, Alexandra McMurdie stumbles into Forbidden Ground where up is down and elements of nature are contested. Though a strong independent woman in the twenty-first century' she is unprepared for life in the 1800s. Her first site of the formidable James Lawrence makes her heart skip a beat, giving her cause to reconsider her desperate need to find a way home.

Born with a silver spoon, James' life was torn apart during the War Between the States. Moving west he vows to put the life he once knew in the past. When he discovers a half-frozen woman near Gold Hill, his heart begins to thaw. His love for Alexandra and his need to keep her from a man who has pursued her through time might cost him his life as well as hers.

A Valentine's Anthology

The Lending Library-a fantasy by Christie L. Kraemer

Faeries try to fit into the human world when the forest where they make their home is destroyed by a mysterious enemy.

Chasing Rainbows-a contemporary romance by Genene Valleau

An eccentric aunt, an inventive uncle, a mother who wears poodle skirts, and a brother who wears pearls provide a hilarious backdrop for the courtship of a young woman who yearns for a "normal" family.

The Gift-an historical romance by Christine Young

A man and a woman on opposite sides of the Civil War get a second chance at love after one final battle returns soldiers to their war-torn homes to rebuild their lives.

A St. Patrick's Day Tale
by
Christine Young, C. L. Kraemer, Genene Valleau

Tumble through time…

…to Ireland in 1817, when tensions are high between Protestants and Catholics and faey people guide the fate of villagers. A lovely Catholic lass stumbles upon the weakly ritual fisticuffing between Irish lads. She falls into the lap of a handsome young Protestant. Family ties, grudges, and two conniving faeries threaten their budding love. But the faeries outsmart themselves when they hijack a time machine that has mysteriously appeared in their forest and are whisked to…

…Eugene, Oregon in the 20th century, amid a property feud between the local faeries and night elves. The conniving faeries from Olde Ireland try to stir up more mischief. However, a warrior gnome convinces the magic folk to control their own destiny, and forces the intruding faeries to take refuge in the time machine again, spinning their way toward…

…A modern day castle in western Oregon. An eccentric inventor is determined to reclaim his wayward time machine and save his beloved wife from her latest misadventure. If only they can travel safely past the black hole…

a May Day Anthology
by
Christine Young, C. L. Kraemer, Rosemary Indra, Genene Valleau

Highland Miracle -- Christine Young

HURTLED THROUGH TIME, Sean Michael Sterling, landed in the midst of a May Day celebration he didn't understand, assuming the role of Laird Sterling.
ILLIGITAMATE CHILD OF NOBILITY, Reagan Douglas searches for a way out of her half brother's house.

Defying the Odds -- C.L. Kraemer

The night elves on the hill aren't happy without their magic. They concoct a plan to punish those who were involved in the act that rendered them almost human. Meanwhile, Uther, the rogue night elf, has returned to woo the Librarian to be his eternal mate.

Love in Bloom -- Rosemary Indra

When childhood friends reunite it takes two fairies and a matchmaking daughter to help them admit their true love for each other.

No More Poodle Skirts -- Genie Gabriel

After drifting for years in the innocent age of the 1950s, a woman struggles to join today's world by finding a career and a new love, with some help from her zany family.

Once Upon a Christmas Moon
by
Christine Young, C. L. Kraemer, Genene Valleau

TWELVE DAYS TO LOVE

When Archer Steele shows up at Calanthe Durand's failing plantation with an alligator over his shoulder, Cali thinks she's never seen a more handsome man. During the war she had to defend herself and her servants from both union and confederate soldiers. Independent and self-sufficient, she vows to never marry. But Archer Steele has different ideas. The first time Archer sees Cali in town, he feels an instant attraction. He decides he will do everything and anything to convince the beautiful Miss Durand he is worthy of her love. During the weeks leading up to Christmas, he gives her twelve gifts in hopes she will fall in love with him.

BOOTS AND BLADES

An ancient evil from the old country has arrived in the high desert of Oregon. Gnome children are vanishing then re-appearing, showing various stages of traumatization. Tiamoon, warrior gnome, will put her skills to use alongside Killian, a handsome warrior, also in need of a cause.

CHRISTMAS PAWSIBILITIES

With their world destroyed and their space ship malfunctioning, the dogizens of Planet Canid have little choice but to crash land on Earth. They face tortuous experiments at the hands of the Geeks in Green...or they can trust an eccentric inventor and his zany family to deliver the Canine Queen's puppies and help them celebrate new lives.

www.ingramcontent.com/pod-product-compliance
Lightning Source LLC
Chambersburg PA
CBHW071446170626
46811CB00007B/2493